Anders Flagstad's

Spare Parts

Book One
of
Principal
Parts

ALSO BY
ANDERS FLAGSTAD

Thad Says Parts Is Parts
(And Thad Is Right)
(Book Two of Principal Parts)

Circles and Wheels

The Chaotic Pendulum

Slip Slide Sideways

The yellow blurs, which if anyone were looking would look something like raincoats, stand patiently across the street and watch. They stand and wait until John is safely wrapped in a wetly twinkling Blue and White cab and tunneling homewards through sheets of spritzing rain. They watch as John's cab splashes and skids, accelerates down the one-way street, slows at the end of the block, makes a tight right turn and drops out of sight as it swings around the corner.

And, if anyone were still looking, they'd see the blurs hanging around a few moments longer, then they'd see them drifting off in the opposite direction, and then they'd see them melting serenely into the pitter-patter of rain slapping the early morning San Francisco streets and sidewalks. Eventually they wouldn't see them at all, anywhere. The blurs would be gone, just like John. There'd be nothing left to see. That is, if anyone had seen them at all in the first place.

Four Compartments, pp.107-108.

Spare Parts

Book One
of
Principal
Parts

Stories and Novellas by

Anders Flagstad

Bubble Eyes Publishing
www.BubbleEyesPublishing.com

Bubble Eyes Publishing

Library of Congress Catalogue Number: 2013936377

ISBN: 0-615-79326-6
ISBN-13: 978-0-615-79326-9

Illustrations and Design by K.P. Anderson

for

L. S. (yet again)

CONTENTS

INTRODUCTION

You might say that San Francisco, the city around which all of these stories take place, lives only in the mind and not be too far off the mark.

Exiles and ex-pats like myself that foolishly put down roots far from the peninsula would agree and might even try to convince you that the city doesn't exist at all - even for the citizens that live, work, and love there. We would say - yes, The City certainly is a mirage. It is a massively multiplayer shared delusion. An exquisitely tormenting dream, an unwanted blessing, a carefully cultivated curse.

San Francisco. This is a city that floats and bobs in the brain and once there doesn't easily get dislodged, if ever. I say this because I know. I speak from experience. In fact, all of us, residents and exiles, speak from experience, loudly and often. The not-so-short short stories and the novella that follow this introduction are voices speaking. Listen to them. Hear their pain. Heed their warnings.

And then, like everyone else, start scanning Craig's List for flat-mate openings close to a Bart or Muni line, ship all your worldly possessions to an ancient apartment on the slope of a nearly vertical street, start figuring out how many dogs you have to walk each day to pay for your 1/8th share of the rent while you surf the never-ending waves of nightlife thundering over you every time the fog rolls in and the sun goes down and you rapidly go through three intense personal-growth-filled relationships that come out of nowhere, fly off into the sunset and leave you changed. You'll find yourself smiling through your tears, crying while you grin.
Welcome to San Francisco.

So.

The City is a city of immigrants. And usually, except for those favored few who are natives, The City generates amazing personal histories (well, amazing to San Franciscans) for every new arrival - how they made the trip, what they did to settle in, how they found a place to stay, where they find cheap food, how they got their first decent-paying job, etc. etc. Most importantly, they babble on and on about what they do 24-7 when they're not working, sleeping, or eating. The City's a very busy, very rowdy, raucous place to live in, even if it exists only in the space between your ears.

San Francisco promises, pleads, pulls, propels, and punishes. It instills an abiding, not-unpleasant state of mental anguish. It is an inchoate yearning. Sometimes it feels like a skin rash that just won't go away, no matter what you rub onto it, no matter how hard you try not to scratch at it.

It's usually about at this point that the sad tales are told of why we were all compelled to leave The City - but that wisdom comes much, much too late. It comes long after San Francisco has been bolted permanently into place among all the rest of your mental furniture, partially blocking your previously unobstructed view of the Universe for the rest of your natural life.

But it's not all that bad. Really. It was probably all worth it, right? No one's complaining. At least not so you'd notice.

Especially not the Texas women finding each other the hard way, the haunted homeless and the lonely, lucky Chinese computer programmers, the circuit party boys gone bad, the evil twins, and the fortunately unfortunate terminally ill. All of them, to the last woman and man of them would say the same thing, if you took the time to ask.

Yes, it's a mental thing, and yes, it sticks *with* you and *on* you like the results of a diet of pancakes and sugar cookies - but come on, think about it, if you have San Francisco as your own personal, private mirage, who really needs reality?

Spare Parts

PART IN THE MIDDLE

Alice has always been better with the inanimate.

It's just how she is. So she doesn't question why the perky home-care nurse Kerri (with an "i") makes her skin suddenly feel two sizes too tight on her, why her admittedly capacious flesh and big bones won't settle for just her own body, why they want more. More of what and where, she doesn't know. All she does know is she can't keep still around Kerri. Kerri is a lot to handle. Kerri makes her want to be up and busy, busy doing something, anything, preferably somewhere else. There seems to be a lot of talking going on around Kerri.

The steam iron feels good in her hand. A simple tool that's solidly three-dimensional and performs a necessary task. Cant' say enough good things about something like that. No you can't. Not these days. The floor creaks complainingly as she shifts her weight from one foot to the other. She wonders if she can get to changing the oil tomorrow in the red Ford truck, but is not sure if she has the tools at hand. Alice likes her tools. She mentally tries to track backwards in her day and tease out where she saw her toolbox last. Alice likes to do two things at once. Even three. Or four. Hank, her husband, and a bookkeeper, does one thing at a time, carefully and well. Hank calls Alice a "multi-tasker." Alice calls herself a worker.

She has a pile of laundry to get through and no time to do it in. Of course, just then the cell phone vibrates throbbingly on her waist. She fumbles for it, attacking her waist with both hands repeatedly until she throttles it to silence with jabs from her fingers. What if it's Billy, Hank's brother? What should she tell him? This time Hank is swollen up and the steroids aren't working like they used to. She can see an Emergency Room visit on the horizon. Those are always a lot of fun. Alice doesn't want to think about it. No point. He always gets better. Always. No point in thinking about it.

Hank is mercifully dozing for the moment so Alice gets to do laundry. Of course, she's still bouncing back and forth from the front room to the back every five minutes, a basketball being dribbled upcourt, downcourt. She doesn't like leaving Hank by himself with his breathing so rough and all. And she has to admit it, she hates doing the laundry. She takes breaks. Hank's usually the one who does it. The laundry that is. He does a much better job. He's fast. Detail-oriented. That's what Hank is. He'll be better. Soon. Just don't think about it.

The tinny voice that bubbles up from her waist is feminine and concerned and business-like and it is Kerri. Her forearms and hands immediately start itching. She finds herself dancing nervously from foot to foot doing that quick two-step you do when you discover your stepping on an anthill.

"Ally" comes floating weakly back from Hank's bedroom. "We have any ice water?" Alice guesses Hank's off and racing again. She likes he's asking for things, doesn't like she can hardly hear him do the asking. He's sounding weaker. No point in thinking about it, though. No point at all.

" Mrs. Cartwright? How are you holding up, today?"

"Or lemonade. We have any of that lemonade left?"

She almost says "Second shelf" but realizes he wouldn't hear her, and what would he do? Jump up and get it? The far-off Kerri-voice is rattling on, Alice's heart feels like its skipping beats, and her knees go weak. Alice looks back and forth from phone to back bedroom to kitchen to laundry to phone and for a second Alice can't move. A frenzy of smashing gears and exploding pistons inside her head and all of a sudden it's all a jumble. It's just too much. Too much.

First, Hank. Hank. Her heart is just racing. She munges the phone shut, misses her waist clip and doesn't hear the phone hit the floor under the ironing board and stumbling, shuffling, she arcs towards the back bedroom through the tables and barcoloungers she's pushed aside to do her work in the living room and their hallway seems long and endless and then she's there.

It feels like all the strength has just drained out of her. Like someone reached inside and pulled the plug. She leans heavily, one hand on the bedroom door jamb above her, and presses her clutched fist against her heart with her other hand, gasping. Her lungs just aren't big enough to get her breath. Then as she goes in, she remembers the lemonade. Hank, quiet, calm Hank with his face and limbs all swollen up, red and tight like a Thanksgiving day parade balloon, Hank's already dozing again in a shallow, wheezing, uneasy unconsciousness. She feels his forehead, checks his pulse, adjusts his sheets.

He calls himself Bullwinkle when he blows up like this. He calls her his Rocky. Parade balloons. It's their little joke. Something only the two of them know about. Although anyone can see Alice is anything but chipmunk-sized. She wanders out, wanders back, leaves a lemonade on his nightstand with a paper napkin wrapped over the top to keep the flies out, listens to him struggling for breath in his sleep for a couple of minutes, feels his forehead, checks his pulse, adjusts the fan so it blows across him and not at him like a hurricane and backs out tiptoeing. She half-closes the door.

The laundry is still sitting there, just where she left it.

She rubs her lower arm where the name "Hank" is tattooed in a clean, economical cursive across the veins on the inside of her solid wrist. It's funny, Alice can't remember ever getting that tattoo. She just doesn't seem to herself to be the tattoo type. And it's doomed her to long sleeves in public her whole adult life. But there they are - perfect letters – and Alice has always been proud of them - letters you'd more likely see above a 3rd-grader's classroom chalkboard than on a person's skin. Only Alice knows they represent the actual way Hank writes them out – it's his own handwriting, truly it is - she could forge his name now just by looking down at her own right hand, if she could twist it upwards and write downwards all at the same time. Not that she would for any number of reasons she can think of.

They are the both of them poor as church mice. Lord knows there wouldn't be much to forge for. And besides, what they have, what little they have, lately it mostly comes from Alice. Alice and the Humboldt "Quick and Dirty" All-Make Automotive Repair Garage and Gas Station in Humboldt, of course. It's her cash-only, under-the-counter employer a few days a week, more or less. Recently, it's been more less than more, but Alice isn't complaining. Pop Grainger lets her sneak in the back. She gets good money to do what she loves anyways – mess around on multi-ton machines with heavy, greasy tools, sometimes run the diagnostics. What more could a girl ask for? She gets a workout and grocery money. Pop Grainger gets hard work for half pay. It's simple. It works. Alice likes it, even if Pop's roaming fingers need to get swatted with a swift back hand from the old hex wrench every once in a while.

They aren't married, she and Hank, not court-house, licensed, blood-tested married. But Alice has been living with Hank in conjugal union for many years now. That's marriage as far as Alice is concerned. Even if East Texas (or Eastex as some were having it nowadays) might have other ideas. She's a married woman. Married for fifteen long and eventful years. And if Hank's Lupus calms down and stays put, with him getting healthier and all, she's fifteen going for fifty, no problemo. Hank's her one and only. The first and the last to capture her heart. He knows it. She knows it. Doesn't matter if the world doesn't know it.

Kerri comes waltzing in, late even for her, and announces the beginning of her second daily visit of the day with an overly casual and neighborly yodeling "Yoohoo." A thundercrack of a screen door slamming into a mobile home's metal-girt frame completes her entrance. Except for the déjà-vu, second-time-around part, it's the usual. Alice is used to it.

But at exactly, precisely that same moment, Alice thinks she hears a voice coming from the humid rooms in back of her, she hears a voice but can't be sure where from. Her head feels muddled in all this heat and for a second, as she turns around peering squinty-eyed into the green-gold twilight filling up her trailer from the carpet upwards, she is positive she hears her duck rifle, hanging in a glassy case on the false, pine-paneled wall in front of her calling out, begging for help, mournful and melancholy, plain as the day is long.

Kerri moves into her line of sight. Alice moves to one side, staring hard at the rifle. Kerri moves in front of her again, looks over her own shoulder at the rifle, back at Alice, then smiles brightly, as bright as she can make it. Something's sneaking up on Alice's back, something nasty and sly, she can feel it. Something that's been waiting there a long time. Watching her. Tracking her. Alice finds it starting to get hard to breathe again. She needs to tell someone. She needs to warn someone. But she knows from experience, there's no "someone" who'd listen to her. Nobody's going to listen to her. Nobody ever does. Especially, not a Kerri with an "i", that's for sure.

"I knocked, but no one came to the door." Alice doubts that. Kerri's just plain snoopy. Always asking Alice about herself. Kerri's eyes are roaming all over Alice's trailer now, looking around. Alice um-hmm's a non-committal sound in Kerri's direction.

Kerri sets her notebooks with all her paperwork down on the kitchen counter and just looks at Alice, up and down, left and right. She's still smiling, teeth as bright as a full moon, her blond hair flying around in the mini-tornado set off by the ceiling fan. Alice feels her nerves rising to the surface again. Her Kerri-nerves. She falls into ironing, a drowning man going after an outstretched oar, not looking back, not looking up, feeling itchy, feeling jumpy.

"Sure is hot today. Y'all have any lemonade left over from yesterday?" Kerri drawls in Alice's direction.

"In the refrigerator. Second shelf. On the left." Alice talks half to the shirt in front of her, half over her shoulder to the kitchen. She can't think. She hears Kerri scuffing her black-soled shoes across her clean linoleum, the abrupt click of a handle being pulled carelessly upward and the slow, slow kissing sound of a refrigerator door ever so weakly being opened. Then silence. Not even breathing. Lord give me strength. More silence. She's not going to find it.

Alice carefully squeezes yet another seam into place with one massive, calloused hand, careful to balance the ironing board's weak pressed-iron legs with her right knee so it doesn't collapse as is its habit - it apparently being a delicate, sensitive, and genteel table unused to heavy and extended exertions such as Alice's. Alice is not sympathetic. The table should have been long used to it, long used to Alice's ways after all these years. Should have, but wasn't.

She hovers over it with her right hand levitated by satisfying jets of foaming steam erupting hell-bent-for-leather out of her ancient Proctor Silex. She's par-boiling Hank's worn plaid shirt to a limp, pliant submissiveness, and filling her tired face with a wall of warm massaging cloud. It feels good. Why hadn't she ever done this before?

A voice from the other room – "Ally." Did she really hear that?

"Mrs. Cartwright, ma'am, you O.K.?" Alice can hear ice clinking in a glass, and Kerri standing close behind her. How long had she been standing there?

Her hand on the seam on the shirt begins to hurt from the heat and she realizes with a jerk of her head and an unconscious waving and wagging in the hot summer air of her semi-burnt digits that she's been a-steam-pumping for a couple of minutes now. She'd whooshed herself up a wet thundercloud here in the front room. She'd pretty much steamed the iron dry.

"You want me to take that iron for you, Mrs. Cartwright?"

The voice again, softer this time – "Ally?"

That's Hank, she hears him now, no rifle pining for cattails, chord grass, blinds or decoys. Hank. What was she thinking? She doesn't bother calling out. He never hears over his fan. And he's not much for idle conversation, not recently, not ever really. He must be needing something. Why does Kerri make her so nervous? Just filled to overflowing with sharp edges and unexpected corners? Why? She can feel that girl creeping up behind her. Suddenly she needs to be somewhere else.

"Mrs. Cartwright? Alice? I can go to him."

She doesn't trust herself to speak. She sets the wheezing, waterless iron down and swears she can feel its mute indignation at almost being burnt out. Guiltily she switches it off, and pushes aside and through various pieces of living room furniture, making a direct line, in her determined way, for the back bedroom and Hank. She is stopped by the body of a large, capable woman in faded overalls coming straight at her, out of the dining room, barreling towards her, a ballistic intercontinental missile shot out of some unseen underground silo . It stops her cold. It's Alice of course. Alice and Kerri behind her wearing an anguished, puzzled expression on her pretty face. She isn't holding the lemonade anymore.

Looking at her reflection in the glass in front of the gun cabinet she doesn't even recognize herself, although, truth be told, Alice hardly ever looks at herself. Why bother? It's the same old face. She quickly traces the straight, honest lines around the eyes – years of squinting, some laughing, a little shouting, short, bristly blond hair with a sprig of gray here and there, same pug nose, same round, tanned cheeks, same worried, distracted expression hanging over it all.

She doesn't look angry, which is what she expected. She looks surprisingly worn. Frayed. Thinning. Unraveling even, she's a work shirt put one too many times through the wash, hanging almost transparent on the line, drying out quickly in the hot July sun. That's what she looks like – dried out. When had she started to look that way? Thirty five isn't all that old. Hell. She can almost feel herself vanishing piece by piece, moment by moment. She brushes the back of her hand shakily across her forehead.

She feels a hand on her shoulder now. She lets out a sigh almost before she can prevent it and takes in a long-shuddering breath. Kerri squeezes her shoulder and pushes on past her into the bedroom opens and half closes the door.

She looks away. The gun case perches incongruously above that old sideboard - dark intricate polished wood designed for the eye of a Renaissance prince, a mountain of babied and fretted-over mahogany that her mother's mother's mother received as a wedding present in Mobile, Alabama from... who? a niece. A former governor. Some personage related in some 2nd cousin-twice-removed kind of way and living in Italy. Or France. Or something like that. No that's not right.

The somewhat lopsided macramé doilies spread on top of the sideboard however, they come directly from Alice's hand. They are the sad fruit of last winter, this spring, and this summer's long days and longer nights sitting by Hank's sickbed. She spies her 3-5/8 oil filter pliers on a mostly clean towel draped over the far side of the marble top. They hide shyly, nestled behind a blizzard of spindles, curlicues and woody whatnots. She'd been wondering where that had gotten off to. Funny, she couldn't remember putting it there.

"Ally." This time there's a lot of strength in his call. Alice's breath catches in her throat.

Anders Flagstad

"Easy there" says Kerri from the other room, "let me do it, Mr. Cartwright. Mr. Cartwright?"

Where is her mind? Her heart skips a few beats, and she begins swimming down the gloom of the back hallway, paddling forcefully with arms and legs towards the half-open door at the back, pushing, fighting, feeling a blast from the angrily buzzing rotating fan hit her from within just as she punches the door wide open. She blinks her eyes closed for a second, rubbing them with the back of her hands, drying and the rubbing the sweat out, the stinging sweat filling in the corners of her eyes and backing up into her lower lashes, covering her sight with an acid, sand-scraping, undeniable curtain of pain. She stands rubbing, the fan comes back and hits her square in the face again. She admits, in the end to herself, finally, that it's not sweat, it's tears. You would have thought she'd have given up the luxury of personal dishonesty a long time ago.

Nothing in her life fits together anymore. To be truthful, nothing ever had, not the way it should have, not, at least, according to the way everyone else thought it should have. But if you are strong enough you force things to fit and hold them tight and guess what? It stays together. The way a ball of sand stays together. Well, a wet ball of sand. It holds. It's recognizably a temporary ball.

And that works, as long as you are strong, and Alice is. As long as you keep your eyes open and watch for things beginning to slip, and Alice does. You watch and grab, you hold and watch. It tires a body out to do it, and work-wise, it's pretty much never-ending. But you do it. She notices – that is, it appears to her, that people around her, well they aren't working nearly as hard as Alice, at all that watching and grabbing and holding. Not nearly as hard as Alice works at it. But Alice keeps on. Alice doesn't give up.

It may feel like sometimes, you're all alone. And sometimes you are. She may be all alone, but what else is new? Hell, she is always the odd extra. She is the fifth wheel. She is the odd-shaped, different-looking piece of the jigsaw puzzle that obviously comes from an entirely different box. She is the black sheep that people pretend not to notice when black is not the kind of sheep you want, not at all, when all you want is to rest your eyes on is a sea of fluffy, brilliantly white backs from the end of your nose to the far, distant, white and wooly horizon.

10

But Alice knows from experience, this kind of thinking gets a person nowhere. Life is about love and you love who's in front of you. The person in front of you. And right now Hank is in front of her. Directly in front of her. She comes in to the back bedroom to find Kerri's tear-stained face turning towards hers. Alice aims herself blindly for the swivel arm chair by the bed and plops down, leaning forward, causing the chair to go through a rapid series of hysterical pops and squeals as it settles down to her weight. Alice doesn't hear anything though, nothing at all.

Kerri backs out, biting her lip and quietly closes the door. Alice doesn't hear her leaving. Alice doesn't see her go.

She smoothes Hank's limp, sweaty hair, brushing and parting it in the middle that way he likes it, fussing ineffectually over the sheets, pulling and tugging and tucking when she glances down and notices out of the side of her eyes that his chest isn't moving anymore. She feels with the back of one arm, laying the big forearm awkwardly but gently across his chest and touching the side of his neck feeling for the pulse. Nothing. He isn't breathing. Isn't moving. He isn't. She finds herself strangely fixed in place, rusted solid all the way through to immobility, eyes closed, listening, every inch of her skin taut as a drum sampling and sieving the air, straining to catch the slightest sound, the slightest vibration. But what her arm is resting on is as unyielding and quiet and amicably composed as any piece of furniture in this room. Maybe more so. This goes on for quite a while. She can't stop. She sits and listens, sits and waits.

Alice. Me. Stubborn as all get out. Everyone says so. Strong and careful and... Hank says so. Said so. Says so. She waits. Hands as big as shovels, helplessly hanging from the ends of these arms. Nothing to do. A strong woman and she couldn't even keep him there in his own bed. Couldn't even keep him safe. She thought "I didn't even see him leave."

A knotted, tangled, irredeemably kinked and twisted ball of fearfulness and anxiousness Alice has been carrying around, an obscene charm on a uselessly large charm bracelet of pain, well it abruptly vanishes. It surprises her. It evaporates; leaving a hole. She feels the air and the light passing right through her now. She's' made it, she's transparent. Holding herself still, poking around carefully inside, up and down, inside and out, her short bristly hair, her strong reliable body, her solid thighs, her legs and strong feet, she realizes that the hole she's feeling isn't the absence of all that fear, the hole is Alice herself. There is an Alice-sized hole in the universe now. The room is empty. Both Alice and Hank aren't there anymore.

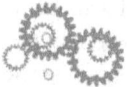

It was a week before she noticed Hank's name is fading out on her wrist. Another name, in a much more swirly, curl-filled, perky illegibility appears on her tanned skin – the letters clearer and clearer, limp alphabet noodles rising wanly to the surface of piping-hot tomato soup. She starts wearing long sleeved shirts.

It's a year and half later, late winter, and Alice and Kerri are eyeing each other over their coffee cups, sipping, glancing, resting elbows on the tiny, scratched and dented linoleum dinette Alice has next to microwave stand, by the dead potted plant hanging in front of her kitchen window. A radio gospel program plays old-timey, four-part, a cappella congregation singing in the background. Alice sometimes chimes in with a tuneless grunting, following the alto, Kerri breaks out in a squeaky, high soprano unexpectedly, from time to time. It always makes Alice jump.

Blowing on her coffee and shifting dangerously to one side in her tiny chair, Alice wants to say "I wish you wouldn't do that" but holds her tongue, Kerri being so nice and all to keep company with her. Kerri's been at it at least once a week, all during this past year. At first Alice wouldn't open the door to her. As it is, Alice hardly says a word. She doesn't know why Kerri puts up with her.

The hymn enthusiastically lurches into another verse. Alice can almost see them. She can almost smell pine-board varnish of pews, hear irreverent, heathen flies buzzing through bands of Sunday Meeting sunlight, feel dozens of lungs pumping honest, sky-thrown melody out of throats used normally for everyday talking, eating, breathing. She listens to the miniature congregation of singers winding up for the final soulful chorus of Precious Memories. She hums a few of the low notes to herself, eyes closed, grinning because she knows she's hit, dead-on, that funny alto harmony that always hangs below the melody with the sassiness of a ripe, glowing strawberry, and looks up, gripping her Knob Lick Mountain Ozarks souvenir mug with both hands (the handle broke off long ago), enjoying the warmth on her palms, the tickling coffee steam in her nose, the river of milk and honey flowing through her mind to see Kerri grinning from ear to ear. She's leaning on the table, balancing that heart-face of hers in both fists and smiling at her like there's no tomorrow. Alice feels a strange shifting, a bumping and a crashing inside her - a storage room door opening and what was inside, packed floor to ceiling, spilling out onto the floor in every direction.

"What?" Alice bites her lip and tries to put a frown on her face but only succeeds in making herself look playful - not the look she was going for - a little girl in a meadow play-lecturing a dandelion on how to behave itself properly and lady-like during a long summer's afternoon.

"Nothing." Kerri sits back and smiles. And then she smiles some more.

"Well" says Alice and sits back, a screw on the chair somewhere pulling sharply on wood and calling out piteously. "Well, well, what have we here?" Alice feels trapped and outwitted someways she doesn't quite understand completely. Trapped the way you'd lure a dog inside on a frost-bitten winter night with loving arms, food, water and a warm rug on the back porch. Trapped. A lucky trapped, possibly. Maybe a safe trapped. If safe is what a person is looking for. Is she looking?

She suddenly has an image of her freedom, wide-eyed, mouth open, face pressed against the window of an express train, barreling away from her forever into parts unknown, waving frantically at Alice standing dumbfounded on the station platform.

"So," says Kerri "did anyone ever tell you Al, that you have the prettiest smile?"

Alice doesn't trust herself to answer. Her smile, which switches up from 30 watts to 120 does it for her. The tracks are empty now. Alice realizes, somehow, somewhere in the last few minutes she made a decision. Why is she always running, trying to catch up with herself? Kerri straightens up, puts both hands primly in her lap and locks her gaze onto Alice's. Alice looks down, and on impulse, pulls her right wrist out of her long sleeves. She hasn't dared look at her tattoo since Hank's funeral . Not even showering. Not even in the tub. Afraid of what she might see. Knowing what it would mean. There it is. Happy, sprawling letters – a signature on her wrist, "Kerri" as plain as the nose on her face, with an "I" at the end dotted with a heart. Always the last to find out. She looks up, determined and ready, the way she looks when she has an old engine to rebuild and weeks of work ahead of her and she may as well get started because the sooner she starts the sooner she's going to be done with this whole re-building thing she's doing and where in the heck did all this come from and why does it always have to happen so fast and why is life so mysterious. Alice asks the universe but expects no answers.

"Move to California with me, Al."

"O.K."

It happens almost as soon as they finish unpacking.

The (very) little they bring with them hardly fills this mind-staggeringly expensive doll-house apartment (really a remodeled garage) they rent in Pittsburg. Yes, Pittsburg. Pittsburg, California that is. No "h" - Alice is reminded of this important fact many, many times. A kind of gentler, stress-less, mellow and centered, Zen-like Northern California spelling, as this is the East Bay – and, after all, Berkeley's just around the corner.

California turns out to be beautiful. Palm trees. Swimming pools. Movie stars. As advertised. Yes, Alice will certainly admit to all of that. But their tiny corner isn't exactly a sand-filled bikini romp through blue-skied, always-summer Nirvanas. A steady hum and whooshing in the background isn't the gentle sound of California surf, it's a mega-interstate humming with wildly-driven metal torpedoes, rubber tires whining continuously, pushing across eight lanes of concrete. A maze of oil refineries' storage tanks peeks above trees in their backyard - trees that look to be a forest in some Midwestern state, cornily pretending to be next to a wheat field when actually they're nestled here among steep, whiter-than-white grass-covered hills. Fingers of ocean water wiggle between the slopes, appearing oddly and unexpectedly fifty miles from any beach. The walls in their apartment, well Alice could put her fist through them and has, by accident while making a dramatic point about the sarcastically high cost of groceries here in the Bay Area.

The transition to their new life, as Kerri puts it, alarms here. It shouldn't be this easy. She keeps thinking she's missing something, something important, something that will come back and bite her in the ankle, pull her down and devour her and she'll wish she'd gone running back to Texas then. She's a little tired of waiting for unavoidable, impending disaster, but one of the two of them has to do it. She waits. Waits and looks over her shoulder. But so far, nothing, nada, zip. The universe and its habit of jealously squashing and obliterating burgeoning human happiness hasn't noticed Alice and Kerri. At least, not yet.

Kerri, sweet and supportive and upbeat, nests energetically. Flowers, new brightly colored cloth prints for curtains, a plaque with two frogs sitting on a lily, rubbing heads, eyes shut and grinning, saying "Welcome to our pad."

Alice sinks into a post-purchase, buyer's remorse, totally-new-life depression, wondering what in the world she was thinking. But between looking for work during the day and re-discovering her body (with much help from Kerri) at night, she really doesn't know whether she is coming or going anymore. She's on Life's Tilt-A-Whirl now, and it's going faster and faster and the scary part is, it's just getting started. It's all blending together into one funhouse blur of hormones, sun and sex and pure, unadulterated terror. What really scares Alice sometimes is that she's actually doing all right. Somehow, someway, the two of them are making a new home together here on the edge of the continent.

And then she notices.

Alice's wrist, with a mind of its own like always, transfers its allegiance abruptly, in the space of a few hours during a single night's sleep , from the unsuspecting Kerri to a mystery person who writes in gawky, lumbering block letters – the shadowy, forceful, and somehow sexy "Deb" – Alice isn't amused. She somehow hides it in the morning, tells Kerri she has a sprain and wraps it with a satisfyingly opaque springy drugstore bandage. She never takes it off now. It only slows them down a little bit in their nocturnal gymnastics. Sometimes, long and late into the night, holding Kerri's blond head against her side with her strong right, Ace-bandaged arm, Alice lies wide-awake, staring at the foam pebbles on the false popcorn ceiling, brushing the short hair on her head backwards and forwards, backwards and forwards (she parts it in the middle now just the way Hank used to part his, a way of remembering him 24 hours a day with a part of her body, although she doesn't tell Kerri that's the reason she's doing it), and she worries.

She is trying to imagine what the face of a Deb would look like, piecing together shapes in the shadows on the bumpy ceiling - shadows cast from the sodium vapor lights clicking loudly on and off in the refinery behind the tiny bedroom of their garage apartment. She does this often and for quite some time. Eventually the low-tide, soft hissing of eighteen-wheelers and night owls sailing over the bright expanses of interstate concrete a couple of blocks behind her will buoy her up, float her gently off, out and away, set her free sailing into the wide sea of California midnight rising in slow swells all about her.

Released. Well, almost. She nearly, but not quite, outruns her worries. She drifts and dozens of Deb incarnations float by her on waves of white noise, as she bites her lip, eyes resolutely closed, thinking of a trusting, sleeping, tenderly snoring head nestled between her breast and bicep.

The night streets are starkly empty, its past ten, and Alice is beginning to wonder why she and Kerri and another nurse friend from the clinic Kerri works at are driving around in circles in this wasteland of parking lots, homeless people pushing marvelously full shopping carts, barred and gated repair shops, condos snugly closed behind steel paneled, bright-riveted fronts. Every so often there's boiling knots of thin twenty-somethings, decked out in various shades of black under pools of neon light. Alice thinks they resemble nests of hungry ants investigating fallen and undefended Jolly Ranchers. She makes yet another right turn – never a left turn - onto yet another one-way. The city of San Francisco hates left turns the way Nature hates a vacuum. They have this zero-tolerance policy towards them. Alice has learned that hard way and has the tickets to prove it.

Annette, Kerri's friend giggles at something in the back seat, and Kerri leans back to get in on the joke. Annette's always giggling. Alice says to herself "Just get through it, get out, and get on the other side." If they could see her face, it would be one of those smiley faces that has the smile that's just a grim, straight, bare line.

"Annette says to turn down the next alley and find an empty spot on the sidewalk" Kerri whispers beerily into Alice's ear, giggling. Maybe those Tecates back in Pittsburg weren't the best idea. Sidewalk? Alice feels someone kicking the back of her seat. She grips the steering wheel tighter. So this is a South of Market San Francisco bar adventure. Annette's eyes had glowed a hysterical baby blue when she heard Kerri and Alice hadn't ventured into the City yet. Hell, they hardly left Pittsburg except for runs to Costco and that was in neighboring Antioch. The Home Depot was only four blocks away. Coming over the Bay Bridge from Oakland, Alice has the strange feeling she's flying an X-wing fighter into the canyons of the Death Star. It's beautiful in ways her brain doesn't have, or maybe doesn't want to have, the ability to register.

Nudge. Nudge. This time the punches seem to be a signal. Alice stops herself from whacking backwards. Instead Alice obediently turns to the left, down a narrow wilderness of chain-link, dumpsters, and abandoned cars left at various angles to the roadway. She starts looking. She feels more nudging, but doesn't see a spot, and then the giggling around her crescendos, twin pistons in an engine about to blow a gasket. Alice restrains an impulse to reach over and pitch them both out the window. She thumps the steering wheel a couple of times. Solid whacks. It feels good. Then she has an epiphany. It gets strangely quiet in the car, except for some muffled gasping. She finds an empty angle between two "abandoned" cars, and expertly slides in and between them, parallel parking, switches off the ignition, declares herself parked, mentally braces herself, and turns around to look directly at Kerri and Annette. Both of them are staring at her with big, moist eyes, biting their lips, unsuccessfully trying to bottle up their giggling and guffawing, trying to let her get on with the very important job of getting them to a club and drunk. The attempt at helping her softens her up some. They burst out of the car into the cool and foggily damp San Francisco night in a cloud of girlish laughter, some of it Alice's. Alice thinks "Well, maybe, just maybe."

The streets they walk are deserted and muffled-quiet in the fog. Alice has all her senses on red-alert, scanning the perimeter constantly, memorizing the way back to the car, looking ahead for roadblocks, imagining darting, skulking forms. Kerri and Annette are huddled, whispering, weaving back and forth gently in the stray waves of fog, black hair mingling with blond, bare shoulder to bare shoulder (they're both wearing flimsy string-tops and tight, bright-colored pedal pushers – like they're sisters - they'd be freezing except they're powered by Tecate tonight). Alice is more rationally dressed in new, bright blue work jeans and a surprisingly clean t-shirt stretched over her ample bosom. You can't even see where she bleached out transmission fluid around the collar.

She feels the vibration of the club long before she sees it. Then, suddenly they turn a corner and there are women everywhere. Solid walls of estrogen stretching in front of them. A line of women outside a long, low building. Tangled kinks and bunches of them in complicated feminine inter-relationships that apparently everyone understands but Alice. As would any worldly-wise, alpha female elephant, Alice, the good matriarch she is, gathers and pulls her little herd closer to her side and slows them all down to a shuffle to reconnoiter the situation with the proper care and caution such a predicament requires. Kerri and Annette ignore her. They squeeze into the knots of women, rapidly wending their way towards the front door and disappear. Alice follows a little miffed.

The doorman (or doorwoman) sports shiny heavy black leather pants, a leather jacket with stainless steel chains dotting and draping the front, and a face that could face down a Panzer Division before breakfast. She could easily wrestle Alice to the floor, and that's saying a lot. On top of it all, this bouncer has obviously bounced and partied a little on her own before she got herself together and showed up for work. Her half-lidded eyes are ogling every girl in line, in turn. They miss nothing. They enjoy all. And when she's done, she starts all over again.

As they get to the front of the line, she ceases sullenly fumbling and mumbling for ID's and awakens grandly from what looks a lot like sleepwalking (or sleepchecking in this case), reaches down behind her, grabs in a kind of acrobatic, alcoholic grace an enormous cartoon-sized bottle of Colt 45, takes a long, slow swig, and stands up a little unsteadily, still holding the bottle, to call out "aureole check." The line is silent for a millisecond, then erupts in explosive conversational exclamations. "Oreo?" thinks Alice darkly, "no one's checking my Oreo tonight."

Apparently the three girls immediately in front of them are having difficulty with the concept too, they don't seem to speak English and their downturned eyebrows and prettily managed frowns rouse the bouncer to further heights of explication. The leather-encrusted one says in a lower, careful voice, a teacher bringing the slow students up to the general-class speed "Nipples, ladies. I'm here to inspect your tits." The red-haired one in front screams, a full-throated exclamation that could only mean yes, scrambles to pull off her shirt, and promptly falls against her friends in a heap. Obviously , someone else had been doing a little alcoholic pre-loading with the cheap stuff before they went out bar-hopping tonight. The friends of the now half-nude woman duck behind and around her in a last spurt of exasperation and disappear into the all-consuming throb and crash of bass beating out of the open door of the club. The swinging doors close quickly behind them with an unheard slam. The red-haired girl is left with one breast cupped by one hand of the bouncer, while she is offered a turn at the Colt 45 with the other. The red head doesn't move, the leather woman says "No?" then glancing down bobs the breast up a down a couple of times and says "Honey I've seen bigger."

A face slap, an explosion of re-robing and a most severe rebuke ensues. The word bitch and what sounds like what just might be long, elaborate insults in a foreign language (French?) punctuated by sharp barks of laughter and pointed head wags goes on for a minute or so until it is drowned out by another voice - a long, drawn out wail of "Deborah!"

The door is open again. The red-head is gone. Popped and propelled by her own invective into the club, a chic watermelon seed that just got spit out, only an empty space remains where the a tornado of Gallic fury once stood. The leather-bound breast-inspector tries to slip her massive bottle unobtrusively between her feet and sit back down on her ancient stool in something approximating a professional, nonchalant pose, but the approaching voice will have none of it. "I TOLD you, Deb, I TOLD you The City's out to get my liquor license. Give me that bottle. In plain sight. On the street. Give it to me! Now! I said Now!" Alice is unsurprised to find out that near naked females on public thoroughfares do not merit even the slightest mention in this town. "Look" says the unseen not-to-be-brooked-no-nonsense mother-voice from beyond the door, now apparently waving a half-empty bottle of beer around "just a fucking fifteen minutes. Barb needed a fucking fifteen minute break, and you, you… just fifteen minutes. I fucking swear…" The door closes, it goes quiet, the fog blows and everyone realizes they are standing out in the cold separated from a warm cube of music, dancing, mayhem, and forgetfulness by one slightly drunk woman who's way too clever for her own good. The line bunches up towards the front and people kind of start to push a little. Alice pushes efficiently but forcefully back and goes about creating an adequate, workable open space in front of the leather bouncer for the three of them.

The bouncer seems to really notice them for the first time. "Ladies" says Deb, expertly eyeing each one in turn and grandly disdaining to closely examine their proffered I.D's. She pauses for effect. She opens the swinging door with the back of one very solid arm. She braces it open for them with a kick of her jack-booted foot, and puts thumb and forefinger together on the brim of her black cap (which looks suspiciously similar to a battered and used Hollywood prop for an SS Storm Trooper's) – a cap she's just put on, just for them, completely covering her spiky, short black hair. Then with an only barely perceptible swaying, she repeatedly waves them in, smiling graciously. Alice notices in passing that she's waving them in with what appears to be another full bottle of Colt 45.

Kerri and Annette squeeze in, looking happily into each other's eyes, beaming the message "and this is the reason you come into the City." Alice pushes in sidewise right after them, unsure whether or not she feels a leather glove grab one denim-covered buttock as she tumbles in, rubs her arm and its Deb tattoo, and realizes she's just met a Deb. No. Not THE Deb. Universe, this is not the Deb you're thinking of. I mean, you meet Debs all the time. They're everywhere. Deb is a very common name.

Alice pads in behind them, thinking too much now, worrying, rubbing her jeans, feeling a handprint on her backside burning through the material and marking her, a cattle brand (she's part of the Deb herd now) - and lights, laughter, music from speakers taller than her, the smell of a hundred close-packed women crashing in a wave over them, it swallows them. Swallows them whole. The door closes and the three of them and their night are safely on their way, journeying through the wilderness to parts unknown.

"You never ask me how I feel."

Alice types her rapid-fire, two-fingered typing, she doesn't bother looking up. Gwen, the unhappy, abused voice across the room doesn't bother noticing that Alice isn't looking.

"When are we going?"

It's hot. Sticky, prickly hot. Unnaturally hot. A keening, squeaky sound, motorcycle tires being wheeled at an angle across polished concrete, hangs in the air around Alice. Her shoulders immediately tense in readiness. She mentally cracks her knuckles and uncrimps her neck. She's ready for a good fight. The air in the room crackles and spits - a violent summer night with a big lightning storm just about to break. Alice just wants it over. Whatever it is. Over and done with.

"Everyone's leaving but us."

It's also Friday night. Alice pulls off her glasses, arranges a smile in Gwen's direction, leans back in a rickety office chair, folds her hands behind her sand-and-salt, blond-grey head, looks out the open office door. She catches Deb waving goodbye, snapping a black helmet onto her close-shaved, black-fuzzed head. Deb scuffs both feet across the floor, revs up her bike, maneuvers the big Honda chopper out onto the sidewalk in front of the garage, motors out and is lost into her weekend. Alice leans forward, listens to the bike's grumbling roar until it's lost in the general traffic noise and hits the switch under her desk that shuts and locks the big front garage doors. She watches them close, making sure no one slides in, under the rumbling doors as they roll back down. They click loudly, shutting them in, tight and closed.

She glances back at Gwen again, who ignores her, and Alice shrugs, smiling to herself, entering bills into her laptop, smelling the honest odor of her labor - black caked fingernails, hands, arms, and overalls reeking of motor oil, grease, more motor oil, and several other miscellaneous chemicals Alice would be hard-pressed to identify without seriously sitting back and trying to reassemble the roster of vehicles Deb saddled her with today. Cars hoot and trucks rumble on Army Street outside. It's rush hour. Another illusory bubble of weekend optimism explodes over San Francisco and Alice. Abruptly everyone's fleeing - refugees from the bitter land of responsibilities scouting out the way to the often-promised, seldom-found land of careless pleasures. Everyone's in movement. Well, almost everyone.

Alice works for a while. Stretches. Gets some coffee. Then works some more. She looks up over the half-moons of her reading glasses and catches Gwen in sullen smolder, glaring now specifically in her direction, her thin arms crossed as she kicks the back of Alice's battered, peeling, only partially riveted leather coach.

Gwen's last contribution to their conversation - "I am so fucking bored" - hangs provocatively in the air - not unlike the unavoidable smell of someone who has just upchucked in the backseat of your car. Gwen doesn't care. She doesn't care because she's beyond caring — she's slowly being tortured to death by the sheer monumental boringness of this oven-hot afternoon with boring-as-hell, businesswoman Alice in an honest-to-God auto repair shop for Chrissake. Gwen wants to know what she did to deserve this. Gwen wants to know when someone will start paying attention to Gwen's needs. And what the hell happened to the genuine redneck she fell for? What? Where did she run off to?

Where is the woman who rode in an all-female motorcycle gang over all of Northern California? Where is the rebel she met in the Castro last month parking her bike in back of Walgreens, offering her a ride at 2 A.M. to the top of Twin Peaks? Not the old lady wearing bifocals in front of her ignoring her new jeans, her new hair color, her new piercing in her left nostril just below the previous one.

Gwen's drapes dramatically over and around and on top of the couch - imitating a viciously spilled can of female paint. She picks away at the upholstery - pick, pick, pick - innocently but rhythmically, methodically and loudly, with a certain directed malevolence, apparently all for Alice's benefit. Steadily, she's worrying a loose seam looser under her weary, uninterested head. Already a little strip of free leather is starting to flop towards the floor. Passive-aggressive unraveling. Pick, pick, pick. Alice won't bite.

Gwen. Twenty-two and tired of it. Tired of waiting. When will her life start and all the things she deserves come to her? The muffled sound of another motorcycle revs into life outside on the street. It sounds like a dirt bike. It doesn't even sound street legal. The ghost of it echoes through the closed and cavernous garage. The hollow sound bounces into the small office slash shack accreted onto the back of the building where Alice and Gwen sit in gray shadows thrown back by energetic fluorescent lamps hanging low from the high ceilings. The sound hits Gwen, a whip hitting her back, and she jerks upright. She re-drapes herself spastically, over and over again, sighing piteously. No reaction.

Alice stays head down, fingers a-pumping away, smiling and frowning to herself at the same time behind the flipped up laptop screen with a half-filled entry form beaming expectantly back at her. She keeps on typing the same thing in again. She keeps on typing it in wrong. She can't concentrate. Now Gwen's nearly upside down in her bored contortionist waiting routine, and Alice finds it almost impossible to take her seriously - not that she takes her all that seriously ever.

Alice is forty-four and knows all about waiting. It's not that she's patient, no, not by a long shot. She's just had to wait. And getting isn't always all it's cracked up to be. You get, and then you get disappointed. Sometimes the best of it was the waiting. But twenty-two doesn't want to hear any of that. So, Alice doesn't tell her.

Alice's office cell phone, by her big binder of invoices, breaks out in a melody from the Nutcracker Suite. It's the irritating ring Alice has programmed for Deb's cell number on Alice's phone when Deb calls her. Deb consistently refuses to notice how annoying The Nutcracker ring is when she chances to hear it, which Deb knows makes Alice crazy. This is how the two of them communicate to the other person that they still love them. Using and ignoring disturbing ringtones. She flips her cell open and jams it into her ear.

" Yeah" says Alice, "Didn't I just see a sugar-plum fairy flit off into the sunset?" She hears miniature snorts and some of Deb's honking laugh, some actual car horns honking and a low, steady purring sound - a hundred cars gridlocked in front of a stoplight and radios and even some yelling going on — you can almost feel the heat lifting off of the pavement. It must be hell out there. San Franciscans hate heat. Alice finds herself listening to the sound of the idling engines and categorizes the various wheezes, coughs, and panting, motorized gasps, estimating how much it would cost to fix each one and what their profit margin might be if they did. Deb's voice booms out at her and Alice pulls the phone away a foot from her head.

"Alice? That you? Yeah, yeah, can't you see I'm on the friggin' phone, you moron. Just go around. "Alice hears honks punctuated with shouts. "You use that round thing in front of your fucking nose, it's called a steering wheel." More shouts. "Yeah, sure. You and who else? Unlock that door and say it again. Yeah I thought so. Go on by. Just keep going. She still there, baby?"

It takes a second for Alice to get that Deb is done for the time being messing with the general public and has turned her attention solely back on to Alice. "Yesss…" says Alice cautiously, knowing two ears on a sofa are soaking all this up with the suction of fresh sawdust tearing into a pool of newly-spilt oil. Deb coughs out a throaty cackle and then yells "I'm on the friggin' curb, you dumbfuck. Whaddya want me to do? You got plenty of room. So what's the arm been telling you these days Al?" Alice maintains an uneasy silence.

"Watch and learn, watch and learn. Cowgirl." Deb laughs softly. Alice hears clicking and beeping. What in the hell is she doing now? Is she calling someone on her other phone? Alice gets the feeling a storm is about to break.

At that precise moment Gwen's cheap phone begins banging out a muddy club beat, and Gwen pulls it out, bored, but looking slyly sideways at Alice across the room, like maybe Alice wouldn't notice the sudden transformation of a garage office into a dance floor.

"Hey" whispers Gwen into her hand, cupped away from Alice so she can't see. Alice can hear Gwen clearly with one ear — the office ear, and amazingly also barely with the other — the one on the phone with Deb. Then Alice hears Deb's voice in stereo. Stereo. From her phone. And from, where? From her couch? Alice thinks "She is NOT doing this."

"Stop it, Deb, I'm warning you." Alice growls. Gwen jumps at Alice's voice, hazards a quick glance back at Alice and the laptop, frowns a little now, hunches back down.

Deb's voice low and purring. "So how 'bout it? You coming over later? The key's under the big round rock by the front stoop."

"Stop it." Says Alice. "Now. I mean now. This isn't funny, Deb." Gwen gets an odd look on her face and looks at her cell and then over at Alice, then at her cell. But she rolls over, stretching elaborately the way a cat does, waking up, and turned away from Alice whispers into her phone "After two, I got like, things to do first. You know."

Alice looks sharply up, dropping the receiver heavily on the desk, scraping the chair out from underneath her and knocking it back, ricocheting it in a sharp plastic/metallic thud against the wall behind her with the precise violence of an eight ball hitting a bumper shooting for the side pocket. The chair bounces off the desk, off the filing cabinet and comes to rest on the floor in front of Gwen.

Gwen doesn't have a chance. She's scrambling to get completely out the side door, as Alice grabs and pitches her ratty, military surplus backpack over Gwen's head and into the twilight of the alley. When Gwen stops to get her breath, pausing in the long string of pornographic names she's calling Alice, some of them even creative - she fumbles at the pockets in her jeans and yells back "hey Elsie, four-eyes, where's my fucking phone?" To Gwen's credit, she catches, doesn't duck and doesn't drop Alice's major league, over-arm, baseball pitch aimed straight at Gwen's young, bored cleavage. Although, Alice thinks, in the dim light of the narrow, urine-scented alley, it looks as if some random pieces of plastic casing may have exploded out of Gwen's hands upon impact. Gwen ends up walking backwards toward the big iron gates that let out onto Army Street, watching Alice carefully for any more ambushes. A quick click, a sturdy slam and then Gwen is gone.

The garage is suddenly very quiet, and a lot more roomy. Alice watches the alley for a second or two, one foot keeping the back office door open, eyes blinking, face reddening, breathing a little rapidly, hands clenching and unclenching in purposeful fists, which now have nothing to hit. When her breathing is more normal, she goes back inside, letting the heavy steel outer door slam violently and satisfyingly.

Her desk is laughing at her. The cell lies face-up on her

keyboard. Alice picks it up and starts looking around the office for her glasses, or the pieces of her glasses. She can't find them. She feels the cover of the phone bend slightly in her fist. She's holding it way too tight. She puts it in her left hand, shaking her right hand above her head to get circulation back in her thumb. In the process, she manages to whack one of the hanging fluorescent lights, and she starts cursing under her breath.

"So girly-girl's gone, huh? Gone for good?" Deb is still laughing.

"Deb, I'm just telling you. Someday. Someday you're going to go too far."

"Girl, I'll always have your back, you know that. I told you she was poison. Pure poison. When you gonna start listening to your Auntie D?"

Alice sets the phone down on the desk and hits speakerphone, looking down at her wrist. It has the look of something an animal has been gnawing and clawing at it – lines every which way – half-formed letters – it's funny, she ought to be laughing out loud it's so funny, Gwen never once asked her about her wrist – she wonders if she even noticed it.

Well - maybe that was an A, maybe a Q, maybe it was a map of the streets of San Francisco starting to wriggle out of the general rat's nest of characters wandering down, up, and around her forearm.

"I can see someone we both know, whose name starts with Gwen, walking right towards me and the bus stop I'm pulled next to. Whoops! Correction! I've been sighted. The target is now high-tailing it down the street the opposite direction towards San Jose. Not many bus stops thataways for Miss Nose Ring. Hope she's got her best walking shoes on." Deb is chuckling, but Alice can hear her working her clutch, yanking the revs up and down, getting ready to pull out into traffic.

Let's see now – Alice runs both hands through her hair and tries to force a part on the top of her head, but it's too short for that - there'd been Kerri, then Deb, then Paris, then Lamansha, then Gwen. Where had Zana come in again? And there'd been that one time with Annette, before Kerri had seen Deb's name on Alice's arm and run off to Annette's condo never to return. The past 9 years were a blur. And now she had Deb's garage to run, well soon Deb and Alice's garage when Alice got that inheritance from her mom settled in Probate, which would be soon if that lawyer from Dallas would get off his behind and actually start working for his money. With any luck, she'd be too busy for girlfriends then.

Alice doesn't hear any more laughing. The speakerphone is silent except for random bursts of static and complaining combustion engines. Alice is weary. She sits in the deepening gloom, her head resting on one hand, listening to the fluorescents hum efficiently above her.

"Yeah that's a turn signal stupid. It means I'm gonna turn. You O.K. honey?" Deb asks into the silence. "Lacey and I could swing by later. You could drive the old Harley. It'd be like old times. Be good for you to get out. Al? Al?"

"You there, Al?"

"Al?"

"I'll be fine, Deb. Just fine."

The reunion is at the County Park this year, out by the reservoir, ringed by white oak, winged elm, and persimmon. It feels like home, but Alice feels different. Alice feels like a stranger.

The humidity is East Texas crazy and the temperature close to a hundred and Deb, Lace, and Alice as long-time San Francisco residents who promptly wilt in weather even 10 degrees above 65 visibly deflate and diminish after they leave the cylinder of frosty air in Deb's Volvo.

Ever since Pat left Alice to go back to her ex-husband in Fresno, Deb and Lace have been pushing Alice. They go at her all the time. They try to get her out, but Alice would rather not. She'd rather work. And what's wrong with that? Working? Someone's gotta do it. The garage has never had a better year, and they know it, but they still have to push her, push new women at her, push vacation getaway folders in bright getaway colors in front of her nose, just push, push, push. But Alice is an expert at dodging. And not a single shove, not a single punch has landed until just recently.

Alice successfully spun and weaved and ducked every push. Every single one. Until just recently. Then she just plain collapsed, gave up. No one holds out against a Deb assault for long. Everyone throws in the towel eventually. Everyone. They were relentless. Three weeks ago, they threatened to hog-tie her, kidnap her, and Fedex her to this reunion themselves. She didn't react. Well, then, maybe they'd just throw her, trussed up in the back of Deb's station wagon and drive on out to the reunion, feeding her a liquid diet of fast food milkshakes and ice cream cones to keep her alive for her family's sake. That'd get her out of San Francisco. She'd been silent. No reaction. Then rope showed up one morning in a neat coil on the seat of her office chair with a well-thumbed Boy Scout book on tying knots and she could see she was going to be on the losing end of the this reunion road trip battle and the rest, as they say, was history.

Now Hank's grand-nephews and nieces are getting their butts whooped at horseshoes by Lace. Deb is over by the beer keg telling tall stories to guys chewing and spitting by the long weeds. Alice shades her eyes and walks purposefully about, scouts around for some fair-sized shade, tries to look like she belongs to this family.

Sometimes Alice feels like multiple people, so many different Alices have lived under her skin in her lifetime, and there were probably more tapping their feet impatiently, waiting and limbering up, ready to jump in as soon as the current one had gotten tired of carrying on in Alice's substantial frame. Well, they were going to have to cool their heels for awhile. Let 'em get used to waiting for a change. The present Alice is feeling generally happy and mostways satisfied, notwithstanding the occasional rough bump and spectacular crash that just makes life more interesting. She's gotten more and more content, with less and less. Someday she'll have nothing and be absolutely satisfied with everything.

Alice's shade tree is not her own. She's found what turns out to be shared shade. There is one little girl who is not playing with the others. One little girl, all by herself, who is running and skipping around Alice's picnic table in breathless circles holding bunches of picked wildflowers outstretched in her hands and singing a song to them. The little girl comes to a halt by Alice's knee and stops to look up, rubbing her forehead with one muddy hand, staring with an intent concentration at Alice's face. When Alice reaches out to touch her hand, she leaps backwards, a trout jumping on a fishing line, starts circling again, singing her serious songs about flowers and bees and fairies.

Part in the Middle

A voice rises from a group of women setting up a very large pile of food on the neighboring tables. Alice scans the horizon wondering where all the Simmons are who will be eating all this baked chicken and rice, shrimp and scallops casserole, potato salad, and jello. "Now, Lisa Kay, stop bothering Aunt Alice. Come here. Show me your flowers." Lisa Kay's song doesn't even skip a beat. The women keep working. Lisa Kay keeps running.

Deb motions for Alice to come over. Alice waves and pretends not to understand. Deb is not fooled. But Alice is seated too far away from the beer for now. Alice is safe. For the time being. Lace is over by the men, hanging around a big pot on an open fire, giving her opinions about how best to spice up this chili they're making. Alice knows most of the men over there, but for the moment Alice doesn't try and mix with them, she doesn't even try to remember their names. She just sits. She just is.

She hasn't looked at her right arm for a year or so again, not since Pat's hysterical farewell note appeared taped to their bathroom mirror one morning. She's not afraid to look at her arm. She's not. And it's not that she doesn't want to look. She does, it's just, it's just... what? She doesn't know. She's doesn't know what she wants. She just doesn't want.

Well, all she does know is she doesn't need bossy Alice appendages making life-decisions on her behalf. Not anymore. Not Alice. Maybe it just that she's being superstitious. By not looking she's not wanting. Maybe by not looking and not wanting, she'll end up finding what she's looking for after all. Isn't that Buddhist or something? Or is it Texan? She can hear her mother's voice saying something about a watched pot. Maybe a pot of chili. She can't think. Lord, it's hot today. And humid. Alice fans herself with a paper plate she finds beside her.

Alice sits back on the picnic table bench, adjusts the purple sweatband she's wearing, which is clearly not doing its job, and sprays herself down with insect repellant. She gets ready to make her move. She'll head over to the chili cookers. She feels the grain of the wood under the flaking paint, and starts to thinking about how much work it would be to sand, fill, and re-stain each table in the park. Or maybe replace them with aluminum ones. Or cast concrete ones. She's stalling, she can tell. She feels a pressure on her arm, pulling it downward. The tiny grand niece-let, Lisa Kay tugs on one sleeve, looks her straight in the eyes and wordlessly puts both arms up in the air. Alice hesitates for a second, then throws Lisa Kay over her back, shouldering her carefully as you would a sack of squirming potatoes and bounces off bucking-bronco-style with delighted high-pitched squeaks and squeals echoing loudly into her left ear.

Alice collapses, gasping, on an abandoned blanket by a tree avoiding someone else's cell phones, sunglasses, and half-empty soda cans, and she and Lisa Kay sit cross-legged resting their backs against the tree and each other, and both remain solemnly silent. They are sisters. Lisa Kay pushes her small hand into hers. Alice hears a tuneless humming from a tiny high voice bubbling up from one side of her.

Well. She'd join in and start singing with her if she knew the song. She looks down at the small hand clutching two of her fingers. Inadvertently, she looks a little to the right and she can see a letter "A" showing on her wrist now.

People always talk on and on about exciting beginnings and endings. Alice is sick of it. It's not the rough startings and stoppings she remembers, yearns for, dreams of. It's the long, smooth middles. She actually doesn't want to know who is going to drift into her life, twist it and take it over again. She doesn't want to know who she, Alice is going to have to please. She doesn't want to know who will be in charge of her happiness and her heart. She doesn't want to know.

Yes, she does. Alice's biggest failing is curiosity. Hank always said so. Deb's ribs her about it whenever she can. Yeah, it'll be the death of me. She closes her eyes. She gently releases the little hand and pushes her right sleeve back up to her bicep, in one quick, strong jerk. The mosquitoes can have a field day now. She can feel her whole arm is exposed. She opens her eyes to see Lisa Kay staring up at her with a wide eyes but a small smile. It's a smile she is sharing with Alice alone on her smooth, upturned face. Lisa Kay makes a grab for Alice's left hand, snags it, and gets it back. The humming starts floating upwards again.

She looks down at her bare right arm. There, plain as day, in her own slanted, sloppy cursive it says "Alice".

PARTICIPLES
(A PART OF SPEECH IN THREE ACTS)

Participle (*plural* participles)

1. (grammar) A form of a verb that may function as an adjective or a noun. Usually formed in English by adding –ing (present part.) or –ed (past part.) to the stem of the verb – *eg.*, *Letting go is hard to do.*

2. One of the more nervous parts of speech. A verbal-noun, implying movement as a verb would, or anchoring a sentence as a stationary noun would, or dangling anxiously and descriptively as an adjective would. Not completely of any single world, huddling miserably in a perpetual twilight, shuffling along somewhere betwixt in a

shadowy and muddled in-between.

3. (pres. part.) A part of speech signifying the middle portion of a movement. Ignorant of its beginnings, uncertain as to its final end, caught perpetually in the process of becoming.

4. (Ancient Greek) Very common way to express a thought without using nouns - *eg., Using your head on one hand, and not running away on the other hand are useful life skills to acquire.*

ACT I

ME AND HARRY

"Adam."

"Not now Harry"

"You're doing it again."

"Later. I'm busy Harry. What am I doing?"

"Substituting. Using sex in place of intimacy. Drinking dust instead of water. You told me to tell you if you did it again."

"I did not. I never told you that."

"You would have, if you'd known what to ask. And I would be telling you, if you started doing it, just as I'm trying to do right this very minute. You know what your problem is?'

"All right, I'll bite, what? – wait, no, I don't want to know. I told you, I don't have time for this Harry."

"You want control over your life, and picking up girls is a way of feeling in control."

"I'm not talking about this. And by the way, if you think hitting on a girl makes you feel in control, well, it's been many a moon since the last time you did any significant hitting. And I don't have time for this Harry."

"That was a bit below the belt. I'm surprised at you, Adam, surprised. You know it's been 1,400 years since I held a female.

That's a millennium and half. Nearly. If you were counting. Which you aren't"

"Sorry."

"That's all right, Adam. I know you mean well. You're probably just feeling lonely and acting out."

"Acting out?"

"You feel out of control, and so you try anonymous sex. But you suspect it might not make you feel better – it might make you feel worse – and why not? - it has in the past. You feel lonely and afraid and so you dangle the prospect of romance on top of the anonymous sex, and suddenly it all seems like a win-win situation. Houston, we have a go, I believe is the saying. And then there's the interesting addition of alcohol to the equation."

"Harry, Harry, Harry. I have so much I need to say about your new algebra of Adam, but I refuse to be drawn in yet again. I am busy Harry. Busy. Yes, with a woman. And you, being a man, or (oops!) having been a man (sorry, again), I would hope and expect that you would understand, scope out the situation, step aside and let me get on with my business here. My business with a woman."

"All right, we'll start again. You know where this is headed, little brother…"

"Don't Harry."

"It's how it always ends. Getting hurt, hurting her, hurting each other. Pushing away, separating."

"I'm not listening, Harry. You're talking to yourself."

"So why not separate now? Save yourself all that trouble? Hmmm?"

I refuse to look at him. He wants me to look at him.

"Because we haven't even fucking gotten together yet, that's why not. We haven't even fucking started."

No response. Now he's sulking. I find myself overloading and exploding, a nobly patient Chernobyl pushed frivolously - and for no fucking good reason - way, way past its operating parameters.

"You want me to save myself, well save your own fucking self, save yourself before you're fucking lost, if you think I'm such a loser. Maybe I won't lose this time. Maybe I won't. I really don't need this, Harry. I don't. This soothsaying. This prophesying. The all-seeing Harry. Harry the Delphic Oracle. Yeah, sometimes it's been fun. And sometimes I've needed a swift kick in the butt. But not here, Harry. Not now. I've got it hard enough as it is. I'm a walking triage unit, a medical non-starter. Back problems. Neck tortures. Intestinal absurdities. I really don't have a place to live, I'm new to the city, no friends, no family. I'm sick. I need distraction. I need a break - a break from reality here. I need a break from life. I just need a break, Harry.

No! *You* listen, Harry. I don't have *anybody*. I am *all alone*. Alone, Harry. No one's looking out for Adam. Nobody. Nobody but me. And I get tired sometimes. Yeah, and lonely. Sometimes I'd like someone to help me out, for once. Someone else to be strong.

Yeah, yeah, well, look you know I'm not complaining. You know that. I'm not complaining about you or my broken body or my broken family or my broken anything. I'm not. It's been this way for years and years and I don't complain. I am not complaining. I'm not. I'm explaining.

No, listen. Hey! Listen to me. I don't need you tearing away at me like this. Ripping me apart, some rabid dog going after a needy side of beef swinging from a hook in the meat locker of life. I swear sometimes you look like you're enjoying it. Enjoying getting a piece of me. Yeah, well I don't need this. I do not need this, comprende?

Look. You and I both know how you can get, sometimes. When you get on a roll. When you've got a point to make and you can't stop. You just go and go and go. On and on and on. Yeah, like me, right now. Right. Like me. Fine. So this time you just don't go. You stop. Stop it Harry. Stop."

"Do you feel better now, Adam? Can we talk now?"

Harry will eventually either drive me to wild acts of insanely centered, one-pointed, Zen serenity, or drive me to become an amoral arch-villain with superpowers and a crazily devoted ninja army terrorizing the earth and I'm starting not to care whether it's the one or whether it's the other.

I feel a pressure on my side, it's her. A hand pulling at my waist. Pulling on one of my belt loops so she doesn't tip over. She's a little blasted. I'd almost forgotten she was here. Fuck you Harry. She leans in close to my head as we walk tentatively up an apparently near-vertical sidewalk, taking little baby steps, just learning to walk. I guess there are two of us who are a little blasted this fine evening.

"Hey, uh…" (She won't remember my name, twenty dollars she won't even try, they never do - she'll give up on it in a few seconds.

Participles

One… Two ..) "Hey, uh, you! Hey you!" (yup, no name - and it's not even that hard a name - two syllables - I hate it when I'm right - if I had all those won-twenty-dollar-bill-bets in my pocket right now I'd be stinking rich - stinking - and I'd be unable to walk upright without limping - even though I limp sometimes anyways - but I digress). "Hey, you. Hey! C'mon. C'mon, look at me."

"Let it go. Let her go Adam. Releasing, walking, little brother, that can be good too. On the one hand feeling the cold air hit your face, on the other hand metabolizing, changing the foggy breath of night in your lungs into strong red blood. Walking away. Just walking…"

"It's not working. I'm not listening, even to the poetry. And I'm not your brother. Shut up, Harry, just shut up."

I say it, but no matter what I say, or how I say it, I know he won't. He never does.

"Who are you talking to, bright eyes?" She's comically searching the far horizons, her free hand up at her forehead shading her eyes in the non-existent sun, peering into the night at imagined shapes, swiveling her head back and forth to get a better view of them. She's cute, in a sort of cheerleader-gone-wrong kind of way. Curves resembling a topo map of the Himalayas, high inaccessible peaks, deep mysterious valleys. You'd need a Sherpa to navigate her. I think I'd attempt her solo.

She's laughing low and quiet to herself, biting her lower lip, swaying dizzily a tiny bit, then hiccupping louder, then coughing even more loudly, then gasping for breath and holding on to my shoulders for support. And laughing. And she's still smiling. At me. Her wet eyes are an iridescent gleam, beaming into me and the night from all the hacking and the alcohol, twin miniature flashlights smeared with a thin layer of petroleum jelly. All for my benefit. All for me. Adam.

My knees go watery and elastic.

I am looking, looking and smiling lopsidedly despite myself, doing the grinning, walking and wobbling thing. And then all that neck-twisting and torso torsions set off the inevitable pain - pain Nazis, once again, in my lower back - a blitzkrieg of nerve firings - accurately shot, all hitting their target, precisely and effectively incapacitating me.

I keep on re-injuring the fucker. I'm lucky, really, to still be ambulatory, to use the Emergency Room lingo which has become my second language. Shit. I'd roll my eyes but I think some vague connection between my eye muscles and my back could make things worse.

A familiar sensation. This jackboot stomping up and down my spinal cord. The Luftwaffe strafing of my lower back muscles. Pain - an old, old acquaintance of mine. And that has to be some kind of record – eight hours without mind-blowing, masculinity-humbling misery. Can the playful nausea be far behind?

A steady not-so-gentle gouging and slashing up and down a couple of lower vertebrae accompanies each step now, but I'll be damned if I'll let her see it. Not now. I can feel rhythmic pain registering on my forehead and cheeks – ripples of grimaces crossing and re-crossing the old facial pond. Closing my eyes, I imagine great gobbets of nerve and flesh sloughing off and falling to the pavement behind me as I walk. I'd see them if I turned around. I would. If I opened my eyes. I don't.

Self: note for future - not nearly enough chasers or beer in that last round of beer and chasers at the club – work consistently towards more quantity, less quality. End note.

"Limping, huh? Hurting and walking again, Adamakes? Not the best thing."

"No shit, Sherlock."

"And it's Adam" I mumble on stubbornly "It's Adam and none of that Greek shit. Not tonight, Okey dokey, Harry?"

I'm looking to my left, but I can't see Harry, even though he's there. Wait, now I see him, just at the edge of my peripheral vision. He's his usual white on white transparency, a spectacularly muscular man-shaped blur in some Late Roman uniform with a perfect face bobbing on its top, his countenance a polite and artfully arranged mask of concern and puzzlement and determination and something else I've never quite figured out. Sadness. Or maybe some unnamed emotion that comes after a long and desperate sadness. Peace? Maybe? If it's peace, it has to be some cruel kind of peace.

Harry doesn't look too happy about it. You can get peaceful just lying in your bed and you can get peaceful lying on the pavement after you've just gotten the shit stomped out of you. I know. I've done both. I think Harry's is the shit-stomped kind. Maybe all peace is a cruelty. Just a break between beatings. You know, that even sounds close to something Harry would say.

Participles

Anyways…like I said, I don't know what it is with him. Sad, peaceful, cruel. He gets me thinking strange thoughts, pushes me, shoves me wandering in my own mind, fumbling down towards foreign places within myself. Messages, miracles, monsters. All at the most inopportune times. Like now. Like right now. I've got to stop letting him get to me like this.

Harry. Well… He has the chiseled features of an angel, or a statue, or a god. He ought to, since he's the ghost of the Roman Emperor Heraclius (or so he claims – how could he prove it to me?), or a figment of my fevered, mis-firing, painkiller-sodden neurons. I can't remember when he first appeared, but it was definitely less than a year or so ago. Nowadays, there isn't a time when he isn't hanging around somewhere nearby, gathering ammunition for his next Adam-harangue.

And from long, past, intimate experience (see – I know from intimacy), I totally get that once he gets an idea into his elegant head, he'll never stop. He can't help himself. He's a fighter. And he never takes a breather. He's an avalanche, a force of nature, a law of physics, a big pain in the neck.

Harry. What can I say?

She leans her head on my shoulder. I'm still busy groveling in pain with each step. "Hey. (cough) (cough) Hey. C'mon, c'mon, just one eentsy, teensy, tinsy, itsy, bitsy looksy, big guy. Hey! Am I alone over here?"

"Letting go, letting her go, it's so easy Adam. Starting, it's even easier. We can do it together. Watch. Moving one finger at a time, moving your hand on a level plane horizontally away from her body, accelerating your walking pace…"

"Harry, for the last time, for the love of Mike, give it a rest."

"You'll thank me later."

She's going to dump me. Before she even picks me up. Right here, right on this street. Literally kick me to the curb - my ghost-infested self. I don't want to look at her. Not yet. I need to see if the old back's going to give Adam time off for good behavior and allow some honest R & R tonight. The prospects aren't good. My back, like Harry, is randomly accommodating – I'd thought pre-lubrication with Heinekens and Cuervos would have outwitted my vertebrae, but obviously I have severely underestimated their deviousness. Again. Now I'm drunk *and* in pain.

She pulls on my ear to get my attention, I tippy-toe up the hill, stalling for time. I'm finding it's also easier to balance on my toes for some reason. I must be really flying.

Bad things come in threes. She, me, we. O.K. Harry, Maybe Another Bad Idea. Maybe One of Many Bad Ideas lately. Drink, dance, debauch, another three Bad Ideas. Look, Adam, you're a fungible good – eminently replaceable by any number of healthy male twenty-somethings out and about in this very city on this very Saturday night circling the streets in Brownian motion hoping to collide with an interested, unattached female. Well, circling on Sunday morning now. The point is… I've forgotten the point.

When am I going to figure all my shit out? Ah, the point is I'm a common commodity. Like pork belly futures. I'm a big, fat pork belly, and in my new guise as said belly, I can feel my walk slowing down perceptibly, as muscle system after muscle system shuts down, legs and back tightening up into stubborn, sullen rigidity.

Tripping, hopping my way gracelessly up the cracked sidewalk now. Scuffling. Slower and slower. Gone are the fluid movements of the throbbing dance floor. Gone the easy confidence of coordinated muscles. But do I stop? No. I continue. Shuffling manfully forward. Onward. Upward. Weaving to the left, weaving to the right. A little heavy breathing here and there. But I keep in motion. One arm still wrapped around her waist. Long blond hair gets in my mouth. I spit it out. Why? Why is home always so uphill when you're so wasted? Everyplace is always so uphill in San Francisco.

"Letting go. Exiting. You can do it. Anytime my friend, anytime."

"Hey, so what are you thinking about, blue eyes? Look at me, you. Oh. Brown eyes. Well, dreamy brown eyes, then. I know you have a place. C'mon. Hey, look at me again. Let me see those eyes. Hey, you over there! Knock! Knock! Anyone home in there?" Laughter. She's talking about my eyes, but her left hand is all over my butt.

Hot breath on my cheek, explosive giggles and then my earlobe is getting nibbled. I stumble again but refuse to open my eyes more than a crack. Is the left side of my back slightly better? As her hand starts rhythmically kneading my buns, I desperately try to shoot healing energy down from the top of my head into my mid-section. Fog and cold night air billow protectively around my exposed left side, my right side is under constant attack.

"Hey, you got a car? Yeah, that's it, a car. You gotta have a car. What kind of guy doesn't have a car?"

"These girls are broken sticks leaning on your broken stick. You learn to be stronger, yes, but at what cost? What a hard way to do it, brother. It doesn't have to be this way."

"And what way does it have to be Harry?" I'm too drunk for this conversation. I decide to ignore him. What was her name? Was it Isabel? Or was it Caroline? Is it so important? I take a long, convulsive breath in, spitting out the ubiquitous hair, shaking my head and immediately regretting it. Soft, comfy pillows of inebriation lazily orbiting in the back of my brain explode and the shrapnel of the headache sets my whole world spinning wildly, faster and faster.

I open my eyes. Bad idea. My night for bad ideas. When they do the film of my life that'll be the title – "Bad Ideas." Not just one bad idea. Lots. Constantly. The ground jumps jerkily toward me, an internet video on low bandwidth. The gray-pink night sky of the city flying high above me and my sweaty forehead, rolling away, and I'm going down. Abandon ship. Adam is sinking. The sidewalk gets closer. Forward locomotion stops. A rapid descent begins.

"This" says Harry.

The pain in my back increases, if that's possible.

"Doesn't" says Harry.

Nausea trails behind me, it's a kid brother the pain can't ditch.

"Look" says Harry.

Shit. My body. Helpfulness. Is that too much to ask?

"Good" says Harry.

A little help, a little encouragement? A single night of oblivious normality? But I've grown used to being betrayed by my body. I am sure I am one, unending, life-long disappointment to my body. My body is so over me. It could have done so, so much better. So much better than Adam.

I feel oddly ambivalent about cracking my head open as I start my long tumble forward. Eyes, bright slits, dazzled and filled with streaks of orange streetlight pregnant with hidden meanings. Skin, vibrating, aware. I, Adam have become that tree, that silent tree that falls alone in that silent forest, a tree falling alone except that I'm not alone, am I? Damn.

I whirl (Terry? Monica? Gertrude?) in front of me with my strong right hand, spin her to my front and off to one side, moving quickly to save at least one of us the indignity of skidding face-first to a stop on wet, disintegrating concrete. And shockingly, I succeed. It's vanity and foolishness, but I do it anyway – I look around to see if someone, anyone is witnessing my chivalrous, acrobatic excellence - even at 2 A.M. – my dazzling alcohol-soaked motor skills.

The rest of me concentrates fuzzily on the falling. It seems to take a long time.

I notice her body twirls and snaps back towards me – probably because she's holding on to my belt now – and suddenly we are, the both of us, she laughing, me gasping, trying to say something breathily directly into each other's mouths. She rotates to a stop and ends up briefly standing squarely in front of me. For the merest millisecond, balancing on my toes, between spinal jabs of pain, she is looking into my eyes and I am looking into hers and I feel half-way like any other guy on a Saturday night holding a girl under foggy skies in this city. That is to say - normal. Normal, a normal guy about to kiss another normal girl. Why in the hell does it take me practically killing myself – why does it take that to get myself to this point?

The laws of momentum ensue remorselessly. The ground moves quickly towards us. Cheerful waves of agony blaze across my lower back, play back and forth, duck in and out of muscles, electric sheets of pain, thin and wide as sheets of summer lightning. She's still laughing. Which is probably a good sign.

We crash together through a sadly small hedge, falling lightly into a bed of soggy iris, I land with my lips and nose nuzzling her warm throat, arms pressed into the muddy earth on either side of her, doing a kind of drunken push-up over her wide-eyed self. The scent of sap and crushed leaves, soil and salt wind blanket our panting bodies in a hushed, frantic stillness.

She stops laughing. I hesitate, and then let my body sink onto hers. I can feel her heart beating clean and strong right through her lycra top, right on through the sweaty, dirty silk of my once-black club shirt. A vein in her neck by my right eye is keeping perfect time with the steady pumping in her chest. The pumping goes faster and faster. An answering pounding accelerates in my own chest. I let my face lie for a second longer nestled under her chin. I count the beats. When I reach ten I find I've decided to kiss the neck. I kiss it then I do it again. And again.

" You don't really live on someone's back porch do you? Not really, right? I mean, how could someone live on a porch? People don't *live* on porches. Right? Right?"

I, Adam close my eyes. I can feel myself smiling my tight, tense, quiet smile. I find I'm biting my lower lip. I stop biting when it starts to hurt. Harry's voice floats back over me, from far away, delicate and thin as a teacup, through diaphanous curtains of fog.

"It's probably all turning out for the best, Adamakes. I mean Adam"

"Shut up, Harry."

ACT II

THE POWER OF MOVEMENT IN PLANTS

"You may have been emperor, but this is not Constantinople, and I am not the Senate. You can't just announce this and order that."

Silence.

"I suppose you're going to tell me Death is not The End."

Silence.

Adam (who has not spoken yet, maybe because he's still drunk and is wondering besides where all the talking is coming from) asks Harry "Who is that?" and "Why am I here?" and "Where is here?" Harry says "Sleeping, that's what you're doing, and you are at the place where you fell asleep." Adam asks "Why do you always start your sentences in the middle?" Harry says "So many questions. Greek is nothing but a string of participles, and participles are always in the middle of doing something, so Greeks are too, always starting in the middle and always doing something and that's how I speak to you and be quiet and listen and watch in silence for a change."

Adam doesn't want to, but his mouth is a forgotten desert valley filled with sand and dying, half-mummified things, his head is an aching, ringing bell that's cracked and consistently off-key, his stomach is a somersaulting fool, flipping itself enthusiastically and badly, over and over and his back is a busy guerilla fighter, making random, sharp, jabbing stabs at an innocent and unprotected pair of kidneys. The kidneys are reacting by being emotionally distraught and preparing a retaliatory bursting. Really, there's a lot going on right now, Adam-wise, so Adam wisely decides to take Harry's advice and stay quiet.

They (the two of them, Adam and Harry) must be on one of their little side trips, their occasional Harry-excursions into the aether or wherever it is Harry takes Adam when they go on one of these crazy things. Adam doesn't know why Harry does it, how Harry does it, or if Adam even likes it when Harry's doing it. It's a puzzle. But it's never boring. Even if you're in excruciating, complicated pain. Adam blinks once or twice, pushes himself up on his toes and peeks ever so carefully over Harry's shoulder.

Charles Darwin glares over his newly-growing patriarch's beard - powerfully bushy in the latest style - as it bunches up against his linen-covered chest and stomach. He pushes smoothly backwards and away from the two of them (Adam and Harry) on four well-oiled wheels. His body, supported by the solid substructure of his office chair, floats across a short expanse of nearly pattern-less carpet - the carpet material worn thin by years of loving dedication to the duty of patiently bearing up under the benign weight of Charles' ever-curious cerebellum as it roams about this room, examining the cosmos, teasing out patterns and relationships. The wheels on Charles' chair stop. He adjusts and re-positions his body in front of a wide and drawer-less desk. He listens for an answer, any answer.

Silence and more silence.

He gazes in satisfaction on this tool, his desk - and he waits. He dares the silence to break his reverie.

He examines the fibrous, closely-grained, carefully shaped plane of plant material from the Quercus Robur (English Oak) a substance useful for any number of purposes. This particular specimen of worked oak, obviously from the heart of the tree and to judge by the plethora of rings visible, ancient at the time of its cutting — this table top is long and broad - large enough to hold multiple projects in a state of mid-prosecution indefinitely, and even invite more. And so it does at this moment. As a work surface, it has always proven to Charles to be an inducement to long hours of welcome labor and fruitful, insight-filled study. Now however, today, it seems hateful to him. It repels him. He is disturbed by it and his apparent inability to work.

"I must finish this first. Surely you can see that. The work must go on. Nothing must interfere."

Participles

Silence.

"That is what separates the scientist from the amateur, from the dilettante, from the part-time dabbler. Willpower. Perseverance. Work." He stops to answer any objections. There are none. He finds he is tapping his fingers in a kind of military tune on one of the few patches of open, exposed, unused desk top in front of him. He stops.

Charles spies the shadowy figure of a female form (the maid?) pause outside his partially open office door. It waits, listening. Tires of it. With a barely perceptible sigh, moves on. Charles shakes his head.

He has obligations to fulfill. Pledges he's made. Here. And here. Editing his researches and the manuscript for his (apparently) last paper – the *Power of Movement in Plants*. He will be damned (yes the language is appropriate) if he doesn't also finish his *Formation of Vegetable Mould Through Action of Worms,* that is: if his effort, decision and willpower have anything at all to do with it. And they do. They will. What could be more simple? Choice and then Action. It's how he's always lived.

He frowns at stacks of miscellany, notes, descriptions, figures, charts, etc. in front of him, all waiting for his (and Francis, his son's) magical organizing touch. On impulse he reaches for the nearest stack of the *Movement* papers. Aims for the first page. Stretches his arm out over the void between him and the desk. Takes it. Holds it in front of his face as he adjusts his spectacles to his nose.

He pauses. Silence. He holds his breath for a second, listening. He half expects to hear a mournful, warning voice echo once again in this, his *sanctum sanctorum,* if an agnostic may use that phrase and remain credible, but he hears nothing. Good. The silence continues, this time, providentially. He is to be free to work. He exhales. He notices the light has begun to fail. It is past sunset. He feels an inexplicable wave of optimism and energy buoy him up, gladdening him. Satisfied again for the moment, he looks down at the sheet of paper in his hand. Frustrated by the general murkiness, he tilts it this way and that towards the lamp on the wall. Finally, upon finding a manageable angle, with suitable illumination, he begins, he reads.

It's not working. The words run together. "The chief object of the present work…" He can't concentrate, can't focus, can't bear down on them as he would like – as he is accustomed to do. "If we observe a circumnutating stem, which happens at the time to be bent, we will say towards the north, it well be found gradually to bend more and more easterly, until... turgescence... extensibility of the cell walls... De Vries... Pfeffer... De Vries... seedling... radicle..." Word, words, and more words. He stops and looks abruptly up.

"What business have you to tell me when I am to die?"

There is no answer, but then, he hadn't actually expected one.

"Seventy is not old. Granted, my health is not at its best, but then again, it never has been excellent my entire life. You, of all people, must know that. I am not too old."

"Moreover, I have too much to do. I have people who depend upon me. It's quite out of the question. Not remotely possible. Not yet. Don't speak to me of it again. Too soon. Too much to do. Too many responsibilities."

He finds he has been waving the paper around in rhetorical gestures to emphasize each of his phrases. He has perhaps been speaking too loudly again also. He puts the paper carefully back on the corner of the desk, balancing it so it won't fall off, and runs his hand unconsciously along the carved and uneven edge of the heavy oak board, his fingers efficiently and accurately tracing each rough-hewn ridge of decoration. He lets his spectacles fall off and swing on their cord to hit his chest.

Adam begins to ask another question. A ghostly hand is placed on his shoulder. Adam keeps his question to himself. He looks over at the hand, surprised by the touch – he's never been touched by Harry before - and realizes he can see through Harry's hand *and* through his own shoulder. He's achieved transparency. That, for some reason, doesn't surprise him. And, the fact that he is not surprised, *that* doesn't even surprise him. The big surprise to Adam is that his head is managing to stay in one piece while simultaneously being drilled open methodically by a maniacal, jackhammering hangover.

A shadow passes the door again and stops, in as puzzled, as questioning and as suspicious a manner as a shadow is capable of. It does not leave this time for quite a few minutes. Charles eases back into his chair. The shawl draped over the back falls off and hangs decorously from his left shoulder. He leaves it there. He looks down at the desk again, one eye closed, shifting his head left and right, eyeing the manuscripts, one hand still moving as if by itself feeling the cornice of the desk, all along its edges.

So. Before this admirable example of the cabinetmakers art, he squeezes his eyes shut, finally settles back. He gratefully relaxes into padded and shawl-covered comfort on this modern, posture-saving office chair. And he thinks. Arms and hands coming to settle comfortably onto his lap. Fireplace hissing its gaseous warmth into the chamber. Lamps hissing their oil gas glow into the gloaming deep.

A surreptitious cough permeates the dimness. Charles doesn't deign to notice it.

Adam is surprised. Surprise number two. He's never heard Harry cough before.

Charles continues to think, or rather he rests from thinking. Slowly opening both eyelids, he allows his mind and eye to wander where they will - in and through the thin winter twilight sloshing about his office now. Cascades of light-particles weakly splash over window-seats covered in their orderly pyramids of cushions and books. He follows the particles as they ricochet merrily off piles of correspondence and papers piled in significant archaeological layers, piled high as the wainscoting, piled neatly tied with shiny black ribbon. He imagines the particles skip and slide over his specially-constructed overfilled bookcases, walls of them, on tracks hiding more overfilled bookcases, in turn on tracks hiding even more, yes, overfilled bookcases - bookcases upon bookcases upon bookcases turned in upon themselves over and over in the infinite harmonic regressions one finds in a nautilus shell - only his regressions are constructed of wood holding pulp and leather which in turn hold knowledge rather than living nautili.

The particles coruscate everywhere – over notes pinned and stuck fast to wallpaper, over maps stacked unevenly in cases, over his poor daughter Annie's little writing box sitting on a shelf above the white marble mantle. Annie. Gone. Gone almost these thirty years. Incredible. Unbelievable. It seems like yesterday. He glances over all of these familiar things and more in the gentle gleam of last light and his eyes gleam back with the increased reflection of unexpected tears. His eyes are closed now. Why don't they let him think? Let him be. Just for a moment. Only for a moment or two.

Adam says "Is he dead?" Harry just shakes his head, keeps his hand on Adam's shoulder.

Another cough. Charles squints one eye, closes the other, and pulls his mouth into a tight, compressed, disapproving line, although the last action is effectually fruitless as no one would be able to tell, after all, what expression, if any, he is assuming using his mouth - a thick, enthusiastically growing foliage of white whiskers now successfully obscures the finer movements of his lower facial musculature. Nevertheless, he frowns, and frowns pointedly in the cough's direction.

"You realize, of course, that a cough for a man in your condition is superfluous and an affectation. What's more" continues Charles warming to his subject, "persons without lungs or indeed torsos do not have the need to reflexively convulse their diaphragms with a view to clearing their squamous epithelial tissue, that is - the alveolar epithelium, or their bronchia."

Charles takes a breath to continue, but hearing no response or protest, thinks better of it, enough having been said, and settles into a companionable silence with any lung-less friends who might be with him, watching the gentle evening become deepest night, listening to the sounds of his household preparing for dinner.

A short while later, the tea boy comes in to take away the crumb-filled plates and empty pot, walking out carefully with a cluttered tray. A short while after him, the parlor maid apparates suddenly before Charles. She startles him and causes him to jump, making the springs of his chair squeak as he smoothly rolls backward on well-oiled wheels. He hadn't even heard her open the door. She apologizes, spirals swiftly about the room, fusses with the fireplace, twiddles the lamps, clucks respectfully under her breath at the mess of manuscripts, rulers, pens, inkpots, and spills spreading over his desk, dusts the only tiny open area in front of him on his desk blotter (examining him, not unlovingly, out of the corners of her eyes when she thinks he's not looking) and retires, closing the door slowly and carefully behind her, so as not to jar him again. She is concerned about him. He has been acting a trifle odd lately. She's not sure what that might mean. She hovers, uncertainly, by the nearly-closed door.

"Understanding what's about to happen, you should talk about it. Begin to let go. Talk with her about what's been, what is, and what's to come. You know I am right. Let go, Charles, let go. Let others shoulder the weight and carry the burden now. Let it go. Let her go. Let them all go."

"You tell me what I must do?" Charles asks in monotone, eyes still closed, "what I must tell my own wife? My Emma? My family?"

The parlor maid re-appears cracking the door open, eyes brightly scanning the room and its dark corners, face fixed in a careful, blank attitude of service, but anxiety radiating off of her as sharp as the stink of a burning rubbish heap. "Excuse me, I'm sure, sir, you were, perhaps, *needing* something else, sir?"

Charles rolls his eyes, and raises his bushy eyebrows, all in the direction of one corner of the room as if to say "Look at this, and you'll be having the servants thinking me in my second childhood again before you're satisfied."

"No, Kate. Thank you, nothing else." Kate leaves the room even more slowly this time. Charles waits a few extra minutes before saying anything else.

"Death. Well, yes, being dead yourself, I suppose you *would* know what you are talking about." Charles snaps these words out cracking them as you would a whip, then instantly regrets it.

Adam looks up at Harry to see what Harry will say, but his face appears as it always does – sad. Maybe a little sadder. The room is relatively silent for a period, except for the punctuated reverberation of a pendulum clock somewhere, reminding anyone who had an ear to hear it, like Charles, that a constant, even, and uninterruptible flow of time courses through this structure.

Time pulses, through this home he keeps in Down House, through this county of Kent, indeed through the whole of England and through all the world from here to the Antarctic and back. It pulses through the whole, through all the wide, wonderful, secret-filled universe. It beats steadily and for everyone and has been beating for hundreds of thousands of years, if not longer.

Time. Time brings change. In general, to species, animal and plant (as he has conjectured and proven, publicly and in print, these 30 years past), and in specific, to this solitary human being, Charles Darwin himself. Time rules all. Time changes all. Time is change.

Additionally, and unsurprisingly, and despite his best efforts to the contrary, time has performed its same, slow, careful work on Charles that it has performed on everyone and everything else it has ever touched, touches or ever will touch. And Charles has succumbed to it. Charles has succumbed to the ubiquitous and all-pervasive effects of time. Charles has gotten old.

Although in his heart he still feels he's twenty-two (and not seventy-one). He still feels literally wet behind the ears, still braving the storms of Cape Horn, still rounding the tip of South America on the spray-strewn decks of the Beagle, still the whole of the Pacific lying before him, full of promise, full of the undiscovered, a golden land of the Israelites, a Land of Milk and Honey, voyages and oceans and lands raising questions in Charles faster than he could possibly write them down. All before him. All awaiting his keen eye. All in the future. What a time that was! What a start! What a feeling! And that which began in the Argentine and Patagonia, that which led him irresistibly onwards, it led, just as inevitably, to this night, to this room, to this chair and to these pestiferous pages that refuse to submit to order. To this theoretical chaos. To this intractable mound of undigestifiable, recalcitrant facts.

Charles frowns, then smiles, then frowns again, but leaves his eyes smiling. Well, now. Really. Charles. It isn't all quite that bad. Not as bad as all that. Is it? Could it be? No. It is not.

Besides, Francis could and would continue wherever he chose to leave off. If he chose to leave off. When he chose to leave off. He sighs.

"How did the work get to be so much work?" His voice startles him. It's irritating, but he doesn't know for a certainty anymore how much he speaks out loud and how much he says only to himself. No matter.

"I am talking to myself." He smiles to hear his clear voice in the crepuscular void which is his office now.

He moves back, then forward, leaning both elbows on a surface liberally strewn with odd plant fragments, intricate pieces of small skeletons, bell jars covering arrangements of preserved butterflies on artfully twisting sticks, small lustrous tools grown patchily dull in odd places from continuous, concentrated use, and page after page after page of handwritten paper - some on foolscap, some on proper folio pages - the last meant for his new books. They sit expectantly in front of him, as did the boulder before Sisyphus. The editorial labor relenteth not. Neither does it falter. The mills of publication grind exceedingly fine. And presently they are grinding me - to bits and pieces. Oh, the tragedy of it. Oh, the drama. He smiles – at himself.

Well, maybe he shouldn't leave it *all* to Francis.

He settles down to work some more, and a woman in a wide hooped, but simple and cunning dress, suffused with a worried, distracted air comes quietly into the room. It is his wife Emma. He looks up, eyes twinkling, questioning and hears her announce they will have mutton for dinner. Then he smiles at her – both he and she know already it's Tuesday. Tuesday is mutton. It always has been. She must be here to check on him. He stops working and talks of this and that with her for a considerable time. Finally she leaves, smiling and much less distracted. Smiling similarly, he goes back to work. But it doesn't come anymore. It's all parts. It won't congeal. There is a difficulty, an continual odd twist to it that just won't parse. It's unnerving. The work feels very nearly impossible.

What's more, he can hardly see the pages anymore. What the devil has happened to the fire? And the gas lamp? He moves to ring for someone to look to it then sees the source of his discomfiture.

"If you would, Heraclius, kindly relocate yourself a few feet to the right. There. No, just a bit more. Thank you. The increase in illumination is considerably helpful and welcome to me, even if my present work isn't. And yes, I will get my affairs in order, not that they aren't already. And yes, I will "let go" as you put it. My boat is drifting away from shore. It would be foolish of me to keep one foot on dry ground and one foot floating away down the stream. Yes, no good would come of that. Even I can see that. You are right in reminding me these last few months. And you are most persistent. I am grateful. Now if you please, I have a great deal of work to do."

Heraclius nods, one eyebrow artfully raised, looking off into the middle distance, not at Charles, not at anything in particular "So, tell me my friend" he asks innocently of the open air in front of him, "is it, in the end, worth all the trouble?"

Frowning his bushy brows, but smiling his eyes, Charles refrains from reply, pins his spectacles, hanging again from the cord around his neck, between left thumb and forefinger, raises them with hardly a shake to the bridge of his nose, puts them on and silently and unfussily returns to work. A minute or so passes. Then Charles, wagging his right hand and pointing at Heraclius and Adam, motions at them with a slightly exaggerated and theatrical scolding motion, index finger wiggling in Heraclius's direction. Charles shakes his head at Heraclius as if to say "How could such an obvious question be asked?" But he smiles as he does it. Then he goes back to work.

He edits another few pages, pen raised and poised, a fencer with his foil at ready, dips into ink, marks a word, scribbles a phrase, dips again, scratches out, dips, flips to a new page, blowing and blotting on the last to dry the ink, marks again drawing a long line to one margin where he pauses, looks up, shrugs his shoulders, removes his eyeglasses so as to expose his bare and expressive eyeballs directly to his audience, stares straight into Heraclius's face and smiles. He smile is rueful and he says "Yes, actually. Yes, *it* - as you say – although I would say *life* – that is - my life, yes, well, *it* was all very much worth it. Even if it has to end. Wait, don't say it, I know you will - I meant to say, even *when* it has to end."

"With whom are you talking father?" Henrietta, his daughter has entered the room and has been sitting on the leather fainting couch in front of one of the bookcases watching him work for the last few minutes. Good Heavens, he hadn't even noticed her.

He laughs, lightly, to allay her fears - they must all be keeping vigil over him now, in shifts. He is a lucky man, to be so cared for, to be so looked after. He is more than that, of course - more than lucky - he is a greatly blessed man. He realizes that, with deeper and deeper conviction, every day now. He is it seems, as of late, doomed to be never alone, perpetually grateful, and unreasonably content. There are worse fates.

Adam feels a tap on his shoulder, Harry is motioning as if to leave, as if they, the both of them, should move off someplace. However, Adam has no idea how he would go about doing that. He has no idea how he came to be standing in Charles Darwin's presence in the first place. He's not big on ideas, just now. He's doing a lot of absorbing. And a lot of not reacting. But he feels a strange sensation begin in his feet and start to wander up his legs. A kind of evaporation. He supposes this must be "withdrawing", this must be "leaving." Charles is still talking in the gloom under a puddling of lamp light.

"I talk to myself, dear Henrietta. To myself, to little Annie, to my mother, my father, brothers and sisters, old friends, old enemies. To all those I am going to re-join in the future. Just an old man's habit." Henrietta crosses over to him and embraces him from behind, laying her head briefly to rest on top of his. "Oh, papa" she says. Charles lays one hand on one of the two soft arms resting on his shoulders – he presses down as he does so, with his arm lightly touching on the hands crossed over his chest – the two hands that are protectively bundled over his ancient, sickly heart.

The clean and orderly garden lying outside his window, quiet in the November twilight shows a bare and frosty aspect that is almost sepulchral, although Charles knows that it is not. The animal and vegetable world outside writhes with life. It is a web. A woven blanket of relationships extending out of the distant past, and completely blanketing the present with dependencies, causes, effects, actions, reactions - a slow dance it is impossible to stop, but whose movements one may follow, if one has the desire, if one has just the right eye for it. He, Charles, fortunately or unfortunately, has had just such an ocular instrument, a lifetime to use it in, and a rebellious curiosity that has effectively redirected his career from the Church to Taxidermy to Natural Science and now, to the venerable and honorable position of Ancient Oracle. He grips his daughter's arm a little more closely, a tad more strongly, but not so tightly that he cannot not let her loose when he must.

But, yes. It is all worth it. Every bit. It's grand. He'd recommend it to anyone.

ACT III

NOT PORPHYROGENITUS

I hear a gas fireplace whispering in my head, feel a winter chill falling off high windows, see a Victorian office, strewn with a thousand curiosities in a dim, fading lamp glow that grows weaker and weaker and then the last drops of light leech out and then I am left in a chilly, lonely darkness, really a kind of unwelcoming half-light.

I realize I am awake. And immediately wish I wasn't.

Blurry and sick, eyes closed, alone, pitching out and rolling from my sleeping bag across some carpet-covered planks, colliding with a wall, knocking my skull against the edge of a much-painted beam. I reach up and surprised can feel a new crease in my forehead. Harry sits meditatively draped and arranged over a table by some of the windows that ring this entire room. I'm waking up on the back porch. I'm cold. I'm hungover. I'm stiff. I'm getting kicked.

"Shit!"

Someone, a familiar voice, cursing under their breath, kicking me again, steps over my prone body, shoves me with the back of their heel and hustles off to my right, conspicuously clomping loudly through my morning, closing and bolting a door with a penetrating and unmistakable firmness of purpose. A strong will lurks behind that locked door.

"Good morning to you, Adamakes. Sleeping well, are we?"

Then I hear something heavy (probably some mass of heavy, glossy motorcycle magazines) hit the plank floor in the bathroom in a dense pulpy detonation that reverberates in shockwaves across the porch, under the door, out to me and on to the far edge of the room where the garbage can is and the long back stairway to the backyard spirals in rickety bravado. The floor jumps. I jump. My back jumps. Harry remains stationary. The built-in alarm clock way down on my lower back goes off, uncorking a vicious tsunami of stabbing pain and nausea on top of my hangover on top of my kicking wounds. Just another day in the life of a *persona non grata*. A day in the life of the kind of guy who lives on a back porch of a flat in San Francisco. And my Sunday begins.

I breathe slowly in and out. Squinting with one eye, directly in front of me, a square of lurid butter-yellow sunlight crawls gamely down the ancient, scarred wainscoting towards the heavy plank floor and also towards me, Adam. I peer around with one good eye, the other closed to tone down my headache to a deafening roar and see no girl. The girl that never was. I am alone. As usual. Of course. I moan out loud my sense of loss. My lost Saturday night adventure. Harry mistakes my groaning and eyeball-rolling for a conversational opportunity.

"I told you, you'd thank me."

"I haven't thanked you."

"You will, you'll see. And you're welcome, you crazy kid. How did you like our little outing last night?"

"I would much rather have had the girl."

"You're welcome again."

"Fuck you."

He's a steam roller. Unstoppable.

I hear a toilet flush and a shower, no a tub begin to splash and fill and more muttering coming from the very angry land beyond the door. That was not *the* girl, although I wish it was, but it is *a girl*

Participles

– it's Patricia (not Pat, not Patty, but Patricia with four fully pronounced syllables – Patricia). She's the landlady, well, one of the two landladies I have.

If you could call someone a landlady when you didn't pay her rent, and she hated you, and your friend Al (Alice) was her partner, and they were about to break up, and you had nowhere, absolutely nowhere to go except here to stay and have a roof over your head in this very expensive and very chilly, but still trendy and artsy city.

But in that case, she isn't your landlady. In that case, she is your lord and mistress and don't you forget it you pathetic freeloading excuse for a friend and why Al why is it that all your friends are such irresponsible freaks and sponging bums and would a little normal a little average be so bad once in a while would it huh answer me huh would it Alice would it?

Patricia talks to herself. More and more in the past week or so. I listen. I can't help it. I am supposed to be listening, apparently. I am supposed to be eavesdropping on these acid monologues of Patricia's burning and spitting fire as they etch the open space of the rooms, burning the very air out of the flat, preparing it - for what? A cleaner, brighter existence. An Adam-less existence. I'd figured that much out, the first few hours I was here. I met Al at a bar over in the East Bay and she said I could crash here if I didn't have anywhere else to go, and I didn't. So here I crash. On the unheated porch. And every morning I eavesdrop on Patricia.

If I act like I don't eavesdrop, things get much, much worse. So I listen, I do. I wince. I react. I tell myself, there are all kinds of ways to pay rent. I tell myself, in these situations you have to be your own best friend. I tell myself, listen and live. Breathe. Breathe, in and out.

However, it isn't what you would call warm on the porch here, I've mentioned that, haven't I? Either temperature-wise, or temperament-wise.

"So what *did* you think about last night, Adamakes?"

I pull the sleeping bag over my mostly naked male body. I let myself be rolled back into the wall and allow gravity to tuck me back snugly in, next to the beam. Only my eyes show through a fold of my bag.

"Adamakes?"

I ignore Harry. I can still hear Patricia through an inch or so of solid oak door asking herself why she had to have unclothed men in her house and wasn't she done with all that and all her friends thought she was crazy to put up with it and she was crazy or God knows she was getting there. I listen and breathe. In and out. Reminding myself (self!) like the good friend I am to myself – know why you're doing what you're doing and how important it is. Know, for the time being, it's a good thing for you to be sheltered in this porch and not living in a car again and crippled and vomiting and visiting the Emergency Room every other day by bus. Listen. Breathe. Squinch eyes to squelch headache. Listen. Breathe. Squinch.

"Adam."

That's an odd, flat monotone, even for Harry. He's really biting down hard and holding on to it this morning. Apparently, he's incarnating the adjective"indefatigable" for my benefit.. A personal performance just for me. But I don't have any fight left in me for this, not this morning. All I have is the desire to appease my rudely swollen back muscles. Breathe in. Breathe out. Press your lower spine against the hard planks. Press and hold. One, Two, Three...

"I'm not just talking to hear myself, Adamakes."

"Adamakes? Adamakes?"

The porch of this top-floor flat lists with a distinct tilt North by Northwest, which is O.K. because it is, after all, a hundred and thirty years old, old enough by now to do exactly whatever it wants to do. And besides it has managed to survive the First Big One (the San Francisco Earthquake) back in Nineteen Aught Six relatively intact - all things considered. That was a feat. And it probably would have remained a feat, a heroic feat, but for one small sinister item lurking in its misty future: toilets. I've discovered, sadly, subsequent owners installed their new-fangled indoor plumbing (the bathroom) on the back of the porch. They installed it without (apparently) taking into account the century-long settling effect of heavy porcelain/iron bathroom fixtures on older redwood substructures. I wonder, I am amazed, sometimes at the naïve optimism and wild exuberance of these early twentieth century bathroom-installer-pioneers - it must have been a golden age of plumbers and positive thinking.

"Adamakes, this isn't funny."

As a direct result of a century of previous flat-owner decisions entirely out of my control, I know in a visceral way that I am currently balanced thirty feet above a brick-paved backyard on a sloping train trestle engineered before the Great War to End All Wars with an angry woman filling an iron bathtub just a few feet away from me on same said sagging, ancient crossbeams. I live in the perpetual knowledge I am only one bubble bath away from a one-way trip to eternity. I obviously think too much.

Harry tries again.

"You know moping around won't get you anywhere."

"Moping is my time-honored way of getting through the boring periods of time between moments of outrageous excitement."

"Life can't all be thrills."

"Is this going someplace?"

"Look, you're a guy in a kayak shooting the rapids. You come to the calm parts. You look around and say where did all the fun go? I feel horrible. Well, what did you expect? You're in a kayak. Sometimes you go fast. Sometimes you go slow. Instead of staring in bovine wonder at your own boredom and pain, remember – the kayak came equipped with a paddle."

"I can tell you've thought a lot about this, and it means a lot to you."

"And…"

"And… just fuck off. I'm in deep shit. I failed miserably last night. My ass may be out on the street tomorrow. I'm sick again. What in the hell do you want from me?"

Something seems to snap in Harry's face. For the first time, I'm afraid of him. It's the act of watching the girder supporting the bridge you're standing on (the one suspended over the infinitely deep chasm) loudly and obviously crack in two. His voice rises to a kind of keening sound, a buzz saw happily chomping swiftly through soft, green wood.

"It's always you. You are the center of your own personal universe. Which, by the way, you are turning into your own personal hell, but that's your own personal business, apparently. Are you other-centered in the slightest? Do you ever think of anyone other than yourself? Their own hells? Their own aspirations. Their dreams. Their conflicts. Do you? Do you ever think about the lives of the people around you? Do you ever, oh I don't know, do you ever think of me?"

He had a point. I wasn't. I hadn't.

"Have you ever even bothered to google my name?"

He had me again. I hadn't.

"You have no idea who I am. Have you ever asked yourself why I harp continuously on your self-improvement? What's my motivation? Why would I do it? Why you? What were we doing in Charles Darwin's study last night?"

That has to be at least five questions in a row. Man! I've completely forgotten the first three before we even get to the last one. With any luck he'll answer them all himself. I therefore, wisely remain mute. I've never seen Harry like this before. He rolls. He just keeps right on rolling. Rolling right over me. I don't think I've ever seen a real, live juggernaut before.

"No idea? Adam? None at all? Were you ever even curious?"

"You're a total waste of my time, Adam."

"My grandfather…"

I could tell something big was looming over the horizon.

"Adam, I'm not *porphyrogenitou* – born in the imperial purple bedchamber – wait - before you ask - that means I didn't inherit the empire. I had to go after it. I got it the old-fashioned, Roman way. I worked for it. I took it. I earned it.

I don't know where he picks up his clichés and his slang. I make an encouraging um-hmm noise and burrow into my bag.

"My grandfather was in the Reconquest. Not that you'd be interested. The African one. I know, I know, you have no idea what I'm talking about. North Africa had been Roman for 600 years before that sad, ragtag, slapdash horde of hapless Germans calling themselves the Vandals (hah!) wandered over from Spain, well Baetica and started smashing everything within reach in drunken wonder."

"They took over. It was not a good time for Romans. Then in the 500's, 150 years later, we came back. Like Macarthur, we promised to return and we were Romans so we did what we promised, and we came back, we returned. It took three botched invasions, but the fourth time we were golden and in only a month or so we were in. We were in for good. The Vandals were out. What was left of the Vandal army became a minor division of the Roman legions serving in a remote outpost in Persia – Iran that is. That was my grandfather. Are you even listening? Adam? Adam? I really don't know why I bother…"

Harry's voice is getting louder and louder. It's kind of similar to this time when I was in Florida once and watching a hurricane approach. First a small cloud, then a gray wall of boiling moisture bearing down on you. Then, it's storm-whipped chaos, everywhere. I can see that roofs and palm trees will be blowing boiling-wild in a minute or two.

"Adam?"

I nod at him, mostly from behind the padding of my sleeping bag, throwing him some morsel of attention to keep him from hitting me (could he even do that?), and try, on the front side of my thumping headache, to compose the part of my face he can see into an attitude of eager attentiveness.

"My father…"

This is going to be a long, long storm, if we're just getting to his father.

"Now, my father – he was Exarch of Africa, after a long, successful military service against the Persians – he was the head of Roman government in Africa, the *capo di capi*, even during all that nonsense and trouble with that bearded, non-entity Phocas from Thrace – well, Phocas tried, maybe, possibly, to be a good emperor, but you can't cut taxes and build an empire and defend it from barbarians all at once.

Anyways… something had to give. And it was Phocas. Father called the family into rebellion. Nicetas, my cousin, rode in with one army and took Egypt, I sailed, by way of Sicily and Cyprus with another and took the capital – Nea Roma, Constantinople, the seven-hilled, God-guarded city. The center of the world. And father stepped back and he gave me the empire. Just gave it to me. Amazing. An amazing and capable man. A Roman. I lost him right after that. And then we lost the empire."

I am nodding now. Nodding off, that is. History wasn't ever my strong suit.

Heraclius looks down at me. I look up. I wish I hadn't. That sadness I always see has disappeared. It's gone. The pain is gone too. What remains is a beautiful, unvarnished, feral cruelty. Kind of close to what the orange-black, fur-covered rippling muscles of a tiger looks like as it lopes efficiently towards you in a professionally predatorial way. Stunning. Mesmerizing. I would've liked to have observed it more closely, if it hadn't been so unreservedly and absolutely directed at me and me alone.

Harry's eyes. Well, they have the impersonal viciousness you see in the eye of a hawk or an eagle. I know I'm changing metaphors, but believe me, narrative consistency is not uppermost in my mind right now. Abject terror, yes, literary neatness, no. I may be homeless, and a college graduate, but the same as anyone else I know when I am lunch.

It is reaching for me. One taloned foot uncurling one claw at a time, stretching across the room, aimed precisely at me in my protective sleeping bag. I pull a blanket over the bag - as if - my impenetrable blanket will protect me. What chance do mice have, really, in an open field?

"So, little Adam. Adamakes. Little Adamakes. Can you ever guess what happened next?"

I shake my head no.

"I can't hear you Adamakes."

I mumble something.

"No, I don't suppose you could."

"Well, Adamakes. We fought. From nothing, and having lost everything we fought – the Slavs, the Persians, we lost almost all our cities and we fought. Whole towns, whole populations were removed to Persia and we fought. They made it to the gates of the city, and I had only a tiny army-let left to me and we fought. Guerrilla warfare. Years of training, planning. Dancing around stupidly fantastic plots and political cabals by Romans behind my back. Persians jabbing at me from the front. We lost and lost and lost. And still we fought for Rome. For the last 1,300 years of history. For all the Romans. For land and people and our country. And can you think what happened, Adamakes?"

"I can't hear you Adamakes."

"No"

"We won. In a world war that had lasted decades, we Romans won. We won over an empire we had been fighting in one way or the other for 600 years. We won. I did it for them. Me. Heraclius. The greatest Roman emperor since Augustus. I, *Basileus*. King of Kings. Emperor of the Romans. The greatest power on earth left standing. Now, little Adam, why do you suppose, hmmm? Why is it, do you think, that no one has ever heard of my name?"

"Why is that, Adamakes?"

"Why, Adamakes?"

"So shy now? Adamakes? Don't be. Now why?"

"Why is it?"

"Why?"

He is fairly screaming at me now, the volume is deafening, it's a runaway freight train barreling towards me, brakes burnt off, wheels sparking and jumping the tracks.

"No idea, Heraclius."

Heraclius glares. And stares. And smiles. Which is actually the scary part. Seems to be waiting for something. I am someone about to be punched. A lot. By someone who'd enjoy it. I try again.

"Tell, me Heraclius. Tell me why."

"Well, Adamakes."

I relax the tiniest bit. At least he's talking now.

"Well, I'll tell you why, Adamakes, I'll tell you."

"Because, after we won, after the empire was safe, after we no longer had to fear the Persians for the first time in centuries, after all that, while we were destitute, poor, war-weary, but proud and re-building. After all that, we lost everything. Not for a short time. Forever. Have you ever wondered why in Egypt and Syria, Palestine and Turkey they don't speak Greek?"

"I know you haven't. Don't even answer that. It would just make me angry. Angrier. Even though they were Roman for 600 years, they don't speak something like Italian or Greek because the Arabs, they demolished us. We lost them. All those provinces. All those cities. They took the whole empire away from me. Forever."

Heraclius is standing over me now, slashing at the air with both fists, kicking the walls, pulling at his hair. I curl up in my blanket/bag in a fetal position and try to protect my kidneys in case a kick or two or a punch or a slash find its way to my section of the floor.

"Just one year after the total defeat of Persia they started. In a decade they were all over us. Persia went. Rome went. I got the empire, the whole, 2,000 mile wide, troubled country of the Romans, and I left it the size of Rhode Island. And my wife and sons ended up bickering and killing each other, and the Romans faded. They faded. Faded away until centuries later, when Romans remembered themselves, they knew themselves to be Roman again and slowly, so slowly built something new and honorable. But in the meantime, everything I did, gone. Everyone I loved, ruined"

Now he's so hushed. He is a little muffled from inside the sleeping bag inside the blanket, but I can still hear him. Barely. It's almost worse than the yelling.

"And you wonder…"

"You wonder…"

"If I can fix anything, anyone. I've got to try. Fix it. Make it better. Make it work."

He stops. There is silence for a long time. I think he's gone.

"Why won't you listen to me, Adamakes? See what is around you clearly. Just try. Oh, Adamakes. Forgive me. Please, look at me. Forgive me, I was wrong. Adamakes? Adam? "

Then it is really, really quiet. There is a quiet space around me, an amputation has taken place. It is quieter than it has been around me for months and months. I poke my head out.

Harry is gone.

It takes me awhile to get myself untangled from my sleeping bag, and halfway vertical again. My eyes feel wet, and I can tell they're bloodshot, and it's not all just from the hangover and the headache. Maybe its tears.

Harry is gone.

I'm shaking. I watch my hand shake. My cheap cellphone starts to vibrate next to my feet somewhere, but I ignore it. A hot shower, an hour of so of self-administered physical therapy, some food scrounged up – these are the daily, or rather today the Sundaily (I also like really bad puns, hey at least I'm trying to get myself together) activities before me. Other activities – hangover recovery, finding a new place to live, maybe writing some poetry, I'll probably wind up going with Al and Patricia and Co. to a Raiders game (the Forty-Niners are too tame for Al) across the bay. Yeah, the game. Probably. Well, maybe. I dont' know. Hell. Shit. Fuck.

I even feel my jaw shaking. I cross my arms in front of me and just try and sit quietly for awhile, rocking in my sleeping bag.

I wonder where Harry *is*, now.

I wonder when he is coming back.

The porch has one original, hundred-something-year-old window in the wall between it and the kitchen. The ancient glass runs earthwards sloppily in a kind of crystal fudge across each pane. A face that looks a cross between a Hell's Angel and June Cleaver watches me and my peering, red-rimmed eyes with a crooked smile.

If I ever need someone to watch my back in a bar fight, I wouldn't have to think twice about the back-watcher I'd pick. I 'd pick Alice (really Al) hands down, every time. Alice looks at me from the other side of the blurred-up window, makes a thumbs-up signal and holds up a bowl and a cereal box in one hand, and a Budweiser in the other.

Where is Harry?

At least I think it's a bottle, box, and bowl. The glass is so warped it could've just as easily have been a kitten, a blender, and a jar of marshmallow topping for all he knows. Al's big German shepherd Klondike probably wouldn't have turned down the chance to puree Patricia's cat Mrs. P. (Patricia's cat is mysteriously also named Patricia). And Mrs. P. has been known to pee on my stuff here, out on the back proch of the flat here. More than once. I'd even say, from time to time. I'm not sure it has always been an accident.

The cat seems to have an entire system of morality worked out that has as its logical center Mrs. P - itself - with the rest of the ever-disappointing world hovering fuzzily about the bright edges of Mrs. P's urgent needs and wants. It's a very pragmatic philosophy and I have to admit I admire the cat's unflagging, unselfish devotion to its own interests. But what Al's holding up - it's too small to be the cat. Isn't it? Squinting and scowling I wonder, hopefully, how difficult could it be, really, for Al to marshmallow a cat for breakfast? Not that much effort. Not really.

Harry.

I lie down, head propped on my fist, elbow on the worn carpet over the slanting porch planks. Bad idea. My neck pops and aches. I lie down, hands crossed behind my head and look at the tongue and groove slats of the roof above me.

Harry.

I feel my eyelids closing again. Damn, it's hard to think this morning. I can't do it. I should do something for stomach, head, back and many other assorted organs of mine. But I can't do it. The beam is feeling great against the back of my head. Steam is rolling under the bathroom door and perspiring off the windows. The square of sun has reached me and I'm starting to get hot, I'd say sauna-hot, in the deep freeze of this back porch.

Still I'm not moving. There's clinking sounds from the kitchen now, faucets going on and off, the smell of coffee and bacon and burnt toast and suddenly a sharp rap on the window. A stern look from the kitchen and a thumb-pointing motion to get-the-hell-in-here.

The unstoppable force of Al beckons. I must comply. Wincing

from the pain, but remembering to put a smile on for Al, I push off. Upwards and onwards. Into a weirdly empty Sunday. I want someone to nag at me.

They get ready to head over the bridge for the game in Oakland. Alice dances in front of the big bay window facing the street, scans back and forth over the so far, non-existent Sunday traffic, a SWAT team sniper looking for suspicious movement. She's double-parked the station wagon in front of the flat.

She waltzes efficiently through and down the long, high hallway. Passes the steep staircase to the street with a wistful reluctance. Putters around in the kitchen listening to Patricia. Watches the second hand on the clock over the stove. Orbits back to the front and starts it all over again. Unfortunately no overly-aggressive motorist or tow-truck driver have appeared as of yet, but Al can only hope. I have often heard her extol the virtues of "clean, honest confrontation." Parking cops are perfect for that. So are angry neighbors. But it *is* a Sunday, after all, and if you're looking for conflict, the overall feeling of peace and serenity seems to be offering slim pickings for the present. But Al's very optimistic.

Front, hallway, kitchen, hallway, front, hallway, kitchen – I stand in the middle of the front parlor and marvel at the patience and energy of the orbiting Al.

Patricia is in the bathroom, talking to herself and to Al two rooms away, engaging in her usual half-hour guilt-fest. Cosmetics, shaving: when, where, and how much, torment her every time she leaves the house.

Subtle and changing questions around sexual solidarity, political awareness, gender roles and what she thought was just good hygiene leave her with a nagging feeling she's allowing herself to go to seed in a stunningly public way, and that she's faking it, and that somehow deep down she's the square peg in the round hole with this new feminist lifestyle she's chosen with Alice. It's only been a year or so. It's all so new to her. She's trying, but she's not sure she's getting it right. What does Al think about her eyebrows? Too much? More?

Participles

Al is indifferent. Well, maybe not indifferent, more oblivious. Personally, Al just makes sure Al has washed off all the motorcycle grease and tire grime she's gotten covered with earlier in the morning and she's done - she's happy - she spent the early morning performing mysterious services to her chain and O rings on their big touring Harley down in the garage. The world is in good working order. Life is a roaring V-Twin, growling and ready to ride.

A sprinting frenzy of soap and water in the sink in the garage and Al says enough is enough. They clean up pretty good, Al and the Harley. At least Al says so. Al radiates healthy contentment.

Figuring as usual, they were about to leave, Al pulled out their beat-up 20 year-old Volvo out of its tiny garage, swung it into traffic and promptly double-parked it. She always does this. If it's meant to get Patricia out faster, it never works. So Al is left orbiting, uncomplaining, but orbiting. She does it a lot. Al has the orbiting shtick down pat. I hear Patricia saying something about eyeliner in a distant, exhausted voice. But Al doesn't hear it, Al isn't in the kitchen anymore.

She's back in the front hallway. Al, looking at her watch, briefly pauses in the latest revolution, hands me a hat, a cap she's picked up from the closet off the bedroom on her last whirlwind trip through. It's branded with some random South of Market feminist wholesale automotive parts shop – a large, somewhat greasy decal of a furious woman military pressing a Mercedes over her head in ferocious day-glow orange on a matriarchal and nurturing purple background. I don't take it right off the bat, but look at her questioningly. "Someone took a magic marker and wrote backwards all across your forehead last night. Just don't let Deb get a gander. She'll never let you out with us like that." Seeing my eyes, she adds "It's faded. It's faded. Faded clean away. You can barely read it."

I don't believe her. "Just take it. Put it on. Go on, you." She looks back towards the back porch and the bathroom and her other half. "It won't kill you." I finally take the cap, adjust the strap to fit my smaller head and jam it on, opening my eyes wide and moving my head around in a sarcastic way to get Al's approval, but Al isn't even in the room anymore.

I move into the kitchen, get a dry tea towel, buff up the side of the toaster oven and lean over, holding my breath. Sure as shit there's a small black line of writing across my forehead. Shit, there's another closer to my hairline. It's a little hard to read in a mirror, especially a toaster mirror, but I have to try. I carefully unwrinkle my forehead, frown to make it smooth and even, look down, and peer through my eyebrows over the top of my eyes into the shiny, dented metal.

The letters are drawn neatly and concisely. They flow in a straight line across my forehead, at a slight angle, as if someone was leaning over me with a pen from the right and was trying not to wake me up or smudge their work as they went. Bastard. Or bastardette. "Why?" is all I can think. Well, that and "How?", "Where?", "When?", and "Why me?"

You could tip me over with a feather when I see the top line looks to be a foreign language – like maybe, what? Greek? Maybe Ancient Greek even? The bottom is in English though. And Al is right. They are backwards. I look like an acolyte for a Satanic Sabbath. They are faded. They look like they're sinking, falling into my head like pebbles dropped into a pinkish mud puddle. I run to Al and Patricia's kitchen table, scrounge a pen from the hills and mountains of bills and newspaper there, rip off a corner of a steam-cleaning carpet ad and run back. On the way I grab a dish towel and wet it so I can start rubbing and erasing.

Adam hears Al calling at the head of the steps in the hallway. "Honey. Honey, how's it coming?" A series of muffled, frustrated murmurings flows outward from the bathroom. Then the door slams open.

I lean over again, blinking, writing and this is what I copy down, just before I attack it.

O AGATHOS H ALHTHHS O KALOS

and

LET GO STOP RUNNING USE YOUR HEAD FOR
ONCE

Patricia breezes past me saying "Aren't you ready yet?" Al runs up the stairs saying "What do you mean, you thought I had the tickets." I stand up, and run my hand worriedly under the visor, feeling my forehead. I bend over, look again, and grab my wet dish towel, buff the oven up with my shirt sleeve to a dazzling silver and start the rubbing at my head again, staring intently into the side of my personal kitchen appliance. Al's looking at me strangely, as she disassembles their kitchen table with all of its assorted magazines and receipts, looking for anything that looks lost, oblong, and printed with football players wearing eyepatches standing in front of crossed sabers.

My cellphone vibrates again. I continue working at my forehead, which is starting to feel sore. Al's land line rings, she picks it up, holding it under her chin, throwing papers left and right onto the floor as she works her way through the piles. Al says "This is who? Bob? Bob who? *The* Bob, Patricia's ex-husband Bob? Yeah, this is Al. Likewise. What can I do for you? She said what? Would you mind repeating that? When? Where?" Patricia yells "There's a tow truck down here stringing up our Volvo." Al looks over at me, past the receiver under her chin, frightens me with the dazed and blurry look of a woman drowning, drops the phone to the floor, clomps unsteadily down the stairs, and then all hell really breaks loose.

I'm sitting on a random front stoop on Market Street, all my worldly belongings in an enormous backpack by my side. My hat is off, packed away, I feel relaxed some, but mostly I feel hot and sweaty. I just got back from the gym where I do my showering when I'm homeless. Which I am. Again. And I'm doing some covert, impromptu personal P.T. (physical therapy) on the hard surface of the steps behind me. I know, pathetic. But hey! Cut a guy some slack. It's the best I can do for now.

A woman with a little girl walks past me. The girl catches sight of my forehead, starts a smile in my direction, the mom follows her eyes and deftly performs a mid-walk save-intervention - averting her eyes from mine, gazing at the horizon, snatching the little girl, whirling her up and away in a smooth arc which lands her far, far on the other side of the sidewalk (and safe from the crazy forehead-tattooed homeless guy writhing around and smiling at little girls on someone's front steps) and then moving rapidly and efficiently off into the distance to complete the rest of their very normal, very Sunday tasks.

Doesn't bother me. I'm used to it.

More people walk by. More people look. There's more rapid walking. More eye-averting. I decide to act. I un-crumple and don my orange and purple femme-friendly baseball cap once more, so I don't end up in jail for being a public menace to foot traffic on Market Street. And guess what? It works. I become invisible.

One problem solved, one hundred more to go.

And those words on my skin, they won't rub off, they won't scrub off, nothing gets at them. I know. I tried. And tried. And tried. I was in the showers at the gym for at least an hour and a half. Maybe I'll have to molt them off. Maybe I won't ever get them off. You know, there are worse fates . And it's not like I don't got other shit to think about. At least I have the cap. At least I have this stoop.

So. I'm nursing a cappuccino and watching these purposeful people with places to live and bodies that function walking determinedly right in front of me on the broad sidewalks of San Francisco, and I'm thinking - it must be nice. They know where they're going, and they know where they'll be sleeping tonight. Me? I don't know either (or do you say neither?) - anyways, I don't know the going or the sleeping part - not any of it, not for tonight. But I'm used to it. I should be by now. And it's not all that horrific. Not once you get into the rhythm of it. I say that at random intervals to myself - to keep my spirits up. It's all in the rhythm. It's all in the rhythm.

And my beater of a car is light-years away, perched high on a hill above the Saturn Stairs, where you don't have to move it every week to avoid tickets when they street-clean. It's up there. I'm down here.

I need to go there. I should put all my extra shit up there. I should. I need to. Now. I should. I should start. I should start right now. Right this minute. Look, here I go. I'm going. I'm leaving now. Bye. See ya' later. So long.

Who am I fooling? It's a long hike just to get to the *bottom* of the Saturn stairs. Now, I know I should go. But I don't move. I don't. Pushing up against the marble and brick wall at my back, I continue un-kinking some of the usual morning knots and jumbled messes in my back and hit a few new ones in my lower back as I think about this afternoon. I squirm and think, squirm and think.

I'm not looking forward to the 560 steps to the top of Saturn, not to mention the steep hills before and after, lugging all my junk, going into contortions to keep my spine in line under my backpack, sweating like a pig, well, like a one-and-a-half-legged pig sweats.

You know, I'm not absolutely sure I can do it.

I hate it when it gets this bad.

The more I think about, and feel around my back, I'm even more sure. I can't do it. I can't.

Shit.

I slowly roll my vertebrae against the side of the steps and watch the street. I pull my cap farther down my forehead just to be safe.

You know, people *are* doing a lot less detouring when they get to me on the sidewalk and I think - lucky me, it's a good thing I held onto Al's orange and purple muscle-woman cap. It's my surefire ticket to incognito this morning, what with my forehead billboard and all. Yup, a good thing. Incognito works for me. Is working for me.

I twist my back around some more. Close my eyes.

So, anyways, Al said to call her in few days. Patricia locked her out, so Al's sleeping at the garage she co-owns. Al thinks Patricia's about to bolt back to Fresno and her ex-husband. Al thinks Patricia's making bad life choices. Al's being driven out of her mind by all this.

I don't what to think.

I actually have no opinion about Patricia. I stay silent while Al explains the latest and greatest wild Alice-Pat escapades. I know Al too well. Al will flatten anyone who questions Patricia or gets in Patricia's way. I, for one, intend to stay unflat, thank you very much. So I stay silent. But I listen a lot.

Al. Hmmm. You know, maybe Al would let me crash with her a few days at the garage. That's a possibility. And her garage is all downhill form the Castro.

Then again, maybe I've imposed my limping self on her already one too many times.

But, then again...

You know what? Maybe I'll just let Al decide.

And so, my event-filled life goes on.

My new mottos, direct from a (hopefully) very short career as a set of forehead tattoos, are - USE MY HEAD. That and LET GO. And then, the ever-popular STOP RUNNING. There are worse words to live by.

And even though I don't like labels, and especially being labeled by other people, I have to say, a friend of mine, and *old* friend of mine helped me out once (this morning) by telling me exactly what I was made of. He labeled me AGATHOS ALHTHHS KALOS which my handy internet foreign language dictionary tells me is Good, Truth, and Beauty. In Ancient Greek. And I think he's right.

It's all there. If I look for it.

It's already inside of me. I just have to figure out how to get it out and make it show. More and more. Every day. Between Emergency Room visits. While I'm doing my endless rounds of P.T. When I'm not scaring children or causing traffic jams.

And maybe someday the person who wrote it there on my forehead, maybe someday he'll even see all that in himself. And maybe he'll stop beating himself up. And maybe he himself will STOP RUNNING. And maybe he himself will finally LET GO.

You never know. I think kind thoughts about Harry and beam them over to him, wherever he is now - my own recipe of homemade joy and hope and strength - and generally I wish him all the help the universe can possibly give him. Heaven knows, he's helped me out enough. Maybe it's time someone gave him a leg up. Myabe that someone can be me. Maybe that's how the universe works. First it was my turn, now it's his.

Who knows?

It's worth a shot.

Anyways.

In the meantime, it's sunny.

I am, for the most part, ambulatory.

And I, Adam, have a hot date with a staircase. Hey, what more could a formerly haunted guy ask for? Nothing more. That's what I say. Nothing more.

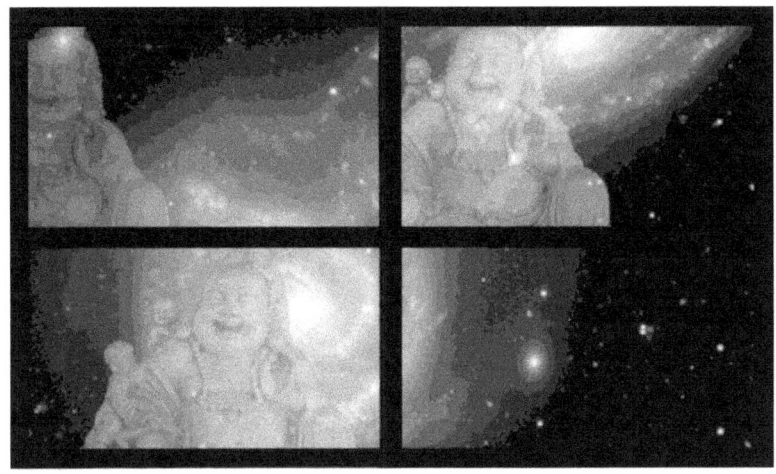

FOUR COMPARTMENTS

1. SPRING

A fat man is farting rainbows.

He walks by quickly, grinning, swinging his arms wide, fists arcing gracefully about him as would orbiting small planets, broad thighs working it, bow-legged as a cartoon cowboy (except it would have taken a hippopotamus to carry him), one mischievous hand running over his bright, bald head and the other blowing a kiss to John as his nearly circular silhouette disappears around a corner in a cloud of self-satisfied, odoriferous phosphorescence.

John stares ineffectually at the abruptly empty corner.

A fuzzy shadow slides directly in front of John. It blocks out his light completely. John notices, watches, slouches and sits numbly unsurprised. He is sleep-typing on his keyboard and can barely keep his eyes open. He waves his hand vaguely in front of his face with the woozy intention of promoting a greater clarity about his person. It doesn't work.

The shadow cuts off the friendly beige light from the friendly beige hospital corridor John's sitting in – well, has been camped out in, to tell the truth, off and on, for the last two weeks or so. It's dark outside, and now it's darkened inside. The shadow's not especially helpful. His laptop is eclipsed and the screen shines brighter, but that doesn't make it any easier to work since John's brain hurts. And it hits John, he's friggin' cold.

John Alexander Chin sucks in his breath and shivers, beginning with his neck, running down his shoulders and arms, jiggling his chest and pelvis, finishing up with his knees and ankles. He taps his feet nervously once or twice on the shiny tiles underneath his chair. His spiky black gelled hair remains unmoving however, even under the ceiling ventilator's small tornado of arctic, antiseptic air.

Rumpled in a thin, white polo shirt, aching wrists arched over his keyboard, squinting, watching, waiting for something else to happen after beach-ball man disappeared, he exhales, too tired to stand up and walk ten paces and peer around a corner. No, too tired to stand up. Too tired really to care about standing up. Scratch that – he's just too tired.

John allows blurry disappointment to settle down on top of him in a comforting, fluffy bedspread of fuzzy discontent. It's the same old familiar feeling. He wants his real life to start. New places. Interesting people. Hallucinated flatulent overweight men do not count as interesting. Not in John's book. He wants. That's it, he just wants.

Wasn't longing supposed to make you spiritual? He's the most spiritual guy he knows. He wants. Something. He doesn't know what that is exactly. He wants something else. Something else going on besides work and doctors and more work and more doctors. There's got to be more… something more out there. Somewhere.

Hands still hanging, mouth still open, John the walking-dead-computer-programmer (which is an oxymoron) frowns and mumbles under his breath - where the hell did all the light go to?

The reason why slowly percolates up through his overworked cerebellum. It's bubbling up through the tumbling universe of computer programming bits burbling about in his muddled brain. Squeezing past the many Do While's. Pushing through the multiplying If Thens, squeezing by the hostile hordes of Method Calls, the gaggles of stubborn Static Constructors - and now, of course, forcing its way up past the ranks of farting, smirking fat men. He slowly realizes that there's a body near him.

A male body. It dawns on him – John's tired, but not dead - this is a cute guy, cute for a white guy, some kind of orderly or nurse, and he's standing in his light. Baby blue pants, an orange-pinkish shirt, bright brown eyes, close-shaved brown hair, small close-set ears, dirty forehead – he really ought to clean that grease off his face, I mean this is a hospital for fuck's sake – the orderly's looking down at John sitting there, looking back at the hall over his shoulder, looking down at John again, who is by now looking up, right back at the orderly.

"They poisoning me"

It's his mother talking. Talking to his father inside her microscopic hospital room in a stage whisper, even though the two of them are alone and the second bed is empty now, thankfully, at least for the time being. John's seated in the stark hospital hallway outside for no particular reason other than a perverse liking for his own sanity.

"But I fool them."

Cute guy looks at the door to his mother's room. John tries to think of something to say. He'd really like to do that – the saying something thing. But nothing comes. A tiny club beat pulses in jewel-like sound behind the orderly's neck. The guy purses his lips, nods some more, smiles at him, an explosion of brilliant white teeth and smile dimples and crinkly eyes. It takes a second for John to absorb it all.

Cute guy subsequently makes a fist and jerks it backwards and forwards at him. John assumes it's a sign of solidarity, and not a request for John to toot his horn – but you can never tell with these white guys – and then he shrugs and nods. The orderly guy straightens up, relaxes out his lifting-safety belt a notch or two, sticks his earbuds (one side repaired with a stripe of black electrical tape) back in his ears, proceeds to walk towards the elevator pushing forward a gray cart full of brilliantly white and patently sterile medical equipment wrapped in mysterious layers of bluish plastic and barcode labeling.

And John is alone again, freezing, with a plenitude of useful, efficient, fluorescent light to work himself to death by.

"I only drink Coke. From machine. From first floor, visitor's room. See. Here."

John doesn't want to imagine how his mother gets down the elevator and through the lobby in a backless medical gown. It probably involves the curtains in her room. She's small, strong, resolute, resourceful, imaginative, and righteous. It's been an effervescent and ever-surprising combination for John, for all the last 25 exciting years of his young life. His laptop screen is flashing at him.

"No, this half-empty."

He smashes his fingertips into each plastic pad on his keyboard, a furious hailstorm of flesh falling on defenseless keys. Clicking, crackling, clacking – they are sounds an aggressive and businesslike plague of locusts might make. John loves it. He makes it louder. The hospital corridor is cold, his hands are stiff, the project's behind schedule, his mother is dying. For the third time in the last 12 months.

The auto-editor flashes red all over the page he's just typed. He slows down. Begins backspacing. Retyping. I won't listen he thinks. Pretend they're talking in Mandarin, no, he'd get most of the words in Mandarin, make it Swedish, Swahili, Suomi. Just syllables of sound. They are as birds singing. Not human. Not his parents talking. Not listening. Not hearing. Working.

"See, I bought two bottles. I not thirsty. Not now."

He's listening. He's stopped backspacing. She's diabetic, sugar should not be on the menu, not bottles of it. His father knows all that. Why isn't he saying something?

His mother knows what her problem is. His mother knows it's not sugar. How could it be? Something that tastes so good? She has a problem with her liver. Or her gallbladder. And dryness. Too much wind, too, little moisture. And now this new thing. She hears her head rattling. That and sometimes some pain. Not so much. Just some. In her head. And more dryness.

She wants John to paint her tiny living room in their tiny bungalow out in the Sunset two light green colors. Better for moisture. More balance. Less dry. They had been picking out the new colors at Home Depot only last week. John's head begins to ache, reliving even a few moments of those two hour marathons with the head of the paint department. It took three visits.

This week would have been the big weekend – a re-painting, everything smelling fresh and new, ma getting plump and healthy, watching her new T.V., scrutinizing the lazy neighbors, basking under her new moisture-attracting walls – finally John would have gotten it all done. John would have been working heroically, the proverbial salt miner in the salt mines, as usual - it would have been typing and programming and painting and sweating for John all weekend long, non-stop. But what else is new? Don't get him wrong, John's not complaining. He's not. Still, it could have all been over and done with. Finished. One less thing to worry about. Another task ticked off the endless list of ma-tasks.

But no. Instead they are all in Laguna Honda Hospital, smelling disinfectant, ma getting thinner, pa getting worried, John not getting any work done at all. The ventilator sighs wearily and switches itself off. Concentrate. There is no conversation. There is only keyboard. The ventilator wheezes back on again in a shower of glacial sputtering. There is no hospital. There is only code. Concentrate. Concentrate.

John's cell begins to vibrate wickedly, making the same sound a phaser does if it's on stun - a text announces its arrival. At first John doesn't look. John doesn't have a lot of friends, but you never know, maybe it's some of the guys at work, going out clubbing on a Thursday night and thinking of old John. "Hey John, how's it hanging? Get your ass down to…" Not that he'd probably go. He never does. And they never do. Actually everyone usually just stays at work and works. Or goes home and works. Or they work on the Muni or Bart commuting to work. There's a lot of work going on where John works. Work and not a lot of clubbing. At least not in John's experience. But John's not complaining. He never does. Does he? No, he does not.

The ventilator turns off importantly with a series of hums and clicks. He still doesn't look at his phone. It buzzes. John listens. Social stuff for John is, well, it's complicated. You know, complex. Multi-layered. The thing of it is, no one knows he's gay, not his parents, not his family, not his friends, John barely knows it. But lately it's been popping up insistently. The couple of times he's gone out with his straight friends here in San Francisco have been torture-sessions of stolen peeks, furiously rapid glances at the wrong sex at the wrong time, frustrated, mismatched signaling displays. Complete train wrecks. Hell, he's never even kissed a guy. He's never kissed anybody. When would he have the time? He's pathetic. All he does is work. And pick out paint. And work. Pathetic.

Speaking of which – he hovers his hand over the backspace key, two fingers twitching. Concentrate. Type. Code. He won't look. Not at the phone. He won't. He'll just be disappointed. Hope and excitement battle it out with realism and a pitiable need for self-protection. He won't look. No. He won't. Stop it. Well, maybe just one peek. Just one.

It's the corporate server machine auto-calling. He closes his eyes. Says "shit" softly to himself. And says it again. And again. And again. It feels good. So he says it faster. It's a sound effect not a word now - a submachine gun, or rather a shit-machine gun or maybe a poorly-maintained Vespa warming up on a cold foggy morning in the Castro. Or maybe... The ventilator abruptly bursts into life above him, sending down a vicious cold front of antiseptic arctic air that John literally experiences as an avalanche of goose-pimples – starting from his head and descending rapidly from there. That's a new one. Shit. John's teeth start to chatter. Shit. Shit. Shit. Shit. Shit.

A thin guy who buffs the floors and rocks and vibrates in a cleaning frenzy at the end of the hall, he looks up at the quivering, stuttering John, shakes his blond, dread-locked head, and moves a little further away from him. It's 10 p.m. and all John's code, the code he's just uploaded fifteen minutes ago for the next software release has sprang (sprung? John can never remember which) a serious leak somewhere. The recompile failed. John's in for it. Bigtime. The whole software push is trashed.

A text from the Team Lead screaming "why?" in a long drawn-out texting-wail is sure to follow. His cell obligingly vibrates. Then doubles up on its vibrating. Other team members check in with him. He sets the cell on the chair next to him and lays his face in his hands, leaning his elbows on the keyboard under the blinking, angry-looking laptop screen. He hasn't gotten more than a couple of hours of sleep on weekdays or weekends for, hell, for longer than John can even remember – months, it has to be months. Between the hospital and the software pushes at work, and... what else? John must be doing something else with his life. He must be. Isn't he?

No thinking. Must rest. John's so tired. Someone did an emergency brain-ectomy on him and John's trying to think with the temporary cotton gauze stuffed in his skull while they get him a new nervous system. The cell phone beside him becomes a maddened wasp, angry as hell and out to sting whoever just rapped and ripped its nest. He's fucked. It's going to be another all-nighter. The cell vibrates right off the plastic chair he set it on, and skitters malevolently across the clean linoleum flooring, buzzing and whining uncontrollably. He's totally fucked.

"'Course, I not have much food. I not eat this trash they give you. Poison. Besides, not clean. Who knows how they make it? Do they wash their hands? Two times?"

John hears his pa's voice right through his hands wrapped around his face and ears, loud in the therapeutic hush of the late night hallway. "Now Grace…" the voice continues in a heroic burst of rational Chinese and both his parents, the two of them, race together to see who can talk the fastest, the loudest, the most authoritatively. It's a foregone conclusion his mother's going to win.

"Rough night, huh?" Mr. baby blue pants (which pants really, really fit him very, very well - lots of interesting shadows, indentations, bulges in this cool, hospital light) stands observing him with what looks like more than a medical interest and a crooked grin. His cart is empty now. He's holding John's temporarily quiescent cell in his right hand. His lifting belt almost unbuttoned. A thin voice above his neck warbles "Throw yo' hands in the air."

John nods, sadly, says "thanks, man" in a surprisingly husky voice as he takes the cell, places it back on the chair, stares down dumbly in amazed incomprehension as he hears mournful, sinister chords ooze upwards out of his laptop. The internet connection's history.

"Shit. Shit. Shit."

More melancholy, wistful sounds and his laptop tucks away all his work, primly closes all his windows, and tight-lipped, shuts itself completely off leaving only a battery light behind blinking a frantic red warning – it has scrupulously morphed itself into an elegant, streamlined, cool, rectangular, matte-black doorstop. John's power cord is ten floors down, two buildings and three parking lots away.

"Life's a bitch, huh?" Blue pants comments, watching John, face cupped once again in his hands, blinking slowly, staring open-mouthed at some point a couple of feet in front of him.

Resembling raisins studded in a slice of bread (which by the way

John hates), miscellaneous English syllables surface in long stretches of solid five-tone wrangling from deep inside the room behind him. His mother's voice gushes out into the hallway "No worry about me. Don't bother yourself. I, O.K. I just die. No worry."

John smiles helplessly upwards, shaking his head. And he wonders if he even brought his power cord in his car. Is it under the front seat? Or was that last week? He realizes someone is still standing in front of him. Takes in a long breath as if he's actually about to speak. Doesn't. Nods generally in the direction of the blue pants, shrugs, can't think of anything more to say, nods and nods again. He tries clicking his tongue. Nods some more.

"Well."

John nods.

"Well, man."

John considers holding his head with both hands to prevent the inevitable nodding he feels coming on.

"I guess, I'll let you get back to work. My name's Adam, by the way, just started working here last week, and I see you here every shift I work, man. Just thought I'd say hi."

John nods, and nods, by this time he must look like one of those wagging-head dolls – the tongue-less wonder Asian nerd programmer painter doll – first of a series – limited edition - get one before they run out .

"That's gotta suck. Sorry. I mean that's gotta be hard. That's your mom, right? Sorry about that. And all."

John finds himself nodding. Realizes it. Stops with a jerk. But still, no words. He tries smiling again, upwards at the amiable pants standing there with the hypnotizing dimples, but the smile comes out crooked and frowning and not the way his normal smile is at all – it must look like he's trying to be ironic and cool and who knows what else. He is a clown. A total clown. A real nut case. No wonder he spends his nights typing alone in medical facilities. John looks down, sighing.

" Well."

John looks up.

"Well, guy, be seeing you."

He nods, of course.

"Later, man."

John mouths the word "bye" but no words come out.

He jumps up, a croaking Chinese bullfrog and belches out "My name's John. John Chin." There. Finally. A noise. A loud noise. In English. If anything he's louder than his mother. But earbuds in earlobes, and a place to get to, Adam, deaf to the world, is walking rapidly away. He's waiting in front of the elevator. He's stepping quickly inside. He and his cart are disappearing. He's gone.

John stiffens into immobility in the empty corridor, stunned, then sits down abruptly. Another text message vibrates the seat next to him. He cocks his head. Why is he perched up here, a pigeon on the tenth floor every night? Trapped and caged in this polar hallway. Why is his ma always sick? Why doesn't he fit into this crazy family? Why is his whole life either a coding crisis or a hospital bed? God forbid John should have more going on in his life than re-factoring code and translating for his parents. Why do people expect so much from him? What's wrong with them? What's wrong with me?

"Jojo" he hears his ma calling for him, a question not a command. What a shit of a son I am. What an absolute worthless piece of shit. His brothers and sisters, they never complain about ma. But then again, they live in other states. Easy for them. Too bad for John.

Why is it always John? Why always me? This whole family shit, it's just, well, exhausting. Just because he's the youngest. Young and dumb. It'd be so much easier to be alone. Have only himself to please. Have only his own pleasures to worry about. At least they wouldn't be screaming at him at work. None of his co-workers, none of his team members spend every friggin' weekend home with their folks, helping out, making sure things aren't falling completely apart. No wonder it's easy for them.

So when? When is it? When is John's life finally going to crawl away from the starting line and begin to limp its slow way down the racecourse? John will tell you. John has the answer. That would be never. Never. That's when. Never, as in - not ever, as in - not in this lifetime, forget all about it, just get through it, just one more night, do what you have to, be responsible, don't let anyone down, be a team player, do the hard work, do the right thing, think the right thing, say the right thing. Never. That's when. Never.

"Jojo?"

John makes a decision. Drops his dead laptop on the tannish molded plastic chair by the door he's been freezing in for the last five hours, runs for the elevator, jabs both up and down buttons a couple of times, breathes hard, sees from the display it's the basement floor Adam's stopped at, grabs the elevator next to it, pushes past a guy with a cane leaning on another blue-panted individual with a pony-tail, apologizes, waits, watches people get on, waits, watches people get off, waits, almost ruptures due to the extreme exercise of patience required of him, finally flies off the elevator and skids into a wall, almost hitting Adam and another guy who are talking and laughing by an open pair of external doors marked "Hospital Personnel Only" and "Emergency" and "Keep Closed At All Times".

John slides and bounces to a halt, legs braced against the slick linoleum tiles, bending over, arms supporting him, palms flat on the floor, impersonating a sprinter, waiting to hear the gun, start the Olympic 100 meter dash, and go for the gold.

"Uh" says John.

Both guys are looking at him now, Adam with his eyebrows raised, the other guy with wide eyes, chewing gum in a kind of astonished way, hand caught in mid-air, apparently reaching for something in his pocket.

"Uh. Adam. Uh. You're probably wondering why I followed you down here."

Adam waits a second, tilts his head, pauses, turns and says something to his buddy who shrugs and heads out the doors. Doors which shut, loudly and mechanically, groaning and shuddering with a number of authoritative, protective, locking, ker-chunking sounds. The corridor hums with an expectant air, John has the bizarre feeling he's listening to an overture at the beginning of a Broadway musical.

Adam waits until the doors are finished with their important business. He leans backwards on the door jamb of the now-closed doors and crosses his arms. It looks like he has a black tattoo of strange markings across his white, high forehead. John wonders if they are trendy Hanzi Chinese characters, saying something along the lines of "Buy More Five Happiness Rice Noodles". He saw one a year or so ago at the gym across the back of a muscley, unsuspecting white guy. He'd been duped into being an unwitting advertisement for trendy prophylactics. John hadn't said anything, although he'd felt bad for the guy and somehow partially guilty for the knowing and the not telling. Should he have said something?

Isn't it better not to know sometimes? Why is it John's responsibility? He straightens up and makes a conscious effort *not* to look, which of course, makes him look all the more.

"Hey."

"Hey."

John can't help himself. It's as if he's undergoing a seizure of involuntary, compulsive idiocy. There is a certain purity to mindlessness. He decides just to go with it. What else can he do? His mind is mush. "Uh, yeah, is, uh, is that a, uh, a tattoo on your face? It kind of looks like words. Or characters. Or words." John snaps his jaws closed with an audible crack - preventing additional babbling and stopping himself from saying whatever-the-hell-first-thing that decides next to wander through his head, out his larynx, and into the open air.

Adam smiles. John maintains the mouth-shut pose. John forgets to breathe. John is such a jerk.

"Well, something like that, yeah."

Adam uncrosses his arms and puts a hand on Johns' shoulder. John forgets everything else, flinches - it has the feeling of a severed high-voltage wire coming to rest on his bare skin while he's standing in a puddle of water. Adam pulls away a little bit, head bent down, smiling from one side of his face, eyebrows up and questioning. A soothing, hopeful series of musical tones burst down upon them. The elevator doors open up behind them and a crowd of noisy riders exit in various directions, including the closed emergency employee doors. The doors open. The hallway empties. Then it's once again, with the long closing process. Finally, they're alone again. Then Adam looks slam-bang, right at John.

"You all right, man? Everything O.K. upstairs?" Adam stops when he sees John's confused expression. Then he laughs. "I mean upstairs, the hospital, not upstairs, your head."

John barks back a tight, worried coughing laugh. "Oh, yeah, yeah, just fine." He pauses. "Well, not fine. Well, yes. No. Yes. No." He pauses again. He's talking in escaped-mental-patient-ese. "No. My ma's real sick. They don't know what's wrong."

"Oh, hey man. That's rough. I'm really sorry to hear that."

John just looks at Adam. Adam looks back then looks ready to leave. John takes a deep breath, closes his eyes, opens them and babbles as if his life depended upon it.

"Yeah, I just, well, If you wanted to go out sometime, you

know, I was, just, I was thinking, well, you know."

Adam smiles as if to himself, looks off to the left, then looks back directly at John. "You mean, out, like on a date going out?"

"I mean, well, yeah, uh, yeah, like out, going out, out you know. Yeah. I guess that's what I mean. No, that *is* what I mean. Yeah. Going out."

Adam takes a deep breath. John takes a deep breath. Adam takes another breath. John doesn't, he's still holding his first breath. Adam looks at John, looks away. Pulls both hands up, pushes both arms way above his head, knits his fingers together, cracks his knuckles. The elevator doors open again. People spill out. The elevator trills and chirps. Someone runs down the hallway to catch it, sliding in just as the doors close. The elevator yells out balefully. The doors open and close slowly, honking sadly the whole time. People scramble past the two of them. The employee emergency doors open, fill, empty and close again. Adam looks at John this whole time. Puts both hands behind his head. Breathes again.

John is dizzy. Adam's going to say no. Adam's going to punch John in the mouth and break his nose. At least if John's going to get hurt, he's going to get it done to him in a hospital. John may be reckless and insane, but at least he's reckless and insane and practical. He gets that from his ma.

"Look, man, I'm flattered. Really." John feels a black hole opening up below his knees. No. No. No. No. No. This isn't happening. No.

"But I'm not gay, man."

John wants to dematerialize into a pile of crushed and blushing dust and be swept away in a dustpan, thrown into a dumpster, trucked off to rest quietly in a garbage dump and listen to the peaceful sound of methane burbling up and into exhaust pipes around his disintegrated self for the next century or two. He finds he can't move. He's grown roots. He's a tree. He's a new kind of tree – Johnus Imbecilus Oakus.

"Hey. Hey. Dude. Chill. Look, chill. It's all good. It's not like you're the only gay guy in San Francisco. And hey, I'm not bragging if I tell you this isn't my first time getting asked. I mean being asked by a guy. No biggie, man. It's cool. So. So, hey, what's your name again, anyways?"

"John." This pops out and then he freezes, an entirely automatic reaction, wholly reflexive, as sure as a soda can falling out of a machine after you hit the big, rectangular Hit-me-I'm-a-Coke-I'm-John button. One action, then immobility. It's lucky John's brain is on auto-pilot right now.

"Hey. Hey, it's cool. Really. No hard feelings, John. Really."

"Look, John, me and some friends are heading out tomorrow night, Friday, come out with us. You in?"

Adam's hand is back on John's shoulder. "Come on, you need a break, guy. Everybody needs a break."

"Say you'll do it, man"

"Say it. Say it."

John nods yes.

When John hears his ma's cutting, chainsaw Mandarin as he wanders off the elevator on the tenth floor, he re-checks his pocket for the seventeenth time making sure he's saved the ripped, crumpled slip of paper with Adam's number on it. His head spins and spins. He doesn't know what to think. Or how to begin thinking. He needs to reboot his brain. Somewhere quiet. Preferably with a bed and a pillow.

"Jojo, that you? You back from dinner? Jojo?"

He walks in, snags his laptop and phone off the chairs outside, more than half-surprised they're still there, wondering if he's completely lost his marbles and his mother shakes her head when she sees him. He mentally braces himself.

"Why you so skinny? Like old rooster, hardly good enough for soup. You eat. Eat more. When I get better, you come every night, I feed you. You get big, round, healthy, big belly, be prosperous, be happy. Not weak like me. Out of balance. Too dry, too dry. Water run away from me now. Not like before. Dry."

"Ma, I go to the gym. I want to lose fat and gain muscle. I want to get strong, not just big." His mother glares at him. John can see disagreeing will get him nowhere, quick, just like it always does. But he has to try. He sees even though her eyes are somewhat feisty and shining, the rest of her looks like it's already giving up. She looks so unsteady, so tired, so breakable.

"And ma, you're not weak. You're fine. You just need to get some rest. Stop working so hard. We can handle it now. Rest. Rest and get better."

"No. Dry. Weak. I weak. Feel." She reaches, quick as a bird and pinches his bicep between a thumb and forefinger. Well, maybe she isn't so tired. John feels skin and muscle caught in an auto factory sheet metal press. She lets go and a big, startled purple bruise begins to bloom on his upper arm. "See? Weak." Then she directs a fierce gaze at his upper torso.

"Jojo. You call these stringy arms and that bumpy chest healthy? You call that strong? You look like your mother. These thin old arms, these twig stick legs. Not so strong anymore. You not be like your mother. Stay in balance. Get strong. Big. Round. Live a long time. Do what I say, not what I do."

"Ah ma." John lays his hand for a brief moment on her shoulder. She tries to continue frowning, looking the stern parent at John, but relents after a moment of internal struggle. She smiles a wan, worried smile.

His pa lays one hand on his mother's other shoulder, she twitches, startles, looks up at his pa in terror, then calms. He rests his hand easily on her pointy shoulder blades under the nightgown with a feather-soft touch. John sees his mother looking back over at him, a newly-energized determined expression on her angular face and John realizes he will be talking about wasting money, gym memberships, and arms for a long, long time. He makes a quick tactical decision.

"Ma, I just saw a fat man, covered in rainbows." John leaves out the farting. Although, from past experience, and knowing his mom, that one detail could be the most essential part of the whole fat man episode – the fart. It probably means he has a dry liver. It could be the key to his health and the chance at a long, lucky, prosperous life. He decides to let it go, anyways.

John is not surprised when his mother is not surprised. She doesn't miss a beat in their conversation, but speaks up immediately.

"Oh, that bad. Did he have sack? Carry something?"

Not wanting the conversation to die, John improvises.

" Yeah, I think so. Carrying a sack on a stick, like a hobo."

"No. No he carry in his hands. Has beads too. That good. Budai. Budai watches you. Good luck. Good luck for you. You always the lucky one."

"But I think I was asleep, ma. I think I was dreaming."

"Ah, that better. You come every night. You come every night and you tell me all your dreams from night before."

Since he was coming anyway, that seems like a good idea. He'd rather talk about dreams than get his appendages blacked and blued.

His pa looks at his ma, who looks at John, who looks back at the two of them. There is a satisfactory silence, as everybody looks at everybody else. And what is more, it being so pleasant and so very unusual, everybody looks pleased.

"Jojo" his ma calls out for him, but looks abruptly over at his father.

Something's up. John realizes he still has the laptop shut and tucked under his arm attached, just part of the John-anatomy, looks for a place to set it down, but there is only the hospital bed. He shifts it to the other arm and holds onto it. He watches his ma doing her eyebrow-moving language with his pa. Ma doesn't look good. He hates this. His ma, fading in front of him. Her strength evaporating. Her wiry body melting into the air – as fast as condensation on the windshield when you turn the defrost on. There's less and less of her. Each day. He wonders if he should really be starting to worry about her. Worry for real. Just look at her. Thin arms, delicate wrists, hard tendons, harsh muscles on her face. She's so old-looking now. So tired. So not his indestructible ma.

John blinks a couple of times, his eyes are suddenly working funny. He rubs his eyes with his knuckles to cover up the wetness, which is a little difficult and requires some elaborate elbow-work as his laptop is still clenched stubbornly between his left arm and his torso. He nearly drops it. When he's done rubbing, his father seems to be trying to leave, pretends to help John to set down his laptop on the chair his pa was sitting on, but leans into his ear, as he sets it down and whispers throatily "She doesn't know. Jojo. She doesn't know. There's not much time left. Don't tell her."

Then he turns and surprisingly moves his head angrily at his ma, saying no, and leaves. No to what? No to death? Johns' mind is swimming and empty and he feels dangerously off-balance and sick. The room is seesawing, swaying, and he finds he's filling up with queasy and slippery questions that can't be asked as he turns towards his ma. There has to be some mistake. Pa has to be mistaken. It's never been this bad before. He needs to think. But John has no chance to think. No chance to ask. No chance for John. His father is already moving away. Moving away from him and leaving. Why is he leaving? There's no time.

But he pauses, his father, he pauses and comes to a complete stop halfway to the door and looks at the floor, wagging his head again, then steps backwards until he's leaning on the door hinges, head tilted slightly back as if to overhear them, hands crossed in back of his waist. John worries his pa might get his fingers caught in the door, starts to call out to him, feels his ma's small hands on his leg, turns around. He looks down at her, she has a pleading look on her face he's never seen before, he looks back up and his pa is gone.

His mother leans forward and upwards, pulling John downwards and towards her at the same time, and as John leans in, he sees her crying and he suddenly doesn't want to hear whatever it is she's got to tell him. But he is her son, she is his mother. He leans in, head spinning, throat closing, eyes scratchy and hurting. She puts her lips close to his left ear. She says "Jojo listen. Listen carefully. No easy way. No easy way to say this. Jojo, you not my son. You adopted."

2. SUMMER

Someone very fat and very round is hiding behind a curtain in the living room.

Not this. Not again. John sees it immediately but no one else seems to want to talk about it. So, John doesn't either. Still, John has to squeeze past the impressive hemisphere of his bulk (it just feels like a him, a him-bulge, so John goes with it) every time John comes through the front door and down the narrow front hallway. It's there, every time he slips past the big hospital bed sitting proudly in the center of the living room. It's there, as he goes past the built in china cabinet across from the big front bay windows. It's there, as he pushes past the two best chairs and the end table.

And then there's this giggling. Little kids, lots of little kids, caught in mid-tickle-fest. He ignores it all. He rubs past, dragging his right arm along the curving contour of the drapes, sure he's bumping over a jumbo-sized belly button depression somewhere right about the middle with his elbow - scraping on, over, and past it, each and every trip, in and out, every time. Bump. Bump. Bump. Giggle. Giggle. Giggle.

"Good morning, ma."

"G'morning Jojo."

The soft voice floats out of a pile of pillows and mounds of tightly pulled blankets on the shining hospital bed which sits in the form of a textile version of the Yellow Mountain in the hopeful morning sunlight spilling and splattering across his ma and pa's living room.

John stops on his first trip in to the living room, as he's bringing in some old towels from the garage, and bends down to hold his ma's hand and she reaches up to brush his hair. John can hear the T.V. babbling in the other room, so he calls out "Morning Pa." He hears his pa harrumph back "Jojo, good, you're here".

His ma is smiling up at him, her head shaking a little involuntarily, her face a fragile construction of fine skin and bone stretched as tight as the blankets she's sitting against. He watches that familiar face smile at him, skin an expensive porcelain, crisp and translucent, draped across her familiar bones. She has her best clothes on today with her green flower-covered silk slippers (green to encourage moisture), and her high lace button-down collar shirt. She looks nearly worn out, faded and fraying and John hates that. But her eyes gleam bright and true in the morning light, and they beam determination and strength up and out of her failing body and into John, offering it all as a gift into her boy's face.

"You lucky. Luckiest one I know. Never forget."

"Lucky. I won't forget, ma."

"Now you go. You help these women. No men here, only women. Why? I ask, nobody know."

"They're all friends of mine, ma. They came to help. Remember? I asked you if it would be all right if my friends helped. You said…"

"I sure not too much get broken. All old stuff anyway. 'Sides, women work hard. Harder than men. Everybody know that. But sometimes not so good with heavy lifting. I not any good for lifting."

"Ma, no one needs you to do any lifting. Just sit back and rest, ma."

" When you a baby I lift all the time. Now, not so much lifting."

"Ma, nobody wants you to lift things today."

"And your pa, he only good for watching. No good for lifting. Never. You go. Lift. Go on. Use your high price gym arms."

"Ma…"

"You no worry. I watch from here, make sure everything done

right, done best way. Only a few things broken. You go."

"Ma…"

"No worry. No worry 'bout me. Go on." Then softly "Go."

"Go", this time even softer.

"You working or resting, John?" A voice calls over John's shoulder.

Al (Alice), gray-blond crew cut already polka-dotted with fresh green paint, has been busy. She'd unpacked half her truck already by the time John had gotten there this morning - she gives him a high five as she speeds by him, which he misses – she's making trip after trip carrying tarps and towels and paint and beer. Another substantial woman or two follows her each trip with just as much stuff, maybe more.

Al and company go in and come out, go in and come out. John stands, watches it all at the front door. He's trying to look as if he's carefully opening a can of paint. What he's really doing is straining his eyeballs scanning the street, scoping out the street corners, listening with his whole body for the sound of a certain voice, straining to make out a certain scrunching and tapping of leather soles strolling down ancient cracked sidewalk, watching for a scruffy head to appear over the top of hedges. He's also trying very hard not to be too obvious about it. He pokes and prods at the can and looks off into the distance.

"Screwdrivers works better than fingernails, John"

Al glides past him and out the door. A second later she and another woman are carrying in two sawhorses and a board.

"Need help? One man shouldn't have to open a whole can of paint all by himself. Could take all day." Al goes out and comes in with another board, followed by yet another woman carrying clamps.

"If I were a betting woman, I'd say what you're doing is resting." Two other women breeze past John and start spreading tarps on the floor, and various cans of paint around the living room.

Al leaves, comes back in. She swats John on the butt, hands him four rolls of masking tape, a six pack of Red Bulls and a pile of untoasted pop tarts.

"Kitchen" she says pointing with her head because her hands are full of paint brushes. John balances everything, then tries to say casually, as he pauses on his walk to the back of the house.

"So you seen Art anywhere, Al?"

"Wow. That's seven minutes. That has to be a record. Seven minutes without one mention of Arthur. Deb, not in front of the front door. You want to step into the cans and end up with lime green leather boots?"

"Al? What about Art? Any sightings? Anywhere, Al?"

"And what are you wearing your riding boots for anyways? Yeah, yeah. I was thinking you would. Barb's got an old pair of mine out in her Volvo. No, no steel toes. What? You welding steel girders today? You Rosie the Riveter? Quit your bellyaching. Yeah, yeah, you and who else?"

"Were all of you born in a barn? Wipe your shoes before you come in. Yeah, you know you love it. Where's Tammy off to? There's some clean-up stations that need setting up in the dining room with Tammy's name on 'em. Tammy! Yeah, you. That's right. Over here, girl!"

"I'll go look for Art myself."

"You just do that. The tarp goes over the chair, not in front of it, babe. What's your name, again?"

John looks in every room, moving clockwise through the house, then looks once again going counter-clockwise, for good measure. The house isn't all that big. It's actually pretty small. John knows, he grew up between these four walls. It would be difficult for John to lose Art in this house. So that means... Artie is obviously missing from the house. Art said he'd be here. Art promised he'd help. Art told John's ma, to her face, in that very hospital bed, that he wanted to help. So where the hell *is* Artie?

He's nowhere. No sign of him. No sly, diminutive body that drives John crazy, no winking eyes that make him forget his name, no shy smile, no smooth skin. No straight-cut bangs to run your nose through. No nothing. No Art.

A vision of Art with his arm nearly severed, lying in a gutter, feebly whispering John's name floods John's brain and kick-starts his adrenal glands. Shit. Art isn't here because Art is hurt. That has to be it. Art could be lying dead somewhere. Or robbed. Or... some kind of car accident. Or a terrorist attack. Or, you know, an escaped rabid elephant from the Zoo. Do elephants get rabies? They must. Sometimes. Well, it's not all that far away, the Zoo that is. And the freeways. God knows what might happen on the 280. John keeps all this to himself, although he's starting to break a sweat. He knows he's being ridiculous, but he also knows he doesn't care. And, there's no mentioning any of this to Al, she'd just keep her mouth significantly shut and do some serious Olympic-class eye-rolling, all in John's direction.

He runs out onto the front yard – all ten square feet of it here in the Outer Sunset – and googles San Francisco traffic on his phone, scanning the street, studying the map, fingering his car keys, thinking about where he ought to begin his search and rescue mission.

"You're hopeless" says Al, carrying a bunch of thin, spindly rod-things into the house. John is googling San Francisco hospitals and emergency rooms now.

"He'll be fine. Stop your worrying. He'll be here. Get your mind off of it. For heaven's sake, make yourself useful, boy. Get what's left in the front seat of the truck, O.K.? Should just be one trip left."

John nods slowly, folding his phone shut even more slowly, gnawing on his lower lip, gazing wistfully up towards the end of the street and back the other way as he shuffles his mournful self to the truck and back. "Just hopeless" he hears repeated behind his back, "And doesn't even know it", Then, quieter and quieter as the voice disappears into his ma's house, "hopeless."

He doesn't even remember carrying back whatever it is Al's got him carrying, rubbing and squeezing past the belly behind the drapes, dropping off his bundle by his Pa, who's staring politely at the T.V. and helpfully not noticing the crowd of unlikely people showing up to make his wife happy and make his living room glow with the healthy shine of an exploded chlorophyll factory.

Then John hears a car pull up and forces himself *not* to run out the front door as if he were fleeing a raging inferno. He stares out the dining room window, sitting backwards on a chair, examining the neighbor's redwood plank garden wall just three feet away, keeps his back to the front door, tries to look casual, hums tunelessly under his breath.

"You know you're facing away from the T.V. and staring at a fence don't you?" says an Al voice behind him.

"Just hopeless." And then John hears only the singsong patter of the sports announcer, and his pa creaking one of the other dining room chairs as he shifts around to get comfortable.

"Hey! It's going to be a little hard to paint, Deb, with the brushes in the dining room and the walls in the living room. Yeah, yeah."

Painting begins in earnest. The front door booms open. John tenses. But it's John's friend Adam that comes in right after that, with a couple of six packs of beer, some soda and a pizza. He heads straight for the back where John and his pa are hanging out and starts commenting on the baseball game – Giants versus the Blue Jays. In Toronto. But the conversation peters out. Pa answers Adam's polite questions in monosyllables. Pa is only half-watching the game. The other half of him is watching his house turning into a wilderness of brown plastic and lesbians. Adam leaves him be after a decent period of game-watching silence and comes over to join John and watch the fence with him.

"Hey geek."

"Hey hobo."

"So John, where's the shadow? Your evil twin?"

"Hey! Adam! C'mon, stop. Art's not that bad. Really, he's just young, young and shy."

"Sure, geek-boy, just shy. Shy like a fox."

"I think that's *sly* like a fox. And I wish you wouldn't be that way. He's not that bad. Really. He's opinionated, he's all by himself, he's new to the City. Cut him a little slack."

"Sure. Sure. He's shy and sly. If that's what you want to call it. And he's got you wrapped around his little finger."

"Adam… C'mon…"

"So where is the little fucker anyway? Wasn't he supposed to be here already?"

A hesitant voice rises in the living room, and Al is shushing everyone and asking an important someone what they want.

"No, big wall only, big one dark green. All other, light."

"So that wall right in front of you is going to be the dark one, Mrs. Chin?"

"Big wall, dark. Rest, light."

"You heard the lady, ladies. Get 'em moving."

The motorized hospital bed is set up - a living, breathing moving thing made up of chrome, cords, mattresses and taut hospital-corner bed linens - in the living room because the living room is the only room in the house big enough to handle such a wondrous complexity. It has become so covered with pillows and shawls, folded blankets and comforters, it looks more like an enormous throne from a 20's film set for the Dowager Empress of China than a piece of hospital furniture. His ma loves it.

It is certainly no longer just a bed. It is The Bed. It has acquired a presence and a personality all its own, in the Chin household, as if it were another person in the room, taking part in conversations, helping out with the painting, demanding respect. His ma delights in getting it to do gymnastics and take the form of all kinds of unlikely shapes with her remote control. John's happy because it keeps his ma upright and breathing easily and as comfortable as can be expected. John's ma likes it because it puts her in the center of the room and gives her immediate advisory and management control over the whole household.

Al looks over and winks at John as she nods at each of his ma's detailed instructions. His ma, sitting at the center of the bed, in the center of the room in her flowery pants leisure suit soaks up all this loving attention - a houseplant set loose on a sun-dappled patio after living for years in a forgotten corner of a dark, airtight, windowless flat.

She is shining today, in her element. And John loves her. She guards the floors, monitors the foot traffic, gives advice about how best to lose weight or gain it. She details minute directions for the timing and the order in which each necessary and important task needs to be accomplished today. She is Madame Premier Grace Chin. Mistress of the Flat. President of All She Surveys.

Al listens, Al watches over her, Al coordinates around her and asks her opinion, although you have to lean in close to hear what his ma is saying now, she's so weak and soft-spoken. John gave his ma's hospice caregiver the day off to keep the numbers down on painting day. Al says she can handle anything that needs to happen. Al says she doesn't mind, she's used to being around people with health issues. Her purple bandana'd head shows up all the time by The Bed, bobbing around his ma all day long, and John is confident no pillow is going to remain un-fluffed for any significant period of time in his ma's vicinity.

John thinks Al would be just as comfortable commanding an infantry division as organizing a painting party. She's strong, reliable, and very matter-of-fact about life. She says she's had to be, since life has thrown so many rocks at her, you gotta be good at seeing what's real and what's not, and get very good at ducking and weaving. She talks tough, but she's always there when you need her. She took in Adam at one point. Adam bunks down with her at Al's repair shop on Cesar Chavez in the Mission, well really Bernal Heights. Al owns the shop with Deb.

John met Al (and Deb) through Adam. And sometimes (well, a lot lately) they go out. Astounding. John Chin going out. Having fun. Bar-hopping. She and Deb and Adam and various girlfriends of Al and Deb and Adam have gone out any number of times in the past six months. Amazing. So much is changing. John Chin is changing.

John used to have a very clean and tidy life. It was neatly divided into four, distinct, completely separate boxes. One box, one part of life. Each part in its own place. Not fancy. But orderly. A clean, easily understood, self-documenting life. Rational. Appealing. Predictable. There was a family box, a school and work box, a friend box, and a romance box. He always imagined them as four huge pigeonholes on a giant's roll top desk. The way they do it in a fairy tale, you know, Rumpelstiltskin or maybe Jack and the Beanstalk, with John being Jack. What can he say? He likes cartoons. And it doesn't take much to make him happy.

Now the boxes are just ragged fissures, piles of shattered, splintered lumber, bullet-riddled dividers and rubble-filled craters – for as far as the eye can see. Not that he was complaining. John doesn't complain. He doesn't. But the family box had been well-and-truly-nuked when his ma told him he'd been adopted from a Taiwanese orphanage. The work box, The Box of No Return, had undergone serious modifications when they'd fired him for not putting in the unofficial, mandatory and continuous overtime that John had no time for anymore, not with a sick ma. John was now a temp. Making next to nothing. The friend box had been more theoretical than real for a long time (if 25 years is a long time) - until of course Adam parachuted into his life at the hospital. And that left only that very abstract and hypothetical container - a little thing John called the Box d'Romance.

Romance and sex. John had discovered them both in a hurry running into Artie at the Crescendo Coffee House and almost dropping his Decaf into Artie's lap, Artie was so stunning. At least to John he was. No, he was to anyone, Art was always getting looks on the street. Art was stunning. Maybe overly stunning. It was sometimes disconcerting to John seeing Artie smile back at so many guys in a single walk down a single block of street - of let's say Market Street around 16th. Last week John had gotten up to 97 men before he stopped counting the smiles and Art's counter-smiles. And that was only in the first 10 minutes.

Still, John had to remember - Artie was new to all this. He was. He was young. That day at Crescendo, Artie had looked down in embarrassment and looked up over his long lashes at John in apology for sitting in John's way, and John had been hooked. Right there. Right in the café. All Artie had to do was reel him in, hold out the net, and he had John. Completely. Adam had been with John that day in the Coffee House watching the whole thing, clicking his tongue, shaking his head. But John didn't care.

Romance and sex. John suddenly understands in an appropriately visceral way the whole *Dangerous Liaisons*, forget sleep, forget food, have sex all day, all night thing – a thing that had seemed a tired Hollywood plot device before, and now is a thing so real, he wonders if he needs to see a shrink and start on psychotropics. What is happening to him? Where does his commonsense run off to? Sometimes John doesn't even recognize himself anymore. Who is this moonstruck, puppy-faced pile of jelly he turns into around Art? He has no will. He has no individuality. He has no desire that isn't Art's when Art is nearby. It's freakish. It's wild. John loves it. He wants more.

Romance and sex. John wants to write a book. They've gone from no nights a week to almost every night of the week, sleeping together, waking up together, and John feels maybe (with constant encouragement from Artie) that John is ready to have Art move in. At least John had been ready up to the point John lost his job. Now John's not so sure. But not Art. Art really, really, really wants to move in. John is thinking – well, maybe, I could ask him this weekend. Art will flip. Just flip.

Art has three flat-mates and it's a fact that it is always a major hassle getting any privacy at all in that crazy house. Always get-togethers and music, arguments and slamming doors and Artie taking courses at the Art and Design College in the city during the day and running to parties at night and worrying if his dad is going to send him his rent check on time and where he's going to get his tuition from and how he's going to pay for food. Art is new to higher education. He graduated from High School, went traveling for a couple of years, courtesy of his dad, and now that he's 21, his father is forcing him to do the college thing, or no more checks.

He started his first quarter, Summer Quarter, two months ago. John isn't sure he's taking to it very well.

This is John's new crater-filled life. Life on the moon. Life on a new planet. Far from the Earth he used to live on.

"Any time now, John" says Al from somewhere off to John's right. He looks and sees her painting around masking tape with dexterous flips of her roller brush in the front hallway.

John grabs a brush in one hand and a pop tart in the other and stands up. The baseball game hits the seventh inning stretch, his dad walks into the backyard, sipping his iced tea and getting out of the way, and John, standing and staring intently at decaying knots in the fence-planks in front of him, feeling miserable, well, John hears a familiar voice. It can't be. He runs the obstacle course of living room tarps, edges past Al and sawhorses and hands his brush to Al and stuffs his pop tart in his pants pocket when he sees a slim, elegant shadow stand limned, backlit by dazzling shimmers of fog-scattered photons, emerging from the San Francisco afternoon sunlight and entering his pa's house. Art has arrived.

"No" John hears Artie saying to someone out in front of the house, "No it's Art, as in Life Imitating Art. I'm the Art everybody's imitating. Art – that's it, you got it."

Art slouches in, gets pushed from outside, and stumbles forward, tripping and briefly going down on one knee on a tarp spread over the entryway floor. Face fairly glowing, bright red in hot, boiling embarrassment, he glares back at the four hands still trying to insert his slight body forcefully through the open front door.

Art shrugs his shoulders, twitching off the pushing hands and composes his irritated face into a smile, throws his head back to get his long black hair out of his eyes, smoothes the sides of his shirt and pants to bring back the crease, checks his cuffs to make sure they're crisp, removes all evidence of his falling and erases any emotion on his face.

Al watches amazed and bemused from two feet away, right arm caught in mid-air as she works a powerful down stroke of dark lime-green through the roller onto the wall separating the living room and the bathroom.

"Better late than never, huh?" says Al pulling the long-handled roller down the wall and into the pan for more paint. Art smiles at her brightly, showing perfect, even, white teeth in a tight, controlled grin, and pushes off another offending hand that starts to grip his shoulder from behind. He chuckles a low, almost noiseless chuckle. Bites his lip. Looks down at his feet. Gets pushed. Looks over his shoulder. Whispers something furiously. Looks back at Al, smiling and chuckles. Looks down again. Looks up. Al just stares and paints.

"You sure go to a lot of trouble, that's all I'll say. So who are your little friends, Art?" Al says, placing the brush carefully on the pan, balancing the handle on the tarp on the floor, wiping her hands on her overalls, and walking over, her right hand out, ready to shake.

"Gwen. And Barb."

"Hi, Al. How's tricks? How's the truck?" says a new voice.

"You're looking healthy. Big and healthy. Emphasis on big." says another. Some soft, hushed, feminine laughter, a chorus of laughter, behind Art's back explodes after that last comment. Then quiet. Then snorting and laughing and more exhaling and exploding. Then more quiet.

Al looks back at John's ma in the bed, watching T.V. on the far side of the room, and pulls Art by the shoulder up and off the tarp-covered floor and out onto the porch in one smooth movement – she pulls him up the way she would pick up a particularly large piece of lint that was dirtying the Chin's clean carpet.

"Art. I'm surprised. Surprised and disappointed. Gwen isn't coming in here today, Art. Barb isn't coming in either. Time for them to go home." Al looks back to see if anyone's seen them yet, smiles awkwardly when she sees John bouncing around them still, a "J" ping pong ball in a Bingo hopper and pulls Art close, whispering through clenched teeth.

"I don't know what you're up to, mister. Or Gwen . Or Barb. But so help me God, it's not happening today. It's over. Done. End of game. I'm on to you and your little friends here, so git! Go on. Git!"

"Al, why you look so purrty? Come over and give me a kiss." says a voice from behind Art's back.

Art says "You're hurting me" and pulls away dramatically, rubbing and shaking his arm and staring at it. It's all lost on John. John only sees Art's brown eyes glowing and smoldering under alternating ribbons of lemon noonday sun and romantic iridescent streamers of fog – John sees the whole sky blowing around in Art's eyes.

"Hey" says John, looking at Art, watching the ribbons of fog flow by them, feeling the cold air blow in off of Ocean Beach fifteen blocks away and not caring if he froze to death out here. He could watch John forever. In fact, he will.

"Hey" says Art, frowning and wrenching his shoulder up and down, in wider and wider arcs, to the left and to the right, gripping it with his other hand, motioning soulfully with his eyes to get John to ask him why his arm is hurting.

"Hey" says John watching the smooth play of Art's muscles in his chest under his shirt, in his shoulders, watching his perfect neck arch backwards and forwards, watching each finger on each hand work, the wrists flex, the elbows bend. John's going to kiss each joint separately and tenderly as soon as he has the chance. Ah. He's forgetting all about breathing again. His heart pounds, slamming his chest, bashing his insides they way those long, high winter breakers pound the wet, packed sand of Ocean Beach. His face burns. Then it feels cold. Then it burns. He's going insane. All he wants to do is touch Art and feel his skin under his fingertips. He blinks trying to get his eyes moist. He can't swallow. He's so dry. He shakes his head.

Everybody should be this happy. Everyone should feel this way. John loves the world. He has Art. Right here. He realizes, as if for the first time (it's not) - Art is the most beautiful man he has ever seen. His body is grace incarnate. He pulls in a deep breath remembering finally to breathe and inhales the sweet, spicy scent of Art's cologne and has to close his eyes before he cries. This must be what it feels like to lose your mind.

Adam comes up behind John and squeezes past to Al. "Is that who I think it is?" Al just nods.

"Why would your ex show up with her new girlfriend when she stole your truck?" Al shakes her head.

"What's the two of them doing with Art?" Al shakes her head again.

"This is fucked up." Al continues her stare-down with Gwen and says "No shit" out of the side of her mouth.

Adam looks back at Mrs. Chin and bunches himself beside Al creating a human wall between the painting crew, the painting management, and the spiteful drama brewing up on the tiny front lawn.

Art stares at John who is holding his breath again, weaving back and forth, squinting under closed eyelids, smiling a strange twisted leer and Art just gives up. He lets his arm drop to his side in a normal posture and ponders what his next move will be. Then Art realizes something. It's quiet behind him. Too quiet. Art cocks his head to the left – in fact, it's been very calm behind him for at least a minute or so.

Then he sees Al's eyes in the form of 125 millimeter smoothbore tank guns tracking the girls' locations in back of him. Art can almost hear the sound of ammunition rounds loading up, guns swiveling and locking, distances being estimated, angles being calculated. There is every appearance of imminent explosions in the near future. And Art is in the way.

All Al's muscles are bunching up, she's a six foot puma getting ready to leap on two unfortunate and nervous jackrabbits standing in her path. Art hears voices, a couple of feet away, and getting farther away, whispering loudly - "Barb?" "Gwen?" "You know Barb… I was just thinking, I think we got someplace we need to be…" and then the sound of a hedge being backed into, branches broken, steps being negotiated badly, footsteps stumbling slowly, then more rapid footsteps, and then quiet and soft traffic noises and only the sounds of distant stereos wafting in from distant lawns. In other words, just peaceful Saturday afternoon sounds.

John hears the bushes crunching and looks over Art's shoulder and his strangely frowning, unhappy face. What's Artie so upset about? Artie's the one who's late.

"Johnny boy, you sure can pick 'em." Al says this under her breath.

"Are you going to let her talk to me like that?"

"I wasn't talking to you, party boy."

"I can bring whatever friends I want. You don't tell me what to do. Who are you? What are you doing here? Tell them John."

John is lost. What friends? Art's alone. Tell them what?

"What's up Artie? What's the heck is wrong?" says John, then adds more softly "Tell me, Artie, just tell me."

"As if you didn't know."

John just stares at Art.

"You don't know? Well, somebody needs to tell you. Who cancelled our plane tickets? Both trips. Who took me out to a Taco Stand last Friday when I wanted to go to that concert down the peninsula? Who, Johnnie? Who? I'll give you one guess. No, you'll need three. Who was it?"

"Artie, I lost my job. I'm broke. I may have to move back in with my folks. What do you want from me?"

"A lot more than *you* can give. I can tell you that."

"Hey, Art, take it down a couple of notches. Lower your voice, guy. Show some respect." Al motions backwards with her hands, shielding them with her shoulders, pointing at the bed and the living room, and the person in that bed.

"Oh. You're tough. You're Big Alice. Gwen was wrong. You're way uglier than your friend Deb."

Adam whispers furiously beside Al "Just walk away, Al. Walk away from it. It's not worth it. He's not worth it."

"Yeah, there's Deb behind you. Yup. Uglier."

John is blinking rapidly now, feeling he slept through half a movie and woke up clueless and confused at the big fight scene. His head spins.

"Why are you doing this Art? Why are you acting this way in front of my mother? You know she's sick."

"She's not your mom. And you're ugly too. Ugly and old. Why are *you* trying to pick up younger guys like me? Find an old wrinkled man to be with you."

John's mind is erased. His mental hard drive has just been reformatted while he was still conscious. Something huge and painful and angry is flipping over way deep down inside of him and coming to reluctant life and John doesn't like the feeling, he doesn't like it at all.

"You know what, John? Just leave me alone. I don't want to talk to you anymore, John-eee."

John moves forward to touch Art's arm and Art watches, lets a finger brush his shoulder, hesitates, then jumps back, a guy who's been poked with an industrial cattle prod at full strength.

"He hit me. Everybody saw it. He hit me."

"Art, nobody here hit you. Nobody here wants to hurt you. You're fine." Al speaking calmly and softly.

"Stay away. Stay away, all of you. Don't touch me. Leave me alone. Don't hurt me."

"Just go Art. There's nothing here for you. You've done all you came to do." Al again, a simple voice, a plain voice, a tolling of a large and heavy and irritated bell. "Go ahead, Art, just go."

"Artie, for God's sake what's going on?" Someone is amputating half of John's body but forgot to start the anesthesia. Once again, he's being dropped newborn on another planet and is having to learn how to walk and talk all over again. Not again. Not again.

"Don't hit me, John. Stay away." Art continues walking backwards. "Stay away." He keeps an eye on Al and Adam and John and backs down the two steps to the street. He stops at the sidewalk and relaxes. He smoothes out his pants, shakes out his sleeves and tussles his hair. He swings a dazzling smile in their collective direction and turns, disappearing behind the hedges. They hear him whistling some theme from a Saturday morning cartoon as he strolls leisurely towards the corner. Then all they hear is cars and traffic and the stereos and the sound of the game from the dining room. Some part of John's brain realizes the Seventh Inning stretch must now be over.

Adam says "What was all that about?" Al says (at the same time) "Like pigs rolling around in their own shit." Deb is saying "I say we go after 'em. We got bikes." Two of the other girls, faces white as sheets, are watching Al break a paintbrush she has in her hands into little pieces.

Al looks into Deb's eyes in an angry, then a pleading way and Deb glares back, then shrugs, grimaces and says "Shows over, everyone. Back to work. There's trim to paint and beer warming up and the good lights not going to last forever. That means you, Tammy and Sue, back inside." Deb hustles the girls in front of her up the steps. Al puts her hand on one of John's shoulders. Adam stands and places a hand on the other.

"But... but... I, Art, we, He's never... I mean... Why?"

"Hey Johnny, you just got your nose rubbed in the real thing." Al talks out of the side of her mouth, still watching the sidewalk, making sure no one is engineering a sneak attack. "It sounds like a corny 40's musical, but it's true. Love. It's great when it's great, but it's a bitch when it isn't. And I wish I could say it gets easier. I sure do. But it's just fucking hard sometimes. No other way to say it. Fucking hard." Al grips his shoulder a little tighter. John begins to worry about bruised bones. Adam squeezes his other arm, holds it a second, then let's go. Al lets go. Turns to go back inside. Stops and talks over her shoulder.

"You know, kiddo. Being able to love wide-open, well, it's a gift. You've got the gift. But you're also wide-open to the pain. Lots of people would give anything to have, to be, that kind of wide-open - the joy and the pain. Lots of people." Al steps forward and she's back inside.

"I just…"

"Yeah, I know. I know, man. C'mon let's get inside and finish up." Adam pulls John around, but John hangs back.

"In a sec…" and Adam heads in as John sits down on the porch step.

John's there for more minutes than he really intended to be. Finally he hears a small voice, over the ongoing hubbub of the end of the painting party.

"Jojo?"

"Jojo?" an almost noiseless noise piercing the engine and tire sounds surrounding John – it comes from out of the living room.

"Jojo, you all right? Jojo?"

"I'm fine ma, really. I'm O.K."

3. FALL

His head tries to unscrew itself from his neck, going round and round in delicious circles, a light bulb unfastening itself from its boring, stay-at-home, stuck-in-the-mud socket. Arms wrap around his neck. Two fingers pull and nibble at his left nipple, which feels exposed and unreasonably cold, but pleasantly engaged. John feels good. Very good. In fact, he's feeling excellent.

Streetlights blink and sputter above him, jets of fog downdraft on top of him, pavement glows wetly and blackly at his feet, a horizon of shadowy buildings and avenues tilt and bend randomly whenever he looks up. He briefly remembers he no longer has a shirt on, finds it tucked into his belt, and promptly forgets. He wonders why he's so freezing.

"A few more feet, man. You can do it."

John smiles at the friendly but unfamiliar voice at his right, and leans his head sideways against a warm and bare shoulder and a comforting bare chest. He snickers to himself and hears someone else chuckling. His head starts bouncing up and down on one spasming pec. For a few moments both of them are standing in the middle of the street, listing and laughing, tripping and leaning, vertical only by virtue of the other's support.

"Hey."

John can't stop laughing up and out of his nose. He snorts, he's shooting torpedoes, gasps explosions with his beery breath, balances his rolling heels on pebbly, slippery asphalt. He needs a Kleenex or something.

"Hey."

"Dude."

"Can't stop here, man. Gotta keep it moving."

John feels in his pockets with his free right hand, finds a piece of paper with airline information logos all over it, drops it, watches wide-eyed as it disappears from sight somewhere below his knees. His left hand is too busy to catch it - it's running over someone's red, buzz-cut hair, a warm velour pillow of head flowing pleasantly under his palm, back and forth, left and right. He could do this all night.

"Dude." The other voice breathes heavily and chortles somewhere to John's side.

"Dude. Gotta go." More breathing. More chortling.

"Move it, move it, move it. Get along little doggies."

"Rawhide" says John and both collapse against each other again, diaphragms aching from overuse, gasping for breath between guffaws. John waves around a pathetically torn piece of white tissue paper in one hand - but has no idea why. They start laughing again. Then, deep, sonorous rumbling, growing closer and louder, throbbing, pumping noises, hissing and squishing of rubber on water, and a piercing, keening musical tone of metal scraping across metal, whine of complaining brakes, and smell of diesel and rubber and heat and electricity over the sleepy smell of moisture and fog. John looks up blinking and fighting for breath.

A floating island of light, a long city bus, is stationary not five feet away, blanketing them in a blinding blue-white glare from its headlights. Enormous, wounded honking sounds prod at them from the bus. John feels a hand and an arm guiding him curbwards.

"Whoopsey" is all John can think to say, which starts him snorting and giggling again, mostly from nervousness, looking in his hand for the Kleenex he remembers seeing there, but finding his hand empty again. His hands are cold, wet, and glow obscenely. He waves his fingers in front of his face, again and again, quicker and quicker, until his hand morphs into a tangerine blur. This is his hand. But not a hand related to his ma or pa. Who is he? For real. What is he doing here? And who is this guy? This is not right. None of this is right.

He feels tears beading up in the corners of his eyes and his sinuses expand, stuffed up and uncomfortable. He snuffs his nose raucously and desperately. He doesn't want to go forward. He doesn't want to go backward. He doesn't know what he wants. He stumbles along, limply pushing himself through air thick as fruit-filled jello, through the pink-orange haze of cones of streetlight, kissed by sheets of fog, slapped by weak, spitting rain.

John sidesteps around an enormous man in a bright yellow raincoat the size of a circus tent, calmly tugging two pint-sized versions of the same raincoat around a large puddle and across the drizzly sidewalk in front of them. It's a low-flying dirigible. What in the fuck are all three raincoats, the monster-beach-ball, the child-beach-balls and everything – what the fuck are they doing out at midnight, South of Market, in the rain - well, it remains way, way beyond John's ability to reason at the moment. He can't even begin to figure it out. He blinks to get dripping water out of his eyes and when he looks around again they have disappeared from sight.

"Almost there."

"One more step, upsy-daisy big guy."

"And through the door."

Suddenly everything is strangely dry. John takes a big breath and looks around at a narrow hallway, a staircase, and a closed door. There are men everywhere – standing, sitting, drying off their hair, re-arranging their clothes, but no one is talking. It smells of wet newspapers in here. That and maybe beer. And something else John can't quite figure out.

It's as if he's stumbled into some midnight fundamentalist church that believes in sanctified foyers and dignified silences. John pries his head from the pec/shoulder he's glued it to, and examines the voice next to him. A rangy, red-headed guy with big shoulders, two dimples, and deeply violet eyes. At least they look violet to John. John doesn't look at eyes all that much, but he has to say, as eyes go, these two are keepers. Stunning. Deep. Mysterious.

Deep. Mysterious. Stunning.

He trips on his own feet as he leans backwards to get an even better vantage point to stare all the more effectively at the aforementioned pair of eyes. Does a little dance step to prevent his imminent upturning and unfortunate crash-ass-landing. Propels himself wildly right and forward to land squarely on Mr. Red's lips. Ka-chunk. A soft, but solid contact, unfortunately with the top of his head and not his mouth. He probably couldn't have hit his mouth on the red-head's mouth if he'd carefully planned it out using AutoCad and a Physics template .

Although, John would try. He'd definitely try. Nice mouth. Nice lips. Nice eyes. John, at present, however, has none of the necessary coordination to properly appreciate and give them the attention which is their due. John decides to rest. Rest there for a second, top of head pressed against nice mouth. Just a second, or two. It feels comfortable. No one's complaining. At least not yet. John feels a smile forming on the outside of his forehead.

"You can't remember my name, can you?"

The closed door opens, and a long hallway appears with a desk, a friendly yellow light and a man hunched over and writing at the end of said desk. And amazingly, John sees yet another small gathering of men, all in a line. It's reminds John of a Victorian woodcut of a dark, Dickensian office, a tall, narrow authoritarian desk, a line of clerks in front of it waiting anxiously to get paid their miserable Victorian pittances at the end of their harshly long Victorian work days. It's beautiful, somehow. It is. In a twisted kind of way, a way that appeals to John tonight. He wants to explain it to Red, but can't remember all the words.

Two men disappear within what John is now thinking of as the *Inner Sanctum* and the door closes on the welcoming light leaving the small, soggy crowd once again expectant and shifting and silent in their humid outer darkness.

"Patrick, or Pat'll do in a pinch." John feels an arm across his shoulder again drawing him close.

"Say that three times very fast." The smile on his forehead grows broader.

Eventually, they both make it through the door, up the line, Patrick transacts some mysterious business with the Power Behind The Desk which involves money and signing papers and getting a small rectangle of cardboard in return with a happy, but dripping depiction of male genitalia as its centrally placed logo, and the Inner Inner Door opens and John sees yet another line. Of patient, silent men.

John realizes, nodding and frowning to himself, with what he thinks is admirable reasonableness, that he is trapped in a series of rooms with men and lines and that's how he's going to spend his night, sobering up, lining up, muddling forward and thoroughly drying out until the sun rises and its Sunday morning in San Francisco, and he needs to start thinking about Monday morning and work and the rest of his rapidly imploding life. That is… If it wasn't Sunday already. Was it? Patrick pulls straggling, puzzled John along behind him. John allows himself to be pulled.

It turns out, they're getting undressed and leaving their clothes in a bag at the clothes check line, and John finds himself wandering into the darkness, his hand in Patrick's hand, socks, shoes, and tidy whities on and nothing else. He ogles left and right. His mind boggles. Neurons fire, but no references for what he sees bubbles up to the surface. Music pulses towards him, through him, and out of him in waves - loud, insistent, full of the sounds of justified hopes, expectations fulfilled and promises kept. The air is warm, fetid even, and it smells like a gym in a whorehouse built in an industrial greenhouse.

John doesn't want to be here. John never wants to leave. Images flash in his head - John wading into a sprawling, murky aquarium housing hundreds of naked, swimming men – they paddle forward and back, propelled hither and yon by unseen pressure-compression waves issuing out of a dim dusty water flowing all around them – he sees them move in languid circles, shoals of sardines, grouping for protection. But protection against what?

Suspicious now, John peers into dark plywood corners, searches high lightless, wood-beamed ceilings, examines cracked, painted cement which serves as the floor. He's ready to leave. This place is a maze, a labyrinth, as unreadable as John's life is right now. The last thing John needs is more chaos.

Patrick's hand grips tighter and Patrick leads him through corners and intersections, through a big two story room with pathways and catwalks, through a small room with day-glo graffiti and cartoons of naked men, outside into a chilly wilderness of benches and walls and tents, in through another door and on to an oddly-shaped room with four doors opening out of it. Patrick opts for the left one, which is a long hallway of swinging, saloon-style doors with various holes cut out of them at waist-level, chooses an open one on the end, slips inside and pulls John in carefully beside him. Patrick closes and locks the door.

An hour later, John pads out, Patrick says you can get water at the clothes check, so John's heading to get his clothes, get some money, get some water, hand back his clothes, and get back to Patrick. John promptly gets himself lost and ends up at one point crunching his way through a room with a T.V., a DVD playing with a lot of moaning going on, and a couple of over-sized barrels of unshelled peanuts. He wanders off, and must have walked in a circle, because he comes right back to it, from another angle. Same nuts. Same moans. John hears a voice rise from over by one of the barrels, coming from the other side of a dangerously high pile of peanuts, and it reminds him of something so he stops.

"Thanks, yeah I get that a lot. You ever hear of Life imitates Art? Well, that's me. Nah, I just got here. Yeah, I've been here before. A few times. Well, you know. Let's just say I know my way around."

John bumps the barrel and sets off an avalanche of overflowing nutty objects which tumble over the side and spill in mighty rivers onto the men and onto the floor by John's feet. His blood congeals and his lungs stop working. The back of a familiar head, the shape of a familiar set of shoulders. He closes his eyes and waits, but Art doesn't turn around. In fact, nobody turns around. Nobody even notices.

"This is my fourth Saturday night. It just gets better and better. I'm real popular. And I don't go home alone. Do you think so? Well, yeah, well, you're cute too. I've got some walking around to do. Nah, I'm not ready to go. No, not yet. Look for me. Later. Before I get dressed."

The hair cut straight on the sides. The slim arms. John sees Art's cute butt outlined in shadow in the flickering light of the T.V. and realizes Art is totally nude. Not even wearing his square-toed shiny black club shoes. He's wearing flip-flops. No Lycra. No nothing. Just like God made him. John has never seen him nude in full light before. He'd always undressed and turned out the light before he let John get into bed with him.

John's more than a little buzzed, so he stares for longer than he should have. John hasn't seen Art, or heard from Art at all in the last four months, ever since Art walked out on him at his ma's painting party. Art hadn't even come to his ma's funeral, even though John sent him an email link to the Funeral Parlor. No, he's not going to do this. He doesn't have to. Not this time. He's not. His stomach starts doing flip-flops. He's going to be sick. He tiptoes backwards, pushing his way cautiously through little hills and larger mountain ranges of peanuts. Inch by inch, feeling his bleary way towards the door he just came in, feeling the floor through the soles of his tennis shoes, eyes all the while on Art's gorgeous back.

Someone starts laughing and walking and John gets jostled, and pushed and finds himself leaning towards Art. With horror he feels himself touching Art's bare shoulder. John's heart stops. Art turns around, a dazzling 1000 megawatt smile on full power – and the smile freezes into place in blank-eyed surprise in mere milliseconds.

Suddenly it's very cold around John. Not just a chilly cold, not just an obnoxious, un-warm, inconvenient drafty kind of cold, but a mercilessly pulverizing blast of malevolent absolute cold - a purity of cold you'd get in interstellar space, out in the holes and empty places between galaxies, where only severely lost and very dispirited photons plow their long and endlessly lonely way across billions of light-years of agonizing nothingness. John feels it. It is that kind of cold.

People talking nearby stop talking. They begin to move away from John. John knows how the surprised and disappointed wooly mammoths, frozen in place by some sudden, natural disaster in the icy wastes of Siberia – well, he knows exactly how they must have felt in the few seconds they had left of their lives before being flash-frozen by the universe while innocently grazing on the Russian steppes.

"You. You again. You always."

"Art, I.."

"Quit following me! When will you stop? Why can't you let me alone?"

"Art, really, I didn't mean…"

"No, get away. Get away from me. This is stalking. That's what it is, stalking. You're a stalker. You know what? You know what I'm going to do? Right now? I'm going to take control of my life. I'm going to report you to the manager. I'm going to walk up to the manager and I'm going to tell him all about you, and how you're a stalker. That's what I'm going to do. You just watch me. You stalker. Stalker!"

Art strides dramatically towards the opposite end of the peanut room, threading his way through the detritus of half-chewed peanuts and empty shells littering the floor in all directions, scuffing his sandals into the dim darkness of man-shapes congregating about John. A big guy, with a long curling blue flame tattoo, tongues of blue fire licking his chest hairs and splaying across his right arm stands and stares meditatively at John – he was Art's companion by the peanut barrel. Mr. Blue Flame looks inclined to want to hit John. Or maybe John is paranoid and dazed and too fucking drunk to know *what* people around him want to do. Maybe. But how could John tell? How?

With those thoughts in mind, John stands and watches the people around him. And everyone else stands and watches John back. It seems to last for hours. The only sound is a heroic wrestling session of grunts and groans coming from the T.V., so John dashes out and retreats quickly back to the safety of the clothes check counter. There, coincidentally enough, he re-clothes. And he does it, with what he thinks is an amazing degree of efficiency considering his befuddled and horny and panicked state. He looks over his shoulder every two seconds, and turns around often and at random intervals so no one will even think about sneaking up on him unawares in the sweaty gloom of the changing area.

He fully expects at any moment for an official someone to clamp their strong official hand on his stalker arm and arrest him and carry him off to County Jail for attempted assault and battery before witnesses. He's sure of it. He can feel their hand on his bicep. It's going to happen. After a long, long fifteen minutes, once he's painfully and finally dressed in his soggy clothes again, he allows himself to inhale and exhale normally a couple of times and he makes a break for it, aiming his body at the first of the many doors he needs to exit to get out of this place and remembers Patrick. Shit. Patrick. Shit. Shit. Shit.

Ten minutes of searching, fully clothed among an army of naked men, and another twenty minutes of Patrick-explaining, and another thirty minutes of mind-blowing contortions in the small space and John convinces Patrick - no, John's all right, no need to leave with John, Patrick ought to stay there.

Then John wanders haphazardly about, and finds himself eventually outside again, in front of the club, with the familiar sensation of water running down his scalp, water flowing between the flattened, mushed, gelled spikes on the top of his bare head, water cascading down his back and over his pecs and down each of his water-logged arms.

However, he concentrates on, and succeeds at keeping his right hand balled in a tight fist – he's intent on keeping his right palm safe and dry for as long as he can manage it. Patrick's number is folded in his right hand, written on the back of a grocery store receipt Patrick has just given him.

There's a row of gleaming cabs of various colors lined up in the rain in front of the club, appearing as if by magic. Across the street John thinks he sees a trio of yellow raincoats huddling happily under an awning in the soggy shadows, but he has important things he has to do, it's three in the morning, and he decides following raincoats is not one of them, at least not tonight.

He has to find someplace dry on his body to transport Patrick's number safely home, since he'd forgotten his cell back in his bedroom at home at his pa's house. So… Pockets, no. Under his belt, no. He can feel the paper in his hand smearing into greater and greater illegibility with every passing second. He pats and prods his body looking for an un-damp fold or pocket, and watches to make sure he's not losing his place in line to get the next cab. It turns out, after exhaustive effort, all of his clothes are still too moist to put anything in.

He stuffs it in under his shirt. Now he needs to see if he has enough money in his wallet to get him back to the Sunset and his parent's house. Then once there, he has to sneak in without waking his pa. Then he has to work on getting to bed and looking forward to a Texas-sized hangover when the sun comes up. So much to do. So few working brain cells to do it with. Wait, does he even have his wallet?

The yellow blurs, which if anyone were looking would look something like raincoats, stand patiently across the street and watch. They stand and wait until John is safely wrapped in a wetly twinkling Blue and White cab and tunneling homewards through sheets of spritzing rain. They watch as John's cab splashes and skids, accelerates down the one-way street, slows at the end of the block, makes a tight right turn and drops out of sight as it swings around the corner.

And, if anyone were still looking, they'd see the blurs hanging around a few moments longer, then they'd see them drifting off in the opposite direction, and then they'd see them melting serenely into the pitter-patter of rain slapping the early morning San Francisco streets and sidewalks. Eventually they wouldn't see them at all, anywhere. The blurs would be gone, just like John. There'd be nothing left to see. That is, if anyone had seen them at all in the first place.

4. WINTER

John is an orphan. John is unemployed. John is a criminal. John is a pilgrim. John is free.

John places two feet squarely behind the safety markings, squints at the grimy nickel-colored tracks on the Bart line stretching away into the tunnel, slouches his weight onto the edge of the knobby, yellow rubber matting, lets his knees go limp, slips his hands into his coat pockets, pins the suitcase weakly between his legs, waits, and stares distractedly at the toes of his feet. And he waits. He looks and squints and peers more closely at his toes and spies a hole starting in the tip of his right sneaker. Shit. He waits. That's the only pair of shoes he's packed. He waits. Where's the train? Only a strong effort of will stops him from looking at the clock every ten seconds.

Bells chiming, an echoing voice, a train on the other side of the platform flies in, brakes, opens doors, chimes, closes doors, flies out.

A heavily uniformed Transit cop strolls purposefully towards him and John winces, straightens up. Art managed to get a restraining order against John, despite the fact that Art is literally the last person on Earth John would want to spend any time with, be near to, let alone even think about. Art is an open wound on John that still hasn't started to heal. None of which stops Art from mentioning his legal problems with John to anyone who will listen. As John has found out the hard way. The cop walks towards John, slows, then saunters by, heads for a locked door in a tiled wall in back of John and disappears inside, letting the door slam shut behind him.

John re-slouches. He's obviously misread the schedule. Or can't tell time. Or just doesn't give a shit. You know, much longer, and he'll miss his international flight. Chiming and another train pours itself into the station behind him. Wrong track. Again. Story of his life. It accelerates with the startling silence of electricity and burrows off with its cargo of satisfied Bart-travelers. He's alone again. Mostly. Just two people texting at the other end of the station. Sundays must be slow.

The cheery and businesslike red digits above him continue to count out the minutes and seconds he's so very late. His trip is getting less and less likely. Really, he should walk the hundred feet to the posted schedule by the escalators at the far side of the platform. He should. He should walk and check and walk back again. But he doesn't.

He scuffs and kicks his soft-sided, lumpy suitcase, and stops, because it's his Pa's and not his property and he shouldn't be messing with it. He pulls it in protectively, squinched between his calves, and holds onto it, a boat pulling on a sea-anchor in a storm. He feels unstuck and unhindered. Freewheeling and fetter-free. All of which ought to be liberating and exciting, but which is actually turning out to be just terrifying and boring. One long slide into the unknown. One long set of intermittent panic attacks.

He wishes he had a job to go to. He wishes he had only one family. He wishes he could have his ma boss him around one more time. After she passed away, after the 60 day probation and getting fired, after the steady stream of temp jobs drying up, after sitting in his Pa's living room watching daytime T.V. for 4 months trying to ignore the big open space in front of him where his ma's hospital bed used to be, after all that, his pa had drifted up out of his own private hell to offer him a choice.

A choice. His pa had proposed it hesitantly 3 months before - dropping Taiwanese travel brochures and airline itineraries about the house, hinting at the weather this time of year in the Eastern Pacific, asking John to look up exchange rates for Taiwanese Dollars, starting conversations about Betel nuts and mobile phones.

But this time, no suggesting. He was his father. He was commanding. John had been ordered to report to Taipei. A bunch of people he'd never met or heard of, the Luo clan, were gathering and planning and creating expectations in their minds right now, right this minute. The Luos were thinking about John, even as he stood here, missing his plane connections, waiting in a nearly empty Bart station. They wanted to meet him. It was done. Did he want a whole new family? He didn't know. But he was going to get one. So here he was.

He's bent, weary and spent. His hand jams through a set of papers in his pocket which he knows is a plum-blossomed adorned airline itinerary with a big sharp staple jabbing him in the back of his wrist, just to remind him of what this trip is costing his Pa. His palm curls around his cell (which now operates in Taiwan also), and his passport rides uneasily in his pocket in back of the cell. Passport. He better have his passport. He checks again, for the third time in the last hour, pulling it gingerly out of the new leather folder his pa gave him to protect it, opening up its crisp, new pages, scrutinizing the photo. There it is, just like before. Is that really what he looks like? When did he get that calm, steady, unflummoxed expression in his eyes?

The cell starts vibrating against his thigh, for the umpteenth time this morning. He knows it's Patrick. He'll call him back in the airport. Or maybe it'd be good if he calls him after he gets to Taipei. Or maybe, just maybe, it would be better to call him when he gets all the way back home again, back in San Francisco. Patrick is way, way too patient with John. Way too patient the last couple of months since that first rainy night. And John knows it. He tries to ignore the buzzing and bites his lip, trying to picture himself landing in Taiwan. A Luo. John Alexander Luo Chin? He just can't see it.

He looks at the stairs longingly. He can't meet his birth family, He can't, no matter how much his Pa wants him too now, even if his Pa loses the price of the ticket he's just bought for him. He'd turn back if he knew how. But he doesn't. He doesn't know how to turn back now. So John goes on. He's stubborn like that, just like his ma. And reasonable and patient, like his pa. Maybe that's the secret, just keeping on, going forward, doing a little bit more each day. Keep pushing. Do a little steering. Enjoy the ride. What the fuck? It's a plan.

The pieces of John's life, one by one, have been split apart from each other, broken loose, mixed together, carried aloft, and now they flap and spin and twirl in the wind, speeding violently towards some end John can no longer even hope to see. If he'd wanted freedom, and yes, he had wanted it, asked for it, demanded it - someone had obviously heard him. He is free. Hooray for John! Hip! Hip! Hooray! Free! And he is lucky. And, most importantly, he is still standing.

He feels a breeze. Which, of course, is impossible one hundred feet underground, so it must be a train, some kind of train, approaching. He steps back a bit, looks for the black rubber matting (he should have already done this before) across the football field of white-veined marble squares, to see where the black is that marks where the doors will open and a train coasts past John at some ungodly speed.

Every window of this brightly-lit express train holds an identical fat man in a hundred different poses with a thousand different expressions and every one of them is friendly and every hand is rubbing an almost perfectly spherical belly and bouncing an irregular sack of lucky beads and goodies and other eccentric whatnots, and ten thousand eyes pin his eyes down with an expectant expression of amused surprise and calm determination. He sees a hundred thousand laughing children bouncing on seats and round stomachs and crawling over shoulders and pulling on ears. Many are the eyebrows wiggling up and down. Many the double chins nodding. Many the hands being pulled on by masses of joyous kids, pointing outwards and upwards and onwards, pointing the way into John's bright future.

And then with a million shrugs and winks, a quick zip and a mini-underground cyclone of ventilated air, the train, the light, the children, and the men are gone, and the tunnel is empty. Only seconds later, John's airport train pulls into the station, and John steps aboard.

Somehow John is unsurprised. It takes a lot to surprise him these days. He is, after all, one of the lucky ones. His own mom told him so.

PARTY LINE

It slices cleanly and easily into his palm. It feels deep. His right hand feels cold at first, then there's a sharp stinging, then a burning.

"Shit." He breathes the word out into air perfumed with decaying waste. He tries not to breathe in. Fails. "Shit."

He doesn't reach deeper into the trash can, but he doesn't pull his hand out either. He stops. His breath comes in shallow spurts, his hand throbs, he tries to be still, he doesn't stick his other hand in. His stomach starts to turn over. He vomits on his arm. That makes him jerk his hand all around the can. He tries to pull it out. More stinging, more burning. What in the fuck is he going to do? What?

"Fuck me. Fuck me." His face burns. He can feel his pulse beating in his palm. Throbbing wetness down there. He can still wriggle his fingers. But the hand hurts like hell.

He can feel the wallet now, his fingers are touching it, it's caught between his pinky and another finger, but it's slippery, and not just with grease. The wallet's slick, with something warm and thick and he can feel a piece of himself, a piece of his skin flapping open on his hand down there, deep down, buried in layers of rotten vegetables, coffee grounds, empty cans, other unnamable, nasty-looking filth and crusted-over, stained towels.

And those aren't twenty dollar bills he saw under the orange rinds, those were cabbage leaves he was groping for in the dark middle of the trash can and he thinks he's going to be sick again, and he does, and he's starting to get really, really dizzy, and then his eyes tear up. He takes a deep breath and holds it. He pulls his hand out slowly, feeling his fingers brush against something sharp-edged and pointy, cutting it some more, and he gets scared and lets the wallet go, and jerks his hand up and out of garbage and gets it free yelling "Fuck. Fuck. Fuck".

Arthur Zhou sinks to his knees and cradles his right hand in his left, and both hands get steadily wetter and stickier and very, very red. It's black, it's so red, and he throws up again, but this time only dry heaves and he pants, shuddering, watches his black pants grow bright with puddles of stains of wetness, and thinks "Fucking idiot. You greedy fuck. You had to try, didn't you?"

He jams his hand under his armpit, and tries to think "What do you do? What do you do? Tie it up, pressure. Tie it up" and "Don't panic. Go slow. Do it right. Slow, and you have to do it right." He jerks his head around. Swivels it up, down, left, right. He's in a fucking alley. Alone. The sun's just set. It's getting darker and darker. He remembers the putrid towels, they look like dish towels, and leans forward and daintily pulls them out with the thumb and forefinger of his (still working) left hand. He keeps his right hand under his armpit. His black shirt, which was already stained is sopping.

The dish towels have pieces of glass in them, tomato sauce, and something black and shiny smeared all over and the towels are dried hard, glued by filth into shapes like crumpled pieces of waste paper and hard as a rock. He almost sobs, staring at them. He lifts his left hand to throw them down the alley as far away from him as possible, hesitates, and instead says "Fuck it" as loud as he can.

"Fuck it." He's talking to the alley now, to the dumpster, to the trash can, the coffee grounds, and especially to the wallet. He starts beating the towels on the side of the trash can, beats them on the side of the dumpster in front of him, beats them, and lets them soak up the iridescent and cloudy, whitish water he's kneeling in.

The water's starting to look pink and then red. He beats them some more. When he can see a mostly white textile showing, he wraps one around his wrist and pulls it really tight with his teeth and ties it off, wraps the second the same way on his right hand, drops it, tries again, drops it, screams out loud, does it again, and finally ties it off and falls back against a brick wall and squints his eyes in the twilight and breathes in and out slowly, frowning and swaying back and forth, moaning obscenities in a quiet voice to himself. His right hand starts to feel numb. At some point he notices the two feet sticking out from underneath the dumpster.

Arthur leans forward, looks beneath the dumpster, sees the blood, not his, sees the sightless eyes turned towards him, sees the arms bent at a wrong angle underneath it as it lies on its chest, and Arthur scuttles crabwise on one arm and two legs back, as quick as he can back, back the whole twenty feet onto the sidewalk again, stopping himself, just barely, just before he launches himself off the curb and into an oncoming cab.

Gasping, swaying on one arm, still bent over backwards, he watches and waits. His head spins. It scares him that he's getting dizzy and he's practically lying down.

The alley is a steep slope opening up in front of him, descending downwards, the sidewalk Arthur slides to a stop on lies at an impossible angle, also steep, steep as a sidewalk would be if it were built straight up the side of an Alp. Except as Arthur knows, this sidewalk is built on a hill in San Francisco. Which for walking or sitting purposes, may just as well be on the side of an Alp, at least to Arthur. It's getting harder and harder to keep his balance.

Two high buildings hang over him in the dying light. People walk around him. Cars labor uphill, cars whine their brakes downhill. A bus comes down towards him, sparking electricity off its overhead cables as it bounces in spurts to the next intersection. He blinks and squeezes his eyes. Gasps and catches his breath. He keeps his hand hidden. He's lost feeling in it. He can't tell if it's bleeding less, or bleeding more. His head is spinning. When he closes his eyes, he expects it to stop, but the spinning just gets worse. Not good, Arthur, not good. He tips over onto the sidewalk. He decides to keep his eyes open, for now.

He's got to get of here. A dead man under a dumpster. Arthur's bloody fingerprints all over what was probably his wallet. Arthur bleeding to death on a public sidewalk during the evening rush hour. He's got to get out of here.

Looking to the left and to the right, avoiding the alley and its contents and the eyes of passersby, he sees a familiar shape in front of him, the neon sign of a Diner, and a short ways off, the half-rusted awning of an even more familiar cheap hotel. And this is not just any hotel. It is The Hotel.

"Thank you. Thank you. God. Universe. Whoever. Thank you."

Arthur scoots against a mailbox, pushes his back against it, and knee-jerks his way to his feet. He has a dirty jacket tied around his waist, he wraps it over his arm and covers at least a little of the blood. He takes a step forward and almost falls over. He closes his eyes and leans back on the mailbox.

"Slow. Do it right. Take it easy. You can do this."

The guy who's letting him crash with him every so often, Frankie, who only brings up the awkward question of sex with Arthur maybe once, tops twice a week, well, that's his hotel not five feet away, a transient hotel, The Hotel Del Mio Cid, but still it's got four walls, a floor, and a roof. The Del Mio's a hell of a lot better than cardboard in a cul-de-sac or a pile of old blankets in a storefront, sex or no sex, and to tell the truth, Frankie's not all that bad a guy. Just a little strange, sometimes. But who isn't a little strange? Arthur's become increasingly non-judgmental of late.

He wonders if Frankie's home as he breathes in, takes a step, breathes out, takes a step, and gradually, dodging home-bound, rapid-walking commuters makes his careful way to the hotel's entrance. Step. Breath. Step. Step. Frankie has to be home. Breath. Step. He has to be.

Since his dad completely cut Arthur off in every way, when Arthur told him he was gay on his 22nd birthday, and since Arthur had gotten sick, and since Arthur had ran out of money – or rather used up all his money - and used up all his friends, and his drugs and his alcohol and his goodwill and his luck – well, since then, Arthur had changed. He'd had to. Since he'd used up everything except his youth, (well, and he was very busy now using up his youth also), Arthur's whole life had turned into a kind of desperate thrashing about, a pathetic last-ditch effort just to keep Arthur himself alive. Alive for what, he couldn't exactly tell you. But for the past year, staying alive had turned out to be his number one priority, and a full-time job.

And now this. If his hand doesn't stop bleeding, well, then it's goodbye Arthur. Somehow, that doesn't seem so terrible. Not now, not to Arthur. And that scares him.

He re-arranges his coat, like he's carrying it draped over his right arm and hand. Then he rushes in, as normally as he can make himself, like any normal working guy wanting to get home and relax, past the front desk clerk, not making eye contact, staring at the elevator, punches the button with his left hand, stands in front of it and waits for the elevator doors to open. He hopes he's not swaying on his feet too much. He can't tell. He holds his breath when he hears the clerk rustling papers in back of him. Then he hears the clerk come out from behind his desk, moving slowly across the torn carpet of the lobby towards the front door. Like he's noticing something. Like something's not right. Arthur's sure of it.

Arthur doesn't turn around. He looks down at his feet. There are drops of blood on his shoes, drops of blood on the carpet. There must be a trail to the front door. There must be. The clerk is coming back, the elevator doors groan uneasily open, Arthur slips inside, punches the tenth floor button with his elbow, doesn't turn around. He can hear the clerk scuffing something with his shoe. The doors close.

Arthur collapses against the graffiti-covered faux wood paneling and closes his eyes. His head goes round and round and round. His hand pounds with pain, it's numb and tingling and wet, and Arthur can smell the fetid dirt on the towels all over it, all over him. He spits, and spits because he can't get the taste of the slimy crud of the towels out of his mouth. He stops spitting when his mouth gets dried out. But he can still taste it. He feels like throwing up, but just gasps and pants instead- a fish out of water, flopping on a boat deck, waiting to be clubbed to death. The elevator crashes and bumps its way upwards, painfully.

The elevator finally sputters to a stop, once, twice, three, now four times, with jerks and whines as it tries to match itself up, unsuccessfully, with the level of the tenth floor. The doors open tentatively and there's a slight step up to get off. Arthur falls forward and out, stumbling down the hallway, escaping before the elevator can break down completely and trap him there between floors like it's done in the past. Like just last week, actually, last Monday at 3 in the morning. That had been fun. Frankie had to pry the doors open for him. Management hadn't done shit. Those emergency phones never worked. Frankie's door is the second to the last on the left, just past the communal bathroom. The hallway's empty. But it's noisy as a bus station.

It smells like damp, moldy carpet. That and old cooking grease, sweat, dust, and blood. How much of that is him, and how much the hallway Arthur has no idea. He stops breathing through his nose. Each closed door of heavy dark wood is a megaphone, what goes on inside each room is public knowledge in the hallway. Arthur bounces down one of the walls as he makes his way towards the bend in the corridor and towards the bathroom and hears T.V.s blaring, music bleating, illegal hot plates boiling, loud, one-sided conversations and arguments. It's like listening in on one of those old telephones that connected a bunch of people's phone numbers all on one phone line. You hear everybody's business.

Arthur is too tired to make it to the bathroom. He thinks he ought to phone Frankie. But he's too tired to look for his cell. Better just to knock. He pounds feebly once or twice and slumps onto a door he's pretty sure he thinks is Frankie's and throws his right arm above his head, resting it on his black, straight hair, holding it in place with his left hand, hoping that that will help it stop seeping blood all over the place and he lets his head fall forward and he closes his eyes and pulls in a deep, deep breath and holds it. Rest, just a little. Rest his eyes for a second. So tired.

No one comes to the door. He tries doing a backhand knock, but it sounds more like a scratch. He holds his breath and then he lets it out in one, long exhausting sigh. The door in front of him and to the right is pretty noisy. He'll wait here. Wait her for Frankie. He breathes slowly and regularly and lets himself concentrate on the voices within. The voices drift over him. He drifts between them.

"And I wish you wouldn't bring your work home with you."

"And pass the sugar please"

"And the salt. And the pepper while you're at it. And yes. I *am* finished. No more. Thank you."

"Careful! - that's the last salt and pepper shaker set I have, you really should start wearing gloves over those bony fingers when we sit down to eat – I know you're tired of hearing it. I'm tired of saying it. But you and I both know you wouldn't be fumbling and floundering about, dropping and breaking things if your grip had any kind of traction at all. You and I both know it. It's no secret to anyone."

"Really? No cream? How surprising. I am staggered, dismayed. Stupefied. Flabbergasted. Yes, yes, yes. For the last time, yes, I'm aware I'm out of cream. Repeating it to me over and over, again and again won't change that fact one iota – my working assumption is the absence of cream in this flat is the reason you asked me yesterday to purchase cream and return home with it. Of course in the note. The note you left on the refrigerator. Written in a particularly livid, dark shade of red ink. I'm assuming it was ink. Yes, I noticed. With an abundance of exclamation points. The hysterical punctuation had no effect, I might add, on my motivation.

No, I don't think you write notes for the exercise. I don't know what you do for exercise. Don't answer that question. I don't want to know. All right, yes, I admit it. I forgot. There I said it. You reminded me, I had plenty of time, I knew about it, I left the apartment, and I forgot. I admit all. *Mea culpa, mea culpa, mea maxima culpa.* I'm only human, after all. And speaking of that, why do you insist on signing all your notes "Death"? I know who you are. We live alone. Who else would be writing me notes, affixing them to my kitchen appliances, encouraging me to a higher level of housekeeping diligence? Hmmm?"

"And the skull and crossbones stationery is a cute touch, a clever one even, I give you that. But who's paying for all these custom notepads? Where's the money coming from? I certainly have no room in my household budget for them. I barely squeak by on the little I get as it is. Any frivolities must end. There is only one corporeal entity I know of in this apartment with access to a bank account. I will say no more. Enough said."

"Come back, come back. I didn't mean it. I appreciate all the things you do. I see you trying, I do. I'm just not one to express gratitude constantly every five minutes. I expect people will see it in my eyes. See the thankfulness, accept it, move on. Without all the excessive talking back and forth. No, I don't expect you to be a mind reader. I said I was wrong. I forgot. I'm sorry. Come back. Sit down. There. Relax. Lean back. You'll feel better."

"How's that? Better? I thought so. Don't sulk. I suppose you *could* tell me all about your day. Tell me about how your work went. For instance, who is this young man of yours? Yes, the one standing by the doorway. What other young man would I be talking about? Oh, you're going to introduce us. Well that's a first. You usually... All right, all right, Introduce us. Go ahead. Tell me about him. I'll listen. Yes, I promise. No really. I want to listen. Really. Go ahead. Let him speak."

"Yes, you are quite good at surprising people, grabbing, and catching them from behind. Although, you've never caught me. Yes, well, maybe the reason you haven't tried is that you know you'd fail. Really? I rather doubt that.

"No, no that's not what I meant. You grab well. You're a great grabber. A grabber's grabber. You are. And I assume the young man is a grabee? Yes? A recent grabee. Yes? How exactly did you make this particular grab today? Tell me. Tell me about it. Give me all the details."

The elevator door opens, but only a quarter of the way. Arthur hears muffled cursing. It's a man's voice, cursing. Arthur weakly slaps his left hand against his own face a couple of times to try and wake up and tenses his muscles. He's ready to lurch and crawl his way down the hallway. Down the hallway and around the corner. But he doesn't have the energy. He doesn't. So, he pulls and stretches the jacket a little more over his head, he pulls his knees a little bit closer in to his chest and he hopes he's looking more and more like a mound of dirty pants and shirts sitting in front of a door. He tries to send out the thoughts of a pile of soiled clothes. His head feels wet and sticky and he thinks it's getting wetter.

He peeks out slightly from under the sleeve of his jacket, thinking he's going to see the front desk clerk's feet rapidly approaching, but all he sees are dust motes rising and falling in the smoky dusky light in the hallway. There's an ancient gray skylight above him. He looks, moves his eyeballs to the left, to the right, but he's still alone. The elevator door is closed again. But for how long? How long till he's caught? He ought to move. He needs to move. Arthur closes his eyes again, and laboriously tucks his hands and arms behind his head, pulls at his jacket and leans back. The voices are still rolling on and on, relentlessly, from behind the door in front of him. Except he hears a new voice. Distant. Younger. And closer to the door. It gets louder. And louder. Then he hears it clearly.

"So…"

"What up bros?"

"The last thing I remember? The very last thing?"

"Yeah. Uh huh. Well, gosh, let's see, what in the *fuck* would that be? That would be your bony hand on my shoulder jerking me backwards so hard you pulled the fucking ball right out of its fucking socket, tossed me on my ass and rolled me down the sidewalk like you was dribbling a basketball down center court to make the winning shot of the homecoming game in the last ten seconds - that's what I fucking remember. That's what my fucking shoulder remembers. That would probably be fucking it."

"Oh. The next to the last thing."

"So, you want to hear the whole shebang? O.K. All right. All right. All right, already. Goddam it, yeah, yeah, I can speak-a-de-english. I got ears."

"Guys, I know how to tell a story. People *like* my stories. Some people even *love* my stories."

"Well, sometimes it isn't short. To do it right, you have to take a little time with it. All right, all right! Maybe not this time. You don't have to yell. I'll make it short. Just put the stick with the curvy knife down, boss. Short. You got it, chief. Short. Short and sweet."

"So…"

"I was outside – but you know that cuz you was there - the day was cool, not too hot, not too cold. Nice. Typical winter weather. 'Course you always have to wear a sweater or something. I had my yellow and red hoody on. Great warm-up jacket, got it for next to nothing at the Goodwill, good as new, except the zipper don't always work the first time, but still, like new, a perfect weight for walking, not so great for running, if you can ever find a flat place for a decent run – but like I was saying, the hoody was a good decision even though it was a little too warm out for the jacket right at that moment, but I knew, I could feel it, the fog was rolling in, it was going to get a lot cooler later, or, who knows? sometimes it don't get colder on a foggy night, it gets warmer, and I figured, hey! with the old reliable yellow and red I'm covered every which ways - warm and cold, fog or no fog. Like I said, what a jacket! Except for that damn zipper. The clerk tried to warn me, but... What? What?"

"What the fuck! Hey. Big guy. Whatcha waving that thing around in my face for? Fuck it. Put that down. Yeah. O.K. Short. Short. I can do short. Just put it away. O.K. Good. Everyone nice and calm? Settled down? So I can tell you The Last Thing I Remember? Fine. Okey-dokey. Then buckle up boys cuz here we go. Yeah. Now. I know. Short. I got it. Short. Can I talk now?"

"So. Where was I? Because I can speak Spanish - look, put it down or you're never going to hear this, do you want to hear this? All right, then – I can speak Spanish - I told you my ma was from Sonora, right? Which is a state in Mexico if you didn't already know that, some people don't, they think it's in Italy or some shit, but it's not – anyways, because I can understand Mexicans when they're talking, I can also pretty much understand them when they're whispering in the shadows in back of a dumpster. Especially when they're whispering really loud. And they're scared. And they're pissed."

"He doesn't look dead."

"Yet, there he is."

"Yes. There he is."

"So."

"So."

"So."

"So - do it, motherfucker."

"You do it. You want to do it so much." "Look, fucking touch his chest, move your fucking fingers under his nose. I don't know. Do I look to you like I'm a fucking doctor? Fucking feel his wrist. Do it. Yeah. Make sure. Now, find the shit, quick and let's go. Good. Turn him over. Look in his fuckin' pants. Look. In. His. Fucking. Pants. Do it, motherfucker, do it. Not the wallet. Throw the wallet away. Not in the street, in the garbage, idiot. You find the shit man? The shit. Look again. Look around his belt, motherfucker. Do

I have to do everything?"

"You get the picture. So this alley opens up between two 10-story fire traps leaning against each other on the side of a hill. But everything, streets, buildings, people - where I live in San Francisco - everything is on the side of a hill. So I really haven't told you much that would qualify as information. Not really. Not yet. But anyways, as I was saying, it's on the side of a hill and the smell of this alley, this fucking alley, let me tell you, the smell of it by the front doors of the transient hotel - which is where I happen to live, it's cheap, what can I say? I'm a lazy fucker, too lazy to move – but by the front doors of my hotel, the smell of it, the mind-blowing, monster stench of it, well, it's just fucking incredible. You have to believe me. One of those, whaddyacallit, E.P.A., Hazardous Waste Superfund sites. I tell you true. No shit. It would knock over professional football players, gold-medal Olympic marathon runners, fucking Navy Seals, knock them out cold with a single toxic puff from out of that cancer sore of an alley. No lie. And the manager won't do anything about it. Won't lift a finger. Nothing. I know, I've tried. Fucking incredible."

"So, I walk past it every morning and the smell of it overflows like a backed up toilet onto the front sidewalk and it leaves your skin feeling impregnated - is that the word I want? – it gets aggressive and sinks into your skin, pushes this oily, clammy shit right through it and into your body – damp, thick clouds of sticky smell – it's not pleasant, I can tell you - at night, during the day, even now, with the sun up for hours. It's bad. It gets into your clothes, your hair, you smell it on your hands. Bad. And there's all kinds of shit back there. People's bags, cans, boxes, or just plain piles of garbage dumped, rotting for days, junk injecting mutant chemicals and foreign odors and who-knows-what-the-shit-else into the city air. City air that I pay good rent for. Incredible."

"But anyways, I'm standing there. My shoes are getting slimed by a trickle of greasy water. I look around and it's coming from that Greek diner on the corner of our building – I love Greek shit, those little pockets made out of bread, that crazy meat on a pole – anywho, the water, it looks like it's pouring out of a broken dishwasher or some shit like that, at least there's pieces of food and shit floating in it, not like you'd be able to smell the water, not next to that shit-hole of an alley, but anyways, the water is running over my feet – and, I might add, soaking up into one of my socks through the hole in the bottom of my right running shoe – they're Adidas, cost a fortune when I got 'em new, but worth it, definitely worth it – so, it's flowing around me and down the red brick gutters down the center of the alley and is getting soaked up in the warm-up suit of the guy laying face-down, whose feet are sticking out from behind the dumpster, he's got on a yellow and red sweatshirt like me. He even has a hole in his right shoe, an Adida, just like me. Weird, right?"

So, the water's flowing fast. My sock is sopping. Geez, this alley has to be a hundred years old, I say to myself. It's falling apart. The brick's are all wavy and broken. The drainage is horrible. And it's steep. Like a staircase. No wonder no one ever comes and empties the dumpster.

"So. I decide I can't wait all day, I think to myself, Jake, you have to cross this alley sometime. Whaddya gonna do? About this alley situation here. Hoof it an extra three blocks to avoid any problems? Yeah, I know Mac doesn't want any complications, but to hell with that. He's not carrying this shit in broad daylight, up and over the fuckin' Himalayas. Nah, Mac's safe back in our flat, safe behind seven deadbolts, and hanging fifty feet above me on the fifth floor of the building I'm leaning my shoulder against. Mac's not hiding behind a corner by the alley. Mac's not gagging on the fumes. I'm the one, me, Jake, who's out on the street walking and overhearing murderers hissing at each other in stage whispers."

"And let me tell you, no one walks around in San Francisco. No one that's not crazy that is. But I do. Why? Cuz I'm crazy. Well, that's true, ha ha, but nah, it's cuz I'm broke. No money. Mac says I make poor life choices. Well, Mac's up there and I'm down here. What does that tell you?"

"And don't even get me started on the buses. They print those schedules, but the only thing they're good for is emergency toilet paper. Well, like Mac's friend J.B. says – I like J.B., he listens to me, unlike other people I know who only like to listen to their own voice talking, not mentioning any names, but their first name starts with Mac, but like J.B. says, if you gots to get yourself someplace, and it gots to be on time, and it gots to be one hundred percent, and, well you know what I'm talking about, no room for failure, a kind of do or die situation, well, if you find yourself in that position, and I do, a lot, if you find yourself in that position you leave two hours early. And you walk. And you avoid complications.

So I'm walking today. And avoiding. Except right now. Right now, I'm doing more standing and leaning than walking. But you get the picture."

"So, I hear these guys in the alley. And I still got five blocks to go to hike to the very tip-top of Cathedral Hill, and I think – Christ on a stick, you'd think they could find a better place to make a drop than the fucking top of a fucking hill, but you know, as the saying goes, I only work here. So, I'm in the middle of the Tenderloin, well, the Upper Tenderloin, there's a million people everywhere and it *is* noon, right? Middle of the day. Innocent, decent people out getting lunch. Me, making a delivery, maybe not so innocent, not so decent. Still. So how dangerous could it be? So how crazy could it get? For the anonymous by-walker/illicit deliveryman? But I'm stupid that way."

"Then the grabbing. And the sore shoulder. Then you know the rest. If you want to tell me what the fuck's going on, I'd be all ears, guys, I can tell you. All ears."

Arthur can't tell if he's asleep or awake. He thinks he's heard the elevator open and close a couple of times, but he hasn't tried to look up. It wouldn't matter if he did. He's not going anywhere. His hand doesn't hurt as much now. But he really can't even feel it all that much. He falls over noisily onto the frayed carpet runner with a wet plop and enjoys the feel of the old hardwood floors and the carpet nails poking up against his cheek and into his forehead. It feels so good to be horizontal.

"Yes, all very interesting, I'm sure. Quite the day's work. Fascinating. Riveting."

"No, I'm not being sarcastic. And yes, I did hear something falling over in the hall. Why do you ask? All kinds of things make noises out there, day and night. *You* have been known to make noises out there day and night. What of it?"

"More work to do? Now? Here? Well, if you must."

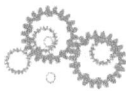

Arthur can hear the sounds of doors opening and closing. Maybe's it's the elevator again. Maybe not. Who cares? But Arthur can also see the battered and scratched door to 1052 opening slowly in front of him. It's really dark now in the hall. Dim. Murky. You'd think the opening to the apartment, whoever's doing the opening, well Arthur thinks they should be brilliantly backlit by a bright rectangle of light.

It should be light enough that Arthur could see what the fuck was happening, but it's exactly the opposite. All he can see is an empty sack of a long, dark material, something discolored and scabby and blowing in a non-existent wind and sighing and filled with inky, oily blackness slopping over the side of the door sill, glopping and twitching as it waddles closer to him.

Well, that's new. He's never seen anything like that before. He feels like he should be reacting to it in some way, but it's just too friggin' hard to keep his eyes open. Too friggin' hard. You know, if anything it's getting darker and darker and the light is almost gone in the hallway. Arthur's content to be in the sheltering murkiness. It's nearly pitch black. Just comfortable shadows of comfortable shadows now, overlapping and intersecting, rolling over and over in front of his eyes, sewing them shut, singing him to sleep. Rest and sleep. Rest and sleep.

Arthur struggles a little. Not much. But a little. The darkness hangs in front of him and he writhes and squirms – he's not quite ready to give up. Not yet. He asks the darkness leaning towards him "Why don't they ever replace the fucking light bulbs in this building? Isn't there a law, or fire department regulation or some shit about light bulbs and hallways?" He doesn't get an answer. And he says "Is this really it? I only get 22 years? I really did everything I came to do?" There's no answer to that either. But Arthur gratefully feels all his words falling away, sloughing off, and he's clean and whole and has no more questions. Arthur feels relaxing carelessness seep into his thoughts and flood over his body and he wants to be smothered. It's O.K. It doesn't matter. It's over. It's all over. Done. Complete. His eyes are almost closed. Now they *are* closed. He takes a deep breath and fights to open up just one eye. One single eye.

He sees something white and shiny. He sees something like polished bone. It glints in the muddy darkness that flows in waves under dirty folds of cloth and reaches for his shoulder. Arthur turns his shoulder slightly to make it easier to reach. He can at least do that. At least that. It touches his shoulder and then the light bursts down all over him and it's the Fourth of July and all the fireworks are exploding at once, and they're all exploding in his head and it's a refulgent, lustrous, white illumination blazing from inside of him lighting up the hallway, the building, the entire city, Arthur is on fire, Arthur *is* the fire.

"For God's sake, Artie, what the fuck?"

Someone is throwing his shoulder backwards and forwards again and again. Someone is slapping his face.

"Jesus. All this blood. Artie. Artie."

He looks up and it's Frankie, talking on his cell, giving the address of the hotel, the Del Mio, red smudges on his face, on his hands, on his shirt, everywhere, it looks like there's some tears in his eyes there too. Frankie. Frankie. He wishes he could speak. He tries to smile. He's too tired. Too tired even for that. But he can watch.

The door behind Frankie is closing, almost closed, the darkness scampering back in. To Arthur, it doesn't feel angry. It doesn't feel disappointed. It only feels patient. After all, in the end, all it has to do is wait.

But maybe it will have to wait a little bit longer for Arthur Zhou.

HIS PARTS IN JOY

1

Nicholas Wojciechowcz met his future husband John Alexander Luo Chin at 5:12 P.M., underground, on a crowded Muni streetcar (N-Judah line) in San Francisco between the stops of Montgomery and Powell. The day was June 14th, a Tuesday, 65 degrees Fahrenheit, a typical brisk summer's evening for the City. Fog was rolling in which meant the temperature might be rising later that night. Unfortunately, Nick, a newcomer to the City (he'd arrived 40 minutes before on the bus) had dressed for a June summer's night anywhere else other than coastal Northern California - in surfer shorts, a thin polo shirt, and sandals (the sandals were Birkenstocks however). This meant he was freezing and miserable.

As the train approached Powell Street Station, Nick tried to open the suitcase he was protecting by sitting on it and stepped on all of John's toes all at the same time. Turning around to apologize he knocked John's laptop out of his backpack, bashed John in the forehead with his own forehead as they both reached down to grab the laptop, and accidentally shoved his knee into John's eye as John bent down again, alone this time, just as the doors opened at Powell Street station. The blow to John's eye socket had the effect, inadvertently, of causing John to groan in blind pain and kick his laptop out of the train, through the gap between the platform and the car, and onto the tracks below. The N-Judah doors closed, the car moved forward, and what pieces of the computer hadn't already shattered in the fall were smashed under the wheels of the moving train.

This incident gave Nick and John a great deal of conversational fodder for the next ten minutes. The incident was also the reason why Nick saw John once a month for the next year as he paid John back in small installments by check, hand-delivered. The amounts of the checks became progressively larger towards the end of the year, when Nick had a better job. The checks stopped entirely after the 13th month, because by then Nick had moved in with John, they had a joint checking account, and both thought it was a little odd to write a check to themselves, endorse it and deposit it.

They stayed together for five years, until John moved to Taiwan for his job, and Nick, being a self-employed designer had to stay behind in San Francisco. That was two years ago. They are still best friends, no, they are family, and the truth is, if John needed one of Nick's kidneys, or both of them, or all Nick's money and worldly possessions, Nick would be all over it in a heartbeat. John would do the same for Nick, unhesitatingly. That's just the way they are. Like I said, they're family.

But now Nick is back in southern Missouri, the Ozarks, Iron County to be exact, taking care of a sick brother, and things are very hard for him, and sometimes he's not sure if he's going to make it, or even if he wants to try.

But all that is in the future.

2

Right now, it's 3:27 a.m., Sunday June 12th, 2 days before Nick meets John.

Nick is sitting naked in a public restroom, coughing, in an uncomfortably wet and stained stall, feeling very sorry for himself indeed, having lost his clothes, his wallet and his enthusiasm for life

– although maybe not in exactly that order. And Nick keeps on hearing an irritable and excitable janitor rattling the doors of each toilet cubicle, double-checking to see if anyone is still back there, and generally making sounds like he's preparing to close the restroom for a seriously thorough and deep cleaning. The janitor's already called out twice. Nick's purposefully not responded. The thick slop overflowing from the toilet underneath him is splashing onto his sandals. Nick is nodding to himself as if he was waiting for this very thing to happen and closing his eyes against the harsh white light. Nick is also talking to himself. Some might think Nick is praying, and there might be something to that. But mostly Nick is thinking.

He has a clear image in his head of his situation. He's a creative guy, an artist and a designer and he can't help getting images in his mind. It's what he does and who he is. This is what Nick sees. A lone man drowns in mid-ocean, gray skies merging with gray water, cold waves rolling over his head, salt water choking his lungs, no land popping up over the horizon at the last minute, icy spray from the crests of waves spreading over his one outstretched hand in grasping little frothy fingers like the Japanese woodblock print from Hokusai's Thirty Six Views of Mount Fujiyama. Lots of muted pastels, a heavier outline around the hand for emphasis, water highlighted around the body. Color the sky - dark, foreboding, pitiless. This man is obviously going down, and going down for the very last time. But this man is going down in beauty. Not like Nick is going down. Nick is going down in sewage. And this is what Nick's saying to himself. What in the hell did he do, what was the one unpardonable act he committed, what was the egregiously cosmic error he made to deserve all this shit? It does occur to Nick how uncannily appropriate his choice of metaphor is.

He's not in a joking mood. He's well and truly up the creek and paddle-less. He sees a police record in the near term. Can prison be far behind? And the person he's talking to – himself – is not being particularly helpful - no brilliant, easily-implemented escape plans, not even a single witty one-line comeback. He squeezes his eyes shut even more tightly, hears the sound of a bucket on wheels squeaking its way towards him, and mutters with more feeling under his breath. This part of the sincere and forceful whispering probably does include a prayer. Nick is an intelligent, respectful, and desperate man. The universe is a big place. He needs some help. His mom always said it never hurts to ask. So Nick's asking.

While he's waiting for signs of divine intervention, Nick casts his mind back a couple of hours. How exactly did he get from where he once was to where he now sits? Set the clock back 3-1/2 hours.

3

It's 12:02 in the morning, Sunday, June the 12th.

Nick is on a bus. Even though it's the middle of the night for most other folks, Nick's night has just begun. Nick has just blown his nose, loudly and satisfactorily, and a favor involving false teeth has just been asked.

"Now, if I give these to you, you won't forget my babies and not keep 'em safe for me, will you, dear?"

Emma, who's smiling and pointing at her gorgeous, store-bought teeth, has beautiful hands, soft skin, and slender fingers. She's very expressive, and even though she's a little heavy, she likes to throw her body around a lot when she talks, especially her arms and those delicate hands. They move and dip and dart in the yellowish, candle-like light (shining down from those little personal light fixtures above the bus seats) like things alive with a will of their own, and they fascinate Nick. Emma's a great one to tell stories, and not always the same stories like some tell over and over again. Lots of times they're different.

"Lord, this pattern in these bus seat covers, it brings back memories – I used to have something just like this in the windows over the sink, by my stove back home. Did I ever tell you about how I found out I needed something to cover up that window? How the meter reader was…"

"Oh, I did? Well, how about the time my sister-in-law, the one who used to break out in hives on account of her delicate nerves, well, my youngest brother and her, them newlyweds and all, showed up one Sunday morning before church services – and you know what? she shows up wearing, if you can believe it…"

"Well, yes, that's exactly right, a dress that matched those new kitchen curtains. Have I really told you all about Tammi Eileen? You sure, honey? Yes, yes I believe she did leave the house and fall down the cellar steps backwards, poor thing crying to beat the band and scratching like crazy. And yes, we did end up driving to the hospital with her laid out in the back seat, covered in coal dust. Never got those back seats clean again. You sure have a good memory. No flies on you, Nickie, that's for sure. Well, dear here's one I know you don't know…"

Emma has a million of them. Crazy stuff. Interesting stuff. She reminds Nick of all his aunts back in Arkansas and Missouri.

"Nickie, Nickie, did I ever tell you how I met my second husband? About the pineapple upside down cake, the missing bars of Dove soap, and the mysterious Emergency Room nurse? "

And because the bus seats are so narrow, and Emma's dress is so colorful (a big, floppy mumu of red, purple, and yellow splotches), and Nick is so tired, he keeps on seeing these double images of Emma tossing her hands around while telling a story and an enormous butterfly struggling unsuccessfully hour after hour to release itself from a too-tight cocoon and fly to freedom. He keeps on wanting to say "Go girl, go – be free! Free!", but since Emma is 75 if she's a day and Nick is trying to be respectful, and Nick really does like her and enjoys her company, he doesn't say anything. He sits. He smiles a lot. He does it in a friendly way. And he takes care of her dentures for her.

A raspy voice bellows over Nick's left shoulder.

"You ever live in Wy-o-min'?"

"Nickie, Nickie dear, could I ask you a little favor? Please?"

"Eastern part? Out on the plains?"

"Nickie, oh, Nickie it's startin' again, Nickie."

"Mebbe the southern part?"

"Nickie, would you just reach behind my head and try and catch my neck pillah? It's fallin' between the seat cushions and I'm afraid any minute I'm gonna lose it this time for good and gone."

"Most folks live in the southern part…"

"You're always so kind, Nickie, there, can you see it now? Just a little to the left Nickie…"

"But then, a lot of folks up north too."

"Just up a little more and to the left, I'm sure it's right there…"

Nick wheezes a little as his head bobs back and forth between Emma and her escaping pillow and his left shoulder and the gravelly voice. Finally he gets on his knees, holding back a cough, balances precariously on his seat facing backwards and tries to root around between his headrest and Emma's headrest, but it's dark and awkward and he can hardly see a thing and it's midnight.

He's trying to think but it's hard. He's tired. Why exactly is he doing this again? He cuts his little finger running it along a jagged edge on the top of Emma's headrest, starts to say something and stops because he's practically breathing down Emma's left ear. He sucks on his finger, backs off a little and breathes heavily instead for a few moments. Deep breaths. In and out. It's no good. With this cold in his lungs he sounds like a leaking accordion.

The voice belongs to the obliquely inquisitive, cowboy-hat-wearing, deeply-tanned, hugely mustached, thirty-something gentleman who is quite handsome, but who also keeps asking suspicious questions and keeps punching his knees into the back of Nick's seat, day and night, night and day. Nick never sees his face for his hat. Although his voice has become more and more familiar. Nick hears from him about once an hour. He still doesn't know his name. Although for some reason he feels he should already know it. Is he some rodeo celebrity? When has Nick ever watched a rodeo? Never, that's when. Who is this guy? The cowboy must be six foot fifteen or something, so that's probably the reason (and it's a good one) for the incessant knee bombardment – but if things don't improve and soon, Nick will be a candidate for receiving a kidney or maybe a spleen transplant within the hour.

He gives up for the moment, twirls and twists around on his knees, plops heavily back down in his seat facing forwards and hears someone shifting and grunting and leaning over into the aisle in back of him, and an object, hard and bony, moves abruptly up and then slowly down his lower back in a kind of thrusting, deep-tissue, kneading motion that pops all his lower vertebrae and leaves him gasping and looking up at the ceiling and talking to himself again.

Nick's private name for the cowboy is Marlboro Man. Which, except for the cancerous connotations one might associate with cigarettes and tracheotomies, in Nick's mind, is nothing if not complimentary. Nick always liked the looks of the Man.

"Oh, Nickie. Now I think it's lying in the row behind us...."

"How's about Cheyenne? Y'ever visit there?"

"And Nickie, while you're up, could you put these away for me? I'll wrap them for you, Dearie. Nickie?"

The Marlboro Man leans forward, Nick peers around the side of his seat at the same time and they nearly kiss. Both bounce backwards and away from each other and back into their seats with a singular energy – looking like two animated electrons colliding in a cartoon physics experiment. Boing! The cowboy's breath smells like tobacco and coffee and a sickly-sweet, syrupy, extraordinarily strong peppermint. Nick gingerly picks up the Kleenex-wrapped package Emma hands to him, stands and carefully wedges it in the luggage rack above them. He doesn't really look where he's putting it. Nick's preoccupied. Nick's busy twitching his nose, partially because he needs to blow it, and partially because all he can smell is peppermint and while he's twitching, Nick wonders what the Marlboro Man is going to do next.

4

2:27 A.M. Sunday, June 12th (2 hours later).

Emma pokes Nick to remind him about her dentures. It's not the most gentle of pokes. She needs them again. Then the bus driver hits the brakes.

Nick contemplates poking her back, but he restrains himself, and his restraint is something Nick is proud of, although he'd never admit it to anyone. He must really be tired. When did he start hitting back on great-grandmothers for crying out loud? Still, Nick decides to ignore Emma and her poking for the time being. Emma's happily listening with her eyes closed to Nick's IPod, snug in her seat, wedged in with pillows in front and back. Nick however, is not braced. The sudden slowing sends him flying face forward into the seat in front of him and a sound like someone pulling a metal skyscraper upside down across a chalkboard the size of a county crashes down on the back rows of the bus as Nick ricochets back and forth. Nick rubs the front and back of his head afterwards and looks to his left, as the brakes continue to scream in his ears. He glances at his fellow passengers and waits. Nothing. He waits some more. No reaction. His fellow passengers fascinate Nick with their imperturbability.

Nick feels Emma administer a motherly pat on his knee – a little sympathy for the forehead bashing - as she closes her eyes again and pushes back into her pillows with a dreamy smile on her face. She loves his IPod. Nicks' been letting her use it since they met in New York City. He charges it when they take their periodic rest breaks, surreptitiously - an electric cat burglar - at truck stops. He probably wouldn't go to all that trouble just for himself. He'll do it for Emma though.

Nick wonders why he can't feel as comfortable and as snug and safe as his fellow bus-traveler Emma. What's the heck's wrong with him? Nick suddenly feels very alone, for no reason at all, except that it's the middle of the night, his neck and head hurt, he's surrounded by strangers – some kind, some not, his whole life is uprooted, he's trying to start his life over in an unknown city, and he doesn't know what he's going to do next once this bus dumps him off in Seattle. Hasn't the least first fucking clue. Not a one.

It's dark. He's thirty-three. And he's feeling afraid. Loose. Wildly and unsafely disconnected. So he talks to Emma, out of the dark, although she can't hear him. He feels like he should talk about what he does know, rather than the thousands of things that are just huge hostile question marks to him tonight. So…he talks about one of the many theories he has about life here on Earth. He has a lot of opinions. Some of them even worth hearing. Things he's noticed about people he's known. About places he's been. It's what he's learned during his brief stay on this odd planet. He tells her One of Nick's Theories of Life.

Nick's Theory of Life #23. Nick has a theory about life – it is like surfing. Stop, it gets better. Really. Not that he's ever surfed a lot. Nick's no surfer dude. Nick just likes surfer clothes. And surfers. But that's another story for another time. Anyways, returning to Nick as he really tucks in and bites a chunk out of this analogy - Nick thinks of life's significant events like waves on an ocean. If you sit on the beach, all you do is sit, and it seems like everyone else is having the time of their lives out there on the water, one perfect wave after another, it's all thrills, bonhomie, good times, adrenaline rushes, the whole nine yards. It's all out there. Waiting for you.

You decide you want some of that. So you get your lazy ass self up and out, onto the water, determined to have fun, ready to bogey with the best of them, and then the waves stop. All you get is flat, and it's mind-numbingly boring and in the midst of all this nada, nothing and zip, the whole surfing experience, in fact the whole wave-surf paradigm seems like such a huge amount of work for such a totally bogus reward that you have to ask yourself the question: why do it? Why keep on trying? What is it all about anyways?

Nick pauses for a second. He can hear the tiniest sound of the world's smallest babbling brook (tracks from Nick's meditation CD) whispering into Emma's ears. Emma's head is angling and bobbing towards the window and her eyes are even more happily closed (if that's possible) and she's breathing slower and slower in gentle counter-rhythm to the sound of water falling over stone. She's also starting to lose her pillow again. Nick retrieves it for her, plumps it, and positions it, and she moves her head, eyes still closed, with a smile as he puts it in back of her neck. She stretches (exactly the way a contented tabby cat would Nick thinks) and she gets comfortable and she promptly falls back towards the window. He continues explaining, speaking a little more softly, into the night around them, spotlit from overhead by one of those small, yellow lights set to dim.

You may say: Why? Why go on? But you have to keep on trying. Many are those who stop at this point. Many are those who miss out. But if you stay out on the water, if you stay out there and you are determined, and you find your balance. If you get the hang of it all and you jump and paddle and dive and do it all over again, and again, and again. Well, while you're waiting in between waves – where before you'd be angry and bored and depressed, suddenly - huzzah, huzzah - you find yourself. You're where you needed to be. You're there. And that's it. You find yourself, and there you are – you are surfing.

He pauses again, Emma is motionless, it's hard to even see her breathing, and it feels to Nick like he's the only person awake in the whole wide world tonight (well, except for the bus driver), but he's surprised to find he's O.K. with that. He continues, speaking even softer.

You surf. Present Tense Continuous. Life is like that. People are like that. Men are very much like that. You have to wait sometimes. You have to wait for the wave. You have to be there when the wave happens. You have to work, throw yourself into it, take advantage of the opportunity of the moment, get your balance right, and then ride, ride, ride, ride, ride. Surfing is all of that - the riding *and* the waiting - it's all surfing - all of it.

Nick finishes so softly his words just sound like soft exhalations and the silence becomes general. Nick is quiet and listens to Emma's breath-lets and consciously tries to breathe at the same relaxed rate. He's exhausted. Really. He feels frayed, and worn – a shirt worn one too many times – so thin, with one good jerk he'd tear in two. Nick notices it's starting to rain. He feels himself getting sleepy, and he thinks back on his day. Nick was playing cards earlier, even though Nick isn't very good at it. Kind of like Nick's surfing.

5

9:48 P.M. Saturday, June 11th – 4 hours earlier that same evening.

On the way back from asking the bus driver, Gordon ("call me Gee Dee") about the next stop and mentioning the odd braking sounds Nick keeps hearing under his seat ("it's like an explosion and getting louder" – GD was not impressed), Nick had been stunned into immobility by a section of seats populated by large biceps, teardrop-shaped pecs, and yards and yards of khaki and camouflage duffel material – some of it covering the biceps, most of it packed neatly and efficiently into the overhead luggage racks in the form of long, lumpy cylinders. How had he missed them before (the men not the duffels)?

He'd just finished walking through a region of the bus inhabited by rambunctious retirees so the effect on Nick was all the more startling as the transition was dramatic and unexpected and, now that he thought about it, not altogether unwelcome. Nick froze in mid-step. A card game among four of the guys was going on in the aisle of the bus in front of him. As he creaked back into motion, carefully stepping over the kneeling men, before he could fully engage his mind and the deep reservoirs of native caution he had available to him, his tongue was moving like it had a mind of its own.

"You need a fifth?" he asked the nearest guy.

Four shaved heads looked up at him.

"Well, that depends, what have you got bro?"

Nick didn't know what to say to that. Michael, the retired baker from St. Paul piped up from behind Nick.

"Hey, no alcohol on the bus. The driver took all our wine and even our plastic cups and stuck them all in a box behind his seat."

It was true. Nick had just seen that box. He hadn't mentioned it to the driver, although Nick had been wondering what kind of party the driver was planning to throw for himself late that night when everyone else was sound asleep. Nick, for one, had not planned on sleeping and giving him the chance.

The four buzzed, high-and-tight heads looked at each other and nodded.

"Regs. Yeah. Sorry dude. Maybe when we stop."

Nick shook his head, opened his mouth, closed it, shook his head again. Although it was still light outside, the evening shadows were falling pretty thick on the interior of the bus, especially near the ceiling (these four marines were using the aisle lights to see and using the floor as a table), so all this non-verbal communication on Nick's part was being lost in the dusky upper regions of the cabin. No one below, playing cards, had noticed a thing. He rolled his eyes and cleared his throat to make a noise (which was a mistake, since it made him start coughing), and waited until someone looked back up at him.

"No, I mean, do you need a fifth player?" No one said anything. "To play in the game." Again, silence. "The card game." Nick knew his weakness for tanned muscles was going to get him in trouble some day. He guessed that this was that day. Or night. At any rate, the oldest, who appeared to be barely out of high school and had a generous spray of freckles across his nose and cheeks and who probably had the skills to kill and gut Nick with a bent paper clip in under ten seconds – this marine glanced judiciously sideways up at Nick without moving his head, glanced down again and caught the eye of each of his buddies in turn by means of rapid eyeball movement alone, then looked back up at Nick again, with the same cool, reconnoitering glance. The whole maneuver had taken maybe two blinks of a civilian's eye.

"You got any money?"

Nick showed him the contents of his pockets, which included Kleenex, cough drops, his ripped and well-folded ticket, and a handful of ones and fives and miscellaneous change, besides his wallet. The guy with freckles nodded, pointed with his head where Nick could squat in the aisle, and the game re-commenced. Nick hadn't really thought that part out very well. In truth, Nick hadn't been thinking at all, at least not with his brain. He played until he lost feeling in his toes and his calves and he was in imminent danger of tipping over. He only lost seven dollars. And, he only pissed off ten or twelve of his fellow passengers by blocking the way to the bathroom. On the surface it looked like a complete waste of time. But Nick knew better. Nick knew he'd just been surfing.

6

Back to 2:37 A.M. Sunday, June 12th.

The rain picks up. Nick looks up and down the once quiet aisle of the bus, as it's hard outside shell is battered by volley after volley of liquid artillery fire. He's awake. He's bored. The bus hits its brakes again. The normal roar and vibrating starts up. This wakes Emma, who bounces into Nick, causing Emma to remember she's going to need her dentures again soon. A sleepy, but not very insistent poking follows. Nick feels his head for more bruises. Nick closes one eye then the other as he tries to figure out how much of the ringing in each of his ears is permanent. He feels his poked and bruised rib. He feels the Marlboro Man re-orienting the entire length of his spinal column with one muscular knee – which is actually quite a feat. Nick yawns, but he doesn't want to sleep, he wants something to happen.

He continues to look up and down the sleeping bus. Just for something to do. It's the middle of the night for Chris sake. This weather's crazy. Do they get tornadoes this far north? Nick can't remember. He should probably ask the cowboy, who would know all about it. Nick can clearly hear the front windshield wipers vigorously squeegee-ing all the way back where he's sitting with Emma. At least he would hear it clearly if his ears weren't being stabbed every few minutes by aural ice picks courtesy of the bus braking system.

At times like this (during the last two days) late at night and sleepless, Nick imagines things. He's good at that, although sometimes (well, most times) it has a tendency to get him into trouble. Last night he couldn't' get this image out of his head.

The bus he is on is actually a large hypodermic needle, sticking itself carefully and precisely into some unremarkable fleshy corner of the North American continent. Painlessly, of course, because nobody notices this bus really. There's a certain anonymity attached to bus-riding, as Nick has discovered. You become part of the highway landscape furniture and you fade away – bus, bus riders, bus driver and all. Even at truck stops. You just blend – blend into an anonymous background. You disappear on a ride on the Great American Transparent Syringe. Nick likes that, since often he feels transparent anyway.

But wait, going back to the needle – a better image, Nick thinks, would be that the bus is a bubble in the liquid being injected by the hypo. That's an idea. Busses are basically hollow, right? Which, he supposes would make Nick some kind of molecule or chemical in the bubble. Yeah, Fantastic Voyage kind of shit. Busses shrunk to the size of viruses. Nick thinks about that for awhile.

Well, yes, but what's more probable, (Nick is really getting off on this metaphor, and at least it's passing the time) is that Nick is an infection in the chemical solution being injected - he is an error. Nick is a malignant oversight. An unfortunate mistake. Something larger than himself was trying to accomplish something important and useful and Nick is consistently and obtrusively getting himself in the way. That thought gives Nick a strange pain in the left side of his chest which winds up under his armpit and continues running down the inside of his left arm like a silvery thread of pulsing electrical fire.

Nick's not alarmed. It's comforting somehow. It's a comfortable pain. It's comforting because at least it's all his – it's all Nick's pain. It makes him feel more real. That's just how Nick thinks. Sometimes he feels invisible – airy, ethereal, more than a little unreal - and at least the pain gives him some kind of outline, something to work with, a kind of neural silhouette. At least Nick is visible to Nick. That's something. It's a definite starting place.

Nick is still bored. Nick looks over at Emma, but she's awake and ignoring him now. Nick thinks maybe she's upset, maybe he shouldn't be so selfish. Nick's tried to talk. Nick and Emma have been sitting in what Nick has repeatedly told Emma is the antepenultimate row (that is – next to the next to the last row - Nick was an English major in college, with a minor in Arabic for all the good it's done him - the occasional polysyllabic conversational ornament notwithstanding – and Nick remains painfully aware of the financial implications of his expensive, debt-ridden education – i.e. ten years later, bankruptcy and unemployment - which continue to obtain despite his interesting and unusual vocabulary and his ability to read a stop sign in Iran).

Well, Emma has proved immune to Nick's tsunami of academic wit over the last forty-eight hours. She never reacts to his adroit conversational gambits. She maintains a modest silence for the most part, when he goes on and on, almost as if she's embarrassed for him and is manfully (or woman-fully) trying to paper over all his social gaffes with unobtrusive and sympathetic silences. Punctuated, of course, lately by the poking.

Or maybe she's going deaf and Emma just can't hear what he's saying very well. Maybe. And then again, maybe not. Who's to know? Nick is always waiting for life (which Nick imagines as an unseen rabid dog salivating significantly just around the corner) to jump up and bite him in his behind just when he least expects it. Life almost never disappoints Nick in that way.

So, take right now. With the obviously failing brakes. Emma has no comment. She doesn't react. Maybe she doesn't need to. Maybe no one needs to when they get as old as Emma. Things don't impress her. Things don't bother her. She nods her head and smiles politely and listens and nods again. Nick wonders what goes on inside her head. He's sure she probably thinks Nick is just a bit strange. A little bit off. One of those peculiar people you sometimes get stuck next to in public places.

Nick must be one of those situations you just make do the best you can and get through it all as quickly and as quietly as possible and be thankful when you're over and done with it Amen. The big thing is not to get these people upset. The big thing is to keep them calm. Keep them content. Most importantly, keep them *occupied*. Keep them *busy*. Nick's positive he's beginning to see annoyance blossoming like mold in bathroom grout behind those pleasing, polite smiles. He's starting to wear her down. He's starting to bother her, get under her skin. He's digging away at the manners and courtesy and starting to hit the real Emma. And it's irritating to her. Well, why shouldn't she be upset? Emma wouldn't be the first, would she? This would not be the first time for Nick. Not by a long shot. Just ask his last boyfriend. Yeah, just ask Chuck. Go ahead. Ask him.

Yes, tonight's brake meltdown doesn't worry Emma. She fits right in with the rest of the bus passengers in that department. No anxiety problems on this bus. It's like they pump Prozac through the ventilation system and follow up with a Xanax chaser. He and

Emma have been sitting in the back rows on the same thinly-padded seats for days now, listening to the brakes, gliding across the northernmost tier of these United States - New York to Seattle. Days. And days. Well, only two days really. Has it really only been two days? How can that be? Just two?

Emma pokes him again and Nick balls his hands into fists and sits on them and bites his lip, forcing himself to stare straight ahead. When the brakes call out yet again like torture victims, he thinks – what would people do if I ran up and down the aisle of the bus screaming "I want to live, I want to live", what? Would anyone even notice? Why is he, Nick, the only rational, reasonable man in this vehicle? Why is he the only one awake, aware, and listening for their sure and impending death? Why? It is a large and complicated philosophical question. Nick ponders it, but realizes he has no answer for it. Well. They're just all very lucky, aren't they? They're lucky that at least one person, Nick, is on the bus and on the ball and is watching out for the safety and wellbeing of the rest of them. Lucky, that's what they are. Nick yawns. Just lucky. Nick tries to stretch, but doesn't want to move his hands, because they're getting warm for the first time in hours now that he's sitting on them.

It's always so cold in this bus. The air conditioning is like an arctic gale out of Saskatchewan. Not that he has anything against our neighbors to the North. He likes Canada. Especially the Mounties and the hockey players. He yawns again. He glances out of the sides of his eyes over at Emma, and decides to shift his thighs after all, repositioning his two freezing hands to get better coverage. He immediately sees he's made a mistake, a grave tactical error.

Emma can see him moving and she pokes him twice, a little harder this time, just so Nick can see that she is looking upwards and nodding at him with shakes of her head loaded with significance. She takes the IPod earbuds out. She doesn't know how to turn the IPod off, so she hands it back to him, playing the sound of tiny waves gently breaking on beaches of Malibu. He stuffs it into his sweatshirt. She gives him a final, meaningful look. She wants him up on the luggage rack, pronto.

Nick yawns again, but it turns into a sigh. Nick goes to grab his ancient baseball cap, which it turns out he's also been sitting on, underneath his gelid hands, and covers his forehead. He's preparing to stand up and make a spectacle of himself, and needs to have his head completely covered first. Nick's a little shy. No, Nick's a lot shy. He's actually morbidly self-conscious. Nick has a purple-red scar just beneath his hairline which runs across the top of his forehead. He got it when he was just a baby, at least that's what his ma told him, and how would he know differently? How? I mean you have to believe your parents, don't you? He's frantically aware of it. He's sure he's horrifically ugly.

He keeps watching Emma to see if she turns away in honest disgust, like Chuck, his ex, eventually did, or is just hiding her loathing, like Chuck, his ex, publicly admitted to doing. He *knew* that Chuck was lying the whole time he repeated over and over again that it didn't matter to him. He knew it. Chuck pretended like he hardly noticed the scar – although to be honest, Chuck and the rest of humanity rarely if ever mentioned it - but still, all the same – Nick knows they're thinking about it. Thinking and getting nauseous. And Chuck's silence, Holy Moses, did that change. Especially in that loud, last argument in the Sushi restaurant around the corner from their tiny apartment. Chuck never could hold his Saki. And it just wasn't funny to unroll raw tuna on your forehead and ask a group of people next to them at the counter - who did he remind them of? Does that sound like a normal boyfriend? Does that sound like a loving partner? Is that unconditional positive regard? Nick didn't think so either. You know, it's not paranoia when they really *were* out to get you the whole time.

Nick adjusts his cap. Emma waits. Nick really doesn't want to move. Nick is, to be honest, miserable and feverish. His eyes itch. His head pounds. His stomach churns. His tongue feels furred and huge like someone upholstered it in used and surprisingly filthy shag carpeting. His throat feels like it's swelled to three times its size and Nick is sure he looks like a six foot blond toad, with goiter-like infected glands horribly distended on his neck and flopping out over his shirt collar.

Nick is getting worse. Nick is not happy. Nick is coughing his lungs up. And Nick is running out of Kleenex.

They brake again, and he squints his crusty eyes in the dim wavering light of the bus, leaning into the aisle, tries to see what the hell they're stopping for now, and surreptitiously moves out of Emma's reach by placing a balled-up sweatshirt between them, as well as two maps of the state of Ohio he found on his seat after their last stop. But he knows he's only postponing the inevitable.

Late at night, last night in fact, Nick had a vision. It was his second vision this trip. His first one came upon him the first night out, but he couldn't remember a thing about it the next day no matter how hard he wracked his brain. It could have been absolute truth in Technicolor, but Nick would never know now. Besides, Nick figures it probably was only a side-effect of the bottles of decongestant he was swigging like they were mineral water all night long.

7

11:45 p.m. Friday, June 10th (27 hours before).

Nick's Vision #2: it is quiet, too quiet, even the Pakistani family's baby (this was before the bus had reached Minneapolis) has collapsed into unconsciousness after a tiring day of non-stop cuteness staged for the benefit of the entire bus load of passengers, driver included. But now, it is quiet and Nick is restless, awake, and alone. Nick feels like the entire universe has condensed, like the opposite of the Big Bang, into a single drop of breathable atmosphere the size of his bus, and he and the other 40 or so travelers are the last humans in existence.

Strangely, he isn't frightened, just curious, and a little sad. The top of the bus peels back like a tin of sardines – the old kind , the kind with a key – and a white light, like marshmallow cream, begins to drip and glop onto the floor, and onto the seats, and onto the passengers' heads, but everyone still sleeps, and only Nick can see what's happening, and for some reason he can't move – he's paralyzed. Suddenly the baby's eyes open, and the baby's mouth opens (but not saying anything) as more marshmallow light pours down upon them, sloshing now at waist level, now under his armpit, and a deck of cards, a combat boot, a full saddle with stirrups and a rosary float and bob past him on sticky waves of light. Waves of light which surge against the back of the bus and bounce back viciously, slapping the back of his head painfully as they travel forward again.

The baby swims past him, in the heavy surf, doing the backstroke, then the breast stroke, then kicking and flinging its arms in a very energetic version of freestyle. He stops just by Nick and brushes his cheek with the back of his hand, soft as a feather, you could hardly tell he'd touched him, as the goopy white stuff rises up to Nick's chin, then to his nostrils, then up to his eyes. The baby looks at Nick, looks into his irises and intones in a sing-song voice "Life's a bitch, and then", and he leans in close to Nick's left ear. Nick can feel the baby's tiny pillow-lips tickling his earlobe as he breathes in and out, slightly out of breath from the exertion of swimming with such short arms and legs and whispers, "and then, it gets better - believe me - it has to."

He comes to with his sweatshirt twisted around his head like the wax paper on a lollipop, and Emma nudging (not poking yet), smiling at him and needing him to move so she can get out of her seat.

8

Back to 2:57 a.m. Sunday, June 12th

Lightning flashes outside, Emma is mesmerized by the scenery outside the window, strobed into a frozen tableau of hurricane-lashed pine forest and flooding highway, and thunder echoes around the two of them and the driver – they are the only souls awake right now. The brakes start up with their noise and stop, start up and stop, again and again.

Utter calm. No one stirs. No one whispers a prayer. No one cries out for help. The thunder crashes again. The brakes complain like it's the Gotterdammerung. Ahead Nick can see the Family Gonzalez he ate lunch with yesterday, konked out like someone slipped them all tranquilizers in their horchata. They are all moving to Oregon to help the wife's brother's cousin set up a Spanish-speaking Insurance Agency/Wire Transfer/Check Cashing shop in some small town in the dry eastern part of the state. Nick wishes them well. His four marines, all shaved heads and tight t-shirts, the three Joe's and a Tom - they were playing cards tonight, after Nick left, just like last night until late, but no more. Hah! Shouldn't they be posting a sentry or something, standing watch for them, and not sleeping their way through danger? And then there's the Pakistani family in the front rows with the famous baby, but no, they'd gotten off in Minneapolis. Minnesota had been where the legion of laughing, winking, dead-serious-about-vacationing Catholic Seniors had boarded, sporting funny hats, brandishing a militant optimism, and quickly absorbing the middle section of the bus in a well-defended fort of pointed politeness and courtesy. They were quiet now too. But Nick noted, at 3 in the morning, he wasn't expecting to hear a lot of activity out of them.

Even the twenty-somethings and teenagers were dead calm. Stoic in the face of their own mortality. There were pairs of them with small backpacks spread here and there - usually whispering, texting, sharing MP3 players – they'd all run out of juice both literally and metaphorically by this time of the night. There was a colony of them in the back of the bus.

And there was the cowboy, the Marlboro Man. Always watching Nick and twitching. Glaring and jiggling his upper lip and performing marvelously acrobatic frowns. Nick figured he'd become particularly pissed after he saw Nick showing off - writing backwards in curvy Arabic for the younger Pakistani Masuds with a stick in the gravel of a parking lot during one of their rest stops. The way Nick saw it – the cowboy was obviously waiting for Nick to pull out his traditional Arab headdress, a copy of the Koran, and the traditional terrorist bomb that must go with it. There was no doubt he was keeping one eye peeled and pointed at Nick. It was either his terrorist tendencies, or his scar, or the fact that Nick was gay, that made the Marlboro Man treat Nick like an ambulatory cow patty. That, or maybe the fact that Nick oozed mucus continuously from his nose, like this bus's own personal Yellowstone geyser of bougars. Yes, there was that. It wasn't pretty. Nick knew it. But you didn't have to hate him for it.

The thing of it was, as has been alluded to previously, Nick was not a well man. This bug or flu was running amok like an out-of-control brush fire, consuming every clean and clear lung in its path. Everyone had it. The bus driver had it. Nick had it. The marines were getting it. The bus had become one surging ocean of germ-filled currents – a maelstrom of wheezes, sneezes, sniffles, and hacking. And admittedly Nick had led the way. Maybe the cowboy figured Nick had given him the creeping crud. Him and everybody else. Well, maybe he had. Who was to say?

The cowboy would say. He would say something. What was up with him? Nick pondered it deeply, as deeply as you can in the middle of the night when you're feverish and expecting to die any minute. Well, maybe Nick looked like one of those blond, blue-eyed Arabs, the northern ones (who were they again? Kurds?). Maybe he looked like one of them. Maybe the cowboy thought he'd seen his face in a foldout in National Geographic standing in some dusty street, holding a sub-machine gun over his head and shouting. Or then again, maybe the cowboy had dated his ex, like every other gay man in New York City and believed all the wild tales of Nick's utter worthlessness as a boyfriend – all the infidelity, stalking, robbery, etc. etc. that his ex, Chuck, told and retold after the third Maker's Mark Manhattan began to have its evil and redundant effect on him.

Or…what? Or, maybe, who knows? All this maybe-ing was making his eyes hurt more. He looked carefully back over his shoulder. The ever-vigilant cowboy was drooling on a neighbor's arm, snoring away. They look so innocent when they're asleep.

And then there was Emma, who hadn't sneezed once in the last two days. Emma, whom he had met forty eight hours ago in Times Square as he ran into the Port Authority, late for his bus and nearly missing it, as was his custom. Emma the poker.

All this twisting and turning and looking at cowboys starts him up and coughing again and he carefully reaches for his wadded-up, well-used tissue paper in the side pockets of his shorts, trying not to disturb his carefully built wall of paper and textiles. However, Emma's finger finds him and easily penetrates the sweatshirt/map barrier. Poke. Poke. Poke.

It's time. Nick's going to have to dislodge himself and make his move towards the luggage racks. Lightning crashes outside the window. The brakes squeal. Are they going downhill right now? God help them all.

"Nihhie, Nihhie, Ah neah wy teaf. Upf theah."

Nick can only look at her. When she has her teeth out like this, he's found it's like she's speaking in some obscure dialect of Tibetan to him. She points upward and catches Nick on his arm as he's blowing his peeling and raw nose into shreds of tissue paper. He jumps back reflexively, knocking both his hands out over the aisle, tossing his Kleenex into the rows in back of him, and ends up spraying his wrists and palms in drippy clumps of yellow brown flu-snot.

He looks at his hands and arms in disbelief, then at her, then back at his hands, then at her, but she's not looking at him anymore. She's watching the lightning outside. Or something. He begins to scrape himself clean with his last Kleenex. She sneaks a few communicative helpful elbow jabs in his direction, but stares in a business-like manner out the bus window and into the dark – although, as far as Nick can see, now that he's interested and looking over her shoulder, which isn't difficult since she can't be more than five feet high, there's only the mysterious blurs of pine tree shadows to be seen, wetly racing past the rain-spattered glass and the reflection of Emma's face in rapt concentration.

He notices she's talking to herself again, breathily, in syllables only the un-dentured can comprehend. Nick wipes and watches and coughs some more. The pine trees fly by. Then there's open space. Then trees. Then a lot of open space. The whole bus throbs with a violent down-throttling. People begin to wake up around him, coughing, sneezing. It sounds like a hospital ward. Emma talks to the window, but Nick can clearly hear the word "teaf" ricochet back towards him in every other sentence.

Nick breathes in and out for a second, and briefly wonders where his Kleenex landed a minute ago, then forgets all about it. Nick does not want to get up. He does not want to begin the Great Denture Adventure. He is tired. He is a walking pustule of flu. He feels terrible. He deserves to rest. He won't do it. He won't. But Nick knows, full well, that he's going to give in.

Emma looks over at him, out of the side of her eyes, an anxious look now on her face. Nick closes his eyes and moans. Then he tenses. With many jerks and piteous cries the bus begins to slow to a long, shuddering halt, and Nick, still sighing and now biting his lower lip, counts one, two, three and throws his aching body up and out of the seat, timing his spring between braking bounces, dancing on the floor beneath him as it rattles, groans and shakes. Emma exclaims beside him.

"Thas wight Nihhie. Upf on thopf."

He coughs, reaching up with one hand, holding onto his seat with the other, grabs randomly along the luggage rack over their heads and gropes various shapes. Nothing small and bony brushes past his hands. Then, over the next row of seats, his fingers enthusiastically plunge knuckle-deep into something soft, squishy and disturbingly clay-like in a thin plastic bag. All Nick can think of is soiled diaper. It can't be that. He freezes. He snuffs in deeply, trying to smell something through his stopped up nose and throws himself into a coughing fit.

When the two men in the row in front of him, a Tom and a Joe, who are wrapped in some kind of greenish-blue blanket, wake up, cussing and jerking their shaved heads at the hacking and the spitting erupting over their scalps and then notice Nick's arm thrust into the packages stored over their seats, Nick understandably jerks his hand free of their possessions, moves to cover his mouth, and realizes he's smeared whatever it was he plunged his fingers into liberally across his lips and face. He coughs into his hand and tries to wipe it off at the same time.

The two guys in front of him get quieter eventually. It takes a while. Tom and Joe probably won't be talking a lot to him in the future. Nick takes in a deep breath, well as deep as he can manage with his tight chest. Then he takes another. Then another. He closes his eyes in the darkness, tries to breathe through his mouth and the bus jumps up and onto a curb with four elephantine oscillations and Nick casually bites down on his tongue.

"Shit" he hisses between his bloody, saliva-covered teeth to the suitcases by his head. "Shit." "Fuck." A soft, but piercing voice emerges from below his waist, punctuated by a few more judicious pokes.

"Nihhie! Nihhie! I newah wiah eath a thing withouw ma teaf."

The entire bus begins to describe a wide, lazy arc to the left and aims itself directly towards a nova-like explosion of fluorescent light Nick can only assume is a truck stop. He bashes his head as it bounces. The bus abruptly turns to the right and Nick jumps to the left. The bus turns to the left again, and Nick pivots neatly, but not neatly enough, and hits his head in the exact spot he just bashed it five seconds before.

"I thuaw I uth em wight up fwonth theah. Hoo thee ything, theawie? Nihhie?"

Nick smiles his politician's Teflon grin as Chuck used to call it, crouching his six foot frame, half-sitting, half-standing under the dented luggage rack and fumbles again blindly above him. One hand bends oddly backwards up and over his head, running his fingers back and forth over shifting, decelerating packages.

The bus stops. Nick, however, continues to move forward. Rather than break his arm, Nick does what he thinks is a skillful pirouette down the central aisle of the bus landing in the lap of a sleeping Latino man (the elder Gonzalez) three rows up who carries a suitcase between his legs. Nick has something in his hand, something resembling a very small, pair of knobby boomerangs wrapped in layers of soggy Kleenex, and Nick experiences a rare spasm of pleasure realizing what he holds in his hand is nothing other than the sweet fruit of hard-won success. A specimen of the rare and almost extinct species - Denturus Vagabondus Terribilis.

He delicately extricates himself from the no-longer-sleeping Latino apologizing in the process and manages to catch the left side pocket of his Quiksilver surfer's shorts neatly on one of the latches of the man's suitcase, surgically removing it and ripping the seam cleanly out of one leg, from waist to hem. This leaves Nick looking like (at least from Nick's right) he's wearing a cutaway miniskirt over a jock strap. His balled up wet Kleenexes spill out onto the lap of the irritated Mr. Gonzalez as it moves up and down in agitated resentment. He picks most all the lumps of Kleenex up, and in a febrile daze puts the teeth and Kleenex back in his now-missing left pocket and thus, once again, distributes everything he had in his hand freely all over the floor of the bus.

Coughing and sniffling, he crawls up the aisle of the bus, banging into seats along the way, retrieving teeth and used Kleenex (until he realizes he's picking up more than his own wet tissue, he's picking up everybody's wet tissue, and he drops the whole soggy mess, all of it, behind a sleeping someone's seat and ventures on) and gratefully pulls himself off the floor as he reaches his own empty seat.

He hands the teeth over to Emma, who says "Tang u theahh" without moving her eyes from the window and he sees a familiar face with an enormous and fiercely mobile moustache, wearing a white cowboy hat glaring at him from two seats back. On the brim of his hat Nick sees a wad of used Kleenex. Nick doesn't say a thing. The moustache is involved in a set of something that looks like frowns that are particularly extravagant and Nick looks up the bus aisle to see what is causing this extraordinary display, but no, there's no one visible down the aisle. That just leaves Nick. Nick and his naked thighs.

Nick pulls and stretches his torn shorts back over his right leg and pulls them down as much as he can, bending over and bashing his head in the process, which also gives him a tremendous sinus headache, and an incredibly compelling need to blow his nose, which he starts to do, but realizes he has no Kleenex. So he stops in mid snuffle/blow.

Then he notices something, bent over in his seat as he is. Even Nick can now smell himself - after two days of riding his odor resembles a pile of greasy paper towels you'd find permanently pasted to the bottom of a garbage can and turning into black slime. His shirt and pants are still a bit greenish from the split pea soup Emma accidentally spilled all over him at lunch. He looks back up and the cowboy is shaking his head. If he were a cow, Nick has no doubt whatsoever, he'd be on a truck for the slaughterhouse and tri-tip steak within a week, if a certain someone on that bus had anything to say about it.

Nick snuffles and clears his throat and closes his eyes as the bus jerks in a final swing to the right and rolls to a finish. All movement stops. The front door opens, and surprisingly more than a few people unbend themselves preparatory to getting off. Holding his pants to his side, Nick moves to get out of Emma's way, he grabs his suitcase and backpack off the luggage rack, to change clothes, and tries to sit down again in another seat, but is instead bustled off by a herd of people texting and phoning and listening to music and finds himself standing outside the bus, wet and cold in a crowd of moist bus passengers as the driver yells out "Twenty minutes, twenty minutes break, everybody."

Nick coughs. He's too sick to think right now. Nick limps away from the bus, carrying his suitcase and backpack for no reason he can ascertain and steps out under the bright sodium vapor lamps of the Pirogue Truck Stop in the pre-dawn darkness of eastern Montana, just in time to get slammed in the face by a mountain-sized fist of nearly horizontal rain.

Acres of wet black pavement stretch around him. Far off, a temple made of pure, wholesome light and stacks of brightly-colored consumer goods beckons. The bus door behind him swings shut with pneumatic firmness, and Emma pulls him, Sherpa-like, on to the end of a line of bus riders trekking fitfully forward, heads-down, eyes half-shut, faces bent away from the wind and rain, in a frenzied shuffle towards a pair of wide, glass doors that open and close over and over again. Nick moves forward. He clears his throat. He coughs. One hand keeps his pants on, the other bounces his suitcase against his right knee. He follows the rainy outline of Emma and they both shamble onward towards the promise of heat and light.

9

The rain soaks through everything in a remarkably thorough, efficient manner. Nick can only hope some of the split pea soup has been dislodged from his clothes. Well, at least he'll be saving on laundry expenses. He hobbles behind Emma, who has made a dash for it, towards the convenience store side of the truck stop, still holding the left side of his pants closed and still clearing his throat as quietly as he can, but managing nevertheless, to sound like a poorly maintained lawn mower that absolutely refuses to start, no matter how many times and no matter how desperately you pull at the cord.

Emma's already inside. The cowboy pushes past him, heads inside, and then astonishingly, holds the first door open for Nick, then the second one also, as Nick damply squeezes past him, holding his breath so he doesn't bark and hack all over him. Nick looks up, then quickly looks down as he sees the pile of Kleenex flattened and now apparently glued to front rim of the cowboy's hat. It looks like a wet paper rose decoration now. At least that's what Nick's going to say if anybody asks Nick about it.

The counter clerk is staring straight ahead, which happens to be exactly where Nick is standing, to one side of the front door - either that, or the clerk is staring directly at Nick. One of the two. Nick holds his breath, trying not to hack and choke, but blue in the face from lack of oxygen, he ends up drawing in a long, whistling breath, and exhaling barking like a dog. The clerk observes him. He is, apparently strangely fascinated by the inventive sounds Nick is capable of.

Nick looks up and over at the cowboy again as Nick barks and whistles. Expressionless, without any moustache motion at all, the cowboy nods at him, with something like a smile this time, and makes a bowlegged beeline for the men's room in the back as Nick breathes out a whispery "thanks" which starts as gratitude and ends up as a magnificent honk. By the time he can yell out "thanks" in a cracked, ten-pack-a-day smoker's voice the Marlboro Man has turned the corner. And he's gone. It's only Nick and clerk now, alone in the front of the store. The clerk is watching him, like he's waiting for Nick's second act to start. Nick looks at the clerk. The clerk watches Nick. Nick feels he has to break the moment somehow.

"Men's room?" says Nick, raising his eyebrows in question. The clerk nods his silent assent.

"In the back?" The clerk pauses, sticks out his lower lip, thinks about it, and helpfully nods again.

"Uh, then, thanks."

"I, I guess I'll just be going."

"Now, that is."

"Uh, yeah, well... thanks."

Nick steps out of the puddle he's created and limps across the vast inner spaces of the truck stop, feeling the clerk's eyes on his back the whole way. One hand faithfully holding his pants up, he quickly maneuvers his way through the store and around the corner and walks right into the rear end of someone who stands in a long line of men that trails down a wide hallway. A face turns to look at him. It's the cowboy.

It's quiet. No one's talking. Nick waits a long time. They move slowly forward in the line until it's just Nick and the cowboy by the men's room door. Why don't they have more than one restroom? Or maybe they do. Nick starts looking around to see if there's another likely spot for a room with a urinal to be placed. That's when Emma finds him. But it's the cowboy's voice Nick hears first.

"You lived in Laramie, I bet, back in '99."

The cowboy has turned around and is looking Nick square in the face. Nick looks at the cowboy in dismay.

"Uh…"

"Sure you did. I remember you now. Sure. Your name is Nick. Or should I say Nicholas? You were awful picky about your name back then. I remember that clear as day. Nicholas."

"Uh. Uh. Uh." Nick is drawing a complete blank. He went his first semester of college at the University of Wyoming – that much is true – in Laramie - which had been a complete disaster – a D minus average and a waste of a couple of thousand dollars he'd saved up, lost and couldn't really have afforded to lose - he'd gone back home to Missouri and licked his wounds and went to Community College there and started all over again. The problem was, he'd come out of the closet that fall and discovered he really did like men, and miraculously men liked him and suddenly he was going out with males of every sort, left and right, in a blurred and energetic dating frenzy that left his academic life fading in importance to non-existence.

Nick was thinking all this with his mouth swinging open as the cowboy grabbed his right hand and started pumping it in a friendly and familiar way. One of the fingers on his right hand has a solid looking silver ring with something blue on it.

"Hey it's Frank – well Frankie back then – Franklin Xavier Carlson. How the hell ya' been Nick? Whatch' you been up to?"

Nick stares. But remembers to close his mouth.

"Yeah, had to quit and run the ranch when my pa died. Must be ten years now, maybe more."

Nick is trying to think of something to say.

"Damn, it's good to see you. Wait, it looks like it's my turn at bat."

The bathroom door's just swung open, and Frank, nodding and shaking Nick's hand is sucked inside – there's a lot of water running and a lot of talking going on and Nick can see it's a busy place for 3 in the A.M. Nick can see for a few seconds that there are a few men milling about, drying their hands, washing their faces, shaving - a row of stalls stretching off to the right, sinks are lined up to the left, urinals are on a far wall. All are occupied – there's a lot of marines, Gonzalez's , and Catholic Minnesotan senior citizens in there – in fact most of the male population of the bus seems to be present, including the bus driver. As the door closes, Nick sees one stall door in the back cracked open and he can see Frank forcing his way through the crowd to get over there. Then the door is closed, and it's suddenly quiet. Nick feels someone next to him.

He'd completely forgotten about Emma. She is holding his suitcase. Nick realizes with a kind of intestinal force – a gut punch really - that he is falling apart at the seams in more ways than one. He must have left it by the front door. What is happening to him?

"Thank you for finding my babies, Nickie. I knew you'd get them." She rewards him with a smile, and a radiant arc of brilliant dentition illuminates both their faces for a moment. And you know, when Emma smiles, she really smiles, a way deep down inside smile. She's got a nice smile, a great smile even. Nick smiles back. He's glad to help. He guesses he's been glad all these past two days to be helping Emma. He truly has.

"I was thinking you'd need some dry clothes. The bus driver says it looks like you're getting off here. Is that so? I thought you bought a ticket going clean through, all the way to Seattle. Just like me. That's what I thought. So this is it?"

"Well, no, Emma, no." Nick feels like he's falling, like he's falling over a cliff. "No, Emma, it's not that, of course I'm going, I was just…", then Nick freezes – mouth open, arm hanging in mid-air, eyes looking at some fascinating spot on a distant, invisible horizon – and realizes he *is* falling and he's about to hit the ground hard.

"Nickie, you O.K. honey? You feeling all right?"

Nick tugs and pulls at his back pocket, on the side that's not ripped (which is actually very difficult to do without pulling his shorts off at the same time - Emma eventually helps him hold down on his sopping pants leg as he yanks upwards on his pocket) and he brings out his wallet, and unfolds a very yellow, very worn piece of paper – wide-lined, written in sloppy black ink (Nick can still remember it being written, the big hand, the silver ring with the hunk of turquoise embedded in it). The paper is so threadbare it almost comes apart in his hands.

"Nickie?"

"Nickie?"

"Nickie, look here's my niece's number where I'll be staying in Seattle. Call me if you need anything, or well, you know. Thanks. Thanks so much. You be careful. You sound real sick. Lots of fluids. Stay warm. Get plenty of rest. Now you listen to your elders, hear? Take care of yourself."

Nick, holding the number in his hand starts to explain "No, Emma, I'm getting right back on…"

Just then Frank and another five men come barreling out and suddenly they're in a crowd, and Emma gives him a big hug and says "I really mean it - take care of yourself, I wished we'd had more time. Bye now, I mean, see you later" and Emma sniffs to herself (were those tears in her eyes?) as she steps back out of the crowd flowing out of the hallway.

Another four guys pile out and a maintenance guy with frizzy white hair comes out and hangs a chain across the men's door which says "Closed for cleaning" and Nick realizes he has to move and move quick. Frank shoots him a big, shit-eating grin as he presses something into his hand (it turns out to be a phone number) and walks backwards for half the hallway watching Nick, just watching him, letting the rest of the guys flow past him like floodwaters flowing around a rock in the river. Frank, the

Marlboro Man wordlessly mouths "Wooeee" and then he flips forward, turns the corner and he's gone.

Emma's somehow disappeared as well. Nick looks to the left, to the left, to the right, sees he's alone now, and ducks under the chain, hitting the door with his shoulder, kicking his suitcase into and through the opening door as it swings wide. He pounces on it once he's inside, kicking the suitcase back and forth with the inside of his foot, like he was back in college and was on the 3rd string soccer team again, and pretends he's working a soccer ball down towards the goal.

10

There's a large stall with a sink in it in a far corner and he flies into it, strips, and goes to open his suitcase before he thinks to look at what's in his hand.

Then he remembers.

Nick used to call him Special FX. His own special Frank Xavier, his own personal Special Effects Department. Nick's own FX. Frank was called that by Nick and others because of his lightning quick soccer skills and his other useful nocturnal talents Nick had discovered FX possessed. Frank was in a grad program in Chemistry, and he used to write poetry to the blond, blue-eyed irresponsible Freshman who was flunking out of the Intro to Chemistry course Frank was one of the teaching assistants of. Nick had seen Frank on campus and thought it was fate that he ended up in Frank's Discussion Section. Nick always sat in the front row. And Nick thought no one so handsome and so smart had ever treated him as kindly and as patiently as Frank was treating him that winter. And you know what? That was probably about right. No one ever had.

And maybe no one ever did, even later on. There was a week or two before Christmas break that Nick didn't even make it back to the dorms, spending all his days and nights at FX's room soaking up as much Frank as was humanly possible. Then the bottom fell away underneath him, he failed all his courses, he panicked, and he dropped out and ran away from Wyoming, too scared and too ashamed to tell FX he was leaving or why. He just left. And that was that.

Sitting on the toilet lid on top of a pile of tissue paper, Nick pulls the paper carefully apart. All you can read is the last square of rubbed-out pulp. It practically falls apart in his hands. But this part, the end bits, Nick already knows it all by heart anyway, so he picks out the letters easily in the dim light.

> Impatient, laughing boy
> walks on,
> me watching
> him carrying
> his parts in joy,
> him leaving
> me following,
> I once was free
> I walked alone
> until I saw
> the laughing boy
> who never sees
> who never waits
> for me

Nick feels like he has something in his eyes – he can't see very well all of a sudden. Then his face is wet. And he hears someone crying. Nick thinks of that foolish young man, of all the love he wasted, of all the chances he let slip through his fingers, of all the people whose lives he flowed in and out of, here for a moment then gone, like he'd never been there in the first place. He really has become the invisible man. He is the man that never was.

He closes his eyes, bends forward and the toilet automatically flushes. He sighs, leans up, forgets, leans forward and it flushes again. This happens maybe four or five times before he realizes his feet are getting sopping wet. He opens his eyes to see brownish water flowing out under his legs, spurting and dripping and spreading onto his suitcase and clothes stacked on top with his wallet, which he jabs forcefully with his heel to get out of the way and pulls up both his sandaled feet up on top of the dry lid. His suitcase with the clothes on it flies under the stall, down the hallway and crashes into the trash can by the men's room door. The lid of the garbage can falls off and bounces like a basketball before coming to rest in front of the sinks. The men's room door flies open. He can see the janitor down on one knee looking under the stalls.

"Is Closed. Quien esta?. Who there? Closed. Closed."

A second later there's some scuffling and then curses in Spanish and then more scuffling and silence. When Nick jumps off the toilet and peers out his door of the stall, the garbage can is gone. So is his suitcase. And his clothes. And his wallet. Nude, tiptoeing ungracefully in his Birkenstocks, holding his mangled poetry between two fingers of his right hand, he makes for the door, hears a noise, ducks in another stall, and stubs his toe in the process, slamming the door, and jumping up and standing on the toilet in his new stall. Silence. Nick has to come up with a plan.

Forty minutes later, he's still there, sitting now, when the manager, leading the janitor and his bucket and his mop back into the bathroom, comes in with a baseball bat yelling for whoever's in there to come the hell out.

Why do these things always happen to him?

11

Much, much later, he's trying to convince the State Trooper that he's actually pretty harmless - the janitor and the manager scowling in the background - when the trooper suddenly takes a call, cuts Nick off in mid-sentence and jogs directly for the door. He looks over his shoulder as he hurries out saying "No more trouble out of you, all right? Do we have an understanding?" He doesn't wait for an answer. Then Nick is alone with the angry truck stop employees.

It's not until he's showered, laundered, and begged and paid his way onto another bus (using up almost all the rest of his money) going to Salt Lake City the next morning that he sees all the police cars and fire trucks by the bridge. It's a couple of miles out of town. Along the Yellowstone River. Nick sees a bus upside down in the water, and he looks away. He keeps the poem. He keeps Emma's number and FX's number, but he never calls them. He doesn't want to know. He doesn't want to know anything.

Nick arrives, not in Seattle, but in San Francisco on Tuesday, June 12th around 4:30 p.m. and, well, you know the rest - John, married life, and now his dying brother in the Ozarks.

12

And how about Nick today?

Seven years later, and helping out his sick brother, and feeling lost and alone and afraid?

Well, his brother will either get better, or he won't. The important thing actually, is Nick is getting to spend more time with him now than he has ever since they were kids. And that's time that can never be taken away from either of them, since it's love freely given and love freely received. Love is permanent. It's indelible. It always is. And really - let's be honest - for the time being, there *are* worse places for Nick to be than in Iron County, Missouri getting to know his family all over again, getting to know himself all over again, maybe getting to know himself and his family better this time around than he's ever known them before. There are much worse places.

And how about he and John Chin (his ex who is in Taiwan)? Well, they will either get together again or they won't. Either way, John will be fine. Either way Nick will be fine. Both Nick and John are safe. They always have been. They always will be. Nick has to decide to believe this - although it will be true whether he believes it or not. Because, no matter how much he doesn't want to believe it, Nick is a magical being. He is much, much larger than the sum of his parts. Much, much, much larger.

He knows it. Or he should know it. Because someone close to him once told him. And it's true of us all.

He is the one who carries his parts in joy.

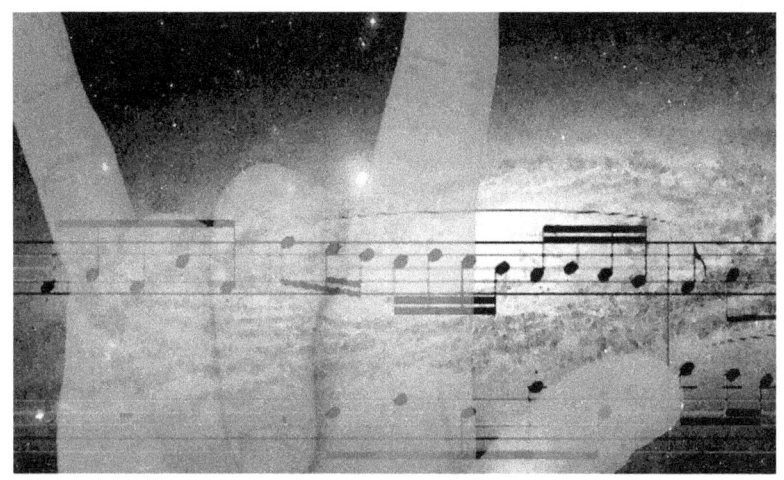

TWO PART INVENTION
(SKAG AND TAG)

1

The window is open. Tom jumps through it. Easily. Naturally.

"Tag!"

What else was a ninja supposed to do?

"Tag! Tag! I know you hear me Tag! You best hope... just hope and pray mom finds you before I do. Tag!"

Armed with fluorescent (orange) sneakers expensively engineered in 21st century waffles based on fractals, sporting his secret smile - the smallest of upturns at the extreme edges of two teenage lips - he executes a perfect 3 point landing (2 feet and a fist) as he slams with a satisfying thud onto dew-spattered lawn, slides, rolls and watches his shadow stretching effortlessly across the front yard - the sun just barely rising - a black edged hulk of a

Tag snapping smartly up against the fence by the street.

Bam! And Ka Pow! And Double Wham! Just like that. He's out. That's how you do it. That's how it's done. He strikes a martial arts pose - a boy-pile of aggressive right angles and compressed muscles, watches his enormous shadow crisply mimicking his young healthy limbs - dappled black stripes falling across a long rectangle of tender iridescent stalks of grass - his family's front yard. And he does a second pose. And a third. Then it starts to get boring. The air gets hotter. His shadow gets shorter. He's still fifty feet tall, at least. Another morning has begun in the life of Tag otherwise known as Tom.

Yup, just like that. Just. Like. That. The sun feels good on his dew-wet arms, it ignites his soaked sneakers into bonfires of red and yellow. He blazes in the morning light and moves his shadow out over the street, punching out cars, trucks, beating down an entire row of trees with a flick of his wrist.

"Tag! Running just makes it worse. You know it, Tag! Tag, where are you?" Tom hears his sister stomping towards the front door.

He slips soundlessly - how else could a ninja slip? - under the hydrangea bush he's just broken, crushed, and pretty much demolished in his recent devious tumbling escape. He holds up a squashed flower and it dawns on him. Fuck! Mom's gonna go ballistic on his ass. Fuck. Fuck. Fuck.

Tom likes cursing. He does it often. He just started this summer and he thinks he's getting good at it. Fuck. And Fuck. And fuck and fuck and fuck.

Ninja cursing. No sound. You do it under your breath.

Unseen. Unheard. Unknown. His sister, helpless. Unsuspecting. How could she know he'd choose such a rapidly executed exit path? He smiles, a wider smile, a smile built for an appreciative audience. He's practicing the smile he'll be using on his friend Calvin and the gang, - later - when Tom beats the pants off them with his brand-new Mark IVXXX joystick - won't they be crazy mad to go up against a Triple X, and Tom the first of them to get one - they'll be hating life at their usual all-day Saturday marathon session of *Antares Troopers* today. His own future awesomeness leaves Tom grinning glassy-eyed at the undersides of some flopping and broken Hydrangea leaves.

But no time for smiling. Ninja's don't smile. They fight, right?

Yeah, no smile, just fight. Even when he tells his buds the Tale of the Open Window Leap Into Nothingness there will be no smiling, not on Tom's face. His will be a blank, unreadable mask - except, of course, for the unconcealable flashes of savvy and cunning deep, deep in his wise warrior eyes.

That's when he notices the smell.

He's just discovered where Dingo - their Irish Setter - has located his new favorite doggy-outhouse area. Tom had been wondering why the yard looked so clean lately. It sure as shit wasn't Tom doing the cleaning, even with Dingo being his dog and Tom being the responsible party, per the parents. Tom's not going to be very popular with Dad. Tom sniffs, squints, sticks out his tongue and gags. He's covered. He's a human litter box. Or whatever the Irish Setter version of a litter box would be.

He hears a door opening and closing, but reacts in a very un-ninja-like way - he rapidly smells various parts of his body, working from top to bottom, hoping some odd piece of Tom has managed to escape unsmeared with Dingo - and soon figures out simultaneously that 1) he's going to have to strip off and burn all his clothes before he goes back into the house, and 2) that someone's standing directly in front of him.

Why Tom looks up, just in time to see the baseball begin the process of mashing one of his eyes into blue and white jelly - well - he doesn't ever quite figure that one out.

2

Typical. So typical.

Bad Juju. Bad karma. Bad reflexes. Just plain bad shit.

The next few seconds seem to hover in front of him, forever, for months, years in fact, when Tom thinks back on it, one-eyed.

The first thing Tom remembers about the baseball, in fact the only thing Tom remembers about it at all has absolutely nothing to do with baseballs. It has to do with fingers. And hands. He feels one (a hand), a hand that isn't there just as the baseball hits. And the hand's pushing down on his cowlick and not un-gently brushing his mop of brown-blond hair from left to right, left to right, touching him exactly the way a dog would want to be touched. He's being petted. And he likes it. It's peaceful. He'd be wagging his tail if he had one. Then everything goes black. That's it. That's all he remembers. One second he had two eyes, the next second he barely had one. Maybe not remembering isn't such a bad thing. Maybe it was good thing. The hand was nice though.

3

Typical. Typical Tom luck. Yet again.

You know, it's always Tom's (bad) luck to be the astonished but excellent eyewitness (pun intended) to the unceasing, obscure and unusual parade of trials and troubles which has been Tom's life more and more, as of late.

Even Tom's friends admit Tom's life has been hard. Very hard. And Tom agrees. Hard and rough and undeserved. In his case, even a ninja would have been instantly granted permission by his master to bitch and moan as much as he deemed ninja-necessary. Tom has it bad. Real bad.

The misfortunes of his young life continuously and wondrously unfold before his amazed, unbelieving eyes. He usually glimpses the next set of disasters just as they are in the process of being gathered together and pressed into some kind of painful shape. Then he gets to watch as they're thrown at him. With unstoppable force. And supernatural accuracy.

Like, for instance, just as an example, say - right now, like right this minute.

But Tom accepts all that. Injustice. Torture. Pointy, spiky karma. Military grade fists of fate impacting unprotected parts of his bruised, long-suffering body. He accepted it - thoroughly - a long, long time ago. He's mature for his age. He can see that's just the way it is. He's a human shit target. Some people are. Some people aren't. He is.

But he doesn't have to like it, does he?

4

He almost has time to be caught in a mid-yell, detonating a mighty obscenity at the approaching ball. But... no... again Tom gets no chance for that. No chance to utter a single lonely cry up to the inequitable cosmos as his ninja-hood speedily evaporates and Tom is successively stunned, felled, and immobilized. Tom gets hit accurately and he gets hit hard and he gets hit fast. It takes a second for his brain to reboot.

"What the hell? What the fuck? He tosses his head back, looks upward, screams and bellows at the universe but as usual, he gets no response. "What the fuck do I do to keep on deserving this? What?"

He scans the yard for the enemy, his sister obviously, tenses for a second attack, but he really can't see. Well at least not very well. It's all a pinkish mist. An insane pressure grows and grows on the left side of his head. And what's that smell? Then it all comes back to him. Well, most of it, anyways.

"Fuck, no. I don't deserve this." he howls, answering himself (because no one else ever does - answer him that is - he'd learned that sad, sad fact of life a long time ago too - Tom's had a tough life, if you ask him, not that anyone in his family ever would dream of doing that - asking him about his life that is - but still, it hasn't been pretty, not at all). Inside his skull, a kind of screaming pain recoils off the back of his braincase and bounces several painful times, spreading outwards into an impressive blossoming migraine. Strangely, at the last minute, the pain wave abruptly swerves, sharply turns to the left, and heads arrow-straight towards one of his eyes.

"Fuck, no" says Tom softly (speaking loud hurts too much), feeling something odd - a fly, or some kind of insect with a tail bouncing or some twig thing, wet and sticky, flopping on the left side of his face. His stomach starts doing Olympic-caliber gymnastic flip-flops. Nasty liquids churn. He can taste his breakfast making its raw, acidic way back up his throat. He's hot, he's weak, he feels himself falling backwards.

He tries to say "No" again, but it comes out a barking moan. Red-hot pain slams into him with a sucker punch, not to his rib cage, but to his skull and topples him into the smells of fresh-cut grass and shit and something wet and metallic and wrong. Tom sinks beneath clouds of gnats and mosquitoes rising in the cool of dawn and can't believe it's all happening again. The bad shit. It just never stops. Never.

He's writhing on the lawn screaming "fuck" and "shit" hoping someone, anyone notices the asymmetricallity of one eyeball in and one eyeball out of a guy's eye sockets. With one hand Tom gropes and feels for the baseball now lying at his feet and as he finds it, cuts himself on something triangular wedged deep into a seam on the ball, something sharp that slices effectively and neatly into one of his fingers.

"What the fuck?"

His left hand is sloppy - glopped with stuff that's wet and sticky, most of it coming off of his face. His heart starts beating fast - really fast - so fast it feels to Tom that it's trying to jump straight out of his chest - so fast in its desperation, that it's trying to explode right out of him onto the bright chlorophyll green (and hemoglobin red) recently trimmed square of his family's front yard. Tom slaps one hand across his left pec to keep his heart inside his body where it belongs. He's never felt anything like that. A machine gun under his ribcage. Panting, he pushes himself up with one shaky elbow, tries to stand, but only succeeds in rolling himself back over onto his back. He feels tears running down his face. It stings like crazy.

He can't see. He holds, no, pushes his left eye back into his face, turns over, throws up (adding more colors to the front lawn), and jerks himself to his feet, starts stumbling for the front screen door, shuffles off in the wrong direction, and promptly falls right over a stopped lawn mower (his own fault, lawn mowing is his chore, but let's face it - everything's always Tom's fault - everything - his Dad fucking yells at Tom, not his sister, whenever anything is left out in the yard and not in the garage or the house or the shed or wherever the hell it belongs - every single fucking time - always Tom, Tom, Tom - always). He steps away from the mower, slips on the grass because, now, his right hand also is blood and glop-covered, pulls and pushes himself onto one knee cutting his other hand on the top of the mower in the process, and starts his stumble forward again. He's not sure where he knows where he's going. But he sure knows he needs to move.

Everything's foggy. A wrong kind of fog. Pink. Painful He can barely make out that a house is in front of him now - he sees a house-shape melting and re-forming and melting again - he hopes it's his house - but it's difficult to see with only a single eye still reluctantly registering photons for the benefit of his optic nerves. That and the blood continuously flowing into over his eyebrows onto his eyeball. He throws up again, but it's just dry heaves. He crawls. Then he starts retching all over again. This time it takes a while to calm his stomach down, and after it's over Tom's up and running. Running and blind and sprinting as fast as he can for the front door and yelling the whole while - Fuck, Shit, Help - somebody's got to notice him. Somebody's got to hear him. Somebody. Anybody.

The white porch steps rise in front of him way too quickly, and way too steeply, and he misses the first one rebounding off the railing, sliding, leaving long dark smears of red on stair treads and banisters. He's more cautious with the next four steps, but still misses half of them. He hopes the screen door isn't locked.

Yelling "fuck" and "shit" doesn't seem to be bringing any help. He tries screaming "Mom" and "Dad" as alternatives. He'll do anything at this point.

He makes it to the door. Both hands being red gory masses he leaves a lot of scarlet handprints. Especially on the door handle. Which is locked. Fuck! He continues to call out "Mom" forgets to call out "Dad" and slides to the porch floor and drips puddles in a bright primary color on the floor of the porch in front of the door.

He passes out, wakes up, passes out again. This goes on for forever. At least longer than Tom can recall.

And his mind starts racing - in accidental, miscellaneous directions - all at once - all the time. Tom can't sit up. Tom can't see. Tom throws up again.

He falls over. Wakes up. Falls over. He pounds one and then the other bloody fist on the porch, on the door, on his thigh, tries to stay conscious. He keeps pushing at his squishy left eye with the fist he's not pounding with. He keeps yelling. He keeps throwing up. He keeps trying. None of this is really getting him anywhere.

5

Tom hears a voice.

"Should have seen this coming, fuckhead."

"Should have been prepared, Tommy."

"Should have fucking been thinking ahead, boy."

Even Tom, even in his present delirium, realizes that this is his voice-of-Dad-in-his-head talking. And the voice is talking nonsense. And the familiar pressure of mind-numbing Tom-guilt and Tom-worthlessness is expanding yet again into every empty space, corner and hiding place in his head. And he's getting angrier and angrier. And he can feel his pulse throb-throb-throbbing, rhythmically, harder and harder, under his skull. And, in fact, his whole head's bursting into flame now - it's all on fire, and he can't stop it and he can't stop listening, and the wrath of Dad beats down upon him, flattening him into sullen silence, helpless fear and the sure knowledge that he will be a fuck-up and a disappointment to his entire family now and always and nothing he can do in the future will change that ever - and it's all the same old garbage, all of it, the same shit, once again, one more time, exactly the same and he's tired of it and he wants it because it makes him feel wanted and he loves it because it makes him feel loved - at least loved a little at least for the moment at least he has this because you need anything you can get when the little you're getting is all you've got.

Dad-voice is not helping. Obviously. He never does. Dad-voice is getting him nowhere fast. All the usual bad shit. But the voice is reasonable and inflexible, just like Tom, who is a lot like his Dad, and it refuses to let Tom speak and refuses to make sense and refuses to shut up.

In fact, it won't shut up. Ever. At least not without a decent fight. All you can do, sometimes, all you can do is sit and listen and try and wait it out. Just like living with his father. Just like it. You've got to sit and take it. Just sit. And take it. And wait. Nothing else works. It's all you can do. That's it. No other choice. No other options. Dead-end street, buddy. Dead-end. Dad wins. Dad always wins. Always.

Always.

So that's what Tom does. Sits it out. Sort of a ninja silence. A ninja quiet. As he makes this decision, the voice rolls on, thundering right on top of him, then right over him, hammering each word into his bleeding face.

"What in the fuck where you thinking Tommy?"

"Where was your head?"

"When will you ever grow up?"

Tom falls back, hits his head on the porch swing, which swings up and back and promptly bashes his head again in the same place it hit the first time. Bash. Swing. Bash. Swing. Bash. It continues to do this repeatedly for several minutes. It should be bothering Tom a lot. He hardly notices it. The sounds his father makes go on and on and on.

6

The voice babbles and rages and rants, mixing it up at times (just to make it interesting) with sly, dangerous, slippery logic that starts in love and ends in rejection which Tom can almost follow but doesn't. Tom responds by breathing in and out slowly, in and out, in and out, and he takes the moments of silence between Dad-explosions to try and figure some of this shit out for himself. Just like Dad wants. So here goes. Here's Tom thinking for himself.

So, Tom, what just happened to you?

Obviously, in retrospect, it was pre-planned. A well-executed sibling ambush. And maybe people who live their lives backwards, in a hind-sighted world, would have been ready for it, Dad. Maybe they would've successfully ducked and recoiled and rolled, and well, who knows what else (caught the ball?) in the millisecond they would have had to choose an action or reaction. Maybe, Dad, maybe.

Who knows what wonders this hypothetical *prepared person* might have been capable of performing had they been in Tom's situation? Who could guess what sensations, what marvels the world would have witnessed from them? It's just too bad you don't have a son that performs like that, Dad. Just fucking too bad. Too bad you ended up with shit for a son. Too bad you ended up with shit-for-brains Tom for a worthless son.

What, tell me, what would an excellent, an ideal Tom have done, Dad?

What exactly, Dad? What?

Wait, don't tell me. It's coming.

I've got it. I've got it. Just a second... Just a second...

Almost have it.

There.

Big surprise. The drum roll please.

Perfection.

That's it, isn't it Dad?

You wanted perfection, didn't you? Didn't you?

The possibilities of perfection overwhelm, shock, and amaze in Tom's family. Perfection is a powerful force, here. It is an awful force. Awful in its uncompromising, immutable, fucking certainty of itself. Awful in its punishments for the weak-willed and short-sighted. Awful in its consequences for the imperfect (read: Tom). Just fucking awful.

Yes, Dad. I can see it. Total perfection. It's out there. Just like you say, just beyond my reach. I know, I just need to try. To try a little harder. Reach out a little further. Just a little. Grasp. Strain. Push. Reach up and out and stretch as far as I can, extend myself towards it, and, yes, I will certainly feel my fingertips touching the soft, even, straight edges of purity and excellence and health. The shape and the edges of truth itself. I know, Dad, I know. If I try. I'll feel it.

I know Dad.

I know.

His vision is getting fuzzier. The pink mist is going kind of gray and shadowy. The edges of the shadows have rainbows on them. Like solar eclipses. No, like halos. Next he'll be seeing unicorns. Or fairies. Or God.

The swing hits him again. This has got to stop. Sometime. Doesn't it? The sun shines right into his one remaining eye. Tom can't tell if he's still yelling anything out or not. He can't really tell if his throat is working. Or if he's silent. Or if he's dying. Or if he's dreaming this whole thing.

7

Perfection.

It rings like a bell in Tom's head. Bong. Bong. Bong.

Tom's got a headache now like you wouldn't believe. The mother and the father of all headaches. He bites his lower lip so hard it starts to bleed too. Bong. Bong. Bong. The swing bangs away at him - trying to remind him of something. Bong. Bong. Bong.

It's not a well-known fact, but perfection hurts. Hurts like a motherfucker. You never told me perfection hurt so much, Dad. You should have told me. You should have.

Tom's dad is a maniac about getting things perfect, a maniac about doing things right the first time. No mistakes. His dad says - it (perfection) takes up a lot of time on the front end. It doesn't just happen. It takes planning. It takes work. Work, work, and more work. Did Tom mention that it takes work? That's what his Dad says. Work. Lots of it. Work, Tommy work.

And willpower - that's also what his Dad says. Willpower, Tommy, willpower. And a lot of it. Lots. And often. Constantly in fact. Applied and used daily. If not hourly. Willpower, Tommy, willpower.

Willpower. Perfection. Truth. Work. Bong. Bong. Bong.

Tom's head rolls to one side and bangs against the side of the house as he flops over. The swing's vicious jabs slow down, get smaller, weaker, eventually come to a stop. Nothing moves. Expectant silence settles on the porch.

8

Then his dad is standing right there in front of him. For some reason he can see his dad crisply, cleanly - he's a pen-and-ink drawing dad.

"But what the fuck is he doing?"

Dad's looking away and holding a calculator and adding. Adding something up. Calculating and adding when he should be figuring. Dad should be figuring a way to get his son into an ambulance and then into a decent hospital and then (as quickly as possible) into an exceptional triage unit with a lot of experienced, underworked, and highly-motivated healthcare personnel.

Tom looks up but none of that is happening.

His dad's usual white accountant's shirt is a blazing arc-welder white this morning, excruciating to look at for longer than a few seconds and starched to the consistency of drywall. Tom's sure his Dad couldn't wrinkle if his life depended upon it right now. Stiff as a board doesn't even begin to describe him.

Tom can see his dad is nervous. But then, he's always nervous. Fidgety. Jumpy. High-strung is what people call him. Tom doesn't like it when he gets like that. Restless. Angry. Betrayed. Tom gets hit a lot when he looks like that. Especially when there's been a few six packs of beer in his dad's recent past. And that's most nights.

His dad looks seriously annoyed at Tom. Like Tom-being-all-summer-grounded annoyed. Like Tom-just-cost-the-family-a-lot-of-money annoyed. Like it was a lot of money they didn't have.

Like Tom really blew it this time. Bad.

Like Tom really, really fucked up.

Bad shit, bad shit. So... One more time... All together now, everybody, for old time's sake - what else is new?

His Dad suddenly notices his son at his feet. He doesn't bend down and pick him up in his arms. No. He doesn't offer a helping hand. Not for Tom. He just yells at him. Tom jumps at the sound of his voice, hitting his head yet another time on the side of the house, leaving a crimson Tom-head-stain by the front door and rebounding again off the porch swing. The swing maliciously comes swinging right back at Tom, but unbelievably misses him and shoots past Tom's one wide open eye, a half-inch from his bright red forehead. It crashes loudly into the side of the house and continues oscillating. Tom senses it dejectedly moving back and forth, slower and slower, somewhere off to the right in his blurred-out peripheral vision. He lets his head drop down onto his shoulder, then his chest, then lets it thump down onto the floor. He slumps the rest of his body onto splintery wood and goes boneless. It feels good. He's not falling down, no. He's blending into the horizontal. He's a ninja floorboard.

Tom's confused. Now why is it again, that Tom is lying on the peeling deck of their front porch? There has to be a reason. Why? Maybe if he wasn't getting majorly reamed by his chemically enhanced father he'd remember. Maybe if his fucking dad would finally shut the fuck up just for a second, well maybe then Tom could get a chance to think for a friggin' second. Or... maybe his dad will just tell him. Tell him why he's here. Maybe his dad knows why. C'mon, Dad. Hey! Drop me some hints. Give a guy a clue. Yeah. Right, Tommy boy. Right. That'd be the day.

"Tommy? You listening Tommy?"

Dad shrieks down at him, talking in a strange high voice.

"Tommy, you have to fucking decide to do something, life doesn't happen by itself. Tommy, when are you ever going to learn? You have to fucking do it yourself, boy. Tommy are you goddam listening to me? Because if you aren't so help me..."

Tommy tries to roll away from the voice. Fails. Tries again.

"Tommy? Boy? Look at me, Tommy. Look me in the eyes. You say you're so smart. Grow up. No one else can do it for you. You have to think. Think it through, all the way through. Life is decision. A long row of 'em, decisions, one after the other. All of them. Your decisions. Yours. You make them. Tommy? One after the other. One after the other after the other. For crying out loud, Tommy. Listen to me. You. Yourself. Decisions. Tommy. Decisions."

His dad leans in closer, yells louder, breathes heavier. All Tom can smell is sour alcohol stink and some old sweat and a sickly sweet odor he's never come across before. He's going to throw up. And it's going to be right in his father's face. Serve him right. His father's crying now. He can feel his dad's tears falling onto Tom's cheeks and neck. When is this going to stop?

"Don't you let them, Tommy. Don't you let them push you around. Like they did me. Listen. This is what you do. Fight. Fight for what's yours. I got fucked. But that's not going to happen to you. It better not, sure as shit it won't. You listening to me? You fight, Tommy. Decide to fight. You listening to me, Tommy? You even hearing a single fucking word that I'm fucking saying?"

"Tommy?"

"Tommy?"

Blah. Blah. Blah. Blah. Blah. Tom's heard all this before.

9

The next thing Tom knows, Dad jams a calculator into Tom's face, practically punches him in the nose and although Tom looks at it, expecting a huge number (his dad had done a lot of finger punching, bashing and poking on it since he'd been standing here yelling away at his bleeding son), but, no, it's not huge. In fact, it's tiny. You know, actually, there's only one lone figure flashing at him in a cool, phosphorescent green - it looks like a single number - maybe a number "1" - he can't tell for sure - no, it has to be a "1" - and for some reason he can't focus on it too well - but the figure keeps flashing at him, brighter and brighter, greener and greener, bigger and bigger and clearer and clearer and joyously phosphorescing with a reckless abandon as if its very life depended upon it and Tom can't take his eyes off of it. What a number! Yeah, definitely a "1". Definitivamente. El numero uno. At least he can see that. At least he can do one thing right. He can see the number "1". I see it Dad, I see it.

"That's all it takes, son. Just one, Tommy, one. Get it? Get it?"

Dad's bushy eyebrows are arcing upwards and downwards, upwards and downwards, in his are-you-getting-all-this-or-just-being-your-normal-wise-ass-know-it-all-ignorant-as-hell self?

The eyebrow twitching stops. Dad puts the calculator away in a pocket someplace. It can't be his shirt. His chest pocket's so starch-stiff it would never open up. It looks like it's painted on.

His Dad leans his face closer and closer to Tom's. Then even closer. In the end, Tom can count the nose hairs in each of his dad's nostrils.

"Tommy, boy, for God's sake, do something."

Dad leans even closer, loses his balance, falls on top of Tom, their heads bash together. But he never stops yelling, and well, passionate conviction in a person's voice cannot be ignored, especially when it's yelled directly into your ear, and originates from a powerful pair of lungs - and you now, his dad's pair of lungs and his dad's nuclear-powered voice really aren't the kind of lungs and aren't the kind of voice that you'd expect in an accountant. At least not what Tom would expect, but there it is. An accountant. And a voice. Omnipotent. Nuclear. Apocalyptic. More beery clouds of spit rain down on Tom, especially around his right ear.

"Listen, Tommy. Tommy? You listening? So you want fucking normal so much. What's the use of normal? Why settle for friggin' normal? Go for the gold. Go for perfect, Tommy. Tommy, look at me! Over here, buddy. Here. That's right. So, smart-ass, what's so wrong with perfect? Huh? What? You tell me. What? Tommy? What's so wrong about perfect? Tommy? What? You listening to me, Tommy? Tommy? Tommy?"

Over and over and over again. He can't hear this speech often enough. Bong. Bong. Bong. It's all just hurting his head.

"Tommy, do something. Say something, Tommy."

"Tommy?"

But Tom stays wisely silent. He won't talk. He won't be fooled into arguing with a crazy person. But he can think. So he thinks. He thinks to himself.

He thinks - what's so wrong with normal anyways? What's so wrong with being like everyone else and what's so wrong with blending in? What? Is average a sin? Is it sinful? That's what Tom wants to know. Is it? That's what Tom asks. No one likes to answer Tom's questions. No one in his family at least. No one. Tom is alone in his family. Tom is alone. Alone.

Suddenly Tom is done. He doesn't have to take this shit, even if it means he's going to get beat up again. And what difference would it make if he did get shoved around and punched and "corrected for his own good" some more? What more could happen to him? Why should he care? Why? I mean really. Just look at him. Really. Look at him and look at his family. Seriously man, how much more messed up, how much more beat up could one guy get? Not much, not fucking much, brother (Tom had heard that last line in a movie - he liked the old-timey gangster sound of it).

Tom looks up. He wants to ask his dad why he never, ever answers Tom's questions, why he never, ever even tries to listen to him, why he acts as if Tom can barely walk and talk at the same time (not expecting a real answer to any of these questions, obviously), and his Dad's gone.

Tom really is alone now. All alone.

Tom finds he's staring close-up at a an enormous blurry knot in an even bigger and blurrier two-by-four board. Intensely. And closely. Very closely. The board is just a half an inch or so from his right eye. And his face is stuck to it. For some reason. And he can't see anything on the left side of his face. For some reason. And it's an odd sensation. That and the feeling that someone is jamming a screwdriver into his forehead. It's all just... odd. And there's no reason for it.

What would a ninja do in a situation like this? With a dad like his? With a face glued to a floor?

10

He feels the hand again. It's smoothing back the hair off of his forehead. He relaxes a little. He lets himself melt into the hot, wet wood of the warm front porch and allows the hand and the floorboards to happen to him. To happen with him. To happen for him. The melting goes on, for some time. Tom continues to let it.

The hand pushes him gently down the stream of time. Gently. Down. Past the pain, past the anger, past the worthlessness into quiet backwaters. A place where Tom floats and spins in lazy circles. A place where all of life, the whole of his existence is a hand. And the brushing. And the stroking. Peace. Safety. Strength.

Beauty. Brushing. Stroking.

11

He hears a sighing sound, looks up, and his mom is standing there, hat on, silhouette bright and hazy against the promise-filled blue sky, washed in waves of color that run in streaks under the clean, even light. A watercolor under a faucet. She's here, but not for long. He can see that. She's fading. Rinsing right out of his life. In front of his very eyes. But at least right now, right this very minute, for Tom, she's here. In front of him. And she's shaking her head.

She has her straw sun hat on, the one that's frayed and falling apart, leaking twigs and chaff in a trail behind her, and she holds the broken rake with the uneven teeth and cracked handle that Tom always promises to fix for her but never does and she is shaking her head. She is looking down at him and frowning and shaking her head. But she's smiling at him too. She's here. She's right here. Tom makes the effort, tries to smile back up at her. He's not sure she can see his smile, but he does his best anyways.

She pushes her hat away from her eyes and he can see she's worrying about him. Sunburned and worrying about him. Her forehead is furrowed with deep mom-worry lines - a recently tilled field of misgivings and griefs and concerns spread all over the top of her face - and the sides and the bottom - all plowed, of course, by the strong iron blade called "The Trouble with Tommy."

Tom drifts.

Tom upsets his mom. Tom gets mad and slams doors and wants to be alone. That upsets her. He can see that. Anguish and confusion, that's what Tom brings her. Now, where's the old, sweet Tom? Her helper? Her little boy? Her only son? Tom doesn't even know where the old Tom went. All he knows is old Tom is gone. Old Tom has left the theater. As much as he wants his old life back, it's walled off someplace, locked up, key thrown away and forgotten. He's barreling headlong into an ongoing explosion - a map-less volcano-filled wilderness - no past, no future, no hope. No nothing. Just danger and loss. And no one gets that. No one. Not in this family. No one listens to Tom. No one.

And his mom says Tom doesn't listen. Hah! He doesn't listen? Tom doesn't do anything *but* listen, 24 hours a day, 7 days a week,

365 days a year. Tom's a listening guru. He's a listening machine.

But she says it anyways. She does. She says Tom doesn't listen and Tom doesn't concentrate. Apparently Tom doesn't even try very hard. Not anymore. He could. But he won't.

And Tom doesn't stick to anything, never sees anything all way through to the end. The smallest thing, she says, gets Tom bored and distracted and wandering off and looking for something new, somewhere new.

Tom is walking disaster, trouble and confusion, generally. For himself. For others. For everyone. Basically, Tom's a miserable disappointment.

And... well, Tom has to agree.

With some of it. At least. Maybe. Possibly. All right, probably.

Tom doesn't concentrate. He knows it, he can feel it. And less and less lately. All right, yes, sometimes it bothers Tom too. Sometimes. Well, a lot of times. Boys distract him constantly. They are endlessly fascinating to Tom now and he can't remember when it all started exactly and he's not sure he wants it to go on this way and he's not sure he wants it to stop. Wait, no, that's not true. He doesn't want it to stop. Or does he? Nothing makes sense anymore.

And Skag, his sister (her real name's Susanne, but just let Skag catch anyone using that Susanne name on her - and Ka Pow! man, Ka Pow! they sure as shit they'll be wishing they'd kept their mouth shut you can bet your life on that) - anyways, his sister Skag just closes her eyes and shakes her head when he talks to her about the growing, formerly useful space in his head where thoughts of men and all things male are pushing out practically every other thought he ever has. He constantly experiences flash floods of overwhelming lust scouring out the flatlands in his brain, leaving un-bridgeable canyons, un-crossable badlands, alarming floodplains littered with wild, unexplored emotions that nobody seems to want to hear about, ever. It's not comfortable, not inside Tom, not even a little, not anymore. But yeah, Skag doesn't want to hear about any of it. Nope. Never. They used to tell each other everything. They used to act like one person in two bodies. They used to be family. That's all past tense now.

It's gone.

Forgotten.

Mental distortion, that's the mildest thing Skag calls it- he's obviously developed some kind of blood clot. Possibly terminal.

He's deranged. There's got to be a pill he can take. Aspirin. Thin his blood some. Get him back some stability. Whatever. Something. Tom should do something. But don't talk about it. Tom should never talk about it. Shit. Shit. Shit.

But guys are so magnetic. The unexpected pulling. The wild head-snapping interest. It has him unhinged. He's a Tom-door flapping loose in hurricane winds, a Tom-house shaking right off its foundations. But Skag doesn't want to hear about any of that. She's not going to save his sorry ass from any lust-tornadoes destroying his life. No she isn't.

He doesn't talk about it. Not to anyone. Why talk if no one hears? And he definitely is not bringing the subject up with his dad. Let alone his mom.

Life has become increasingly non-verbal in the Tom family.

Generally on shoving open the back door, seeing either a mom or a dad hanging about, he directs his looks at the scuffed, hardwood floors, makes a beeline for his bedroom, closes his door tightly (and locks it if he can get away with it) and throws his gangly body in irritated, tumbling flight towards his unmade bed. Sometimes he hits it. And the male nudie magazines "hidden" under the mattress spill out in multicolored, irresistible profusion. So he has to gather them up and re-stuff them. Of course, first, he has to look at them to see that they're not ripped or torn up or something. Sometimes the looking part takes a couple of hours. You know, just to be sure. Sometimes he just has to double and triple check them.

And then, sometimes, he doesn't hit the bed. If it's a miss, he makes a refreshing loud boom that everyone in the house can hear as he bounces off the furniture or into the walls. It's a big noise. Clear as a bell. Always gets a reaction. It shows he exists. It shows he's home. It's just something he does.

His dad sure likes it. Notices it every time.

Loud ricocheting. Helps him feel better. Why doesn't anyone understand that?

You know, Tom didn't ask for any of this. You would think at least his mom would try and understand him. She was young once, right? She had to have been a teenager at one time. Whatever happened to sympathy? Whatever happened to walking in someone else's moccasins for a mile? What? She's his mom. She's required to be sympathetic. It's part of the mom job description. Isn't it? But no. Why is that?

Tom looks up and his Mom is gone too.

Tom is alone.

Everything's quiet.

Tom eventually sees something. A shape. An object.

He thinks he sees his mom's sun hat resting a few inches from his right eye. Why is he looking at it? And is it a hat? Is that straw? Or is it a piece of wood? Or..., what the hell is he looking at? Tom ponders this.

Well, he's pretty sure it's brown. Or brown-ish. Isn't it? But it could be anything. Anything at all. So hard to tell. Takes so much energy to look. So much energy. Too much. And now he's forgotten why he's looking. Again.

So.

What is he doing here?

12

Skag.

He starts thinking about Skag.

So, then there's his sister, his younger sister, well, really his only sister. You've met her already. Her name is sometimes Susanne, always Skag. And he's Tag. Skag and Tag.

So, O.K., it's his twin sister. And this sister, well, this is a person who is really good in the concentration department.

She's good at concentrating specifically on getting Tom not to concentrate. She gets him manic, psycho, disordered, depressive. She tortures him with amazingly complex and imaginative ploys. She schemes. That's what she does. Schemes and strategizes. And that's just for starters. She can get him worked up, calmed down, then wind him back up again in 60 seconds flat. Tom's a yoyo of stress and Skag can play him all day long. She can, and she has, and she will. Skag's a force of nature.

She's absolutely everywhere. And into everything. All his shit. But that's what little sisters are supposed to do, huh? Right? Apparently. That's the Little Sister job description. But what if they're only 15 minutes younger? Tom thinks it must have been a very critical 15 minutes. She's definitely the youngest, and she's definitely a pest, and he's definitely the oldest, and he's definitely a punching bag.

Wait. Wasn't she just standing right in front of him? Yeah, he remembers that. Sort of. Kind of.

And now she's run off. She's gone too. Where did she go? What did he do? Why is everyone disappearing? Why is the world abandoning Tom?

But there's no one to ask. Tom is alone.

13

Tom breathes in and out, in and out.

Each breath pushes his chest up and makes his head pound and makes him regret his need to use lungs to accomplish anything necessary or useful. Shit that hurts! Shit! Tom tries taking shallower breaths. The pain is less. But it punches him in the head more often. Tom never wins.

He closes his eyes. Or at least he thinks he does, it's hard to tell.

He can see his Dad's face floating above him. He can see his Mom reaching down to grab her hat. Now he can clearly see his mom's hand coming towards him. It's reaching, reaching.

Would a ninja just lie here and close his eyes and do nothing? Not even move his hand up towards his reaching mother?

No.

No a ninja wouldn't just lie there.

A ninja would try.

And no, Tom is no ninja.

In fact, Tom is nothing.

Tom is nothing at all.

Forget it mom. Stop. I'm just not worth it. Let me go.

He is a piece of work. His life is a piece of work. It's clear to Tom. Tom's fucked up. Majorly fucked up. Not worth it. He's worthless.

That he's fucked up makes him feel good in a fucked up kind of way. It makes so much sense in a senseless kind of way - even, no especially - to someone who's newly blind - physically, emotionally, every way-ly.

The hand that isn't there keeps smoothing his brow, brushing and rubbing quietness and hushful stillness into Tom's psyche through his hair - it's a spiritual hair-gel, a generous application of non-stop peace and restful contentment and Tom's grateful for the hand and grateful for the peace.

Really, he is.

He's in agony, but he's grateful and it's all so weird and then it's a new hand touching him, it's his mom's hand, and Tom's opening up one eye to peer up into his mom's shadowy arm blocking out piercing bright early morning sunlight.

He screams when she touches him.

14

The frantic ride to the Emergency Room in the old Volvo is silent. Almost. Skag is beating something rhythmically, obnoxiously, a little dismally. Tom doesn't look at her. Not much. Tom isn't making a sound. Well, some moaning, but that doesn't count. Blinded ninjas get to groan. It's allowed. A little. At first. If you really need to.

They are the both of them (Skag and Tag) in the back seat, belted in securely. Their mom is a little paranoid about car safety, although she seems to be driving a little jerkier than usual today - and she's not driving her usual slow-but-steady pace- in fact she's speeding for her - almost 5 miles over the speed limit. And it sounds like she's breathing funny up there in the front seat. Breathing funny - or maybe choking a little. Or maybe, crying?

Tom notices it, and it makes him even more angry and more scared. But not angry-scared only for him, for Tom. He's angry and scared for his mom. He hates hearing her this upset. Hates it. With every cell in his body. And she doesn't need this. She doesn't. Dad's drinking last night was hell enough. Now this? She doesn't deserve this. No. Tom is angry. He's angry and he knows who he should be angry at.

She did this. Skag did this. Skag.

Tom beams animosity towards her, he shoots his righteous outrage over, into, and on top of his sister's tall, slim, all-tendons-and-muscles body belted tightly into the seat next to his. He glares and glares and pushes the animosity intensity way past 10, way, way past it - he keeps on increasing it until it's right off the old animosity dial and approaching extreme hyper-animosity. He's that mad.

Skag, on the other hand, looks like everything around her is happening to someone else's family. She's not here. She's watching it all on a video. It's on the internet. And it's boring her.

She looks cool. Cool as a cucumber. Cool as a cucumber sitting on of mom's famous summer cucumber salads - one of Tom's favorite things. There is, actually a real cucumber salad, a salad, by the way, that is sitting, currently, un-eaten and forgotten in a bowl on the middle shelf of their ancient, wheezing fridge in an alcove in their patched-up but antiseptically clean kitchen. A salad, mind you, that is waiting to be placed on a picnic table in the back yard on mom's prized red and black checked laminated tablecloth. A salad created for a lunch that will never happen now. And look at Skag. Skag certainly doesn't care. Tom can tell. Lunch cancelled by diamond-sharp slashing baseballs. Skag is cool. Skag doesn't care. Skag isn't even here.

Tom looks at Skag. He doesn't look away anymore. He points repeatedly and wordlessly at his overly-bandaged eye, which is throbbing and pounding madly with each jarring thump of his rapidly beating heart, throbbing and pounding with each smash into the car door as they squeal around a corner, throbbing and pounding with each bump in the road as their mom flies over gutters and forgets to avoid potholes.

His head and eye are wrapped tight to his head round and round with masking tape which Tom is sure will rip the hair right off his scalp when they get around to cutting it off at the hospital. Tom is trying purposefully to glare efficiently and effectively at Skag with the other eye. The good eye. And he thinks he's having some success. He opens that eye wide, wide as he can, and stares balefully at his sister. He stares and he lets the blood soaking through the bandage drip down his cheek so she can see it. He stares, he drips, and he points. And then he does it some more.

However, Tom can see that there's not much reaction going on over there, way over on the other side of the back seat.

Skag is pounding her new, her favorite, long-awaited baseball mitt to break it in. She's waited 9 months for it. Which in adolescent-years could almost be a lifetime. Skag loves that mitt. Pound. Pound. Pound. Tom used his wood-burning set yesterday to write "Skag" in big block letters across the back strap for her. It had taken a while to get it right. Lots of practicing on some plywood scraps in the basement. Her eyes had practically glowed in the dark with beaming pleasure when he'd showed her the lettering late last night. Glowed. You could have read a book by the glow of them.

The lettering job had been very nice. Even Tom had to admit that - he'd done a good job. And no, it wasn't a perfect job, it wasn't. But someone might call it a close-to-perfect job. Tom might call it that. A ninja-quality job. And he'd say so, say so to anyone, given half the chance. He would. Look, people, look family - sometimes I can concentrate. Sometimes I can get it right. Just look. C'mon. Look.

He can see the glove with its lettering very clearly with his one good eye. He opens that eye wider. Skag continues in a very methodical and systematic way to condition her glove. Pound. Pound. Pound. She's oiled it down. It shimmers. It shines. It's getting softer. The hammering's driving Tom crazy. His eye hurts like hell. The sound of her fist hitting leather drives spikes of pain directly down what's left of his left eye straight through the eye socket and into his screaming headache. He can taste blood now, dripping over his lip and into his mouth. He doesn't try and wipe the blood off. Ninja he thinks - what would a ninja do? He blinks (they would at least be allowed that) and stares harder (he knows they would do that).

She peers at him sideways, once, twice - now she does it every time she punches her glove. She has no expression on her face. He continues pointing at his eye bandage and the blood continues dripping and his glowering irradiates the back seat of their mom's car - a nuclear spill of poisonous guilt and accusation and pain and Tom is surprised the entire rear portion of the car isn't glowing - pulsing and red and angry with sick Chernobyl-like luminosity.

And then Skag stops moving. Which causes Tom to pull back involuntarily deeper into his car seat for protection. He waits. He tenses. Waits some more. She looks dangerous. And strange. The skin of her face has a kind of a disturbing gleam to it.

Skag stops punching. She looks straight at him. He stares back, ready for anything. She freezes, looks at her glove, starts punching, stops, shakes her head, leans towards him and quietly drops the glove in his lap. She pushes it into his lap. She places it there and lets go. This is Skag giving the glove to him. Tom doesn't touch it, at first. He's shocked to his teenage, twin core.

Then she very gently touches his bandage. He can see she's

crying, or at least her eyes are shining in the dim back seat, it's hard to see with just one eye, and his eye is starting to water too, which hurts like hell. He blinks a couple of times, makes the pain worse, and now he can't see at all. He hears Skag take in a long shuddering breath.

He thinks he hears her exhale slowly. Then she holds her breath. Tom reaches over to touch her face and bends towards her, wiping his uncovered eye with his sleeve so he can get a good view of her and figure out what the heck is going on with her with the one good eye he's got left to work with. The car jerks slightly and he falls towards her.

Their mom is reaching back (having watched them in the rear-view mirror) starting to warn them to stop it, starting to yell in a strangled voice to stop fighting. That's when the delivery truck runs the red light and hits the driver's side door panel the way a pile driver pummels a massive tree trunk into sand and muck to make a foundation for a skyscraper. It's all over in seconds.

It feels like it takes hours and hours though. Tom remembers it all. He re-lives it all. For the rest of his life.

That's the first time (or is it now, maybe the second or third or fourth or fifth - he's not sure - he doesn't know - everything's all so fuzzy to him - nothing is clear - nothing) but knows he feels and remembers the feeling of someone running their fingers through his hair and brushing it back from his forehead and he wonders, as the car flips over and the sidewalk becomes the sky, then the ground, then the sky again, how they're doing the brushing and running thing with the masking tape bandages in his hair and all - the tape is so tangled up in his hair and he's wondering who's doing it and he's thinking about it because he doesn't want to think about what's going on right this minute and he can't see his sister and he can't see his mom anymore and whatever the fuck's going on outside the car window makes no sense to him no sense at all. A tree rapidly appears. It gets closer. And everything smells like dog shit. And the tree disappears as the car turns over, then it reappears, much, much nearer this time. Tom can clearly see every crevasse in the bark. And then its' right on top of him, and then it's dark. And then it's all black. Everything. He can't see a thing.

And he's not touching anyone. You know, he really can't even feel the car seat anymore. And there must be sounds, but actually he can't hear anyone anymore either. No, there's doesn't seem to be anybody around him. There's no one nearby. Nobody. No one. Tom's all alone.

Except for the fingers in his hair. And a perplexing feeling of quietness it brings to him. It shouldn't be so quiet. He shouldn't be petted. He shouldn't feel good. Not here. Not now. He can't remember why he shouldn't but something tells him it's not right to feel that way. But it's so peaceful. So soft. So settled. It's home. It's all right. It's O.K. And that's all he remembers of that.

15

The next time he feels it is a couple of weeks later. The forehead-brushing-back-the-hair thing. It should have scared the bejeesus out of Tom. However, Tom barely noticed. Not concentrating. As usual. But at least he has a reason this time.

It's night outside, but the stars aren't out yet, so maybe it's not really night yet.

It's the evening after the funeral, and there's so many people in the house, so many relatives staying over, so many self-appointed helpers and worriers and sympathetic somebodies rattling around them - suggesting, meddling, admonishing, advising, commiserating, the whole shebang - that except for loud whispers that end abruptly whenever the two of them enter a room, Tag and Skag find themselves invisible and forgotten. They're ghosts. In their own house. Living ghosts. They camp out now in their basement. A kind of hunter-gatherer existence. They're on their own. They take care of themselves. They're wild things. They're alone.

Alone, that is, except for the constant company of a malfunctioning flatscreen TV blasting away with French subtitles, stuck on a very political news channel from where? Argentina? Uruguay? They sit and sit and sit. Well, Skag lies down. On the floor. On something. Tom scrunches into a sleeping bag. Which is starting to smell. A sleeping bag which in turn drapes over the sofa, and then drapes over a wobbly coffee table with three legs. Tom rocks the table back and forth for hours and hours and stares squarely ahead of him. Maybe it's Peru they're watching, Tom thinks. Maybe it's the Philippines. Bangladesh? Singapore? Budapest? He can't remember how to change the channel. He'd have to search the basement for the remote. If the remote's even in the basement. If it hadn't been thrown away. If it had working batteries still. If it would even make the T.V. work anymore. That was one too many ifs for Tom. So Tom stares and stares. He stays stationary and anesthetized and scrunched.

Tom watches images form. They dissolve and re-form and nothing makes sense. It's a window into nothing. A sharp rectangle of nowhere. The TV makes no sense. Where is Tom? How did he get here? He just wants it to shut up. It mutters and curses, invoking who knows what demons, plagues, evils and horrors upon the unsuspecting watcher. It mutters, it talks to itself, filling the room with filth and garbage that keeps on piling up higher and higher and it never shuts up and Tom can hardly stand it. He knows he wants to scream. And he knows he doesn't want to move. That's all he knows.

Tom doesn't stop it. Skag won't even try to stop it. Neither of them really has been watching it. They've been not-watching it for hours and hours, for days and days. They just lie there and point their faces at it, not-watching.

No signs of life down here. The house above them has the sounds of life. Upstairs that is, life happens. But Tom knows it's a lie. It's all a lie. And downstairs there lives creeping horror and shame and death and decay. That's their life, their subterranean life. It's all around them, all the time, everywhere they look - or don't look. All this week. All last week. Or maybe it's been for 10 years now, the two of them and the basement neck-deep in the rot and the corruption and the trash. Or maybe it's been fifteen minutes. Tom can't tell anymore. Tom doesn't know anymore. Tom doesn't care anymore. He wants to scream. He wants to never move again.

It's all a lie. A lie. All of it. The house. Their dad. This family. A lie. The lying part used to make Tom sick. Now he doesn't know what it makes him feel. He doesn't know much at all to be honest. He's thinking through concrete. Not much moves, not much punches through a concrete mind. It stays pretty motionless, most of the time. No, all the time.

He adjusts his eye patch and looks over at Skag. His face is always itching now. Especially around his left eye. Scratching the constant itching and enduring the ensuing pain gives him something to do. It's an occupation of sorts. Watching and scratching. He rubs at his face, around his forehead. He rocks the table a little faster. He watches Skag for awhile.

Footsteps dart back and forth on the ceiling above their heads. They move on seemingly important and critical errands while muffled syllables bark and twitter above them in self-assured monotones. Skag eyeballs the half-window on the far wall of their basement and waits. Skag's lying on top of her zipped-closed sleeping bag in the cold and the damp, on the concrete floor, hands folded behind her head. She's squinting, mumbling softly to herself and watching the full moon rise behind some garbage cans.

The cans block a rectangle of dirty glass in the rusting window frame which opens up on their backyard driveway towards their neighbor's house. The yard through the glass - the tops of trees, the back fence - goes grayer and grayer - blanketed in the palest of neon lunar light. Skag watches and watches. Tom finally pulls his one-eyed gaze away from her and looks up at the dusty window to see what's the fuck's so damned interesting on the other side of that window. It takes a lot of mental effort to move. He wants there to be something exciting up there. A something that makes a guy feel something. He wants it.

But there's not anything. Actually, nothing's out there. Nothing at all. *Actually* most of their neighbor's house remains in deepest shadow. The moon's obviously not doing its job tonight. Tonight the darkness is winning. Winning easily. Tom wants the darkness to win. He follows the purplish-black bruises of night shadows growing. They stretch horribly across the sky, injuring the blue, making it hurt. They inflame the outside with vile greens and clotted dusky reds and Tom hates it and Tom loves it. It makes him breathe funny. But he still doesn't know what Skag is looking at.

Tom wraps himself deeper, sinking out of sight into his own sleeping bag, jamming himself into the couch - a couch upholstered in a pile of Skag's wrinkled and knotted clothes from two weeks ago (laundry his mom never got to fold). Tom watches Skag watching the not-bright moon not-correctly illuminating their red-black backyard. The T.V. babbles. Skag stares. Nothing happens. And then more nothing.

It's gets later. Occasionally someone cracks the basement door open above them and checks to see if they're asleep. They never are. But the checkers don't stop checking. The door is always quickly creaking open and not quietly closing again and the both of

them stay not asleep. Tom rubs his good eye, scratches around the
bad one, and pulls on the string holding the patch on his head and
lets it snap back viciously onto his head. He does it again and again.
Fuck, that hurts. He knows Skag can hear it, but she's ignoring him
now. Ignoring him all the time actually.

The pain feels right. It makes him feel alive. The eyepatch is
slick and sweaty over his bandages, and it doesn't smell so good
anymore. Like the sleeping bag. Like his clothes now. He should
wash it. He should. And the eye hole, where a healthy eye once
was, it throbs and throbs. Tom has a ghost eye now. A ghost eye
for a ghost son in a ghost family. All lost, all missing in action.
Holes where important somethings should be, but aren't.

Tom's buried under a black patch, and no one knows he's still
there, hiding somewhere around under the patch, blind in a new
kind of darkness, blind in a total kind of way that the still-living
can't understand. People (by people of course Tom means the
school counselor who happened to stop by when the two of them
failed to show up at school) say these kinds of thoughts aren't
going to help him, they won't bring him happiness or peace, they
won't make it any easier for Tom to get through all the shit that's
happening, they won't make it anything any better. Tom needs
some other way to cope. Some other method of getting through
each day. Some other life. That's what people say.

But these dark thoughts, they make Tom feel good in quirky,
twisted, painful ways. And at least they're his. They're his own
thoughts, his own pain. All his, all Tom's. It's Tom's new home - in
the dark and staying in the dark and living in the dark and hurting.
All Tom's, all his.

And Skag sure isn't with Tom now.

Tom's all alone.

To Skag, Tom's non-existent.

Tom's alone. He's alone.

Fuck. Fuck. Fuck. He gets no enjoyment now out of cursing. It
causes no emotions at all. That's so pathetic. He should at least be
guilty. Or something.

Tom is so lonely he could cry. And he does. In the dark.

The basement window is almost black now except for the
merest hint of reflected moonlight brushing the world with a filthy
coat of faint, fluorescent ash. Ashy light. It's a kind of obscenity.
No, it *is* an obscenity. Tom snaps his patch over and over and

curses, feels nothing, and waits for something to happen.

16

Then someone is standing right next to the basement stairs. They turn the doorknob three times. In a nervous kind of way. A hesitant kind of way. A high-strung, anxious kind of way. Only one person Tom knows would open a door like that.

It is his dad.

Tom looks up, Skag looks up. Tom could swear he sees Skag stiffen, strain to squeeze out of her bag which she'd zipped herself into, fly up, peel out, make a run for the stairs. But she doesn't. And the door doesn't open. The doorknob stops turning. Someone is being shushed, pulled, even dragged away from the door. There's a two second moment of complete quiet.

Then, suddenly, two or three heavy footfalls run at the door and there's a dragging sound. Then more feet. Then there's some shouting, some running, a violent thumping. A door slams. More doors slam all over the place. People move to the back of the house, then move to the front of the house, then back, then front, then here, then there, then back and forth and up and down and there's yelling and talking and odd laughter and crying and they hear their dad's voice yelling something, it sounds just like dad, it sounds like he's yelling "Skagtag", but it could've been anything. Anything at all. Or nothing. Probably that. Nothing. And all of this, all of this at once. And Tom watches Skag.

The whole while, all through it, Tom watches Skag closely. Skag's expression doesn't change. She's back to looking at that fucking window. She doesn't move a single fucking muscle, not a single fucking one. Tom decides he's not to going move a muscle either. Two can play at this game. But he doesn't look at the window. He looks at Skag.

Then they both hear the backfiring of the old red Ford truck, their dad's Ford, as it peels away, wheels spinning up the gravel and throwing out broken chunks of concrete against the house and against the dusty glass of the basement window, and the vehicle torpedoes down the alley, barely making it around the sharp turn at the corner, screeches, hits something (garbage cans? a fence?), stops, sputters, stalls, and roars to life again, thunders off uncertainly into the distance, into a very distant distance. They listen for it, they listen for a long, long time. It takes awhile, a long while, not to be able to hear its chugging, choking sounds as the motor spastically carries their dad very far away, as far from the two of them as it possibly can manage

Tom's never certain when he stops hearing its anemic puffing and growling. He hears it to this day. And there's the outcry, the moaning, the complaining and the shouting and more sounds of people running and more cars starting and more yelling and violent arguing, and this goes on for quite some time.

Skag doesn't say a thing. Tom would be crying but his eye hurts too much. Both eyes hurt now, the ghost one and the living one. Skag focuses on the window as if she's willing it to talk to her. Her eyes gleam, a wet and terrible sight, a wicked sheen that Tom can't find anything good to say about.

The Argentineans end their news with a flourish of trumpets and follow up with a loud and opinionated soap opera. The screen's filled with scantily clad females and men with enormous moustaches on mysterious errands. There's brilliant black eyes and arms and hands that do a lot of moving around and bodies that talk as much or more than voices. There's crying. There's hushed conversations, there's meaningful silences, there's eyebrow raisings. There's pointing and screaming and deceits and secrets and surprises and vengeances and to Tom it looks a lot like a South American version of his life right now. Too much like his life actually.

He's having trouble breathing again. Why is the universe showing this to him? What is he supposed to do with this? He snaps his eyepatch again. Ouch. Fuck. Then again. Shit. Ouch.

He looks over at the floor. By soap-opera-illumination he sees Skags eyes - closed now - that's never a good sign, never.

Tom holds his breath, no, he's not holding it. He can't breathe. He tries and tries but his chest has forgotten how to move upwards and downwards. It's on strike. It won't function. It's given up on him too. The TV rants and raves, oozing black emotion - disgorging raw, dripping, pooling toxic crud into this refrigerator of a basement and this burnt black cinder of an evening and these two empty people in front of it. Tom hits his chest with his fist over and over again. Still no breathing.

There's a flash of light, an actress woman screams, and

cascading guitar music drenches them, bursting out of nowhere and quickly filling the room floor to the ceiling with a solid volume of shrieking arpeggios. Skag jumps up with the speed of a tightly coiled mouse trap recently and lethally triggered (her normal velocity) and proceeds to kick the shit out of the TV - slamming into it with her foot the way pros cleanly propel a ball into the goal for a winning point in a World Cup Final. Tom can only stare in amazement.

He watches Skag neatly sever the fucking thing right off of the fucking wall. It's beautiful. In a scary kind of way. She does it with a perfectly executed, extremely violent swipe of the side of her right foot, jumping and twisting in mid-air, pushing off the wall with her left foot, landing perfectly back on both feet square in the middle of the basement floor. The T.V. hangs in place for a millisecond, then drops to the concrete below. Tom can only stare at the blank spot on the wall where once a T.V. was.

Then Tom's laughing and laughing and laughing. He doesn't know why he is, but he is. He tries to yell "Goal" but he can't, he tries to stop laughing and he can't and he starts gasping so hard he can't laugh anymore, so he just moans and rolls and moans in his sleeping bag, dismantling forever the broken three-legged coffee table in the process. Funny how his lungs suddenly started working again - too good as it turns out. He looks up, coughing and choking, eye streaming tears.

There's some sparks, but the woman's still screaming, the music's still climaxing and Skag's aiming her foot at the screen on the damp basement floor in the semi-darkness and kicking it again. The T.V. however is still going strong. It's a fighter. So Skag hits it hard, in the back. And hits it again. And again. And again. Tom laughs on and on, not because he likes the laughing but for some reason because he's required to laugh. Really, he's chortling now, and not very convincingly, and his chest and his eye are really hurting bad. He loses his eyepatch somewhere and the bandage on his eye flops over to one side and his empty eye socket wound is open to the air. But Tom can't stop. He won't stop. The laughing's a sickness. He's crying. He's shaking. He's holding his belly. His stomach muscles are cramping. His missing eye starts to bleed and seep again and Tom's ready, more than ready to stop, if someone would just let him.

After a few more kicks, and some significant stomping, finally, the tired flatscreen begins to fail. Trailing a long wire hanging out of a hole in the wall, Tom hears it die with shrill whines and grinding sighs - it speaks to Tom - despairing and groaning to itself at this - this, yet one more example in a long string of unending injustices meted out with violent regularity to a peace-loving silicon-based world that bears all this maltreatment, all this oppression with signal grace and patience. It groans that it must die, that it must do so in anguish and sorrow. It groans that its considered opinion still is, has been, and always will be that it is absolutely impossible to expect any honor, any respect or any compassion at all from carbon-based creatures at any time, or any place, and that anyone or anything that does expect compassion from them is a fool and an idiot and deserves whatever punishment they may receive at the hands of a such fickle, self-absorbed, sadistic and vicious beings.

And with that, with one more flash of light, with one more static-filled, electric moan, and one more eye-blinding fireworks display the T.V. lies at rest, at peace, fractured, silent and dark in the now pitch-black basement.

Tom knows just how the flatscreen felt. He couldn't agree with it more. The world and the people in it are just like that.

Yes, he agrees with it. With all of its accusations. With all its bitter discouragements. Yes, people can't be trusted. They are self-absorbed, pleasure-seeking, pieces of shit. The T.V.'s just learning that. The hard way. Well, at least it's getting to learn it sometime. That's important information to have, however painfully acquired. Tom ought to know. He's attending the same cosmic class.

The silence is a kind of permission - a permission to stop - and eventually, Tom's convulsions slow down. He's able to work his aching chest muscles again, for regular breathing purposes that is, but not with any real enthusiasm.

Sputtering fireworks and flashes bolt out of the defunct T.V. at random intervals. Skag cuts the wire to the wall with a broken piece of the T.V.s own casing. Then the T.V.s just junk - a lifeless pile of glass, plastic, wiring. It gets very quiet. Except for Tom's breathing.

Tom's worried. He exhales and inhales with the loud, muscular sound a whale makes when it breaches in mid-Pacific, maybe after being chased by a Japanese whaling factory ship all day, maybe with a harpoon hooked deep through its windpipe. His chest isn't working too well. His chest fucking hurts.

Footsteps upstairs. Then, quiet. Too much quiet. Too quickly. Skag's tense. Taut. Rigid as one of those braided wires holding up the Golden Gate bridge. You know, one of the really big motherfuckers. Rising and disappearing into the fog. Vibrating and singing in gale force winds. Tense. Poised. Ready. Immensely strong. And immobile. Not about to give. Not even a damned inch.

That's Skag. That's Skag all over.

Why can't Tom be like that. Tom holds his stomach, feels nauseous, struggles for more air. Tries not to think of dying whales and circling harpoon boats.

17

The door above them opens and Tom can see at the top of the stairs one of their many aunts from their mother's side (it must be Aunt Delphina, the one who lives in California) outlined in the light with her very circular outline, a pear-like outline, with big hair, plump hands resting on round hips and sturdy legs. Aunt Del stands there for a minute. Then she begins, cautiously and delicately, stepping down the rickety stairs one by one into a damp and smoky ozone smell of shorted-out electronics. She doesn't seem to like it. Who would? Part of Tom hopes she steps right through the rotten boards three steps from the bottom and breaks something. He holds his breath again. But something or someone warns Aunt Del to stop descending just before she reaches that danger point. Tom exhales quietly. Aunt Del stops and Aunt Del waits.

At first she's not sure that anyone is really there. Has everyone upstairs been pulling her leg? Then she hears Tom bouncing on the couch (trying to breathe), and she starts calling out to them.

To Tom it sounds like she's trying to round up some kindergartners. Tom hates her. Tom hates her voice. Tom hates her silhouette. Tom hates the smell of her perfume as it drifts down and settles heavily into his nostrils. He hates the light she let in when she opened the basement door. He wheezes his hatred out into the darkness and wishes the wheezing would make her go away. Make her disappear. Make her gone.

Skag is quiet as death.

"You down here, kids? You awake? Hello? Anyone here?"

Skag kicks the flatscreen one more time, precisely, flawlessly, brutally. It skids, no it flies across the stained concrete floor and explodes into piles of soggy books decomposing on the far side of the room.

"Well" says Aunt Del, "Well, well, well. I guess you're up."

Aunt Del's starts babbling. Babbling about how they will be living away from their dad for a while, just until everything settles down, but they only have room for one with her, for Tom to stay with her in Alameda (isn't that a pretty name for a town? - it's in California, kids, right across from San Francisco - right on the bay - the bay of San Francisco - it's famous - the bay - the city - you kids will love it).

Tom will stay with Aunt Delphina (herself), which isn't all that far from San Mateo where Susanne will be staying - with Aunt Bryony (that is, of course, the name of the city where their Aunt Bryony lives, right next to San Francisco too, real close, they'll see - it's all on the bay - on San Francisco Bay - Aunt Bry lives on a hill - you'll be able to see the whole bay from her house - you're so lucky), and when you think about it, it's all for the best and really it's only going to be for a short while, your dad just needs some time, some time to himself, it's all been so quick and all and everyone needs time to adjust, everyone does, absolutely everyone, and soon it will all be better, and you'll see, and everything will turn out for the best, you know it always does, and... and... and...

Del runs out of oxygen. She stops for a second, and holds her chest and gets her wind back. Where are those kids? Why is it so dark down here? It's like a tomb. So dark. So cold. So wet. It is. It's a grave. Del hits her chest with her right hand. Stop it, Del! Just stop it!

She'd promised her sister she'd help if anything happened. She'd promised Jasmine - her little Jazz - she'd promised her on their father's grave she'd make things right and so help her God, as long as Del had breath in her body, Del would keep that promise. Always. No matter what it took.

The earth by Jazz's grave this afternoon had smelled just like this. She hates this smell. Soggy, moldy, rotting. Oh, Jazz! Jazz! Erased. Dissolved. Her dear, sweet, youngest sister buried under rock and dirt and her, Del, the older one still walking about in the sun. It just wasn't right. It just wasn't.

And now tip-toeing down into a coal-black basement to bring

the ungrateful living, kicking and screaming, back up into the light. Well! These kids! These stairs! Oh, her poor sister. The cemetery. Oh Jazz! It was so cold. So wet. The grave was so deep and dark. And it's so dark down here. Oh Jazz! I don't know how I'm going to do this. I just don't know.

Del! Stop it! She has just got to stop. Got to. Stop thinking about herself. Stop it, Del! Stop! They need you. Do you know that? Do you realize that? These kids need you. Now do what's necessary and do it right away. Do it, Del! Do it!

Del takes a tentative breath or two, resting her hand on the none-too-steady railing which gives slightly every time she exhales. Comforting. Steps creaking. Staircase shaking. What a house this is! She'd best get back upstairs before the walls collapse in all around her. How had Jazz lived here? How had she gone up and down these stairs every day? How? Her dear sweet Jazz! How had she done it!

Hideous silence hangs in the darkness of the basement. Well, she might as well be talking to the walls. Or to the mice. Who knows? Maybe she is. Maybe she's chatting with rodents.

Del listens. Springs on a sofa squeak again. A soft series of coughs erupts, sounding muffled, from somewhere deep below her. It certainly sounds louder than what a mouse would sound like if it were having a coughing fit.

Those kids! Someone's got to get them before they run wild like stray dogs. Strays get shot. Think of the kids Del, think of the kids.

Although truth be told, the two of them weren't making it any easier on her, or her big sister Bry, that's for sure and no lie.

Still Del can't blame them, not really. Losing a mother is a terrible thing. Terrible. Too terrible for words. And the boy and his eye. And the way Jazz passed. It's all too much. Too much, too fast, too soon. She'd just been arguing with Jazz last week about how she was raising Susanne. Who lets a daughter run around with a name like a skin disease? Not Jazz's worry anymore, though, is it?

"Now, Jazz, honey, I'll try." Del closes her eyes and sends a kind thought upwards. "I'll do my best. You just watch me." From out of nowhere the sobbing starts again. Why she hadn't cried in at least a half an hour. But it happens all by itself now. Del waits for it to calm a bit - a momentary thunderstorm, a downpour, that's got to let up - that's all it is. But she's not fooling anyone. It's a few minutes before she can trust herself to open her eyes again. A little longer before she can speak.

18

Oh Jazz! Oh Jasmine!

The basement waits, glaring at her, rejecting her, willing her to leave.

Del starts to walk back up the stairs, but she's not really watching where she's stepping. She misses a step and sits down abruptly and stops, just stops right there in the darkness. Her cheeks are wet again and getting wetter, but she knows no one can see them or her or anything else in the midnight of this basement. Oh Jazz! When, Del wonders, when does the hurt start to get less? Sometimes she doesn't know if she can stand it.

Jazz. Such a good mother to Tom and Susanne. Del misses her, misses her something terrible. Jazz was always the heart of the family, the center of it all, the rock you could always lean on. What is Del going to do now? How is she going to make this right?

Now she's crying again in earnest. A real deluge, a real downpour. She better finish up here quick. She can't even see the stairs anymore. Oh lord! Can she even find her way back up? It's all a shadowy, watery blur. Before she can stop herself she's babbling again into the malevolence in the basement.

"And so... well, and so Skag can come with Aunt Bryony and stay in the old room Bryony made up when she bricked up her garage (you remember that illegal bedroom Uncle George built for her - you know, the one for her mother-in-law with the club foot, well, she passed years ago - but that's the room, it's nice and cozy). Well... anyways... Susanne's can stay there. And Alameda isn't so far from San Mateo. You'll see. You'll love it. It's only for a little while. You'll see. You can see the bay from there. From Bryony's house. Did I tell you that? It's on a hill. The town it's in is called San Mateo. Such a pretty name. I think I told you that already. Anyways, it will all be fine. Just fine. You'll see. Fine."

Aunt Delphina starts to explain how to get from San Mateo to Alameda over the San Mateo bridge but suddenly stops in mid-sentence. She just stops. No warning. Nothing. And her voice was starting to sound funny. Then Tom hears her carefully getting up in awkward silence and walking upstairs and even more carefully closing the door at the top.

Tom had tried to listen, he had, but none of it had made any sense. There was a lot of sounds coming out of Aunt Del, that was for sure, but Tom wasn't positive they were all in English. All Tom hears is Skag breathing out "Hell no." She does it about once every few seconds. No one else hears it. Who else was there to hear it? Maybe even Tom wasn't supposed to hear it.

There's a warm, buttery light coming from the kitchen, spraying out under the crack under the door at the top of the stairs. It feels like life. It feels like a beginning. And there's low voices. More whispering. One of the voices is Aunt Del's. Tom thinks maybe she was, maybe she was crying before, maybe, a few seconds ago, on the stairs. Somehow thinking that makes it even harder for him to breathe. He tries to think about what he and Skag are going to do next, but it's hard to concentrate. In his mind he sees a kitchen table and people around it talking and he wonders what they're talking about. Maybe he should go up and see. Maybe he should take Skag and go up and see what people are doing.

Tom snaps his eye patch, squeezes his eyes shut when the pain hits and sits in the dark listening to Skag muttering.

19

Skag's still saying "Hell, no" with a metronome-like regularity. But she's' getting louder and louder. Tom can pretty well guess what that means, and starts spastically unzipping himself back out of his sleeping bag (which is of course stuck and refuses to open) to prevent from happening, well, whatever the hell thing Skag is about to do to herself or to Tom or to the both of them. But Tom's already way, way too late. Just like always. Fucking Skag. Fucking, fucking Skag.

It's dark outside now. The moon has set. Within 60 seconds of Aunt Delphina latching the basement door behind her, Skag is running across the floor, vaulting up onto the wall, scrambling and squeezing out the window. The darkened window swings closed with a bang and shuts with violence - a permanent kind of locking-breaking-crash and Skag is missing. Vanished. Like the missing moon. She's moved out of Tom's life. She's gone and it's like she'd never even been his twin sister.

So.

What if he needed her? Did she ever think about that? What about Tom?

Skag has left him. Skag has left Tom on his own. Tom has to fend for himself. Tom is alone. Most definitely alone. Half of a matched set. A broken set now. Fucking, fucking Skag.

He snaps his eye patch up and down, up and down. It leaves marks on his head. Now the pain reminds him he's still trapped and he's here and he's stuck in what used to be his family's basement. Fuck. He even used to have a family. Or part of one. Until a few minutes ago.

He starts crying, a little at first, then a lot, then he can't control it and he stops breathing and he doesn't care that he stops breathing. In fact, not-breathing feels good. He hopes he never breathes again.

Then the petting. It starts. He feels the hand on his forehead, stroking his hair, pulling stray strands out of his eyes and out from behind his ears, pushing and patting and smoothing with sincere, persistent effort but little success. You know, he only remembers it years later. And even then, he's not quite sure it ever really happened. Not like that. Not at that moment. But he definitely notices that twisted sense of peace again. And the crying gets to be more normal crying, and he starts breathing, and eventually he gets very, very still. Very, very quiet.

Did it happen? Just like that? Did it happen that way? He's not sure. Then later, much later, he's very sure it happened that way. Exactly that way. But we'll get to that, we will. All in good time.

All he knows, right now, is that it's quiet. Calm. Peaceful. Everywhere. Inside and out. Inside and outside of the basement. Inside and outside of Tom.

20

Whoosh. Whoosh. Whoosh.

It's a few years later. Maybe more than a few years. And it happens again, the stroking of the hair thing. This time (the fourth time, the twenty-sixth time?) he doesn't feel it. Not the same way. It's different, somehow. The hand through the hair thing. The caressing acceptance. It's less... what? Definite? Convincing? What?

It could be the wind. Seems to be a lot of puffs of air and whooshing going on in the near vicinity of Tom. And yes, there's that sense of stillness, calmness, peace, but the stillness could just as easily be his recent, chronic numbness.

Whoosh.

Correction: no, it *is* numbness or rather, *more* than numbness. Tom would call it now a vastly satisfying emptiness, if anybody asked him (which nobody does). He feels, or rather doesn't feel, something on the other side, way on the other side, well past and beyond the borders of a mere quiet, a mere non-movement. It's pure, perfect numbness. Tom is, in fact, anesthetized. That's Tom's conclusion. His feelings are medically inert. He's stopped. Finished. If Tom were a movie, the credits would be rolling now. Tom is tired. Tom is through. Tom is done.

Whoosh.

He should be telling all this to Skag. Wait. Wait a fucking minute. Isn't Skag supposed to be nearby? He can't see her anymore. It's getting dark, and where the fuck is Skag? Where has she friggin' wandered off to?

He hears whooshing sounds in his ears all the time now. The hands, well he almost never feels (he thinks) the gentle hands, but the whooshing, that's a constant for him now. Maybe it's just the wind. Maybe it's just the cars. Maybe it's something or someone else. Blowing his hair. Whooshing his eardrums. Playing with his mind. Emptying his insides. Preparing him for something. For what he has no idea. But it's there. It's coming. And it's coming for him. It's arriving, very, very soon.

And... Whatever it is - it's far from perfect. It's imperfect. It's a corrupting empty - a nothing, an ambiguous, rotten, ending kind of thing. Tom knows it. It's coming for him. Yeah that's it, that's the whooshing sound. That's what's blowing through his greasy, unwashed hair right now.

Whoosh.

But... Still... He feels a hand is up there. He feels its quiet, its calm, its acceptance, its giving.

So, where the hell is Skag?

Whoosh. Whoosh. Whoosh.

Or...

Maybe the whooshing is the backwash from the street traffic (Tom's standing on an oily gravel shoulder) - the wake from a passing R.V. - or the heckling from another out-of-control teen-filled car like that Mustang last night that tried to run them down and sprayed them with beer. Or? Or what? Who knows what the whooshing is, what it means? Who could possibly ever figure out all this shit? Whooshing. Who would want to? Who would have the time? Who would even have the energy? Who cares?

Not Tom. That's for sure.

Whoosh. Whoosh.

It's annoying. You know, highways are breezy places. Always have been. Crazy windy and sometimes, no strike that, almost always dangerous places to stand next to. And they're kind of empty. Kind of like people in that respect. Lots of motion. Not a lot of meaning.

You know, there are people who die here. All the time. People die here. Tom said that to Skag earlier today but apparently Skag didn't hear him. She didn't even look at him. Typical. She's always doing something else, something more important, something always non-Tom related these days. No more Skag-Tag time. No more, not for Tom. And definitely no listening. Tom may as well be by himself.

Which he is, actually. Since Skag's upped and disappeared.

Whoosh. Whoosh.

Disappearing and dying - they're a lot alike in a way.

Similar, in a lot of ways. Tom feels a familiar pressure start up in his chest. It starts getting difficult to breathe.

Well, now, says Tom to himself, just a moment here. There's a thought. Death. That's definitely a thought. Tom's chest gets tighter and tighter. He should stop. Stop thinking about all this. But it feels good somehow - it's a kind of relief to him - it's a relaxing - a letting go - a final letting go - it seems to help - he wants it to help - he really wants it to help. His heart beats louder, faster, more insistent, compelling. His heart wants him to do something, to act, to move, he can feel its sickly longing for some kind of resolution, some kind of rest. Tom wants it too. He desperately wants it. He wants it now.

Abruptly, Tom feels emotions lurching into awkward motion, lets go, lets himself be carried off, off and away and along the long, dusky road he's been down so often and knows so very well. He bites his chapped lips, which promptly crack, open and bleed (the pain feels good, the raw, red taste in his mouth makes his heart beat even faster). He squints his one scratchy eye into the wind, which hurts like a motherfucker but he does it anyways. He frowns his taut and aching face - his cheeks billowing sails tightly-stretched by sunburn and windburn. He can feel his head pressurizing, expanding outwards in every direction, getting ready to pop. He's going to burst. He's going to explode. He wants to explode. The headache starts as usual.

He wants to scream. He never wants to talk again, just yell and yell. And he feels alive for once. Alive. He feels he occupies space again - just for this moment - space in the bigger, wider world. He feels he's here, right now, by this highway, in this place. Even if it's a pain-filled place, at least it's not empty anymore. Tom is in it. Tom is here. Tom is alive and he's here.

His cheeks are wet and dripping. He licks his lips and tastes iron and salt. Blood. And tears. Fuck! And he hates it, really hates it when he cries. Of course, thinking about that just makes him sadder and he feels more and he cries harder. His heart beats louder. His headache pumps his head to basketball size. His lips drip and bleed and the wind drops more cornea-scouring grit onto his remaining eyeball. Jesus Christ! What a shit-for-brains wimp he is! What an incredible loser! What a fucking, pathetic, worthless mess!

No wonder Skag took off.

Before his head can shatter into fragments Tom realizes something. There's an opportunity here. Now, Tommy boy, here's a solution, right smack-dab in front of him. Yeah, not much of a solution. Tom nods his enormous head admitting that. Not great. But still, (and Tom closes his good eye to concentrate harder, which grinds the pain-filled piles of grit growing in drifts on his eyeball deeper and deeper into the soft tissue - which all feels good, so good, he's alive, he's here) - there's a solution. A *kind* of solution at least. That's fine for Tom. Tom will take whatever he can get.

Tom leans forward. People die here. He tilts his head and chest farther over the shoulder out into the highway. These places are graves. He slides his body at an angle towards the traffic. Death happened to his family. He leans a little more. It happens all the time. He leans and leans, inch by inch, and his feet start to slip. He hears and feels thunderous pulsing in the pavement at his feet. More leaning. A massive diesel engine pounds his left eardrum into mush. He leans, finally loses his balance, tumbles forward and flies head-first, right towards a chuck hole and pitted, broken pavement and the approaching hiss of eighteen avenging fat tires roaring above him and below him and through him and he closes his eyes and falls and waits to hit the asphalt and waits for whatever else comes after.

21

Skag vigorously yanks Tom's shoulder, jabs her foot in the back of his heel and flips him violently and quietly and with what Tom thinks is awe-inspiring efficiency, off the shoulder, away from the highway and into tar-covered weeds on the steep down-slope by the side of the road.

He somersaults once, then twice and flops into a drainage culvert, face down, cutting his forehead and almost losing his old, mismatched, off-color and more than slightly frightening glass eye. Skag follows him down, beating at his head with her heavy backpack as he tumbles and rolls - not in an especially friendly way - just so he understands - effectively and completely - exactly what she thinks of him right this very minute.

"Were you really trying to walk in front of that truck, or are you just playing at being stupid?"

Tom picks himself up. His heart is pounding, but his headache is completely gone. He feels warm all over and soft inside - a marshmallow dipped in warm chocolate. It feels weird. It feels wonderful. Skag tries to glare at him, but ends up scrutinizing him with her twin's-X-ray-eyes - a thing she does in a kind of telepathic way when Tom's acting stranger than the usually strange way he acts. She sees right through him, of course. She always has. She always will. Tom gave up trying to fool her years ago.

She's biting her lip and her tongue at the same time and squinting at him, all over him, up and down. She's still hitting him. Then, she's frowning with her own red, tanned and sunburned face pressed close to his. Skag's contemplating. Trying to figure something out. Puzzling. Planning. Thinking. She's the thinker of the family. She finally does figure it out and stops squinting and stops slapping him. She gives him a hug instead. He feels tears in his eyes (Fuck! not again!) and turns his face away from her. But the hug feels good. Real good. She must have figured that one out right. She knows her Tag.

The hug pulls off his eye patch again so Tom readjusts the straps, uses that as an excuse to wipe his eyes dry, both of them (he really should get a new glass eye, one that doesn't scare small children, but they're so broke right now, so very extremely flat broke, that he doesn't even bring it up, doesn't even allow himself to think of it), brushes the thistly burrs off his socks and shirt and tries to find the shoe he lost in the ditch by the highway when Skag flipped him with her usual unbeatable skill. It takes a few minutes but he finds it. Skag is still staring at him from the top of the ditch. Hasn't moved an inch. And she's frowning again.

Tom makes an effort to stare back at her. He tries to frown. He manages a stare. But it's pointless to throw up a hard-assed attitude when you're still feeling somewhat warm and gloppy all over. Tom gives up. But by then Skag's not looking at him anymore. Guess the hugging is over, huh? Guess that was all the apology he was going to get tonight. Was he really expecting more? Yes. No. Maybe. His heart slows down. The fuzzy warmth fades. A more wintry numbness pokes its fingers into Tom. He sighs, a small sigh, to himself. His stomach cramps like it always does. His head feels heavier. He's a little dizzy, a little woozy. And scratched and dented. And he keeps losing his balance. He puts on the prodigal shoe and rejoins her (falling down a few times crawling up the slope to the shoulder of the highway) and wonders what in the fuck comes next.

When he looks up, after he scrambles to his feet, Skag's contemplating him again, one eye on him, one eye on the highway. She positions herself between him and the traffic. Tom stares back at her. The emptiness is back. It's much easier to stare. He can even frown now.

Except, the lights from the oncoming traffic make the staring at Skag a little difficult. Like maybe impossible. All the headlights are behind her. She's the image of a radioactive, multi-phasic creature vibrating with energy from another world (Tom likes to read science fiction). Or a blob of pure thought bobbing up and down in front of him made up of whole new spectrums of energies from totally new and unimaginable dimensions never seen before by Homo Sapiens. Or... Or... Tom runs out of ideas. She looks supernatural though.

Skag can see right through him. She sees him floundering and drowning and motionless and struggling and screaming all at the same time. Skag understands Tom is always in the past. Their past. Their land of the lost. Skag knows it. Tom knows it. And Tom is O.K. with it.

Skag, on the other hand, is tomorrow. She's the future. She's filled with hidden projects - plans and goals only to be revealed when they absolutely must be, plans revealed with as little detail as possible, and at the very last moment, and with precise and calculated timing. Skag is pure movement and purpose and forethought. Skag is the dawn. Skag is the ticket to a new day - the wild ride to that bright land of promise and safety and happily ever after their mom told them about, the place their mom said awaited each of them when they grew up. That's what Skag is - mom's hopes, alive and fighting and grabbing at life. Tom loves that about Skag. You know, he just plain loves Skag. He does. Has for the last 17 years. Which is to say, of course, his whole life.

Tom knows he'll find out the truth eventually. Why they came to this highway on this particular day. Why they're standing on this shoulder right this very minute. But he'll find out only when he needs to find out. Or rather, when Skag thinks he needs to find out. Which is actually (once again) O.K. by him. At this point in his young overly-eventful life, Tom's just a chip. A wood chip. A not-very-important, tiny flake of tree floating down a raging flash flood towards a very large, very loud, very final waterfall. He has one goal right now: try to stay on top and not sink to the bottom. Every day he wakes up (alive) is one more day of victory for Tom.

All that other stuff - perfection, concentration, truth, blah, blah, blah. He doesn't even think of that shit anymore. Just makes your head seize up and your lungs stop working. Just a lot of pain there. A lot of suffering. And for what? No point. Why do it? Why?

And why in the fuck did he used to worry himself sick about all that shit, anyways? Why? What did he fucking want? What? What did he need? Something. Something about his dad. Something from his dad. Well, yeah. Shit. For sure. Fuck. They hadn't fucking heard from him in years, had they? Tom can't even remember that friggin' far back. Couldn't remember fucking far enough back to remember his fucking dad talking to him. Shit. Barely remember his face now. All in the past. All ancient history. All finished. Old. Forgotten. The places they used to live - ruins. Words they used to speak - a dead language. Dead. Gone. Forgotten. Why Tom can't even fucking remember when...

Skag is touching him on his arm. Not even hitting him. He looks up and over at her, his eye open wide, not seeing her, his mouth silently working at words. He's breathing in short gasps.

"You O.K., Taggers?" She waits. Waits some more. She doesn't move until he starts speaking.

"Yes, Skag, I'm O.K., hunky dory, in the very pinkest of health, a veritable credit to my twin-ness, my twin-osity, fine - more than fine - fine and dandy."

Skag just stares at him. Then she giggles (she never lets anyone else except Tom hear her giggle). And keeps on giggling. He shakes his head. Tries to look severe. Tries to hold it in. Eventually they're both laughing so hard they're begging each other to stop.

Tom's got his headache back in full force. The numbness too. And he feels alive, just a little, and without all the twisted tightening in his chest and without the bittersweet aching. He tries to get his breathing back to normal.

Skag looks away for a bit, Then Skag looks back at him and puts her serious face on - she calls it her "game face" - he calls it her "bar-fight" face.

"We gotta stick together on this Tag. We gotta." She stares some more. She waits. She bites her lip. He finds himself biting his own without meaning to.

You know, she waits for him. She always waits for him. When he's coming back from his dark places. O.K., if she's waiting, he'll come back. He will. Right now. O.K. All right. He kind of shakes himself all over - slaps himself mentally a couple of times, tries to pull himself together and get his scattered thoughts marching in one direction. For her. It's really hard. But he'll try to for Skag. His Skag. He concentrates.

Then Tag nods - a little slowly, and with a little difficulty, not due to his pride so much - God knows he doesn't have a lot of that, but because his neck hurts like a sonofabitch from his recent dive into the gully and the weeds and his thorough backpack beating. It hurts, but he nods. He nods so she can see it. Plainly. A very plain nod.

Skag blinks once to acknowledge the acceptance of the nod. That signals it's a solidly accepted plain nod. A solid blink followed by a solid nod. A contract has just been made. And you know what? Tom has no idea what the contract is he's just agreed to. But he knows he's going to do it. Whatever it is. He's in. Like Flynn. They're both still biting they're lips. She keeps her eyes glued on Tag's pupils.

"Now Tag." She's using her explaining-to-a-toddler-Tag-voice. "Just stay with me Tag. You hear me? You listening, bro? Stay with me. We gotta get outta here. Now." She sticks her thumb out again at the oncoming traffic, but keeps one eye on him still. She looks at approaching traffic, looks at Tag, looks at approaching traffic, looks at Tag. Skag is a very careful person.

Tag watches. Watches and waits. But he doesn't try and wander in front of vehicles any more. Apparently, he's part of a much bigger plan now.

22

Tom pumps numbness through his veins. It's a part of his blood. It's easy. And it works.

He doesn't feel much. Really, he hasn't felt much of anything for months. He's the amazing hollow man. Boy. Man-boy. Whatever. Who knows what he's capable of right now? No moral compass. No morals to speak of really. And he's letting Skag do all the steering at the moment. Skag's driving his life. But then again Skag knows how to drive.

He and Skag are standing by another interstate. In the middle of nowhere. Tom doesn't even know the name of the highway they're standing next to. He doesn't even know the state. All he knows is there are a lot of hills around heres about. More than was absolutely necessary in Tom's opinion. And the big trucks trundling by, they trundle at a snails' pace. The two of them stand on the crest of a serious upgrade. They need a ride.

So. Skag and Tom are standing next to the trucks, and well the trucks, they're having to take it a tad slow if they want to see the top of the pass here without burning some vital engine part out on the way up. Which is probably the reason why Skag chose this place, which is probably the reason why Skag is jerking her thumb out at the trucks and simultaneously waving something at Tom's nose.

She's doing it purposefully on his left side - the blind side (he knows she's doing it on purpose) so he can't see what's moving back and forth in front of his face. She knows that Tom knows that Skag knows that Tom hates it when Skag does that. She's good at complicated, well-thought-out twin-torturing. It's a gift she has.

Tom smiles at her, watches nervously (as she waves whatever-it-is at him), just making sure no passing car/truck pulls off into the shoulder and turns them both into puddles of bright red splattered intestines on the pristine gravel by the this freshly-paved roadside shoulder. Pristine that is, except for the glitter of broken beer bottles, cigarette wrappers and crushed aluminum thingamabobs scattered tastefully around them. Tom observes them faithfully every time a sweeping flash of blue-white headlights illuminates the two of them with God-like power for half a minute. There's even a decaying mattress and unidentifiable textiles in the ditch in the long grass beside them turning into weed mulch and topsoil. Pretty.

Tom figures it must be past midnight. Or even later. It's getting a little cold.

No one stops.

They sleep under some bushes that night and start up again at daybreak.

23

Another night. A couple of days later. Different highway.

Did Tom mention that Skag is on the run?. Which means Tom is on the run too? Maybe that's pretty obvious by now.

A month or so ago they'd been safely if not happily ensconced at Aunt Del's and Aunt Bry's. For over three years, actually. Then, quick as a lightning strike, Skag corners Tom, gets Tom upset, browbeats him, pleads, threatens and gets him in the end to run off with her after school one Friday night. That was a couple of weeks ago.

Then, a few days ago, Tom's scared shitless (well, maybe not shitless, just nervous as hell) when - from out of nowhere - Skag waves multiple rolls of twenties wrapped in frayed and rotting rubber bands in front of his face. He figures out what they are when she finally decides to wave them on the right side of his face where he can see them. Shit. He wishes she'd kept them to herself. It makes him edgy. It makes his stomach hurt. So, of course, Skag makes a point to wave them at him at random intervals, just when he's not expecting it.

But where the fuck did all that money come from?

All Tom can think about as she weaves them in patterns of greenish blurriness in front of his one good eye is - what happens when the rubber bands break and there's a tornado of folding money blowing onto the windshields of passing cars causing a legendary pile-up on this un-named road. What happens? They get arrested, that's what happens. Skag of course is not thinking of that at all.

Where did she get all that money? And how? The rolls of twenties had to come from somewhere - and it wasn't her allowance from Aunt Bry, or her part-time job at the auto repair shop.

And it doesn't happen of course - the breaking, the tornado, the interstate pile-up. Things like that don't happen to Skag. Skag is lucky. She is luck incarnate. She's the goddess of good fortune and barely-squeaking-by.

But Skag wont' tell him where or how or why the money's there. All she'll tell Tom is that they're running away. Starting over. Together. And this is how they're doing it.

Tom accepts it. As usual, what choice does he have? She's his sister. And she's the one with all the luck.

Later that night, at a seedy truck stop motel Skag admits someone will be looking for all that cash, and they're going to have to find a way to pay it back at some point and they better start watching their backs. Tom sits and listens and thinks and to Skag's whole spiel and decides he is unsurprised. He's not being asked to make a decision. It's not really his decision to make. He's in it for the long haul. He's along for the ride. Wherever that takes him. So he's not, you see. He's not surprised.

"But what choice did we have, really, huh? Tag? Huh? Really? When did we ever get a choice?"

Tom mulls this over as he falls asleep to the gentle snoring of Skag which resembles the down-throttling of screaming air-brakes, brakes on concrete trucks negotiating particularly vicious downgrades, maybe somewhere high in the Himalayas. It sounds a lot like the traffic on the interstate right outside their one boarded-shut motel window, and the other cracked and partially boarded window in their hotel door.

Tom doesn't get much sleep. Not because of the snoring (he's used to to that), but because of the certainty of painful death in both their near futures represented by the lumpy rolls of what he assumes are unmarked, much-laundered drug money resting under both their pillows. It's a long night for Tom. There are a lot of breaking and entering sounds outside the thin glass of their one surviving motel door window. He keeps seeing the room's doorknob turning and stopping, turning and stopping while suspicious footsteps crunch back and forth on the gravel parking lot pacing outside by their room. Back and forth, back and forth. All night long. He memorizes every crack in the ceiling and every stain on the walls. By morning he's a mess.

Dawn brightens the torn curtains of their little bungalow without Tom ever having closed his eyes once. Skag claims she'd heard him snoring half the night - that Tom kept her up - that Tom was the proverbial log when it came to the sleeping department. But Tom doesn't believe a word of it.

He's dead-tired. Skag is not. Skag is beaming at him and bouncing about the room and enjoying the morning of a person who has slept the sleep of the innocent and the unworried and the perpetually lucky.

Unfortunately, that's not a sleep Tom is awfully familiar with.

24

The Aunts (Delphine and Bryony) find them six days later, two states away. Or rather the police do. It's a lot less dramatic than Tom expected. They're treated like six-year-old runaways. Aunt Bryony keeps dragging Tom around by his ears - she wants to kick him, she wants to put him away in Juvenile Hall and erase him from their lives, it's all his fault, corrupting his sister, committing who knows what crimes. Aunt Bry all the while hugs and kisses Skag - tells her not to worry, not to cry, Aunt Bry will make it all right.

Aunt Del lets Aunt Bry wind down some before she jumps in.

Skag somehow finds a way to hide the money. Tom doesn't ask how, or where, or when. Neither does anyone else. And Skag doesn't offer to tell.

Aunt Del winds up just shaking her head a lot and sighing and frowning at Tom and Skag, at both of them, in a way that seems very disappointed. But she also seems frightened and bewildered and at the same time filled with a kind of biblical prophet's displeasure. She looks like she wants to turn both of them into pillars of salt. Or feed them to bears. Or commit them to a mental institution. Or give them both a couple of hours worth of hugs and kisses and sit down and have long talks together. Aunt Del has very complicated looks.

Tom watches Skag grinning when she thinks Aunt Bry isn't looking, crying when she feels Aunt Bry's gaze settling in her direction. Aunt Bry (Tom is sure of this) thinks Skag is scared, inconsolable, weeping because she has such an infamous juvenile delinquent for a brother. Aunt Del, well, Tom doesn't know what to think of her. Aunt Del observes all - sees all - says not a word - but you can see nothing is escaping those vigilant eyes of hers and there's a lot of figuring going on behind those suspicious, sad, calculating irises. Skag is no mystery to Auntie Del, no she isn't. And neither is Tom.

As hard as it is for Skag not to laugh, she has no problem forcing Tom to swear never, ever to tell about the existence of the rolls of unmarked twenty dollar bills. She's a maniac about secrecy. Twin's secrecy. She's a lot like Dad. Full of secrets. Tom's not going to cross her. Besides it being too dangerous, it's just not something that would occur to Tom to do. Tom loves Skag. He does. It is the one constant in his young life. Skag is the blazing center, the heart of him. He'd be the first to admit it. And, as he's said before, Skag is Tom's future. The future he was promised. The future he's going to get whether he likes it or not.

He swears never to talk about the money - a thing which frankly is not a difficult thing to swear to - who was he going to tell anyways? And why? Tom will learn who and why soon enough. Either Skag or The Future or the men wearing ski masks who will show up and kill them will tell Tom. Or not. You know, sometimes you just get shot. Or stabbed. And you don't get told. It happens.

Still, Tom's willing to wait. He's been through worse. He'll live. For the time being. He will.

25

Sometimes Tom's future doesn't look exactly bright, or even well-illuminated - but Tom doesn't know that - not yet. The unclarity of the future, well, sometimes that's a blessing to be sure. Not knowing - it's a great gift - given to most of us, many times, over and over again in our lives. It can save a lot of wear and tear on a person, not seeing the future too clearly.

And (again, for most of us, and for Tom) the present isn't all that well-lit either. Yet another blessing. We live in the present, surrounded by invisible blessings, invisibly given, wrapped around us tight as twine tied around a package. They're holding us, carrying us, keeping us going - keeping us safe for ourselves and from ourselves as we stumble forward through semi-darkness moving, hoping and believing we're pushing on in something approximating the right direction.

It's hard to see them sometimes. The blessings. The unearned gifts the Universe showers down on your head and shoulders. You have to know where, and when, and how, to look for them. Sometimes they're small and cleverly hidden. That takes some work and some prying to get them loose so you can see them. Sometimes they're so big they aren't visible because they're taking up all the space around you and they're right in front of you, and underneath you, and on top of you - all at the same time. You need some perspective to see those. That takes time too. Hindsight's always a big help - and Tom's found that out already - although he doesn't exactly realize it yet - in seeing, really seeing your uncovered blessings.

So, sometimes the blessings are easy to see. Sometimes not. And sometimes, you just don't want to see them. But they're there, working for you, 24 hours a day, whether you choose to acknowledge them or not. Blessings are funny that way.

The important thing about blessings - something Tom is learning right now - is that they're free. Absolutely. No strings attached. Freely given help from the Universe - a kind of love you can take to the bank. Every day.

Well.

So much for blessings and Tom and the Universe. Tom feels he has a lot more pressing things to think about than Gifts From Above as he makes his way back, well, to where? Home maybe? Aunt Del? A penitentiary? Somewhere. He wonders how he's going to jump-start his life yet again, when the inevitable S.W.A.T team-ambush-kidnap-maneuver Skag is planning for Tag and Skag (he's sure she's doing it) is going to go down. How long will this brief pause of family peace last? Just how is Skag going to hijack his entire life again, and do it with her usual spectacular sense of drama and inventiveness and...

Well, you get the idea. It's a lot to think about when you're handcuffed, and becoming an accessory to a crime, and agreeing to your own future death by violence and being mauled by your very own aunt in a very public manner in front of very unamused police.

26

It turns out the aunts offer to take them both back. No Juvenile Hall. No jail. No Reform School. At least this time. Second chances all around.

Tom says yes. Tom's used to taking whatever is given to him. What else can/could/would he do? Skag is giving him meaningful keep-it-secret-just-you-wait-be-ready glances. What other choices does he have? She's his sister. He has to have a place to live, doesn't he? Aunt Del actually loves him. It's a no-brainer to Tom.

So. In plain light of day, on the morning they are found, Tom takes his second chance and goes back to Del and Alameda in Del's old VW van.

Skag doesn't even think twice. She and Bry are in a station wagon and on the road for San Mateo in 12 minutes flat. Skag knows which side her bread is buttered on. Aunt Bry, on the other hand (Tom thinks) is in for a wild ride in the near future, even wilder than the one she' been on up till now. He'd hint about it to Aunt Bry if she ever asked him. But she never does. Too bad for Aunt Bry.

And you know, it really is true - as Tom will later freely admit - ignorance is bliss - and (as Tom will later also freely admit) the future always catches up with you. Both of those things are true. Always. In every case.

Well, maybe in almost every case.

But it's not such a bad thing, being caught-up with. In fact, sometimes it's the best thing. The best thing that could've happened to you. Tom also admits that, having just experienced it.

He accepts it and he admits it. Tom has to. He has to since he's going to have to live through the next part of his life no matter what he chooses to accept or admit or reject. That's just the way it is. He could deny it all and go crazy. But he accepts it. It's easier. It's cleaner. And it's the road to his future. Apparently.

27

Fast forward a month or so later.

28

The first thing Delphine remembers is that she is dead, but that's the way it always starts. It's worse when she imagines she's alive.

But this time's she's dead. So there she is, and no matter how many times Bryony asks, Delphine can't ever tell her the hows or the why's, let alone the whats or the wheres. She only *knows*. She's dead. Del has this knowledge. She knows, and Bry doesn't get it.

Or doesn't want to get it. But Bryony is her oldest sister, and, as anyone in the family would tell you, Bry always wants to be the first in everything, the one in charge, the head honcha - even when she can't be, maybe especially when she can't be - but even more in situations like the one at present, in Investigations into the Supernatural.

Still, Bry has to try anyways, bless her heart, doesn't she? Yes, she does. She will try.

So, back to Del. Del is dead. Or is going to be. And Susanne (or Skag), sister Bry's adopted daughter, is in trouble, or will be. And Bry needs to do something about Skag, right now or in the near future - or... or something awful, something just terrible is going to happen, to one or to all of them, Del is sure of it. She's sure this time.

Well, maybe Del's not so sure about the part where Del dies. That part's fuzzy. And Del is the first to admit that, yes, she is always expiring in these visions. But as for the rest of it - by golly, it's all as clear as a bell to Del. It is.

Besides the dying part is just the vehicle (she read that someplace) for Del to Pierce The Veil and See Through To The Great Beyond. Del's aiming for the regions of deep, deep blue in her second sight. That Deep Blue of Eternity where Questions find

Answers. Del thinks she's possibly seen at least a glimmer of the blue a time or two. It's a kind of pleasant indigo color, with hints of aubergine around the edges and navy blue streaks running all through it, here and there and everywhere. Like that piece of cloth she cut up into triangles for a crazy quilt she did with her church sewing circle three years ago. Cheerful. Nice. If you like that sort of thing.

Del does. And she'd like to see more of it. So she keeps on trying. And Del's explained all of this to Bry at least a hundred times if she's done it once. She's gone hoarse explaining it. But does Bry listen? No. Bry stopped listening to Del the day she led Del by the hand to Del's first day in kindergarten. And Bry wasn't all that great a listener before that. In fact, Bry's never been much for listening at any time in her life, now that Del sits and thinks about it for a while.

But Del has a story to tell. Something Bry needs to understand.

So... Bryony doesn't want to hear any of it, none of Del's premonitions, let alone an entire Del dream. Bry's convinced that Del's having a spell, like their Great Aunt Mary used to get, the day before they'd have one of those heat waves and the family would end up having to sleep with all the windows open because Aunt Mary was convinced all the oxygen in the air was being sucked out of the house, south along the bay, and out and under the Golden Gate Bridge, heading straight over to China and who knows where else beyond. They'd all be dead in seconds (seconds!) if they didn't get the windows open on that house immediately (immediately!) and forestall the satanic power of the Chinese vacuum of death falling upon them from the heavens above for sinister purposes of foreign governments - purposes one could only guess at but never know completely.

But that was Great Aunt Mary, Del reminds Bry.

Del is not Great Aunt Mary. She is not. Del is Del. Bry says patiently yes, she knows that, Del is a different person. And then Bry goes silent. Del is suspicious of these silences of Bry's. Del is not so sure of Bry when she oozes sincerity and sweet reason and politeness and quiet and calm, and well, silence.

Del waits. Bry says, hesitantly, dear, maybe it's not a spell, maybe, well, maybe honey it's something else. It could be something else. Now really, it could, Del, just be reasonable. It could be a feminine problem, a woman's trouble. Moods. Water retention. Cramps. Now, Del, be reasonable.

So Del has to tell her, for the fourteenth time that Bry doesn't know what the heck she's talking about. And Bry has to insist, in her gentle, motherly, nurturing voice, that yes, maybe she does, just a smidgeon. And Del has to sternly remind her that she knows what she knows, and then Bry usually starts a sentence, stops four words into it, and with a little hiccup of a suppressed sob, halts - leaving the familiar sound (or non-sound) of hurt and sisterly silence on the other end of the phone and Del with a decision to make. The silence is interrupted of course, by faint sniffling and delicate gasps that has Del biting her lip, and tapping her heels on the floor and batting her forehead with a pencil in order to stop herself from answering Bry back - answering with something that would certainly take two weeks of negotiating and numberless unanswered phone calls and emails to apologize for sufficiently.

Sometimes, someone's got to be the adult in these situations. Del guesses it may as well be her. This time.

So, Bryony thinks she knows.

But Del knows Bryony doesn't know.

She would know, if she'd only take the time to shut her mouth and listen carefully and discriminatingly, like any normal family member would. All she has to do is listen to Del. Just listen. Like the time Bry used ExLax (mistakenly - Del is sure it was an error) in the chocolate icing instead of Hershey's unsweetened squares, even though Del had seen their second-to-youngest brother Grant switch the two (the chocolate squares and the Ex-Lax) and Del told Bry all about it hours in advance of the whole cake-making operation. Hours. In advance.

But was there any listening going on, any heeding on that occasion? To Delphine? At all? Papa's 40th birthday turned out to be, to say the least, a memorable one, at least for the plumber they had to call in at 10 P.M. that night (time and a half at that hour, and every bathroom in the house plugged up), and Momma still won't let Bryony bake a cake in her house unsupervised, but Bry did not, will not learn anything from that painful family memory.

At least not yet. Del waits a second and catches her breath, tapping away at her head with the stub of a pencil. Bry continues her masterful non-communication. In two houses, in two rooms, many miles apart, the same painful expectancy floods to overflowing, freezing two people into silence and immobility. Del sighs. Bryony responds by inhaling meaningfully. Del sighs again. Bry exhales. It seems the ball is now in Del's court.

But, as mentioned previously Del has something important to say, something more important than winning a staring contest with a sister who never loses. So, she says as sweet as pie "Can she tell her story now?" Bry responds as if nothing had been wrong, ever, in their sibling relationship and asks if it's just a dream. Del says no, there's a lot more than dreaming involved, it was too real, it was Premonition. And there's more. Bry says she doesn't know what to say to that.

Del wants to say Bry doesn't have to say anything to that. Bry just has to use her ears. And stop using her mouth. But she doesn't say that. Any of it. She bites her lip again instead.

So. Can Del continue without interruptions? Bry is silent, but silent in a way this time that seems a trifle more hopeful - a way that seems the tiniest bit more promising to Del than the ones that came before. It's a different silence, a different kind of silence (Bry is a woman of many silences) - and it's not exactly a yes. But it's plainly not a no. So. Del plunges ahead, carefully and patiently.

29

So Del is dead. Bry stops her and says so this is a dream after all and Del ignores her. Del starts over. Bry sighs loudly. Del wishes fervently Bry would go back to using the weapon of silence.

So... Del starts, then stops. She waits. Nothing. No interrupting. No comments. Golden silence. So far so good.

So, Del is dead. And she's positioned high above the city of San Francisco in mid-air at night and she's uncomfortably cold. She knows this. It's happening. She has goose pimples. On her dead body. Bry begins to make a doubting noise on the other end of the phone - it's the sound of a seal with a cough breathing underwater and makes Del crazy in the head (Del knows Bry knows fully well how it drives Del wild - but she does it anyways).

Del asks the Lord to give her strength under her breath. After a moment of reflection she gets the strength and Del ignores the cough (barely) and forges bravely on. Bry's always making noises like that during Del's stories. Del's a much stronger person spiritually for it.

So... She has the sure knowledge that she, Del, floats slowly and a little uncertainly through a starry night sky. She's skimming gracefully over undulating lines of pink and yellow points of light. There are fistfuls of air punching and pushing through her - imagine Bry, the feeling of water flowing through a sieve of silk, it's like that. Soft. Even. And there's double yellow dots of blue (or are they red?) scampering like roaches distantly beneath her forgotten, transparent feet. These are the streets of San Francisco from the upper atmosphere. Very cold, but very colorful.

Then, it gets even colder. And wetter. There's foggy clouds cutting through her with a strange and unpleasant sensation – soft felt razorblades shredding her into tiny Delphine slivers. Slivers of delight. She's ripping joyously apart in pain and she can tell she doesn't have much time left. Not much time at all. She forces herself to drift downwards, down, down, towards the streetlights of San Francisco far below. She has a mission. Something she must do.

How? I don't know, Bry, I don't know how I do it, how I force myself to descend to the earth. Holy dust? Spiritual flippers? I don't know. Really. May I continue? Please? Pretty please? Thank you.

Del is being drawn somewhere, pulled towards something and she doesn't want to go as she's sliced into smaller and smaller pieces of spaghetti. Del-spaghetti. She's dead. She should be at peace, Del feels she deserves that much at least. So what is all this wispy flittering through the night about? Where is that bright white light everyone says you're supposed to go towards? Where's the tunnel, and her grandparents and the golden outlines of kindly, welcoming relatives beckoning her onwards and upwards towards her just reward, her long-deserved rest, her full and satisfying start of a life everlasting? Where? Where is it?

Del stops her story and waits. Nothing happens.

It's at this point in one of their little talks, that Bryony usually begins her random inquiries. It's like she pulls these questions out of her hat (if she ever wore a hat - Bry hates hats except on Easter). She'll pick a word, any word Del has said and ask her what she meant by it. And Del tries to answer her at first, but Del can tell when Bry's not really listening to her. She can tell Bry thinks Bry is being extraordinarily polite and ladylike and charitable in a deeply *spiritual* sense towards her affected younger sibling – poor, weak-headed Delphine - to ask her about her *special* stories. Del expects her to say - now how could you be dead? You're talking to me on the phone. Who ever would want to cut you up? And when did you start to use a word like "undulating"? I hope you don't say things like that in front of your Tom or my Susanne.

Susanne's (Skag's) first name is Diana, well, Diana Susanne Emily Lela (Diana after their mother, the rest being names of lady authors Jazz especially liked - oh Jazz! How I miss you every day! My little Jazz!), but Bry never uses it. She thinks it's bad luck. Why it's bad luck makes no sense to Del, but Del doesn't correct her, and doesn't answer any of her attempts to distract her and is silent at the end of all Bry's sentences ending with delicate verbal feminine question marks.

So anyways, it's always Susanne to Bry. Never Diana, never Emily or Lela. Certainly never Skag - never - not if Del wants to talk to Bry during the next 7 - 10 days.

But no questions this time. Del's concerned.

"Listen Bry," says Del finally, "Bry? Bry? Bry!?" Where is she now? Bry better not have put the phone down, turned on speakerphone and wandered off into another room dusting or cleaning or washing her face like she likes to do - but Del hears a telltale cough and plunges on before Bry gets the chance to derail Del with a question about double coupons at the local SaveMart or the best way to get rid of a bunion or something similar. She would do just that, given half a chance. She would and has.

"The twins, Bry, are in trouble. Big trouble. Maybe the kind where someone gets killed. Susanne and Tom. I've seen it, Bry. It's coming."

Then Bry gets cranky. Especially this early in the morning. And yes, this is an early morning call. But Del and Bry are sisters aren't they? Who else can you call at 6 in the morning when you're half worried out of your mind? Blood is blood. You have to answer the phone for a sister. Del would do the same for her. Sure she would. She's done it. Many times. Hmmm. She'd just have to think about that one for a minute. Has Bry ever called her this early? As early as 6 A.M.?

Bry clears her throat. Bry's got to get to work. As if Del didn't have to get to her job as well. Yes, well, maybe Del doesn't keep the books in a big law firm like Bry does, but there's plenty of people who appreciate having an alert and organized person handling the payments of their parking tickets for the City and

County of San Francisco in a modern official government office building by an official government officer. Or employee of an officer thereof.

Plenty of people appreciate that (well no one really likes paying parking tickets, but Del tries to be as helpful and efficient as possible during the whole process). But Bry goes on and on about how early in the morning it is and how difficult and tiring and *stressful* double entry bookkeeping can be, and eventually Del ignores her. Bry winds down (it sounds like Bry's washing dishes in the sink at the same time), and Bry reluctantly allows the description of Del's latest flight through the afterlife to continue. She clicks her tongue and says "my!" even through the parts about Skag and Tom and their imminent deaths. Del thinks Bry must be pretty tired after all.

Del, apparently, is being allowed to rave on through Bry's breakfast. Now Del can hear her pouring coffee and making toast for her kids. Her husband's saying something too, about auto repair shops and airplane tickets. Del pretends not to eavesdrop, but she does anyway. It's not so wrong. They're all family, aren't they?

Still, Bry has just got to listen to her. This is important family business. It is and Bry has got to listen. Or try to listen.

This is actually the whole point of their early morning chatting – the part that comes next. Del wishes Bry would let her get to that. This is the important part. The beating heart of her story. All right, maybe she should have said it earlier. Maybe she should have told her this part first. She allows that she gets easily distracted at times. But who wouldn't, talking to Bry? Who?

Del tries to slow down and make each word count. But she can clearly hear Bry putting the phone down this time (she's not even trying to hide it) on an end table somewhere, pushing the speakerphone button on, and running around the bedroom now getting dressed and brushing on her makeup. Bry takes pride in her appearance. Always has. Now her voice is echoing. Bry must be in the bathroom. The grouchy voice of her husband is calling out for one of his shoes. It's muffled, like his head is stuck under a bed.

No, listen Bry. I'm still here. Just woolgathering. I know, I know, you have to go. But anyways…

So, Skag, no I meant Susanne. I'm sorry, I'm sorry. Yes. Susanne. I meant Susanne. I did. Really. Del hears the sound of a front door slamming shut.

No. No, Bry listen to the story. You can catch the next bus. Listen. All right, I'll speak faster. You listen faster. Now don't get hit crossing against traffic. I can hear those cars flying past you like guided missiles. You just watch out, look both ways and take your time. Be careful Bry! San Mateo drivers are crazy. You know they are, Bry.

Yes, the story, the story. I'm getting to it. It's almost over. This time it's true. By true I mean it happened, Bry. No, no flying involved. It really happened. I'm not lying. Last night. Skag, I mean Susanne (sorry, sorry, sorry, I am really, now listen Bry, listen!), Susanne used a fake I.D. and got herself into that same bar South Of Market like she did last time. You know - the Biker's Big Behind or something or other. Yes, I know you don't go to places like that. I know. Just listen, Bry! Susanne got thrown out in some kind of a knife fight and spent the night downtown, courtesy of the city jail. Someone, a friend of hers, a parent, who knows, got her out. She got home, to my home, your sister Del's home, an hour ago. No, she wasn't spending the night with her friend Elizabeth. She was spending the night with her friend the policeman. Stop yelling at me Bry. I wasn't the one publicly knifing citizens of San Francisco at 2 A.M. last night. And no, Tom wasn't there. I don't care if you don't believe me. He wasn't. No, Bry, he was not.

Del hears a noise behind her and stops for a moment looking up.

Skag enters the dining room. Del switches to speakerphone herself, tired of being caught in the middle again, between these two stubborn, strong women, and excuses herself, doing small busy chores at the stove and at the sink as all the mother-daughter buttons are pushed one by one in ascending order and the nuclear explosion finally occurs.

30

Del stops and waits. Bry and Skag talk more, which, of course, leads to more screaming arguments and uneaten breakfast cereal and fantastically burnt toast and frantic emotional text messages by Skag back and forth to friends (how do kids these days type so fast on such small keyboards?) as more toast burns and more cereal turns to mush. Eventually Skag limps down the hallway pulling on her shoes as she goes, tucking in a loaned shirt (Del's late husband's work/uniform denim with "Marvin" stitched across the left chest pocket) and with a great deal of door slamming and stair clomping Skag's gone. Del hopes it's to school. But doesn't think it likely. Bry hears all of it. She's missed three buses by now. At least. She's back home. She's crying.

This is a first. All this on speakerphone. With Bry. Bry talking from her beautiful hardwood-floored breakfast nook overlooking the scenic hills overlooking downtown San Mateo.

Well. Del is exhausted. She has a right to be. She has Skag's shirt, dried blood on it and all (is it Skag's blood or maybe some other nameless bar fighter's?) hanging over a chair in her dining room. She tells Bry about the shirt. In great detail.

Bry is still crying. What to do? Del can tell - Bry is at the end of her rope. She asks Bry if she is going to need Del to take care of Skag tonight for her (she stops even trying to call her Susanne). Bry says yes so quickly Del thinks Bry's telepathic.

Bry asks if Skag can stay over there in the East Bay for a little while. She's going to be working late. Career stuff. For quite a few weeks. You know. Projects. Work trips. Career stuff. Retreats. Conferences. Annual meetings. Stuff.

Bry is giving up. Or cracking up. Or both. Either way, Del is not impressed. Not at all. She can see where this is heading. She can see exactly where this is heading.

Del realizes she's still talking on speakerphone. With windows open to the balmy 69 degree air of a summer morning in Alameda. At least the burnt toast smoke is clearing some. Well, a little. It's almost gone really. And the neighbor's now have mucho to chat about, enough to last them for weeks or even months, concerning the future of Del's family and its rich history of recent prison records.

The speakerphone continues broadcasting into Del's bloody-shirt-decorated kitchen. Del waves a towel to get the rest of the toast smoke moving out the window and away towards the Bay Bridge.

Del hears Bry start running down the street (again) for a bus of some type. Or a taxi. Anyways, she sends a prayer out that Bry makes it safe and sound. She can hear horns blaring and the sound of Bry breathing heavily as she throws her briefcase in front of her and keeps a sighing, hydraulic-wheezing bus/tram/taxi door from closing on her as she jumps up the stairs and lands in front of the driver. Hydraulics and stairs must mean it's a bus then. The bus driver is asking her something. Bry is mumbling something. Bry talks right at the phone and says she has to go. She'll call Del later. She loves her. And you can get blood out of a cotton shirt if you spit on it, rub it and soak it in cold salt water. Then an engine rumbles and roars and there's more mumbling and then the line goes dead.

Del stares at the phone. She's holding it one hand. The shirt is in the other. The house is quiet. A clock ticks then chimes the hour the next room over reminding Del that Tom's at school and not at home, reminding her that Del's not at work and that she should be. Very soon.

She has second shift at the Van Ness office today (she's rotating between offices until she gets enough seniority to stay put someplace and make a sane life for herself - until then... this hobo life, a constant rotating uncertainty). She looks at the phone, spits on it, shakes her head, spits on the shirt, says "what am I doing?" and starts crying, but as usual she starts laughing before she's done with her tears.

Now all she needs to do is jump into the ocean holding the shirt and it will be good as new. She sighs and squeezes her eyes shut and lets the tears run down her cheeks. She'll have to go fix her face before she leaves.

She thinks, yes, I can put Skag on the couch in the living room. She thinks, yes, and I will clean this shirt.

She wonders what happened to the Bry she grew up with. Where has her sister gone? Where's the woman who loves like a lioness guarding her cubs? Where did she go? And when did she go? And why didn't Del notice it? Why didn't Del step in and help her if her oldest sister Bry was in trouble and drowning? What was so important to Del that she missed that? Del's not laughing anymore.

She doesn't see Skag peering in over the windowsill, dangling one-and-a-half stories above the flat street, tip-toeing, balancing, dancing back and forth on the rotting lacy fretwork that holds up the tiny false balcony overhanging the front door that looks into Del's living room. A hundred-year-old spindle breaks, then another and another, and Skag lightly vaults into an ancient cypress and slides fireman-pole style down the branches to a cracked brick sidewalk below. The heavy scent of pine tar and a not-so-gentle shower of large broken branches follow her down and settle at her feet in an aromatic pile of cypress kindling.

Then, in a split second, in the merest moment she's gone - her back set in such a way and her head tilted forward in a certain manner that would make it evident to any casual observer that this is one person who leaving and isn't planning on coming back anytime soon. This one's gone. This one's gone for good.

Del hears nothing. She's staring at her phone like it just bit her in the hand and watches spit drip off of it. Then she's using the blood-stained shirt to dry the brightly colored keys.

31

Skag tells Tom she has a plan. Tom's listening. They're meeting in an auto repair shop Skag's friend Alice owns in S.F. Alice turns out to be a big girl. With a crew cut. She looks just like the kind of woman who would own a garage that specializes in Harleys. And guess what? She does.

It's a place with steel bars on the windows, heavy automatic metal shutter doors and foot-thick cement walls. It's down by old Army Street which Alice calls the Chavez over by Hunter's Point. The neighborhood, well, Tom guesses it's not the safest place in the city. But it's not the worst either. It's available. It's private. And Skag likes it here. Tom decides to let it grow on him.

Alice has a buddy Deb (another big friggin' woman) who keeps on trying to trap Skag in a corner, ply her with beer or just plain push her up against the wall in a playful way that could easily become even more or less playful depending on Deb and Skag's chemistry and the amount of alcohol in their bloodstreams - but, and this is a big but (no pun intended) - if Skag has anything to say about it (and she does), the playfulness ain't about to happen. Tom can see this little chemistry experiment of Deb's is about to blow up in Deb's face.

A few less-than-gentle jabs with Skag's elbow to Deb's solar plexus, and then a few more with a professional, business-like martial-arts-film attitude has Deb winking, smirking, and backing off. It takes a lot to slow down Deb. You can see in Deb's eyes Deb is thinking "yeah, maybe a little later and this filly will be a little more interested." Tom knows this, because Deb says it to Tom. Tom has to admit Deb has balls.

Alice backslaps those thoughts out of Deb's head (what were you thinking, girl?), then a throws a couple of beers Deb's way for good measure, and brings a new smile to Debs face as Alice and her (Deb) back into Alice's office with a full bottle of Tequila and another girl that appears out of nowhere and follows the two of them like a lost puppy. Deb is all over this shit. Shouting and back-slapping ensues, and someone kicks the office door shut behind them. Alice manages to give a high sign to Skag just as the office door closes.

Tom sniffs, suspicious at the unfamiliar smells of oil, rusted iron, sweat and a lot of other chemical vapors which Tom couldn't name if his life depended on it. It's a big space, and in the echoing emptiness he doesn't hear Skag's first few sentences over traffic thundering on the other side of those heavy iron doors, padlocked and chained with oversize forged-metal shit. What in the hell are they trying to keep out? Or keep in?

It all feels improvised. Piles of stuff everywhere. Things hanging randomly from the ceiling, shit bolted here and there on to the walls. It certainly isn't perfect. Far from it. It is chaos. Barely tamed. Straining at its chain and watching for the first opportunity to break loose and get itself free and mangle anything that got in its way while it scrambles madly for open air and independence.

Tom sways on his feet, dizzy. He', out of balance and way, way out of control. Tom's out of his league. As usual with Skag. Tom should leave. Leave now. Leave while he still can.

Is Skag saying something to him? He can hardly hear her.

But Tom will never leave. He knows that. Tom rolls his one good eye back towards Skag, but quickly looks back down at his feet again because he's feeling nauseous and the floor seems to be tilting away from him, more and more and it's getting harder and harder to stay vertical.

Skag still seems to be talking.

Well, here we go, ladies and gentlemen. Keep your hands inside the ride at all times.

The roll bar is down, the roller coaster is starting up its impossibly steep slope, the track stretches off into the clear blue sky and Tom is locked in - chained and padlocked in - and there's nothing left to do but ride, ride ride - ride this one out, ride it all the way to the end.

The absolute, very end.

He hopes Skag knows what she's doing.

She better.

Or what Tom? Or what? What will you do when it all falls apart?

What? What will you do then?

32

"Tag?"

"Tag? Look at me. Tag?"

"What?"

"Tag?"

"Yeah, what?"

"Tag?"

"What the fuck Skag? What do you want?"

"So. Tag. You on planet earth again? You finally back here, back with the rest of us in San Francisco? Where the hell do you go when you float off like that, Taggers?"

Tom doesn't respond. It's starting again. It's already started. He can feel it.

"Someday, Tag, you're going to hurt yourself and someone else, probably me, drifting and dreaming just like that at just the wrong time. Do you want to get hurt, Tag? Do you? You want me hurt too? Huh?"

Tom keeps his mouth shut. He knows Skag. Something painful and sharp is headed his way. Well, both their ways.

Tom eyes the door. Not that he could get through all those chains and locks. Still, Skag steps in front of him, blocking his path, and spreading her legs, hands out from her sides, ready for any move he might want to make. She's good. She knows him like a book. Skag leans forward.

"Listen to me, Tag. It's going to happen, Tag. It's going to happen in the next day or so."

"Yeah, well..."

"Well, what?"

"What in the hell are you talking about, Skag?"

"You got ears, just like me. You just heard it, older brother. I told you everything. Plain as day. I've been explaining everything for the last five minutes. How many different ways do I have to tell you everything? How many?"

"Say it again. Slowly, Skag. So I can let it register and sink in, deep down, where I can feel it."

"Feel it? You want to feel it? It's not that complicated. It's called robbing a liquor store, big brother. That's R. O. B. Rob. Loot, burglarize, hold-up, steal, break-in, strip, take-the-money-and-run, you name it. You deaf or something Tag? Or you just gone stupid?"

"I'll take door number two. Stupid, Skaggers, I'm stupid. Hey, its' not gonna happen, Skag. Not this time. I can't Skag, I can't. I really can't do it."

That's when he notices the emergency exit, a small door in the corner with a faint red glow over it. Tom moves to push his foot behind hers and trip her and wrestle her to the floor (so he can make his escape out of this poisonous steel-reinforced bunker) but she double-crosses him, twists her foot between his at the last minute and it's Tom who ends up looking at her athletic legs from the dirt and stench-encrusted concrete floor lying in some kind of drying puddle of yellow lubricant.

Skag takes a short step forward and stands directly over him - grinning at him, clicking her tongue, hands on hips, shaking her head, bouncing a wide-eyed stare off of him. His eye patch floats a couple of feet away, sinking in yet another dark, mysterious pool of liquid. Skag doesn't try and get it for him. She doesn't even notice his left eye hole anymore - covered or uncovered, filled or unfilled (he lost his glass eye months ago - being pulled into a brawl at a bar with Skag). Skag just sees Tom. All of him. Tom and Tom alone. And Tom can't help himself, Tom loves her for it.

"That was easy. Are you sure you're Tag? How long you been rotting at Aunt Del's? You're going to seed big brother. A big seedy bush. You may be getting taller, but you're way slower than you used to be. Slower and a hell of a lot more predictable."

Tom stares up at her, waiting. There's more.

"You know, bro, bushes like you - the weedy kind - the kind that just aren't making it anymore, the pathetically thin and weak ones that aren't worth a rat's ass to anything or anyone, well, they hack them down to stumps. Then they chain the stumps to a tractor and pull 'em up. Then they burn the pulled-up stumps, and use the ash for fertilizer. You want to be useless? Burnt and mixed with shit to make plants grow? That's the only place you're headed, Taggers, at Aunt Del's. The shit pile."

Tom claps slowly. Then faster and faster.

Skag just watches him.

Tom clambers up onto all fours and gropes for his dripping patch, he looks for something to wipe it with, gives up, wipes it on his pants, grimacing. Lubricant stays in his hair no matter how much he pulls and tugs at it. Sweet. Great. Now he's got toxic hair gel. Now he's capable, probably, of killing cockroaches just by shaking his oily head at them. Slipping and sliding, he stumbles off his knees and onto his oily feet.

"Skag, graduation's in a few months, remember? Don't we owe it at least, owe it to the Aunts to try and see this shit through to the end? Skag, what... oh just fuck it - they fed us when we didn't have any food and gave us a roof over our heads when no one else would and that means something. It has to count for something, doesn't it, Skaggers? Doesn't it?"

"You'd look good as a stump. Hey stumpy. My bro Stumpy."

She laughs, a fake, cartoony laugh and Tom looks at the ceiling and rolls his eyes and spins around and throws a punch at her. Which, of course, misses wildly.

"Try it Skag, call me Stumpy one more time."

Skag does the fake laugh again. It makes Tom sick to hear it.

"The Aunts, Tag? Well, Del maybe. But Bry? Bry? Get real Tag She's kicking me out. As soon as I'm 18. Right now if she could. Maybe she already has. Who knows?"

"To where? To who? Who would take us, Skag?"

"Me, not us, stupid. And she's giving me to Del."

"Well, we two stole Bry's brother-in-law's car last winter. Bry was a little unhappy about that, if you remember. Breaking down in San Diego didn't help. Skaggers she's got her reasons for being mad. You know she does."

"Well, so do I. I got my reasons. And so do you, Tag. Everyone's got reasons. Everyone's got a right to be mad as hell. No one's innocent. No one doesn't have scars they don't deserve. It's all a crock of shit. But you don't have to stand there and take it. You don't have to let them beat you up. Bro, really, you're going soft. Soft and squishy and not worth a damn. Not even as a stump."

"Enough with the stump shit Skag."

Skag throws herself at him, out of the blue, wrestles him to the ground, and easily flips him over, his arms twisted behind his own neck. She has a strange light in her eyes, nostrils flaring, mouth slightly open.

Tom's not worried. He's seen that look his whole life. It's her night-of-the-living-dead look. Scares the hell out of the unprepared. Tom's prepared though. He has to say, though, she certainly looks hellacious. Who's she been practicing that look on lately? Tom doesn't want to think about what that could mean. Where has she been hanging out? And with who? And why? And why didn't Tom know about it?

It hits Tom that he's tired. He wants to stop playing. Tom's not fooling anyone. At least not anyone in this room. Skag wins. She always does.

"All right Skag. All right. But tell me one thing first. Why?"

"Does there have to be a why, Tag? Does there have to be a because?"

No, Tom realizes, no there doesn't. Tom, admit it, you've totally lost this round. Lost it to Skag once again - what does this make? Round 1,247 over the last 17 years? You don't ever win. You don't. Stop it. No. You don't win. Ever. You never do. Just give it up, Tom. Just give it a rest and let it happen. Let go. It's easier that way. You'll see. Easy. Easy as pie. Let go. Let go.

"Just be ready, big bro, be ready this weekend. That's tomorrow bro."

"Really Skag? I'd forgotten that."

Skag knuckles him on the arm for that one. That'll be a bruise by morning. As if Skag cares.

Tom's cell rings, it's Aunt Del. He doesn't answer. Skag is still sitting on Tom, she lets him up, but gives him a severe warning look as she releases him. And she does it very slowly. The slow warning look. The even slower release. Tom understands. He'd have to be an idiot not to understand it.

But he ignores his cell phone. There's no point in it now. It's part of his past. If it's past midnight (and it is) it's already the weekend. His old life ended already. His new one is beginning.

They both go knock on Alice's office door to get someone to let them out of this metal-bound motorcycle jail of a garage. But it's hard to get anyone's attention inside with so much laughing and whooping and fist-fighting going on. It sounds like beer bottles are breaking and some heavy furniture's skidding around the room. Skag is smiling. Wider and wider.

In the end Skag just boots the door open with her famous kick, splintering a few things in the process, and joins in the general mayhem.

Tom watches, waits, gets bored, falls asleep. A couple of hours later, Skag tattered and just a little cut-up and bloody and Tom just a little too quiet, trudge down Cesar Chavez street. The streets and sidewalks shine purple and pink in the Saturday pre-dawn light. Skag radiates out a kind of hysterical hope - she's her own personal sun this morning - she can't stop talking, she struts and sings and her hands fly out and her arms point and Tom ends up having to duck a lot. Tom shuffles along, less radiantly, at her left side. They turn a corner and disappear into empty streets in Hunter's Point.

33

The weekend comes and goes. Skag has a broken arm from jumping out, or rather through a liquor store window in Berkeley. Tom, who arrives characteristically (even stylishly he thinks) late is left behind at the store after all the excitement is over, standing in stomped-on snack food and broken bourbon bottles, and freely improvising - specifically buying Cheetos, bean dip, and Red Bull from the hysterical clerk and complaining about being forced to hang around as a witness and generally trying to hide the fact he's scared shitless.

Skag in the meantime is racing madly downhill towards the bay on her skateboard. Or maybe she's climbing a tree. Or maybe she's robbing another store. Tom never finds out. He doesn't really want to find out.

Tom has a new glass eye in. A surprise graduation present from Aunt Del. His patch is at home and he feels almost as anonymous as everyone else around him who has two eyes. He's not a pirate anymore, or an Arabian sheik. He's just Tom. It's a good feeling. It makes him feel happy, even a little giddy. It doesn't help his nervousness. He laughs too much. He smiles too much. The police stare at him more than they should.

The police are working their way through a mind-numbingly

boring set of questions soon after they arrive. Tom free-associates his name and address and family members from brand names he sees mounted on (now) torn-up displays at the store. It's not all that hard. No one's really paying that much attention to him. Tom looks pretty innocuous. Tom starts getting creative. Which is pure stupidity. Maybe Tom should be a fiction writer, but not now, not to a governmental authority just for the hell of it, and especially not when he's the twin brother of a thief caught on surveillance cameras and an accessory to a crime the police are closely questioning him about. Just stupid. Stupid. But Tom can't seem to help himself. Does he want to get caught? Maybe. His breathing has gone all funny again. He's giggling under his breath. Stupid.

Luckily Skag and Tag now have two different last names, addresses, cell phones. Even if the police find out who they are, it'll take more than a little searching to connect them. Wouldn't it? Tom thinks about it between questions. And giggling. And trying to breathe.

34

It begins innocently enough. As planned. Skag knocking the usual evening clerk's glasses off "accidentally" with her backpack as she steps up to pay for her gum. The clerk's lucky he doesn't lose an eye. Skag's not so careful in the eye department. Tom would know about all that, of course. The clerk was damn lucky. And also blind, now that he has no glasses.

And Skag's lucky she's so slim. She looks like anybody. Sexless. Boy or girl. Well, a muscular boy or girl. Especially with her knit cap pulled over her short hair. Tom sees it all like he was watching a play, observing through the floor-to-ceiling plate glass windows from across the street, shouting obscenities because, of course, Skag was starting without him. Typical. Typical fucking Skag.

He dashes off the curb and almost dies under the wheels of an Ethiopian taxi cab. Then the light changes and he couldn't cross to win the State Lottery without ending up in an emergency room with the imprint of a car's tire tread mark, complete probably with brand name, permanently affixed to his liver.

So he waits. And waits more. And watches. And says "Fuck" every few seconds, jumping from one foot to the other, swiveling his head back and forth scanning the impermeable patterns of laid-back Berkeley traffic flowing purposefully in both directions in front of him. He's not going to get across this way.

Eventually he just steps out, and (since this is Berkeley) traffic stops for him, but not without a certain amount of polite drama. He guesses it doesn't help that he's dressed in student black. Hysterical hand waving gets their attention eventually. He crosses alive.

Amazingly (well, they are twins after all) Skag's also saying "fuck" every few seconds (their vocabularies are remarkably similar in that way), holding her prize skateboard, winging her backpack with abandon, waving her hands, watching the clerk duck, and trying her best to look discombobulated.

This helps with the mounting general confusion. Tom can hear her as he crosses the street. Skag's pretty loud. Pants belted halfway down to her knees, IPod blaring, an old hoodie ripped and stained. And the full voice treatment. That and the fact that she fakes her throaty rendition of an elliptic fit for the benefit of the camera and the clerk makes it a command performance. A performance to remember. The clerk frowns and stares.

Tom can see the clerk-guy's not exactly convinced of her seizures until she foams the toothpaste in her cheeks all over those little dollar bottles of scotch they always have in big clear plastic containers by the cash register, and spazzing around before falling on her back. The fall into the potato chip rack's pretty spectacular. Puffy bags of salty goodness protect her fall, and make quite a racket (and obviously instantly become a complete financial loss to the store) even though they are also providing key injury prevention for any potential customers who have serious nervous disorders that involve a great deal of random flailing in front of their cash registers.

At this point the myopic clerk loses it. He buys her story and thus, with that simple act of will he becomes another actor in Skag's theater, just one more bit character in the latest Skag play.

Just like Tom did, only Tom did it years and years and years ago. Farther back than even he can remember.

35

The guy (clerk) vaults over the counter. He seems like a nice fellow (which makes Tom feel like a total turd later that night after the police arrive). He has been nice enough to stuff one of those expensive cherry-flavored plastic-tube-wrapped cigars in her mouth so she doesn't swallow her tongue, and he's trying to hold her head up off the dirty linoleum floor while she thrashes left and right and mutters nonsense and rolls her eyes up into her head so all you see is white. He's looking like he's going for his cell (to call 9-1-1?) when Skag turns into a different person.

She just stops moving. Then she smiles, although you really can't see her face very well under that hood. Then she moves her hand under her hoodie.

This is the key part - getting him to believe Skag has a gun, getting him away from any gun he might have had himself, getting him away from any panic button he might have pushed under the counter. Tom can see her face, covered in toothpaste foam, but cool and calm, and yes, now she's laughing. He can see it all clearly. From the wrong side of the window, out on the street.

Ferociously angry is an understatement - describing the expression on the clerk - when Skag points her finger from under her grody sweatshirt and makes the clerk reach back over the counter and pull out his twenties and tens and fifties and hundreds and whatever the hell else he has back there and stuff it in her backpack. Skag also helps herself to some vodka in miniature bottles (illegally - she was under-age after all - but that was the least of her worries), and does a somersault (just to show she can) towards the front door. But she misses. Instead, she efficiently slam-kicks a new door out of a floor to ceiling window. Tom sees all this - as if it's on T.V. - from the sidewalk outside.

That's when Tom wants to smack her unconscious. She doesn't even know Tom's there. Why exactly is he here? And Skag's going to get herself killed. And all she can do is laugh. Laugh and laugh. Tom pushes through the front door, it's opening and he walks in and acts like he's going to run like hell, right back out, as Skag flips into the street followed by a blizzard of shattering glass.

The clerk yells at Skag. The clerk yells at Tom. It sounds

Nigerian, or Swahili, lots of k's and l's rolling hysterically off his tongue. He yells and he starts grabbing at something. Behind the counter. Something that probably involves deadly force. And this guy, he can't see. Not really. Not well. His glasses are still sitting under a wine display at the other end of the store.

Aunt Del calls Tom again - she's calling him like 10 times a day now at least - as Skag does her Olympic-diving-back-flip thing through the plate glass window and the clerk finds his rifle or his bazooka or his flame-thrower and aims at Skag, and Tom throws himself on floor, which smells like Tequila, and all hell breaks loose.

Tom hopes he hasn't sliced his face into a million Tequila-numbed pieces as he closes his eye and carefully squeezes his cheek muscles to hold the glass eye in so he doesn't lose this one too. Which is odd. It strikes him as odd. Since that's probably the least of his worries right now. But he does it anyways.

And Tom also doesn't answer his screaming phone. Luckily the clerk slips back, jumping over the counter and Tom throws his attention-attracting phone out the newly broken window and covers his head with his hands and tries to get as flat as possible and he hears a gun shot and he presses himself into the dirt and the alcohol and the glass and his own blood and he waits to see if he still has a living sister.

He never finds the phone again. He never really looks for it. It's probably a very flat piece of expensive plastic embedded decoratively and permanently in the well-maintained asphalt of the Berkeley's streets to this day.

He does, however, manage to hold onto his new eye. And he holds onto his sister.

36

Tag and Skag were out all night.

The next morning, the Aunts are furious at, guess who? Tom, that's who.

But what else is new? Aunt Bry's certain he attends Black Masses and sacrifices neighborhood pets every full moon at a convenient neighborhood coven. Aunt Del's just very disappointed. Again. And exhausted. Again. And afraid. Again. For both of them. They should've called if they weren't coming home. They need to be more responsible. They need to think of other people, not just themselves. Sakes Alive! If they only knew...

Skag calls it justice. Everyone getting what's coming to them. It's all justice. And Skag is sure Tom and Skag deserve what they got - the money, the power, the possibility of freedom, the means to start over and make a new life for themselves. Skag's positive. Skag' sure. It's all good. It's justice, bro, justice. Tom's not so sure.

Who did they take that money from? Who owned that store?

The universe will work it all out. Justice. Responsibility. All of it. It's the universe's hobby. Working it all out for itself. Working its own slow, fine grinding of human lives into miniscule particles of karma and dharma - just more fine grit, more lubrication, for the ever-efficient meshing of the gears of the gods. Right? Right. Tom's been ground steadily to shreds by the universe's finely meshing gears for years. Going on decades now. For his whole life, really, his entire fucking life. Tom has been ground painstakingly to tiny, guilt-filled bits.

Which is to say (as Skag likes to say it) we are, all of us, dust. Dust of the Cosmos. Cosmic dust. Dust and more dust. Dust to dust.

And Tom agrees. That's how Tom sees it. It's not about justice. No, Skag, it's always about dust. Just dust. Skag laughs at him when he talks like that. But she remembers what he says. She sees Tom. She hears Tom. And Tom loves her for that.

37

But that was the weekend before last. Now it's an eternity later, and the Aunts have kept them separated for more than a week. Tom called Skaggers at home, but Bry found out and locked Skag in her second-story bedroom. Skag crawled out through her window.

Skag whacks him with her cast (which is in a sling, but that doesn't slow her down) when she sees him crossing the street. She runs across the street through heavy traffic to do it. Van Ness is not a narrow street. The traffic is not light. Skag dodges with the grim look of an avenging Fury finally finding the one who is fated to die by her hand that very moment. Tom's caught totally unawares.

"What the fuck? What the fuck were you thinking? Why did you call? We were supposed to lay low for awhile." Skag asks over and over as she brains him with it - the cast on her arm that is - it's bright red because that's Skag's favorite color. And because he's her brother she avoids his left eye and the false eye buried in the socket and just batters and beats at the top of his head. But he can tell her heart isn't in it. After hitting him, she does kiss his forehead. Which is better than nothing, Tom supposes.

They're across from a McDonalds where a lot of homeless people hang out - milling about, looking bored and hungry and sometimes hopeful. Tom looks up carefully after she's done beating and kissing him. You've got to stay alert around Skag. It's a survival instinct you have to develop. Skag smiles even more broadly now. Tom wipes his bruised head with his sleeve.

"Tag, what do we need more than anything right now?"

Tom takes a step back.

"I have no idea."

"I'll give you a hint, bro, it's in my cast. Go ahead, Taggers, guess."

Tom takes another step back looking at the cast on Skag's arm.

"Think. How are we going to get enough money to get out of this place for good? Stay with me Taggers, stay with me. Think. How?"

Skag swings again. Tom dodges backwards.

"I don't know Skag." Tom steps back again and one foot goes over the curb and he's whirling his arms and stepping into traffic and he's losing his balance. He's breathing in short gasps. Skag catches him easily. Tom stares at her as he catches his breath. Skag sighs.

"You're worthless, Taggers. It's plastic bags." and she punches him with her good hand, winking at him at the same time. Her smile brightens even more .

Skag pulls something out of her cast - Tom peers at it.

"It looks like you stole restaurant bags of salt Skag."

"BRRRRT. Wrong answer. Try again." She's still smiling way too much. The bags fall back into some recess in her cast. Tom tries to look out of the side of his eyes and see if anyone's watching them. Certainly any eyes peering at them from over at McDonalds should recognize exactly what's going down here across the street as easily as... Well, let's just say it's not very subtle. But then again,

Skag's not very subtle. Unless she's trying hard to hide something. And she's not trying at all right now.

Tom knows what those bags are. He knows very well. He starts looking around for policemen. Someone's going to be wondering why a strapping teenager like himself is being beaten to a pulp by a handicapped blond crazy girl. And why she's pulling plastic bags out of her clothes and displaying them. Won't they? Isn't anyone paying attention? He peers over at Mcdonald's. Maybe this happens every day, all day long on this street. Didn't he see a police car parked across the street a second ago? Maybe an unmarked one?

Apparently not.

Skag always has the luck.

Skag continues her careful explanation. Tom scouts the surroundings for snipers getting into firing position and for guys in camouflage rappelling rapidly down the sides of buildings.

"Not just bags. Not just salt. Tag, you know what I'm talking about. The big time. Bags with powder. Expensive powder. Powder that makes this city go 'round. Powder which makes us free."

Tom gets the point. He does. He wonders how many different groups of people are after them at this point. He wonders if he still has time to escape to a safer place - like Redding or Buenos Aires - and he thinks, maybe, maybe he should have given this more thought in the past - you know - to being a twin, to Skag, to wild energy and wild times, to schemes and plans and hopes and dreams and futures and happily-ever-afters - maybe he should have thought two or three times about everything before he jumped into all this, before all this started. But that was a decision he would have had to have made, when? A long, long time ago - maybe 18 years ago - like at birth - too late now. Way, way too late now, for Tom that is.

"So what do you say, Taggers? Are you in?"

Tom doesn't even answer.

38

Bry calls Del using her office cell phone, but it's strangely echoing, and Bry's even more strangely talking soft and sexy - just breathing out each syllable in a series of passionate, extended sighs. It's disquieting. Especially in a sister. Del can hardly hear her. She doesn't understand a word she's saying. It's a breeze talking to her. It's the air explaining things to her. She's disquieted. That's a good word for how she feels. Disquieted. She just read an article about that in Readers Digest.

"Why are we whispering Bry? Your voice is so soft and faint, I feel like I'm talking to a leaky tire. And that sound - is that a stream?"

"It's none of your business what that sound is - and soft and faint is all your going to get right now - I don't want the whole world knowing my business."

"Honey, even I'm not going to know your business unless you speak up."

Bry is silent. Del starts feeling anxious. Bry breathes more and more heavily.

"What's going on, Bry? You can tell me. What's all this about?"

Del swears she can feel an electric charge bulding up, crackling and hissing and buzzing right down the phone line from Bry's mouth to Del's ear. It tickles and it hurts at the same time. It doesn't do Del's anxiety any good.

"What's all this about? What's all this about? I'll tell you what this is all about, Del." The whispering's over. The yelling's started.

"You want to know what am I talking about, Del?"

Del doesn't have a chance to respond.

"Del, what am I talking about? Are you asking me that, Del? Why don't you tell me? You tell me Del."

Del opens her mouth, but Bry is too quick for her.

Where is my sweet daughter? Where, Del? Where?" Bry's voice is even louder, if that were possible.

Del is completely lost. She hears a toilet flushing again, twice. Then three times.

"You're whispering to me in a bathroom stall about Skag?

Bry's voice rises to hurricane levels.

"YOU KNOW VERY WELL WHAT I'M TALKING ABOUT DEL."

"No. Bry, I don't. Tell me Bry. What? What do I know?"

Your son has my daughter IN JAIL. That's WHAT. Can you HEAR me now? She's in JAIL." Del can hear Bry sniffling and crying and hears the toilet flushing over and over again very near and very loud. She doesn't think Bry is going to fool anyone with all the loud water flooding her toilet bowl every two seconds. Anyone can hear her. And now she's crying too.

Del maintains a moment of difficult silence. Then she hears distant flushes, faucets turning off and the sound of multiple expensive shoes clacking off in a hurry into the tile-covered distance. A door hinge opens repeatedly and then shuts with a tired hydraulic wheeze. Feminine whispers rise and disappear. More footsteps. Bry's still weeping.

"Bry, Susanna's not in jail. She is not there. She's here. Both of them are. Skag and Tom are both upstairs."

Del can tell Bry doesn't believe her. Bry gives out a short exasperated laugh, a condescending bark-laugh. Then she cries some more.

"Bry, they're studying. Or something. I can hear them. They're talking upstairs right now. Today's a school holiday. They're upstairs. I'm in my bedroom. I'm getting ready for work.

Bry laughs again, but less certain.

"Del, you really think so?"

"Look, Bry, what is it exactly that you want me to do?"

Suddenly there's the abrupt sound of a door being knocked on, then a fist slamming (politely) against the metallic, hollow wall. Bry's voice assumes a sweet, syrupy sincerity - something she's particularly good at. Del holds her breath.

"Why, hello officer. Well, Del, there's a policewoman, a security guard out here and... yes, of course I could. Just a moment."

Suddenly Bry is whispering again - why Del has no idea. Surely the policewoman/security guard can hear every word Bry is spitting into Del's ear. "Wait sis, I can't talk right now. I'll call you right back. Now, what was that honey?"

Del can hear the a door being unlatched, opening slowly on uneven hinges. Bry must be upset, she forgot to hang up the phone. "Why no, Whitney is it?, No Whitney, I'm not talking to myself, I'm dictating a letter. You know, idle hands, the devil's workshop. Even a restroom can be a time for inspiration. Work. Work. Work. Anyways, wasn't that a session at the last corporate retreat - the Idle Hands Symposium? You don't know? I'm sure it was. I'm just positive I saw you there. No? Really? Well, yes the toilets are a little on the loud side, no, I don't spend all my time here, but... Oh, yes, I still have the darn little thing on. Well, O.K. if you say so. I'll turn it off. Now, just where is that button I have to hit. Oh, here it is. Nope. There. Now, Whitney was it? What were you saying? Wait, it's still blinking, it's not off yet. You know I..."

"Call me" is the last hissing command Del hears before the line goes dead.

Del heads upstairs to see if she's going crazy. She listens by the doorknob of Tom's door and hears music and Skag and Tom's voices. Then she notices something peculiar, a little bit odd. The twins are still talking about some party Skag went to three months ago where she threw up in the pool. Del remembers it because Bry never stops talking about how much she had to pay for the draining and cleaning of the entire thing, including the hot tub.

And the music sounds familiar. Very familiar. The conversation sounds familiar too. Del waits. Skag's going to laugh like a hyena in a second then suddenly stop. Skag laughs. She stops. Del pushes the door open.

There's no one there.

A flashing tablet lies on Tom's desk, half hidden under some school notebooks and it looks like it's playing something. At least there's a lot of colors flashing on and off across the front screen. There's a pause. The music starts over again. Skag starts her story all over again from the very beginning. The twins start laughing. Only it's the Bluetooth speakers all around Tom's room that are doing the laughing. It's Tom's laugh. And Skag's sarcastic sniggering. And it's everywhere around Del and it's digitally perfect.

Del has been had. The music and the conversation repeat for the (probable) 829th time. Since Del doesn't know how to turn off the speakers, she just takes the IPod out of its case and steps on it. Nothing happens. The music blares on and on and on. She keeps on stamping, harder and harder on it until Skag and Tom and the music stop and there's an honest silence in the room.

Del's back on the phone with Bry before Bry has a chance to dry her hands on those crazy blowing machines she hates - the ones they put in restrooms these days that practically remove the first three layers of your skin along with any water within a 6 foot vicinity. Bry gets hysterical. Del suggests she get herself out in the hallway again and talk like any normal person would. Bry agrees.

But then Bry forgets, she doesn't leave, and things rapidly go downhill. She stays put. She stays by the sinks, in front of the blowers, and even occasionally turns one on when someone wanders in.

It's funny. Even over the blowers, the sisters can hear each other fine. Bry calls their conversations exchanges of opinion. Del calls it yelling. The rest of the office calls it disquieting and avoids the women's restroom on the 14th floor for the rest of the afternoon, or at least until after the security guard returns with reinforcements and suggests in a polite, forceful, and un-refusable manner that Bry move her communications and her voice to a more appropriate location. Like maybe the middle of a football field during a playoff, or a rifle firing range, or the center of a tornado.

Bry says she doesn't have to. She's already there. It's where she lives 24-7.

But she takes Del, her phone, and her rapidly disintegrating world out to the parking garage. It's going to be a long day.

39

It's a blue light. Maybe a liquid, gin-like hue that some trendy-twenty-something would dream up as the next cool, must-have color. Tom feels cold, wet, underwater - a gilled organism - a lonely, doomed fish in an aquarium set up with a fake pirate chest blowing clouds of anemic bubbles into a fake blue cube of slimy wetness he shares with his equally doomed fishy friends.

That is, if he had any fishy friends. Does he have friends? Tom starts to think about it. But not for long. The light is hateful. At any rate it's very fluorescent and very ugly and nauseatingly self-assured in its very blue way. Tom's stomach feels like it's going to turn inside out. Soon. He doesn't feel well. He looks around for a place to throw up.

It's actually a bar. There's alcohol on the table in front of them. That's because they sell that shit here. That and other "stuff", Tom is sure. Everything's various extreme shades of blueness, blue-osity, blue-tivity and Tom feels dizzy and the place smells like vomit and piss. Could it get any worse? Could it get any dirtier?

Well, he's got to admit, there's a hint of disinfectant in the air at times. Puffs of it. Someone's trying. Just a little. Creating the appearance of cleanliness. But not very convincingly. And not very enthusiastically. That has to count for something though, doesn't it? Effort? You get credit for that, right? Even if you're not winning? He sure as shit hopes so. He's trying. He's making the effort. And he's not winning.

Tom and Skag seem to be alone. Swimming alone in the fetid, aquarium blue-white light that makes walking feel like drowning. For the last 20 minutes it's been just them and the bartender, and now even the bartender seems to have become very scarce. Tom wonders if he should be worried.

Ding! The answer is - yes. Tom should be worried. Very worried.

You could get murdered in a place like this. It probably happens here every day.

Skag just shakes her head when Tom tries to talk about it. So Tom gives it up. He looks around. He watches the exits and entrances. Makes sure the back of his chair isn't facing any obvious doorways. He tries to read a wet and blurry newspaper he finds on the chair next to his. But he finds he's not making much headway in the fashionable aqueous dimness he's immersed in. He has to decipher it letter by letter by letter. It's slow work. Very slow work. And the article's boring. A not-very-well-thought-out rant on proposed re-zoning in a city down the peninsula. He can't tell - are they for it? Are they against it? Does anybody care? Does he care? But hey, at least it's something to do. At least it's something besides twisting his head around every 5 seconds to make sure someone isn't sneaking up on him soundlessly with a 12 inch gut hook skinning knife clenched in their capable, experienced and determined assassin hands.

Maybe he's obsessing too much. Possibly. But maybe he's obsessing because Skag's herself has brought a knife with her tonight. A big one. Skag is playing mumbly-peg with a very sharp knife she apparently found somewhere (it's pretty beat up) and is slowly reducing the tiny table they are both sitting at to a wobbly structure of interconnected splinters.

She throws the knife up with an almost invisible twisting motion of her wrist. It comes plunging down and Tom sees it only after it's vibrating point buries itself in the table. She throws it up. It plunges down. Up. Down. Up. Down. She keeps on hitting his newspaper. On purpose. She doesn't apologize. She smirks. Tom keeps watching out of the side of his eyes. Nope, the bartender is gone. This doesn't look good. No, it does not.

She keeps on telling him - "Badger may get here, but maybe we won't."

He looks up. "And that's because..."

She smiles and flips her knife up at the ceiling again. It comes back down again, as all things must and he dodges it, barely. His forearm gets missed. His sleeve takes a direct hit. He pulls and tugs at it and tears the knife out. What a gash it made. It looks like a mortal wound to his shirt. Skag rolls her eyes. Tom looks at her likes she's a crazy woman.

"Look, I have one question. Tell me again, Skag, why are we here?" "Isn't this place closed?" How did we even get in here?" Who do you know? Why would you fucking pick a place like this and...

"That's at least four questions bro."

He throws his slashed up newspaper at her, but the slivers of current events and editorials never even get close to hitting her. She's too quick. And Tom's been sampling the glass with yellow, urine-like liquid in front of him. It tastes watery. It tastes foul. It tastes like pine-scented turpentine left out in the sun too long. He hates it. He takes another sip.

Skag never drinks. She's playing with a glass of bubbly water and watching both the entrances to their ever-so-blue room (she pinned the entrances down right away) and throwing her knife up in the air and dodging his pathetic assaults with newspapers. Just about par for an early-night study session with Skag.

Then there's the ever-so-quiet sound of some swinging door whining as it very slowly opens on un-oiled hinges. Tom's heard it a couple of times already and hardly notices it, but suddenly realizes Skag is nowhere to be seen. She's gone. Tom feels a strong arm pull his legs down (which pulls his body down) into a puddle of unnamed liquid under the bar table they've been sitting at and Tom collapses in a heap next to her, huddled in crouched posture, hidden behind their chairs. She's ready to jump out. The knife gleams a cool, scratched titanium glow in the shadowy spaces under the chairs and table. It glows deep blue-black in the runny wet blue-black light all around Tom. It looks like it's laughing. It looks like it's having fun.

"Stupid, slow, and struggling to be my twin. How did that happen all at once I wonder Tag?"

Tom starts to answer, then realizes he's being stupid and slow still struggling to be her twin. Skag doesn't even have to "shush" him to get him to shut up. So he shuts up. Mouth closed. Eyes on her. She smiles at him. Encouragingly. Like he has unseen potential. She runs one finger down his nose and smiles. He smiles back. They look into each other's eyes and both eyes are wide and glowing, cool and clean and dark, like the knife and Tom swears he can hear her voice in his head saying "Is this cool or what?" and Tom can swear he answers her "I wouldn't miss it for the whole world" and they hold each other, calmly and safely, in each other eyes and it's all right for Tom, it's all right for now, for now it's enough, it's more than enough.

In the meantime, someone is skimming on the top of their shoes, tip-toeing or some shit silently across the streaked and stained linoleum floor. Looking. Dancing. Searching. For something. Or someone. Or two someones.

40

This shadow moves slowly, swiveling its arm in arcs, smoothly and professionally, walking backwards, forwards, sideways, holding its breath, holding one arm steadily in front of it which in turn holds a small black heavily potent object, which is in turn, carried on its side. Tom can see it whenever it crosses what little light feebly filters down to the floor from the few working light fixtures humming ineffectually above their heads.

Tom can also see Skag listening, that witchy way she has - bright eyes staring at nothing, head twisted sideways, ears almost popping off her head, and then in the dim duskiness under the table he sees Skag look directly, precisely at him, which means he, Tom, needs to relax and quickly, because both twins are going to be moving at near light-speed in a very few seconds.

Tom is oddly ambiguous about all this.

He's trying to feel panic rising, but he isn't being very successful.

He feels, as much as he feels anything right now, a mostly restful tension. And there's the sure knowledge, deep in his belly, that he's about to die. Life. Death. He weighs the two. He's oddly, well, ambiguous is as good a word as any. Probably not the best attitude in the face of a life or death situation. But, what's an all-devouring love of life supposed to feel like anyways? He's never felt it. Survival? Future? It all seems hazy now. Kind of theoretical. Maybe the same as taking a class in Tibetan on the off-chance you might visit there someday. Not very likely. Not very practical. You never get to travel to Tibet. It never happens.

Skag waves her hands in front of his face ever so slightly.

She mouths "You still here. Taggers, still with me?"

He nods with a mime of enthusiasm, a little overdone, and a wide, affirming smile. He finishes with a thumbs-up signal. It doesn't fool her.

She rolls her eyes, and looks right at him. Mouths more words.

"Taggers. You here? You ready?"

He waits a millisecond, then he nods again. Simply. And exactly this time.

And this time she just nods back.

Then all hell breaks loose.

At least that's the way Tom sees it in the pulp detective novel spin his life has been taking on lately.

A gun fires and it's bright in the submarine gloom. Skag rolls towards the door. Tom doesn't. His arm feels wet. There's another flash and his shoulder isn't there, or at least not where it should be. He can't find it exactly.

He looks for Skag, sees no one, but there's a shadow moving towards him, a straight arm swiveling in a familiar kind of way, like its holding something like an oddly-shaped metal cup. Or a like a weird flashlight. Or maybe like a gun. Maybe exactly like a gun.

You know, he's seen that action before, that behavior, that movement, that shape, that trace of a shadow. It has a certain beauty, a certain grace to it. You don't forget it once you've seen it. And he sees it's searching for him. You know, he's sure now. He's sure of it. He remembers it all clearly. The image. The shadows. Somewhere. Recently. He's sure of it. He remembers shit like that.

He has seen this all before.

The swiveling stops when the gun points at his chest. Or is it his face?

Then the shadowy (man's?) torso's above him, a face hanging over him, smiling, or maybe just squinting in the stupid aquamarine darkness, it stops. There's the arm with the gun (surely that's what it is) pointing at one of his body parts. It's all so familiar. His shoulder is starting to really hurt. Familiar. So familiar.

Then there's something sticking out of the chest of the guy's torso - a wickedly sharp knife - and another bright flash and Tom feels the top of his face go numb and then there's the hand on his forehead again, and the feeling of someone brushing his hair and for the first time in years, really it's been years, he feels the peace, the gentle peace, and there's tears on his cheeks, and this time there's definitely a strong feeling of contentment and security - which is really strange - because there's nothing theoretical about this feeling, nothing at all, it's here, it's all his, it's appropriate, it's practical. And it's real. And it's very, very familiar. He realizes it feels like something. It feels like a home. Tom is home.

He feels tears and more tears.

Except he can see the tears are Skag's. The hand isn't Skag's though - it's someone else's - it looks like his own hand, and someone with a gently nodding face smiling wryly into his own - he can see it too, and it's not Skag's face either. It's not. It looks like his own face. It looks like himself. In fact, it *is* himself. It *is* his hand. Then he knows why it's all so familiar.

He was safe. In safe hands. Safe. And he had been the whole time. His whole life even. What a time to figure that one out. But you have to figure it out sometime, Tom supposes. It may as well be now as later. Although, technically, there isn't going to be a later for him, not now, Tom figures. There's no now. There's no later. Not anymore. There's just *is*.

It starts to get darker and dimmer and fuzzier in a good way. He sees clearly another transparent hand, another head of hair being stroked and quieted - it's his sister's. She's crying, tears rolling down on him in a warm, salty waterfall, and someone is brushing and touching each tear of hers as it rolls down her cheeks before it falls onto Tom's nose and his lips. The hands brushing and holding Skag look like his sister's, but they are not his sister hands Not exactly. The pained but smiling face floating above his sister's face is also his sister's face. But it's not her face. Not exactly. But that face isn't crying, it's shaking its head, it's smiling softly, it's using its hands to do a lot of brushing of tears and hair stroking and touching and... well, a lot more that Tom can't see at the moment.

It all doesn't make sense. And yet it does. Tom watches Skag watching Tom. He feels the hands. He feels the tears. He sees the hand touching Skag. And he's afraid for Skag. Skag will be so alone. Skag's never been alone before. Not really. Not without her Tag.

But maybe not. Maybe, Tom guesses, Skag will somehow be all

right, she'll somehow be safe. Skag is safe. She is. She always has been. She always will be. She just doesn't realize it yet. Skag will be O.K. So will Tom. They all will, every one of them, be O.K. Even the shadow with the knife sticking out its chest. Even him. That's when Tom relaxes. Maybe for the first time in his life.

And then he feels one more brush of his hair and a brilliant light which he realizes was inside himself the whole time and it explodes and burns away the pain and confusion and agony leaving behind only bright strong things for which he cannot find a name.

41

Bry won't go to Tom's funeral. She plants voice-mail depth bombs in Del's phone messages late at night which blaze up and ignite Del's mornings in a spectacular way every day now. Del's almost getting used to them and the new slightly off-kilter Bry. It's becoming a part of the rhythm of Del's long, empty days. It gives a shape and a form to her new bomb-cratered, burnt-out ruin of a life.

There's a lot of blaming going on in the early hours of the A.M. coming from the direction of the Bryony household - blaming life, blaming San Francisco, blaming Del, but mostly blaming Tom for putting Diana (now she refuses to call her Skag or Susanna) in such inappropriate places in the first place.

Del knows the anger is there because something bigger is scaring Bry. Del knows Bry's scared of being scared and she's scared of being sad, and she's scared of losing Skag. Probably mostly the last one. And Bry's loud when she's scared. Always has been. Loud is Bry just trying to through the next year as best she can. It's Bry using all of her skills and experience to make it through just one more day, the same as the rest of them in this shell-shocked family.

Del knows it. Nothing you can do about it. It's just the way it is. Del'll put up with constant emotional explosives being lobbed her way. She'll stay put and endure it. She will. And she'll do it gladly. Well, mostly gladly. She'd be more upset if Bry was silent. A quiet Bry, now that would be a catastrophe, that would be a cause for concern. Then they'd really have a family emergency on their hands. A five-alarmer. Del will take the yelling. Yes she will. Hands down.

Del plod through each day (somehow), an hour at a time or when it gets bad, a minute at a time. It makes for long days. Overtime at work helps. Scrubbing the floor and doing the dishes and shopping for food and sleeping and eating help too. Doing the necessary helps. Sometimes. Sometimes not. Well, mostly not, if she were honest about it.. But necessary passes the time. And passing the time is the only thing Del knows how to do in a situation like this.

Necessary also kicks you in the behind. Necessary gets you moving. Although moving never really makes anything better. Nothing makes anything better it seems. Nothing. Del admits it. Better just isn't on the menu anymore. Not in the near term. At least the big kind of better, that is.

But the small kind of better, well, that happens a little more each day. Every day is a tiny bit better. Just a bit. And that's all you need, really. Better is getting through the next 15 minutes without sobbing like a crazy woman. Better is sleeping most of the night without waking up seven times in a cold sweat after another heart-stopping nightmare. Better is just breathing, in and out. Better is waiting. Better is just learning to wait.

Skag has a peculiar, uncanny look about her now, in her eyes, in her mouth, her eyebrows, even her hair. The old Skag's shifting, blurring, and fading out. The new one is nowhere to be found. At least, not yet, that is, as far as Del can see. There's a whole lot of something going on in that girl, and it's happening fast and it's happening now and at least it's movement. So Del's glad for chores, glad for Bry's rants, glad for Skag's odd sideways glances. She's glad for motion. She's glad for flow.

Del feels like life is lurching forwards all around her. Going somewhere. Moving someplace in spite of itself. Del is going to move right along with it. She's decided. Like she said, it's all she knows how to do.

And where there's movement, there's life, and where there's life, there's hope. Right? Isn't that the way it's supposed to work? Isn't it? Del says amen. Del says yes.

Well, what can you do? Just give it some time, that's what Del thinks. Time and patience. Patience and time. Those are Del's unfailing answers to most of life's unrecoverable disasters.

42

So... It doesn't surprise Del a bit when Skag disappears for good (or what looks like for good) two weeks and three days later. Del figures Skag has a lot of work to do. And so does Bry. And, while we're talking about it - so does Del. Time and patience, thinks Del, patience and time - time to have the patience to love.

The letters from Skag start coming a year later. They're always addressed to both Bry and Del. Del thinks that's a nice touch. Actually she bites her lip and bursts into tears when she sees both their names on that envelope. She does it every time. So, yes, Del thinks it's good. Del thinks that's a very good start for now. It's a nice start for all of them.

SPARE PARTS

I am a spare part.

An extra thing.

An unnecessary item.

At least Kev calls me that. But he calls me a lot of things. He smiles when he says it though, every single time. He has this talent - he smiles with his eyes, not moving a muscle on his face - just beams pleasure and satisfaction straight out of his irises. Guess I'm his favorite spare part. My Kev. He's magic. Him and his sorcerer's smile - he can do it with his lips too - the normal way - that smiling thing he does - but the eye thing, that's the sneakiest. There is no known defense against it.

Kev. And those infinitely deep brown-green oceans he calls eyes. Within them lie overpowering surges, overwhelming rip tides, roaring waves that are ridiculously easy to sink into, sheer hopelessness to get out of, a drowning pretty much assured once you fall face-forward and down. I lean and plummet, dying there often. Daily in fact. Not that I'm complaining.

And there's that dimpled chin I push my cheek against as often as possible. And that hair. The blackest, spikiest hair - irresistible and bristly - hair that screams (to me) for a talented and motivated hand (like mine) to run its wriggling fingers through it, caressing every sharp and pointy strand of it. Repeatedly What a trip! However, that last part, the delicious wriggling, Kev usually gets me to stop that shit pretty quickly - generally by putting my forearm in some kind of complicated wrestler's wrist lock he knows how to do. So, wriggling is something I don't get to do very often - except in random, delicately timed, and sometimes successful surprise attacks.

You see, Kev's neat, not mussed - I'm the opposite. I'm permanently mussed, scratched, and bent. Maybe that's why we're together. We're two different kinds of parts. The bright and shiny and the slightly bruised and used. Maybe I figure it's my job sometimes to open him up to new things, to things a bright and habitually shiny part might not get to see too much of. Maybe it's my job to trip the two of us into different experiences, maybe plunge us unexpectedly into places where there's a bit less order and bit more, what? - spontaneity? Maybe. But, well, that's not how Kev sees it. It's all muss to Kev.

Lips. I forgot about the lips. How could I forget about those? Kev's lips - under a nose that cries out to be slowly massaged with the end of another nose, those lips that are waiting patiently beneath that pair of extremely unsafe (previously described) eyes - lips capable of expressing every emotion known to man, and a few not even conceived of yet. Pillows of desire. Talented muscles of pleasure. Soft, hard, and everything in-between - separately and all at the same time. And smiling. Smiling for me. Even when they're not wanting to smile.

And... What else? - his small, alert ears that catch everything - the merest hint of a whisper of a rumor - way too much really - I never get away with anything.. And the razor-sharp, barbed-wire, blue-black stubble he sprouts every couple of hours. And... well... Kev's face is just one fascinating place. Kev himself is a fascinating place. And we haven't even gotten below his chin yet.

But, as I was saying, Kev likes to say I am one of those extra parts in the world. I'm a spare part. And he's another kind of part. Lots of different parts out there in the world. And you know, if you take two parts, fit one part into the other part and if you get lucky, well, sometimes you get a something else - another part, a bigger, better part, a surprise part, a new part. And it's more than what you started with. A lot more. And you're not quite sure what to do with it. And it's comforting and annoying and it's scary. And it's huge. And sometimes it even works. Sometimes over long periods of time. Sometimes even for a lifetime.

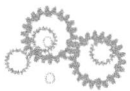

Kev says...

I am one of those odd light bulbs in such a fanciful size and loopy glassy shape that you can't even imagine what kind of appliance it could possibly have once screwed into, or how in the hell the screwing-in part would have worked out exactly, even if you had the said unknown appliance sitting in front of you, bulb-less, broken, and waiting for repair. I am unimaginable.

Or...Kev says I am one of those mysterious, mesmerizing half-used, half-squeezed tubes of glue with the tops permanently bonded shut and the label instructions for medical emergencies long ago rubbed past illegibility into the realm of the invisible. To Kev they are irresistible - these mysterious tubes of chemicals - meaning, of course, me that is. Kev says you just want to try me out, see if the glue works, squeeze the tube, but do you dare? What if it explodes in your hand? What if you glue your hand to your private parts? That's me, for sure. The treacherous, alluring unknown adhesive of doom. I am irresistible.

Or... Kev says I am one of those bewitching handfuls of lost and leftover nuts and bolts and washers and screws and other whatnots piling into drifts of rusty windblown metallic snow in corners and crevices of your house - to be discovered, sharply, by bare feet in the depths of the night as you make your way in quiet desperation towards what you think is a bathroom door. I am rusty. I am dangerous.

Kev says I am a spare part.

But, Kev says a lot of things.

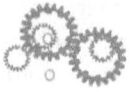

Kev always slams the front door when he comes home, making me jump. I hate that. But the slamming is fine, because I always leave my shoes by the front door in piles which get progressively and riotously higher and higher, peaking and spilling into the hallway in broad talus slopes of leather and rubber as the weeks wear on. Kev hates that.

I know. I know. My laziness betrays me and leads me down the garden path into trouble, worry and strife, again and again. It does. I admit it. It's just that I find it's always easier to locate your shoes if they're always in the same place in the same pile by the only front door you own (or rent). Easy works for me.

So. Kev slams. I pile. But Kev and piles don't mix. One day I come home, middle of winter, and they're all gone. Disappeared. The whole mountain of them. Absent. Decamped.

At first I think I put them away without remembering. Then I think maybe I forgot where I put them in the first place. Then I just start wearing other shoes. I don't find them outside under the front stoop until it's spring already and they've been gradually composting back into the soil under our sagging front porch for 6 months, in the mud, under the front steps, right where Kev threw them. Kev says he warned me. Many, many times. I have to take his word for it. I don't remember.

Later Kev promises - a promise he keeps most faithfully - he says yes, he'll stop slamming the front door upon arrival. The yes occurs when I ask it of him at the PayForLess Shoe Emporium as we are waiting in line at the cash register. It's a reluctant yes, but it's a yes. We are in the process of racking up a large dollar amount on my debit card. It's the considerable re-stocking cost (and we're not a rich couple) of replacing and re-supplying my now mildewed and fertilizer-grade footware. Kev promises. I accept. Life goes on.

And he keeps his promise. So I promise about shoe-piling. Not to do it, that is, especially by front doors. And I keep my promise too. Well, for the most part. I only lose one, (tops, two) pair a season now to the front stoop. Sometimes I even find them before they've entirely decomposed.

Kev can be pretty long-winded when he wants to be. But he's great with the non-verbal too. In fact, non-verbal is his specialty. Have I told you about his eyes yet?

Anyways, Kev calls me S.P. - our private name for me - sometimes pronounced "sp" a noise which frequently in public looks and sounds a lot like you're about to hock something up and spit it right out on the floor at your feet, in front of anyone and everyone. But really, it's my name. Me. S.P. The spare part. The extra part.

That's what Kev says. That's what he calls me.

And you know what? - he's right.

I am one of those extra spare parts. And that's O.K.

Why?

Because there's more. This is where he sometimes gets long-winded.

Kev says spare parts have a strong tendency towards the stationary. They stick to one place. And by cleaving to one location, even accidentally, nature will use them. Nature re-envisions and re-invents, re-assembles and re-organizes, re-creates,. re-births, and releases. It's just one of those things, one of those processes that the big "N" can't help doing. She just does it. It's her thing.

Nature uses worthless, motionless potentially unnecessary objects - parts - and builds and builds and builds on them, and - bam! - something else takes the place of what was once there - something new - that's just how nature or the universe reacts to something standing still for too long. You stand still, you get changed. Something new emerges.

Spare parts get used.

Nature. You gotta love her.

Lately Kev's not smiling. He's crying sometimes, argumentative other times, he's afraid. He's trying like hell to balance on a mental tightrope, but the rope keeps getting thinner and thinner and he's taking smaller and smaller steps. His chest tightens and non-stop panic overwhelms and Kev is sick. Sick and tired. And then he's not working. And then he can't sleep. And then he can't stay still. He hates moving around. He hates being in one place. Night and day both become endurance tests - marathons of willpower - long series of mysterious emotional and physical punishments. He's sick a lot. Sometimes all I can do is hold his hands.

His doctor says it's stress, which doesn't make a lot of sense, and gets him on some drugs. It seems to help. Then it doesn't help. Then it does help again. Then it doesn't help. Like I said. Sometimes all I can do is hold his hands.

It's a rough year.

Like I said, Kev says a lot of things.

And now that he's on Disability for a year to try and get better, he says even more things. When he's talkative that is. He's also got this new mute side to him that has me more than a little worried. Even his eyes get silent. Quiet-like. Too calm. Too still. He's somewhere else and I can't find him. All I can do is be here. So it's what I do. I stay.

However, lately - thankfully - there's been more of the old Kev-spiel going on than the new Kev-silence. All in all a good thing. At least, I think so. And I tell him so too. I point out how much I like his loud, raucous, endless blathering. A wrestling match usually ensues afterwards, if Kev can catch me. I make sure he does.

But, as I was saying, Kev is convinced, as I pointed out already, that we are both spare parts in the greater scheme of things.

And spare parts, lost parts, well, nature erodes, and erodes, and keeps eroding them until long after they have a new shape, a new place, until long after they have a new purpose.

Usefulness through erosion. Place and purpose through constant change - that's the ultimate destination of unwanted parts, of extra parts, of spare parts.

And I am one of those parts, along with my once constantly verbose partner, who is a little quieter now but still rowdy, and who is hopefully getting healthier and stronger and more comfortable week by week, day by day, hour by hour.

You know, people say we're all junk, that people are all junk - semi-pointless - random and useless - surplus things which maybe shouldn't have been made in the first place. That we're extra. Extra parts. Not needed. Just spares. Crouching in the corners. Hiding in the bottom drawers. Not hurting much maybe, but not helping much either.

Well you know what? That's all horse shit - a pile of equine farm manure the size of a football field. The technical name for that is crap.

Kev says - we're parts, parts with a future, parts moving towards places, parts filling up, drop by drop with unplanned but powerful purposes. You just have to look for the dripping sometimes - you just have to look really close to see it. You have to want to see the dripping. and then - bam! - you get it.

Future, place and purpose.

That makes all the difference. To me at least. To the superfluous majority - the superfluous you, the superfluous me and the superfluous Kev.

'Cuz, I'm not the only spare part hanging around out here. We're all spare parts on this tiny ball of rock spinning through the expanding cosmos on pressure waves of cosmic dust, moving rapidly towards God knows where or why.

So - greetings - fellow spare parts!

We are, in fact, the spare part continuum.

At least that what Kev says, when he's in one of his talkative moods.

And I believe him.

And, also, by the way, my name is Lars.

And, if you're wondering, this is my story. My true story. Our true story. Kev's and mine.

So, while you're reading, go easy on me, O.K.? After all, all of us, all us spare parts, we have to stick together, right?

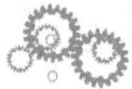

There was a time, long ago, when I lived in San Francisco and still hadn't met Kev - but as Kathryn Hepburn once said in my most favorite film of all time (*The Lion in Winter* in case you were wondering) - "that's prehistory lamb, there are no written records." Only slight exaggeration. But B.K. (Before Kev) seems like an eternity ago, a time out of legend, a cartoonish existence to me now.

Still...

I remember that first time.

The first time I saw him.

Kev is a revelation to me.

Kev says hello to me and I nearly jump out of my bus seat. I'm not used to talking to people. And never on the bus. And never in a crowd.

Then I do get out of my bus seat. I get up, and let an old(er) woman with two bulging plastic bundles of oddly shaped food collapse into my now-empty plastic-molded bench. Some oranges jump upwards and away from her, rolling off her knees making their bid for the floor and freedom and I cut off their escape route with one quick scoop and swipe, dust the truants off and gallantly hand them back to her. She nods and reties her sacks. Twice. Then she does it again, nodding, tying, talking to herself in Chinese I think.

I watch her. Try not to think about Kev. Try to ignore his hello. But then I think maybe it's impolite to be staring at this woman continuously knotting her bag into a kind of plastic neo-macramé. So, I look elsewhere. I watch the ceiling. Nothing up there. I look at the floor. More nothing. I close my eyes and try to think. Oranges. Blue skies. Railroad tracks. Spaghetti and meatballs. Anything. Nothing comes. I can feel the laser beams of Kev's eyes burning into my skin, sweeping back and forth, scoring my torso, leaving long criss-crossing trails of burning hot Kev-ness all across my body.

"Hey" says Kev again to the back of my neck.

I turn around, my face flushed an iridescent red. I look like a stop sign.

"Hey" I say, my mind a blank. Waves of heat roll off my face. I try to manage a weak smile, but achieve something more like a facial tic. I decide to stop smiling.

Kev's face is open and friendly - an unclouded sky. It's a summer sky, full of potential and bright with possibilities. The bus-air around us however is not - it's close, hot, and passively hostile. It's angry, but it won't tell you why. The air crackles with irritation.

Not a lot of joy here. People pushed tight against each other, you can't do any inhaling unless you pull in the air of someone else's exhaling - pull it down deep - way down deep into the furthest reaches of your lungs. Chronic coughers make it even more fun. I tend to hold my breath a lot on the bus. Especially now, especially at rush hour. Holding your breath cuts down a great deal on conversations, I've found.

I can feel Kev's eyes still on me.

I look up and then I see it - there's a blotch on his forehead. I notice it, because I have a twin blotch on my own. In the same spot. Then it hits me (I know, a corny metaphor for what I'm about to explain, but bear with me).

I met Kev already.

I met Kev staring at my own shoes. On the bus. This very same bus. During rush hour. That is, I was bending down to tie my shoes (or latch them - bind them - whatever the correct verb one uses to describe the act of re-tying a velcro shoe), and simultaneously Kev was doing the exact same thing (except with laces, not velcro, and to his own shoes, not to mine). So, it wasn't exactly a meeting we had so much as it was a mutual forehead bashing. The bruises on both our faces apparently didn't go away for a week or so. They're still there, it not being a week yet. And we're back on the same bus. And it's rush hour. And we're standing very, very close to each other. Again. And Kev is watching me.

That first time, Kev scowled, then saw the rank fear bubble up and cover my face and Kev's face changed instantly, scowl replaced by astonishment, knit eyebrows replaced by eyebrows raised, eyes slitted and narrowed changed to wide and accepting and - of course - eyes smiling their secret smile. His eyes are smiling and smiling. All by themselves. I stared. And he shook his head, ruefully, observing me in my confusion and I braced myself (for what? I had no idea for what), and then he laughed. I jumped backwards. That was the first time I heard Kev laugh.

He called us the "Bruise Brothers."

I clearly remember him saying that, I can hear his voice to this day over the grinding gurgling sound the bus engine made changing gears and over the ebb and flow of odd phrases popping up all around us - exhausted but animated people babbling away on cell phones. He said it at least twice. Maybe three times.

I could think of no reply to that observation. I gazed at him with injured bovine vacancy. The bus jerked to a halt and just at that moment, I literally launched my body at the double doors as they accordioned open, rolled down and off the bus steps and found myself draped over a metal bus bench. The doors closed. The bus rumbled off. I'd exited twenty blocks early. It was a long walk to where I lived that evening. Lots of time to think. Not that it did me any good. And my head hurt. And later that night my forehead blossomed with a ferocious bruise.

I went on dazedly for the next week with my job as a bookkeeper - I'm not the best or fastest accountant, but I'm not the worst either, decent is what I'd call myself. Workmanlike. And I circled about the city in the small cautious routines of my life, maybe a little more anxiously than before, uncomfortable somehow, having an itch but not knowing where or what to scratch - you know, *that* kind of thing. Upset. Perplexed. Desperate. But just as quiet as before. I'm a quiet guy. I was an itchy, upset, perplexed, desperate, quiet guy.

I wasn't happy. And I didn't know why. And I wasn't sure I wanted to find out why. But as I found out later, I didn't have much choice in the matter.

And so the universe arranged matters (like it usually does) such that "why" eventually was staring me straight in the face whether I wanted it to or not.

Kev studies me (this second time around) and I try to think of something to say. Is that studying, or more just looking that he's doing? It's getting weird again. I examine his expression more closely. Kev waits. I wait. Even the orange bag woman is looking up at me, questioningly, clutching her tightly bound fruit and waiting, waiting for me to do something.

Hey! - I think to myself - give me a break! Look, I just rattle around the big city here, just one very small piece of hardware in a big box of millions of pieces. And I'm nothing special - I know that. A little scratched here, a little dented there, bent about the edges some, but shit, it works for me. O.K? I'm not much, but I'm all I've got. Really, I'm not all that interesting. Really, I'm not.

Kev continues to study me - I decide it is an act of studying. Well, it's better than a disinterested act of looking. At least I hope it is.

Hey! I think to myself - let it go guy. Just leave it. Let it be. Let me be. Sorry about the forehead lumping. Sorry for the constant squishing and squashing against you like this. Sorry for the breath-of-death (I had garlic Szechuan beans for lunch). Sorry for everything, but this is what San Francisco life looks like and smells like and this is me and just let me be. Please.

Kev stares. Maybe's he's going to belt me one. Who knows? I mean, who really knows what's actually going on inside your very own skull, let alone what shit's running rampant in a total stranger's? I think - what does this guy want? What do I want? What's happening? My stomach's doing somersaults. Kev frowns and smiles at me at the same time.

The Asian woman scrutinizes the two of us fascinated by our wordless conversation. Another woman (her friend?) pushes through the crowd to get next to her and peers over at us, trying to figure out what the Asian woman is watching so intently.

I clear my throat. I cough. I try to watch the street life streaming continuously past the windows, without much success. I keep looking over at Kev out of the side of my eyes.

This friend of the Asian woman starts a long explanation of some sort of health problem involving shoes. It's very involved. There's a lot of pointing down at the floor, lots of foot tapping and ankle rotating. Then they're both on their feet, moving towards the middle doors (we're slowing down for the next stop and I'm getting pressed harder and harder into Kev) and then the bus slams to a halt, I rotate around - a spinner in a children's game - right into Kev's face, and mash into his chest. I gasp out my spicy breath into his nostrils. Then I try and hold my breath. I must smell like an unwashed frying pan in a cheap diner - old cooking oil laced with decaying food particles. Kev thinks and looks, thinks and looks. More people get on the bus. Kev and I gradually get melded into one single wad of human commuter. I feel his lips moving down by my shoulder, his breath tickles the hairs on my neck.

"So how's the bump?"

I look out of the side of my eyes and see Kev folds his eyebrows together in a pretty good imitation of a daytime soap actor's expression of deep, sincere, heartfelt concern. He's still smiling. Eyes and lips both. We're kind of tucked into a corner of the bus now, facing two blank white walls of polished metal, pushed against a thrumming vibration - the beating of huge pistons pushing tons of steel and humans over the cracked pavement on the hills of San Francisco. There's a vague smell of lubricant and grease and Kev's sweat condensing in a cloud about us. His smell hits me first - with the force of traffic safety vehicle hitting a concrete wall at 60 miles per hour. Kev reaches over and touches my forehead, then touches his. I quiver. Something I don't usually do. His finger brushes me again. I quiver some more.

"The bump. Remember?" he says.

I smile, a real one this time (smiling always seems a safe thing to do, except when a bunch of guys are surrounding you and look like they might be getting ready to beat you up - then - as I know from experience, smiling is not the biggest help, but even I can see that in this case the smiling will probably have a different effect). I attempt a brighter smile. Kev waits. I smile. In retrospect, I have to say, Kev is the most patient man on the planet.

The bus starts. Stops. Starts. Stops. We get crushed. The wall of the bus gets hotter. I start sweating. Start wishing I hadn't worn a my sweater. Typical ride home, public transit style, on a week night.

You know...People baffle - they're wonderful, interesting, a puzzle and a pain and a big question mark with me - the connection between their actions and reactions is pure randomness - one of the great mysteries or tortures of my life. I just don't get it or them or what they want or what they mean, or why they want it or why they need it or why I never learned any of this shit when I was younger and people were more obvious. I didn't learn it. I never seem to learn it. People baffle me. I freely admit it.

Social shit. It's the same as being taught exquisitely complicated brain surgery watching through frosted glass windows covered in petroleum jelly. Opaque doesn't begin to cover it. Blurry slow-motion movements. Blobs of wild and moving shades and colors. None of it congealing, none of it making a lot of sense. Bafflement. Total bafflement. It's always the same with me. I'm socially baffled.

I realize I'm practically digging a divot with my chin into Kev's forehead, staring at the ceiling again.

Kev is still waiting. Then suddenly, he's done.

He pulls my head down and gets my eyes to look into his. Tender and harsh at the same time. He touches his bump, then mine again. "Mine's bigger" he says.

I keep on smiling. I couldn't stop if I tried. And I don't look at the ceiling anymore.

Why is this happening to me? I'm a people-avoider. I avoid. It's what I do. People hurt. It's painful to be in close proximity to people. I tell myself that, but I don't believe it.

Kev is a revelation to me.

The bus lurches to a stop. I'm shocked to find myself still standing next to him when it starts up again. Even more people press us up into the windowless corner. My nose is squashed into Kev's left cheek.

It feels good. It feels right. I relax for a second into his face and close my eyes. I feel his face relax. Pressed by dozens of anxious, tired commuters into a corner, two men manage to relax into one another and become one. The universe for one second begins to make sense to me. Then two seconds. Then three.

Kev gently pushes my face down and kisses the bump. Then my nose. Then my lips. I forget to breathe. I forget how to breathe. I kind of go limp. I'm finding I'm liking losing consciousness pressed against his face, wasted on the mechanical fumes of high-voltage electrical motors, full body-pressed against a handsome man - suddenly it just doesn't seem like such a bad way to go.

The smell of Kev's neck and sweaty shoulder blades bash into my cerebral cortex again - a pressure wave of nerve pleasure pulses and I let go. I let it all happen. That's when it all started. Me and Kev.

I do. I do let go. Maybe too much. No, there's no *maybe* about it. I start to drop to the floor. Eyes closed. Blessedly not thinking of anything. Without warning it's very hot in here. I feel sick and weak and remember I should have eaten more spicy, stinking lunch today instead of balancing inventories and munching bag upon bag of potato chips. I should have had less caffeine and more water and - I don't know - I should have certainly been breathing more in the last 60 seconds. So many things I should have done. All I do know is I list to one side, then I droop and then I sag. I don't care anymore. I don't want to care anymore.

Kev's arm reaches around my waist to steady me. He pulls me back up towards the vertical and we stay that way, two pressed sardines in a train powered by lightning, two faces pressed cheek to cheek, two Fred Astaires dancing the light fantastic in a corner of a public bus. This goes on for several stops. Then several more. By the time we get off, after the bus has lumbered up and over and back down a number of hills, we're the last ones on. Gliding through a neighborhood I've never seen before. Still in our hot, sweaty corner. Still pressed together. Still fitted - a couple of jigsaw puzzle pieces snapped into place one against each other. The bus wheezes to a stop. Kev takes my hand. He leads me off.

Kevs a revelation to me.

I scrub Kev's back in the shower, moving slowly down his spine, concentrating on massaging his lower back, the strong cords of muscle feathering out from the center, then the mounds of his lower lats, then the knobby tailbone, pausing for the usual major muscular reconstruction project I make out of his ass (my favorite part). Much later, I make my way down the inside of each of his thighs, running smoothly and efficiently, compressing and releasing, sadly seeing the end of my journey as I come for his feet when I notice a large purplish lozenge shaped thing (well, large, meaning it's at least a quarter of an inch long, but like a missing tooth, it looms huge on his cantaloupe-round, always-impressive calf muscles). What is that thing?

I stop for a second, but Kev tenses, complains, the hot water's starting to run out, so... my hands work quick imaginary Chinese ideograms firmly, deeply, and repeatedly across the pleasing rotundity of his muscular lower legs. Kev likes that better, melts and softens and the whining stops. But his lower legs, well, they seem a little swollen and the lavender lozenge looks angry somehow and I still need to get to his feet. The shower decides at that point to go completely cold, Kev moans, I stand up and in doing so get distracted a little higher up on his body - above his knees, below his belly button, a common problem spot for me when I'm massaging/washing. We jump out of the shower, and soon I've forgotten all about it.

Kev says - spare parts aren't entirely useless. He says - they give us a memory of who we were and are.

Kev says - you know, these things are collections - spare parts that is - they are groupings of miscellanea that grow and grow and get more and more unwieldy and bulky as the snowball of your life rolls downhill and this *stuff* attaches to you. They represent your history, you, your self, your personal narrative, the story of your life you tell yourself to make your life bearable, to force it to make some kind of sense, to require it to impart to you a purposeful direction, a reasonable and rational hope.

You carry this stuff, these things, these parts about - adding to them, moving them from apartment to apartment as years go by - as your living situations multiply - as your life complicates, and your friends and partners turn into different people, leave, return, leave and return again - as you yourself turn into different people and you get older and your priorities assume a certain order and then re-order and re-order themselves and things change and change again and change yet again as months, then years, then decades pass through you - burning life into you and innocences out of you.

Spare parts help you to remember. Spare parts are necessary.

Kev yaps at me about his boss. An old story. We're at a bus stop.

Kev is back at work. But Kev is not happy - not being home much, not putting in anywhere near 40 hours, but putting in more like 70 on an architectural proposal that fell through at the last minute. Kev knows that his boss, ("Reginald, you can just call me Reginald") knew the project was a goner from the beginning, but being his helplessly vicious and rabid self towards those he employs, Reginald tortures Kev's impressive work ethic with impossibilities, with multiple, simultaneous sure-fire failures, with intricate project plans that will never see the light of day but must be finished on deadline, with sketches of fantastical ideas Reginald dreams up in his morning shower and drops on Kev's desk to be done first thing after lunch. Reginald sucks. Reginald, is certifiable.

Reginald is Lord of the Unfeasible. I see it. His other employees see it. Kev refuses to see it. Kev is dead tired but crawls to the gym anyway, he's a homing pigeon when it comes to gyms and comes out of them vibrating with adrenalin. You can see the electrical jolts hitting him for an hour or two after he gets home. He bounces from room to room. I'm sure he's permanently injured the stair master he was abusing, beating, pounding, and body slamming - getting his job frustrations out through the soles of his sturdy feet.

He looks ridiculously tired and his glazed eyes have a manic gleam under the pinkish street light illuminating the bus stop. I step back and look at him.

Kev is naturally muscled and wiry since I've known him, although he hasn't always been like that - but now it's like his body's made solely of tiny pulleys, thin strips of wood, and extra-thin cabling. He's moved way past the "slim" region and into a new territory altogether. I'm more than a little concerned. I feel like I need to do an intervention or something, but what would I suggest he stop doing if I did? Should he be gaining weight? Should I be force-feeding him Belgian chocolate? Kev is still going on and on about his last project, then he starts in about the next gig coming up next week.

Kev, covered in sweat, his dark blue shirt a dark sodden sponge of sweat, says he feels like he could have gone another hour, or another day on that torture machine he uses to hike imaginary staircases at the gym. This from a man who used to weigh over 300 pounds. Kev is psyched. Kev wants to forget Muni and jog home. His energy comes in waves, this must be the high tide. Low tide will probably hit later tonight when he falls asleep at 7:30 P.M. right after dinner. This has got to stop.

I am thinking of ways to engineer a carefully-timed push. A

gentle nudge as his boss - just beginning to descend the steep and slickly acrylic lobby stairs their architectural firm has just installed in a fit of trendiness in their new offices - you know, the safety treads aren't even on yet - well, just as his boss throws his foot out into space over the first stair - I want to insert a shove. I don't want to kill his boss - no, I just want to put Reginald in an intensive care unit for a week or two. Or maybe a month. A full Reginald-body cast would work nicely, I think, to give Kev a much-needed break.

Kev is screwed up tight as an overly-wound watch spring. A walking explosion. He talks and talks and talks. He sounds like he hates his job but I know he loves it. Kev - the stress machine. Our bus appears and Kev's hand's in mine and we show our bus passes and squeeze in next to each other, lost in the moment again, and the lights of the city smear by the scratched bus windows and we glide through the night up and down stupidly steep streets towards my flat tonight - towards dinner and bed.

Kev gets quiet. I look out the window for a time, feel a thump on my shoulder, look over and see Kev's bonelessly slumped over, leaning on me, once again, asleep and snoring and drooling on my white dress shirt.

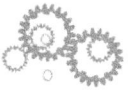

Kev sees the possibilities. I see the complications. We twist and turn our way through our separate but now un-separated lives in a city that makes it as difficult as possible to get affordable roofs and walls securely around you - finding an apartment to rent or even a room is an expedition as labor-intensive as arranging a safari to the top of Kilimanjaro by cell-phone texting alone. Worse even.

But it's worth it. In fact it's rapidly becoming obligatory.

Kev is a fourth primary color to me now. I look at the world through his eyes and see and hear and touch and smell a whole new planet. I have 4 legs, 4 hands, and 40 fingers and toes and that's a joy. A new joy.

I tell Kev, I see endless dilemmas. I don't want to lose my lease. I don't know how I'll get my bed out of my bedroom (a long story there). But Kev doesn't want to wake up without my hair tickling his armpit and my legs braided through his in a half nelson. So we sit, metaphorically, in a stare-down.

I already know I'm going to lose, I'll move in with him.

And that means I already know I'm going to win.

We load up the car with way too much stuff and all Kev can say for the first 50 miles is "Lars, this is way too much stuff." A road-trip to Lake Tahoe, shining interstates running uphill away from the setting sun. Ropes of concrete tying together the impossibly precipitous hills of Northern California. Bridge after rusting bridge crossing and re-crossing the many-fingered SF bay. Then it's delta country, flattened by water and shining wet, then the capital city, full to overflowing with decisions and deciding, and Kev is barefoot, feet up on the dash, singing off tune to the IPod and I realize I'm happy.

I realize this when we stop at a rest stop and Kev muted and sly, sneaks an enormous pine cone (it must be a foot long) onto the driver's seat while I walk the pine-tree-columned path to the men's room, listening for the famous frogs of Mark Twain. You can hear them, but you can't see them. There's a million families travelling this afternoon and they're just as loud, louder than any frog possibly could be.

I get back in the car. I pretend not to notice the oblong object pressing against my rear end and start to pull out of the rest stop. Kev says he's obviously broken me in, down there, in that department. I rock to one side, snatch and toss the prickly missile at him, it flies out the window, and hits the driver's side door of a parked Highway Patrol car. Masculine, hat-shaded, testosterone-filled eyes lift, bore into mine, then lower again (writing a ticket?). Kev snickers, I punch him as I carefully signal getting onto the highway again (for the benefit of the hat-shaded eyes) and we continue up and over the granite saddle of the Sierra looking to drown the lustful noise of San Francisco in the blue mindlessness of selfless Lake Tahoe. Kev finds another pine cone, this one even bigger, and it ends up on a shelf over our bed in our new room we're renting (we found a new place together, a place that would be belong to both of us) using almost all our available and unavailable income to pay for it. Joy. And more joy. For those who know how to grasp it.

I mentioned already, didn't I? My name is Lars. Lars Suneson, recovering Minnesotan.

You ever have the feeling you're looking down on yourself, from someplace way up high, seeing someone else, a complete stranger going about his business but using your body to do it in? You're looking down, squinting to watch your miniature-self working his way through his miniature life in a miniature movie on the teensiest, the tiniest of T.V. sets and it's strange and it's wonderful, and at the same time deeply disturbing to know that it's *you* you're watching from on high?

No?

Well, how about seeing yourself in a mirror and not even recognizing your own face? Seeing someone or something else - larger, wiser, sadder, happier - I don't know - coolly examining you, looking back at you out of your own eyes, waiting for your next move?

Not even that, huh?

You know, I see that stranger all the time. For me, that T.V. set is always playing in the back of my mind. I watch my own life and see - what? A small-Lars, the other-Lars getting through another of his tiny 24 hour days and I think - who is this guy? Who am I really?

Like today.

I can see him, stranger-Lars. Sitting at his desk at work, this small Lars, this other Lars.

Other-Lars is remembering his father.

Why? Because Lars seems to be turning more and more into his father the older he gets. He's not sure what to think about that.

Lars remembers him - laughing eyes, an even more amused mouth, a sharp wit, and a man prematurely bald in his twenties who pulled the corporate plow like an ox, unshaken and uncomplaining for more than 40 years. Working hard was a given. It didn't need to be spoken of much less taught. Maybe it was in the DNA. Anyways, that's Lars's father. And Lars is just like him.

And respect was earned. What Lars's father taught his sons was to disrespect authority and he regretted it only slightly, and not so very often as he got older and his sons took authority-disrespect seriously. Even when it came to questioning him. Lars is still like that.

The written word and books reigned supreme in Lars's house. Bookcases abounded everywhere and were overwhelmed by the sheer mass of printed paper - books pushed into snowdrifts along the walls, under beds, behind dressers. Lars's mother was not amused keeping up with the literary hurricanes regularly heaping collapsing pyramids of paperbacks in unexpected places and unprotected corners.

Lars's dad worked from home all the time (unusual back then) and when he wasn't working he was reading and when he wasn't reading he was raising subversives (sons) with the unfortunate confidence that truth is self-evident and lies are the refuge of the weak.

He freely infected them with the idea of the supremacy of truth and decency and "nice" - a wonderful and horrible virus to give to a child, especially one's own - doing so with the unquenchable optimism of a son of the Upper Midwest. The Upper Midwest - of course - being a place where the concept of "nice" is so very obviously the only sure foundation shoring up our shaky civilization from century to century, that you don't even have to talk about it. Nice, like truth, is as conspicuous as the nose on your face. Obvious. Useful. Crucial. And - The Upper Midwest meaning, of course, God's Country. And - God's Country meaning of course, Minnesota. Lars has to admit that he continues to believe - no matter how hard he might try not to - he still believes whole-heartedly and has an unshakeable, quiet confidence in the natural sovereignty of "nice", truth, decency.

Lars also learned the inevitability of justice. It follows if truth is certain, and if nice is not an abstract term, but a pragmatic philosophy to live one's daily life by, then justice is an absolute -

absolutely possible, absolutely necessary, absolutely required. Lars is right there with his dad on that too. As he's always feared, he truly is turning into his dad.

So Lars was subverted three times - by truth and nice and justice - a condition he was never to recover from. And something for which he blesses his father's name every day of Lars's life.

Although these convictions could and often would make a life exceedingly more difficult than a life might otherwise have been, well, Lars isn't complaining. First, he isn't complaining because he's half-Minnesotan and Minnesotans don't complain. Second, he isn't complaining because blessings and difficulties are not opposites. In fact, they usually occur simultaneously - difficult blessings, blessed difficulties. At least that's been Lar's experience. Maybe not yours, but it's definitely been his.

Lars is remembering his father. As Lars turns into him. It all seems so self-evidently necessary - walking backwards mentally through his life, smiling, gazing, examining his actions in his own past - seeing the importance of things - work, truth, nice, justice, blessings, difficulties. Yup, all there. All important stuff. All necessary. Intellectually Lars can't argue with his dad. He has no desire to. The tricky part Lars finds is the walking forwards and still doing the same self-evidently necessary things, day by day, day in and day out. Especially when life doesn't come so easy. Harder to smile then. Much harder. Much, much harder.

Still, Other-Lars thinks, (I can still see him sitting at his desk at work) - if his dad could do it for all those years, why can't Lars?

It's a couple of years ago.

I see Other-Lars is up late at night again - trying to force-fit the puzzle pieces of the events of the last week into a picture, of something, anything that makes some kind of sense - alone except for the thpt-thpt-thpt of distant marine helicopters (deadly dragonflies) buzzing and talking angrily at each other across the airy distances of midnight. Lars keeps company with the friendly sonic booms of massive artillery exercises beating back the defenseless hills of California chaparral deceitfully besieging and raiding a marine base (which is only a mile away) in a loud and mighty early morning sneak-attack.

In other words, the marines are at it again - practicing. Target practice. With missiles. Lars doesn't hear it, not anymore. It's all white noise. Background. He kicks the chair he's sitting on, slides it back on two of its feet and balances on a pitted and greasy linoleum floor, daring fate to break his neck, or the back of his head.

He's been visiting his friend Thomas down in San Diego who is visiting his sister Susanne who is staying with an old friend of hers she just met last Saturday at the Flame in Hillcrest in San Diego during a half-remembered night of jello-shots of Tequila and a lot of near-nude dancing. Susanne likes to be called Skag. The old friend from the Flame hasn't given out her name yet. Lars has stopped asking.

Thomas is alternately a sexual carnivore, pouncing puma-like on Lars when he least expects it, and then morphing into a solid wall of glacial disinterest - a one-two combination that has Lars pretty impressed. Thomas does both acts in public, *and* he does both in private. Thomas is consistent. Lars appreciates the consistency. Thomas is living two lives at once (at least two - maybe three, maybe four) and doesn't even realize it. It's like there's multiple Thomases and five-plus people, not four living in this crowded stucco bungalow - a pink cube softly decaying here with termite dry rot in North San Diego county in a place the name-less Flame person calls "the dump" when she's drunk, and "the womb" when she's not.

So. Tonight, it's not only Flame's womb, it's Lars's womb too. It's the place Lars is doing his thinking in, his laborious pondering in, his kitchen-chair sitting and chair-leg bouncing in. The Marine assault reaches for a new level of hysteria. Doors seem to open and then slam themselves shut. The ceiling seems to inhale and exhale whole room-fulls of air all by itself. It's evident the U.S. military is teaching a whole new crop of 19 year-olds how to kill more efficiently than they ever thought they possibly could - and convincing them not just a couple of times, no, convincing the 19 year-olds all night long this time. Lars closes his eyes and feels the explosions puffing and popping against his eardrums and thinks and ponders and thinks some more.

Lars can tell - Flame could have painted it in big block letters a foot high on the front door, and Thomas wouldn't see it, and Skag would see it but wouldn't care, but Lars would see it and Lars can tell - he knows that they all - all the Thomases, Skag and Lars will be homeless persons soon. It's going to happen. It's just a matter of time.

Flame is not putting up with Skag's casually wilder and wilder chaos, not for much longer. At first, maybe, Skag caught Flame by surprise. Flame loved the line of women walking in, through, and out of Flame's bedroom (in a Skag-Flame bear-hug as they crab-walked their way through) that conga line snaking nightly, confidently, constantly, at first. Now the conga's slowed and stopped in the last two days and alternate silences and furniture smashing sounds have taken its place.

Thomas (and Lars) grow less and less interesting to Flame and to the womb. Lars can feel the house rejecting them - wrapping them in silence the way white blood cells wrap bacteria up and hustle them out of a diseased body. Thomas and Lars and Skag will soon be history - be extra-womb.

In the literally booming silence of the night Lars works all this out in his head. He bounces forwards, backwards, back and forth, then a particularly percussive explosion rolls impressively over the house and Lars manages to tip over, bashing his head on floor as he crashes to a stop and the chair skids across the slick linoleum tiles to smash into the cupboards under the sink. The loud sound of his sliding arrival on the kitchen floor is covered by the even louder sound of teenage target practice. Both explosions - pain and military, unexpectedly jog some long-dormant brain cells into action. Lying on his back with a possible concussion, he realizes he is deciding.

Through a walloping headache, Lars is sure. As he lies on the gummy kitchen floor he sees a future - Lars isn't going to be having breakfast this morning. Lars will be the breakfast. Lars is toast. Breakfast toast. He has to do something. He has to act.

So where is Kev?

This is pre-Kev. B.K. Lars's one attempt at debauchery while on vacation from his debits and credits back up in the City by the bay. Thomas - a brand new acquaintance - invited him and Lars thought to himself "what the hell?" So here he is. Lying at midnight, head stuck to a stranger's greasy kitchen floor. What an exciting life he leads.

The problem is Skag has the car. Thomas has the keys. Lars came along for the ride. And he's found out he's not much good at lush disorder, no matter how much he tries to keep up with Thomas and Skag. He wasn't cut out for this kind of thing.

It wasn't a mistake. He just added the wrong columns. Now he has a lot of different totals - different totals for the same pages of columns of numbers and he has to decide - which one of the many sum totals is the correct one?

As the sun comes up, Lars's backpack seems to get heavier. It's probably because he's hiking into Oceanside along Highway 76 and if the sun's coming up he's been doing it for a couple of hours now, marching in synch to the destructive blasting rhythmically shredding the dim dawn-shadowed hills to his right. Lars can see distant puffs of smoke across the wide and sandy expanse of the dry San Luis Rey river. Or at least he imagines he can see them. He can sure as shit hear them. He slogs forward, feeling like a refugee in a WWI movie.

He finally crosses train tracks that head north, careful to step on each one, balancing on the balls of his feet, mashing each heel of each foot solidly on the shiny steel - steel that reflects and beckons and welcomes the new morning sunlight. These metallic things have the ability to take him home. Back. Back to where's there's some kind of wholeness. Back to where Lars can place puzzle-pieces - people and places - into a picture of something.

A picture. A new picture. It's waiting for him. Lars thinks maybe something waits up there, up north, and all he has to do is get back to it. Up north. Back to the cold and the fog and the spreadsheets and the careful life he leads. The tracks seem to promise, but won't say for sure. Well, that's good enough for Lars, good enough for now.

The bungalow's fading into a cracked memory, falling to pieces in the back of his head, crumbling into dusty ruins. He lets it. The tracks hum him north , the sun pushes him west, Lars's legs pump up and down and he runs vibrating in sunlight to a station hearing the sound of a train heading up from the south behind him, heading away up the coast, heading back up to Los Angeles.

He's worried about Thomas. He hopes Thomas makes it. At least one of the Thomases. He hopes it will happen. Lars stops and pushes out a good wish for Thomas - sending hope spiraling out from Lars into the universe and towards Thomas specifically, and then he starts running. Running again along the blinding blue-white train tracks to try and catch his ride home at the Oceanside station.

So much for Other-Lars. My younger self sometimes doesn't even seem real to me - the past all distant and fuzzy and blurred out of focus - it's really hard to see what was going on. I can watch the emotions, I just can't feel them anymore. And the motivations for what I did - what was I thinking? All of it - all lost, rationalized and long forgotten. I wonder sometimes if I will be as strange to my future senior self as my younger self is to me now. Probably. I'm strange enough already in the present. I've got a gift for strange. I do.

A gift for strange. That's something else that Kev says. But Kev (as we already know) says a lot of things.

I love Kev's real name - a lordly two syllables (well umpteen syllables, counting all his names) - Joaquin. Kev is Joaquin something something something Ocampo, but everywhere he goes, he goes by Kev, except when I'm mad at him, then he's Joaquin, and I'm rabbit-punched.

Kev's part Filipino, part Japanese, part something else, and part three or four other something elses, and he's all mine. Me? I'm just a lost Swede, a Lars Suneson, part of a family who stumbled drunk over the Atlantic one night 150 years ago and forgot how to get back home again. The brilliant blue eyes of the Sunesons gazed for generations at the flat white tundra horizons of North Dakota (and later Minnesota) until one son (me) jumped ship (metaphorically) and swam west until I ran head-first into the city of Sin Francisco, or rather San Francisco - the mother land of gay men (and women) - our home land, our natural habitat, my new native country.

I hit San Francisco and for the first time I fit in. Completely. Effortlessly. I wasn't dating the tens of thousands of men jumping through the city in herds as do the gazelles of the Serengeti. Not at all. But at least I was in the majority. I was home. Among my own kind. I grew my first (nearly invisible, almost non-existent) blond moustache. I kept at it, growing it, for years. That was the moustache that first met and approved of Kev's cheeks. In the back of the commuter bus. By the pistons. Against the white metal walls.

I didn't know it back then, but I was already permanently pierced and pinned - a chloroformed butterfly (or maybe a moth, I'm not all that handsome really) by Kev's pair of sword-sharp smiling eyes plunging straight into mine, affixing me to the wall of the bus. I haven't been able to move since. I'm his. And that's my Joaquin - my samurai of the smiling eyes.

Kev's doing chemo today, usually if you're positive, and you have KS legions, they fade after a year or so (after you get on one of the cocktails), but Kev's cancers are as stubborn as Kev's personality, so they're hanging in there for the long haul. They're comfortable. They've got a nice home and they've made a good life for themselves and no one is going to throw them off their own property, Goddamit, without a fight.

Apparently they don't know Kev very well. The new post-positive Kev. Kev is out for blood (so to speak). Kev is going to win. Kev's got his game face on for this one. The cancer's in for one hell of a fight.

I offer to go to the infusion center with him, when he goes for his half-day of boring chemo-sitting and drug-infusing, but he always smiles and says no. Smiles with his eyes, and says no with those famous lips. We're up to our 32nd trip, well, Kev's 32nd trip. Chemo's no fun. Sometimes Kev complains and snaps and snarls - about as easy to live with as a Great White shark with a sprained dorsal. Best a guy can do is paddle out of its way, as fast as you can, throw chum in its path every so often, and wait for the pain and the attitude to fade a little.

Then, sometimes you wonder (I wonder) if he's really going to the infusions - he makes it seem easy - he acts the way you would if you were just getting your teeth cleaned at the dentist. But I know better. It is the annoying calm and patience of a Buddha. But a smiling Buddha. My smiling Buddha.

It's weird to me how the harder it gets, the more unbreakable our relationship becomes. We two are joined by something, something solid. Something harder than the hardest thing on earth - spiritual diamond? I don't know. There is, now, literally, no thing that can scratch it - it being our relationship. Are we unbreakable? I don't know. But this unconditional assurance, this love that's there, it's totally unexpected to me. Not how I was taught, not how I was brought up, not my experience in past relationships. But there it is. Sometimes the universe gives you a break.

Still - Oh Universe - did you have to teach two persons such a cool lesson in such a harsh way? Cancer? Couldn't it have been something a little less - oh, I don't know - deadly? Although, I have to admit, you have to hit a Suneson (especially a Lars Suneson) at least a dozen times with a two-by-four on the forehead with great force to even begin to get a portion of his attention. So maybe the universe knows what it's doing after all. Maybe it's all part of the Universe's Lars Suneson-Kev plan.

And what about Kev?

He swore if he ever turned positive, he'd commit suicide before he'd let himself become a prisoner in his own body. But somewhere, somehow, he's learned to fight. And he's still here. And he's fighting. My Kev.

There's more than a silver lining thing going on here, it's as if Kev turned inside out and he's made of it - he's made of silver. A magician's trick. Ta! Da! He was silver all the time. We're all silver all the time. Surprise ending. Got it. It's the fucking universe again. Always teaching. Doesn't it ever fucking let up?

It's my birthday and I know what Kev's planning, but I bet Kev thinks I don't know what he's planning, at least not yet.

He should know I do, it's always the same. Nearly. And I wouldn't have it any other way.

Usually dozens of roses, embarrassingly colorful stuffed

animals, cards that laugh and shriek at you, balloons that sing at you, and enough calories in triple-chocolate cake and twice-the-cream gelato to get us both uncomfortable in our waistlines for a month or two. We do it to each other, for each other, every birthday. We diet at least four months out of every twelve. Caloric penance for our genuine happiness in just having the other guy in our life for one more year. It's worth it. It's always worth it.

And it's always supposed to be a surprise - snuck into the house while the other one wasn't looking - never spoken of ahead of time - as if the whole birthday thing had been accidentally overlooked for the first time this year ("Oh, I'm sorry bro, was that your birthday last week?") - some shit like that.

I'm coming home from work (bussing it as usual) when I hear a singing balloon burst into a country western song from somewhere within the dense crush of people that for some reason always stand around the driver up front and don't move towards the back of the bus, no matter how much the driver pleads for people to move back. Kev is hiding out up there. I know it. Late, as usual, trying to be inconspicuous carrying flowers, cakes, plush toys, escaping globes of various bright colors entwining themselves into and among every other passenger in the front of the bus. People laugh. People talk. It's Kev. I'm sure of it.

I get off four blocks early and walk the long way home.

I can hear the helium-filled singer balloon crooning away inside our flat even before I get to the top of the stairs. I can even smell the roses.

I am an extra part.

A spare part.

An unnecessary part.

See me. My unnecessary self. See me like a picture you would accidentally glance at in a newspaper in the trash, or in some miscellaneous magazine at a checkout counter, or on some random someone's blog. See my unnecessary left hand twisting the pitted brass doorknob on our ratty front door. See my right hand rattling the heavy deadbolt open with my keys, hinges groaning as I push with my unnecessary right shoulder and step inside our flat into a suspiciously gloomy room - a duskiness lit only by the fluttering glow of candles (too many candles) on a barely-visible, whitish cake-like object. You can't hear it, but a single smiling voice booms out of this twilight darkness and starts singing. Singing to me. Singing for me.

See it. Imagine it. I don't' have to. I'm living it. But if you're seeing the picture in your mind, add one more item.

The caption would read (and what a surprise it has been to me to discover it's true) - "Spare Part Finds Home."

ABOUT THE AUTHOR

There's really not much to tell. Anders lives a fairly routine-filled, somewhat solitary, very ordinary life. He'd like to say he regularly goes spear-fishing-scuba-diving - parachuting backwards out of vintage WWI biplanes into shark-infested stretches of the mid-Pacific armed only with his trusty toe-nail clippers clenched carefully between his molars. But he doesn't. The clippers would most likely only chip the enamel on his teeth, or he'd end up swallowing them (and wouldn't that be interesting), and all the fish would probably be schooling 1000 miles away near five star resorts enjoying the white sandy lagoons of Fiji.

Mostly Anders stubbornly carves a life out of the 24 hours he's been given each day, sometimes painfully and with great effort, sometimes ludicrously easily and without even knowing he's doing it. But, he supposes, that could be said of anybody.

And then there's the writing, which is a relatively new thing, and the jury is out on what, if *any*, future there might be in that department.

In the past, there's been the burger-flipping, the accounting, the landscaping, the delivery-van-driving, the Medieval History teaching, the computer programming, and a brief stint around the turn of the century turning countless boxes of mortgage papers and documents into spreadsheets that he was told were to form the backup for a new type of stable international financial product, a kind of security – the bundled mortgage (who knew?)

The truth is, this author has had the incredible luck to find integrity and honesty much more common than he was led to believe, that even though the world is a dangerous and scary place, you don't have to become dangerous and scary yourself to live in it, and that sometimes, if you're persistent, you can find love in all the wrong and in all the right places.

www.ingramcontent.com/pod-product-compliance
Lightning Source LLC
Chambersburg PA
CBHW071308170626
46809CB00001B/369